Dear Reader:

You've already met Special Agent Griffin Hammersmith from the San Francisco field office, in *Backfire*. Savich recognized Griffin's special abilities, along the line of his own, and recruited him to come to the CAU in Washington, D.C. But Griffin doesn't make it.

Fifty miles from Maestro, Virginia, where his sister, Delsey, is studying at the Stanislaus School of Music, Griffin gets a call from Agent Ruth Noble telling him Delsey was found naked and unconscious, lying in a pool of blood, after a wild party. The blood, fortunately, isn't hers. So whose blood is it? Griffin realizes that his sister is in big trouble, and it's up to him to find out why.

Meanwhile, back in D.C., FBI agents Savich and Sherlock have their hands full when the grandson of a former Federal Reserve Bank chairman is found murdered, every bone in his body broken, his frozen corpse left at the foot of the Lincoln Memorial. Was it revenge against his grandfather for the banking crisis, or something more insidious and personal? Then, more inexplicable deaths come fast and furious. It's a brutal winter, and in the endless cold, evil lurks.

I do hope you enjoy *Bombshell*. The mysteries will stump you and you'll be turning pages so fast you'll get thumb burn. I would like to know what you think, so e-mail me at readmoi@gmail.com or visit me at facebook.com/catherinecoulterbooks.

Catherine Coulter

THE FBI THRILLERS

A BRIT IN THE FBI THRILLERS (WITH J. T. ELLISON)

BOMB
SHELL

CATHERINE
COULTER

JOVE
New York

A JOVE BOOK
Published by Berkley
An imprint of Penguin Random House LLC
1745 Broadway, New York, NY 10019

ISBN: 9780425267783

G. P. Putnam's Sons hardcover edition / July 2013
Jove premium edition / July 2014

Printed in the United States of America
7   9   11   13   15   14   12   10   8   6

Cover design by Steve Meditz
Text design by Kristin del Rosario

*To my very clever
best friend ACP*

CHAPTER
1

Maestro, Virginia
Very early Saturday morning

She'd drunk way too much. She was an idiot. Why had she, Delsey Freestone, a reasonably intelligent twenty-five-year-old supposed adult, swan-dived into those last two margaritas? *Because the big cheese director of Stanislaus was treating you like his favorite student, making you his special margarita recipe, that's why, and you were afraid to turn him down. To be honest, you were flattered, too. And what was in those margaritas that tasted so good?*

She was very sure at that moment she didn't want to know.

She didn't understand why Dr. Elliot Hayman, the new director of the Stanislaus School of Music—*Call me Elliot, my dear*—had appeared to want to cut her out of the graduate student female herd at the party and bestow his margaritas and attention on her. Not only was Dr. Hayman in charge of the prestigious music school, he was also an internationally celebrated concert pianist, with a libido, she'd read in a critic's review, to rival his glissandos. When it came to renown, he was in a different universe than hers. She and Anna Castle, a violinist from Louisiana and her best friend in Maestro, had decided Dr. Hayman enjoyed the role of director because it appealed to his vanity, but they also both acknowledged it was only the older graduate students, like herself, who believed that he was, at the core, faintly contemptuous of the students. On the other hand, he was a sharp dresser, dropping in conversations that he shopped twice a year in Milan for his suits, always fashioned for him by Bruno Giraldi himself. Whoever Bruno was, Anna observed, Dr. Hayman certainly dressed to impress.

So why had Dr. Hayman dogged her all evening, giving her entirely too much attention until she was certain every student within hearing distance now hated her guts? *Thank you, Dr. Hayman—Elliot*—that was just what she needed. And what would Anna say about him when she told her about his behavior tonight? She'd laugh and say something like, "Smile, Dels, and suck it up," stretching it out in her lazy Louisiana drawl until Delsey would want to yank the words right out of her mouth. She'd wished all evening that Anna had come, but no, Delsey had had to fly solo.

Delsey supposed the sudden waves of gut-wrenching nausea combined with her flatlining brain had been heaven-sent, since it had gotten her out the door of Professor Rafael Salazar's sprawling ranch-style home on Golden Meadow Terrace in under a minute, with no one the wiser, only one arm in her coat when she'd quietly closed the back door behind her. She'd sucked in the cold winter air, grateful to be out of Professor Salazar's whooping hoedown, away from both him and his twin brother, Dr. Hayman, and wasn't that a hoot? Twins! Separated as boys and ending up with different last names. The only thing they had in common, as far as she could see, was their incredible talent.

She drove very carefully until her head was pounding so hard and she was feeling so woozy she was swerving like a drunk, which, she supposed, she was. *No cops, please—too much humiliation.* She eased her ancient Spyder to the curb of Tinsel Tree Lane and shifted into neutral. She pressed her forehead against the steering wheel, willing the world to stitch itself back together for her, swearing to any power listening that she'd go back to her one-drink limit. She'd made that promise when she was only sixteen, after sharing a bottle of hooch with her boyfriend Davie Forman and wanting to die, certainly not to have sex with him in his daddy's Mustang. Tonight was the first time she'd broken that promise in nine years. *What an idiot you are; you deserve freezing your butt off and having your head explode, and the misery of hugging the toilet in the morning.*

She finally cracked an eye open to see the half moon

crystal clear overhead. It looked as cold and hard as the solid mountains of snow that blanketed everything around her—trees, street signs, cars, mailboxes. Big snow, the locals called it—unusual, the locals also said—yet here it was, a big honking snowstorm. At least it had stopped pelting down for a while, but they said it would begin again hard near dawn. She'd come to realize after the first heavy snow in December that if she hit a snowdrift, she and her Spyder wouldn't be found until spring.

Looking at the unrelenting white made her miss the warm salty air of Santa Monica, scented with the night jasmine trellised on the stone fence surrounding her former apartment building. To top it off, her car heater was struggling to stay alive, her Spyder no more used to this circuit-freezing weather than she was. She sure wasn't helping any, staying out all hours of this frigid night—it couldn't be more than ten degrees, and counting down. *Houston, we have a problem*. She squeezed her eyes shut; what should she do?

She became aware of how very quiet it was, not a single owl hooting in the snow-drenched trees, not a single car or truck engine tunneling through the snow on the interstate only a quarter-mile away. No wonder; it was nearly one o'clock on Saturday morning. Only people she didn't want to know about were up this time of night. She looked around and sent a silent prayer of thanks upward that there weren't any cops, either. She knew she wasn't up for convincing anyone she wasn't drunk. She'd probably shatter the Breathalyzer.

She raised her head after a few minutes, held perfectly

still for a moment, noticed she didn't feel as dizzy and, blessed be, her headache was throttling down. She shifted the Spyder into gear and drove slowly, in a perfectly straight line, as only those who are impaired and know it do. After another six blocks, she turned off onto Hitchfield Avenue and then onto Lonely Bear Court. She saw her building up ahead on the right, a duplex with her one-bedroom unit on the bottom and Henry Stoltzen's on top. Built as a solid red brick back in the twenties, it had been split up in the late nineties by the heirs to the old lady who'd lived there all her life.

She looked up to see Henry's light on. Henry and his prized six-inch goatee had helped her move in the day she'd arrived in Maestro, fed her hot dogs and beer, and quickly become a good friend. He liked the popular songs she wrote and sang, even though he sat solidly in the classical corner, a gifted cellist who adored playing Jean-Baptiste Sébastien Bréval's Sonata in C Major.

He seemed oblivious to most other people around him, only his music and his iPod tethering him to planet earth. She turned into her parking spot next to Henry's, drew a deep breath, thanked the Almighty she was still alive, and even better, not in jail. She promised good works she told herself she wouldn't forget by morning, as she slogged through the snow to her front door. She was shaking with cold when she finally fit her old-fashioned key into the lock and the door opened. She stepped into a blissful seventy degrees.

She locked the front door behind her, slipped on the two chains, and shoved the dead bolt home. She flipped on the light inside the door in the small foyer. *Home and warm. No more margaritas, no more one a.m. parties. I'm now a sensible woman, resolute and determined, and the director of Stanislaus can go compliment someone in the reed section.* She saw Eileen Simons of clarinet fame in her mind's eye, and knew she was interested in Dr. Hayman—*Elliot, my dear.* Why hadn't Director Hayman loaded Eileen up with booze this evening and stayed away from Delsey? Eileen had been at the booze-fest, as drunk as everyone else and giving Delsey the "die, bitch" eye all evening.

Now I'm safe.

Where had that left-field thought come from? Well, from being out alone and drunk in the boondocks of Virginia in the middle of the night, that's where. Delsey bypassed the living room and went straight to the kitchen, swallowed three extra-strong aspirin and drank two full glasses of water. The tap water tasted nastier than usual, but she drank it anyway. She wiped the back of her hand across her mouth and walked through the hallway to the bathroom, turning on lights as she went. When she flipped on the bathroom light she saw the colorful South Seas shower curtain was pulled closed around the bathtub.

She never left the shower curtain closed because it made the bathroom look too small—well, unless she hadn't cleaned the bathtub. Had she? Her brain was still fogged, and she couldn't remember.

A hot shower, that was all she could think about, jets of hot water pounding her face, clearing out her head, making her want to live again. She stripped off her clothes, paused on the clip of her bra when she heard something, movement, something. Maybe a sharp breath? She didn't move, listened hard. No, there wasn't anything. Her brain was still squirrelly with tequila. She got her bra off, left her clothes in a pile on the bathroom floor, pulled back the shower curtain, and froze.

She'd never believed she was a screamer, but a scream ripped right out of her mouth, and then another, her brain screaming in tandem, *Not possible, not possible.* Her breath caught when she heard the sound again and whirled around, but she didn't have time to be afraid before something hard as a brick smashed her on her head, and she didn't scream anymore.

CHAPTER
2

Northwest of Maestro, Virginia
Saturday morning

Special Agent Griffin Hammersmith drove out of Gaffer's Ridge at nine o'clock, after chowing down the best blueberry waffles he'd eaten since his Aunt Mae's famous Sunday brunches. He'd stayed with a college buddy, Jennifer Wiley, who happened to own Jenny's Café in the quaint touristy center of the small postcard town set among low mountains and rolling hills. Since the café was filled to bursting at seven-thirty every morning, it seemed the locals agreed with him.

He'd enjoyed his trip from San Francisco across

the country, seeing friends and relatives on his way to his new posting in Washington, D.C., but he realized after two weeks with not much more to worry about than his Uncle Milton's arthritis in Colorado Springs, and catching up with a couple of old friends, pleasant though it was, he was getting antsy and ready to get back to work.

Griffin looked up at the bloated dark clouds pressing down, promising more snow. He hoped he'd get to Maestro before his world turned white again. He eased onto State Highway 48, planning to cut across to the highway.

Griffin was sipping at coffee from the Thermos Jenny had handed him on his way out the door: "Rich, thick, and dangerous," she'd said, and winked at him.

His cell buzzed. Since traffic was building up, Griffin pulled off the interstate. He saw the call was blocked, and that was weird. "Yeah? Who's this?"

"This is Ruth—Agent Ruth Noble. I would have called you sooner, Griffin, to see when you'd be arriving in Maestro, and arrange to meet you, but we've got something of a situation here, and I'm helping my husband, Dix Noble—he's the local sheriff—figure things out."

Her tone made his brain buzz. "A situation?"

"More a puzzle. It's pretty weird, actually. A Stanislaus student was found unconscious in her bathroom with a head wound. Usually that would mean she slipped and struck her head on the bathtub rim or somewhere else close. But the thing is, the neighbor who lives above her heard her scream, found her, and called 911. If she'd just struck her head, why would she scream? And there was no evidence she's hit anything. All the blood we think was hers was found on the floor around her head. The puzzle is that there was a good deal of blood in the bathtub, probably not hers, like someone else had been bleeding in there and then left or been taken away. Dix saw the blood in the bathtub and of course he realized the implications.

"The back door was jimmied. So was it a burglary gone bad? Well, whatever, it wasn't a simple burglary, what with all that blood in the bathtub.

"She's not with it enough to tell us what happened. She's in Henderson County Hospital. I'm here with her, waiting for her to wake up.

"She lived alone, so there's no roommate to call, and we don't know yet if there's a boyfriend in the picture. I'm also trying to get hold of her parents, but no luck as of yet."

"Any sign of a blood trail outside the bathroom?"

"Nothing obvious, but we're bringing in the Henderson County forensic team to analyze the blood and go over the young woman's apartment. They'll check to see if any blood shows up under Luminol outside the bathroom."

"It went wrong in the bathroom? That sounds strange."

"Whatever happened, that person might have been

injured or died, and was then hauled away. Don't know yet," Ruth said. "It snowed heavily last night, and any evidence outside the duplex—blood trail, tracks, anything—is long covered up. At least it stopped snowing here an hour ago, so the plows can catch up before the next storm comes in."

Griffin felt wired. He loved puzzles; the more convoluted, the bigger the rush when he figured them out.

The bathtub puzzle sounded complex enough to fit the bill. "I can be there in an hour and a half, if it doesn't start to dump snow on me. Have you talked to the neighbor who called 911 yet?"

"He's next on my list. Dix talked to him at the scene, but he was so upset Dix couldn't get much out of him. He's had some time to settle. Hopefully he can fill in some of the blanks."

"I'd be glad to help when I get there if you'll let me. Who is she?"

"Her name's Delsey Freestone. She's a student at Stanislaus, like your sister."

Griffin's heart flatlined. "Ruth," he said, and the words hurt coming out. "Delsey Freestone *is* my sister."

He heard her sharp intake of breath. "I'm so sorry, Griffin. But listen, don't worry, the doctors say she's going to be okay, I promise. You all right?"

Griffin couldn't wrap his brain around Delsey being attacked in her own bathroom. And with all the blood— maybe a body?

"Griffin?"

"I'm okay, Ruth. Hearing this, it's difficult."

"I can only imagine. But like I said, Griffin, your sister will be fine."

He was silent a moment, calming himself, then, "Don't bother trying to reach our parents—they're in Australia, in the outback for another three weeks or so, out of touch, no cell phones.

"As far as I know, there isn't a boyfriend. She told me she had a nasty breakup in Santa Monica and swore off men for the next five years."

"All right. Get to the hospital as soon as you can. I'll be here with her, room three-fifteen."

Griffin punched the accelerator to the floor. A burglary, it had to be. He felt a hot slick of fear roil in his belly. Who had been bleeding in her bathtub and why? Was it the person who'd struck her down or another victim? She'd surprised someone? Why hadn't he killed her? None of it made sense to him.

He knew in his gut he shouldn't be surprised that Delsey was involved. She was, in fact, the perfect candidate, a Trouble Magnet—that was her family nickname, and it had all started when she was sixteen. She'd witnessed a convenience-store robbery, managed to escape whole hide, and was the main witness at the trial that sent two felons to jail. When she was seventeen she was proudly depositing her first checks for delivering newspapers in the local bank when two robbers came in with semiautomatics. It turned out she actually knew one of the robbers. She delivered his papers. "He always gave me great tips," she'd said sadly.

"You think the money was all stolen? Will I have to give it back?"

Even her breakup with her boyfriend in Santa Monica hadn't been because of something common, such as the guy sleeping around on her or being a control freak. No, Delsey had managed to hook up with a guy who ran a car-theft ring and sold guns for his Mexican buddies on the side. "What a bummer that gorgeous red Ferrari belongs to a shopping-mall developer," she'd told him when she and Griffin watched him leave the courtroom in shackles.

His parents had celebrated with champagne when their daughter was accepted into the Stanislaus graduate program that emphasized instrumental composition, what she'd wanted to learn more than anything, she'd told him when she'd applied. Delsey had been so pleased she'd kicked up her heels and announced, "At last, I'll learn how to score 'Eleanor Rigby' for the tuba," and she'd laughed. Stanislaus was not only the most prestigious music school in the South, it had the added advantage of being isolated, a very safe place on the planet, far away from big-city crooks and wackos—and trouble. Griffin agreed. Delsey had assured him during her once-a-week phone calls that there wasn't a single criminal in sight, she had a great girlfriend who played the violin and waitressed in town—everything, in short, was so normal he should worry she'd get bored, not get into trouble. And so he'd arranged to stop off in Maestro to meet Agent Noble and visit with his sister on his way to Washington, D.C.

He was a moron. And now this.

Luckily for him and the other drivers on Highway 50, snow didn't start falling again until Griffin pulled into the Henderson County Hospital parking lot. He'd made it there in fifty-eight minutes.

CHAPTER
3

Henderson County Hospital
Maestro, Virginia
Late Saturday morning

Griffin ran through the hospital lobby, saw a dozen people staring up at the three stationary elevator arrows, and took the stairs two at a time to the third floor. He'd spoken to Ruth two more times on his wild drive through the mountains to the hospital. There was no change in Delsey's condition; she was still in and out, still groggy when she was in.

He ran down the corridor, ignoring a nurse's voice behind him, and opened the door to room 315 to see a tall woman in a white blouse with a black cashmere V-neck sweater, black pants, and boots standing close at the foot of Delsey's bed. She was fit and slender, her short dark hair waving around a strong, intelligent face. She looked over when he came in, and smiled. "You must be Griffin Hammersmith. You didn't let any snow melt under your tires—that was fast."

Griffin realized she had to be Agent Ruth Noble, but all he could do was nod. He felt frozen, not from the cold but from gut-wrenching fear for his sister.

He said, "Yes, I'm Griffin Hammersmith. You're Ruth Noble."

He shook hands with her even as he looked to the bed. Delsey looked to be asleep, or out of it. There was a large bandage on her head. "How's my sister?"

Ruth said in a calm, steady voice, "Dr. Chesney's telling us Delsey will be all right." She knew she sounded mechanical, words spoken to a family member scared out of his mind and not a fellow agent, but still, they were true and they calmed him.

Ruth had seen Griffin Hammersmith's photo, but she doubted she'd have recognized the wild-eyed man who burst through the door still wearing a fur-lined parka over jeans and boots. Ruth looked at him again when he tossed the parka on a chair, and was surprised at her next thought. *Wowza, your photo doesn't do you justice, señor.*

His attention turned immediately to the doctor who walked into the room, an older woman wearing a white coat, a stethoscope around her neck. She was plump and pretty, a pile of curly white hair thick on her head. She smiled at him, patted his arm. "I'm Dr. Chesney."

"I'm Griffin Hammersmith, Delsey's brother. What's going on with her? Agent, ah, Ruth said you believed she'd be okay, but she's not awake."

Dr. Chesney automatically lowered the pitch of her voice. "We've done a CT scan. She has no evidence of a skull fracture or of any bleeding or contusions in or around her brain. She had a laceration of her scalp that required stitches, and she's suffered a rather severe concussion."

Dr. Chesney saw he'd taken it all in, and added, "We gave her some medications for her pain, though we have to be very careful with that. She's still groggy, not completely oriented. It's hard to predict how long that will last, after the severe blow she had. Maybe hours, maybe days, even weeks."

Griffin knew all about concussions, since he'd had his own bell rung more than once when he'd played high school and college football. Mostly he remembered having nagging headaches and not feeling quite right. Griffin looked down at Delsey's face, leached of color, winced at the white bandage. His fingers hovered over her cheek, then touched her warm skin, maybe to reassure himself she was alive. He closed his eyes as his fingers lightly pressed against the pulse in her throat. Slow and steady.

Dr. Chesney lightly touched a spot above her left ear. "As I said, the wound required stitches, but it looks a lot worse with this big bandage than it really is. We'll change it out tomorrow for something smaller. The blow jarred her brain, of course, so we can expect short-term symptoms even after she's fully awake, like difficulty concentrating, dizziness, nausea, and balance problems.

"But she will recover nicely in time, Agent Hammersmith. Right now, she's still confused. Having you here will help her. I understand she's a student at Stanislaus. I doubt she'll be up to performing for a while. What is her instrument?"

"She plays both the guitar and the piano, but she's mainly a singer and a composer," Griffin said.

"An opera singer?"

Griffin smiled, hearing Delsey say as she rolled her eyes, *The Good Lord save me from climbing to high C every other note, except for the National Anthem. Hey, Griffin, wouldn't it be great to sing the National Anthem at the Super Bowl? I wish I knew who to kiss up to to wrangle that.*

He said to Dr. Chesney, "She could have been an opera singer, but what Delsey really likes is to compose and perform popular music. She's already had some success. She's at Stanislaus because she wants to learn everything she can about composition and instrumentation, ah—" Griffin's voice fell away, and he swallowed. "She's very talented. She's like our grandmother."

Dr. Chesney smiled, showing a wide space between her front teeth. "Your grandmother? Freestone?"

"No, Hammersmith."

"Hammersmith? Goodness, Aladonna Hammersmith is your grandmother? Oh, how I wanted to be an opera singer after I first heard her perform at Carnegie

Hall, but alas, even the shower water turns cold when I try an aria."

Griffin smiled. "She was Miss Aladonna to all of us grandkids. She made the best chocolate-chip cookies in the world."

Children, Dr. Chesney thought, had their own criteria for what was important. She remembered Aladonna Hammersmith had died of heart failure in the early nineties. In the years that followed, she'd seen a good half-dozen retrospective shows about her life. "I look forward to hearing Aladonna Hammersmith's granddaughter perform when she's up to it. If we're lucky, she'll be back to normal before you know it, so please don't worry too much. I'll be back in a couple of hours, unless she needs me. They can reach me on my beeper."

She turned to Ruth. "I hope Dix can figure this all out. We sure don't want a repeat of anything like last year in town. Talk about horrific. At least she won't die like the others did." Her eyes flicked again to Delsey. Dr. Chesney left the room, leaving dead silence in her wake.

Ruth shook her head. "Talk about a klutz thing to say, but that's Dr. Chesney. She was probably still so excited to hear her patient is the granddaughter of her opera goddess she forgot you were here."

He said, "What did she mean, a horrific time last year? Was another Stanislaus student hurt? Killed?"

"There was a murder—well, several actually—but that's all over and done with. If you want to know more about it, I'll fill you in later."

Murders at Stanislaus last year? Did Delsey's being struck down have anything to do with that old trouble? Had she somehow managed to start up with the wrong person? He wouldn't doubt it. The Trouble Magnet could sniff out a bad apple in a sealed barrel.

"Tell me, Ruth, that the murders last year were neatly solved and the killer sent to prison."

"Well, all of them were resolved except the last one; well, there are still some questions in my husband Dix's mind and the primary suspect is in the wind, but far away from here, we think. Trust me, it has nothing to do with this."

Griffin realized he was probably being paranoid and tried to turn it off. But a cop is a cop, and he wanted to hear all about last year's murders. But now wasn't the time. He pulled up a chair and sat beside his sister. She was sleeping, her breathing slow and regular. He pulled her hand from beneath the hospital blanket, looked at her long white fingers, magic fingers that made such beautiful music the angels wept, and when she sang you wept along with them. He slowly began to rub the back of her hand. "My mother told me when a person is down and out Miss Aladonna had told her it helps if you can hold their hands, that they somehow know, and she did that for my grandmother when she was very sick. I haven't any idea if it's true."

Ruth pulled up the only other chair and sat on the other side of the bed, picked up Delsey's left hand and began rubbing it. She looked over at Special Agent Griffin Hammersmith. She imagined that when he walked down the street women nearly got run over staring at him. He'd rolled up the sleeves of his blue shirt to his elbows, and his jeans were old and fitted him very nicely. He looked, she thought, very fine. He was as pretty as his sister, with all his thick blond hair, his eyes as green as wet grass, a small hollow in the middle of his chin, and cheekbones sharp enough to slice a lemon. He was saved from being too pretty by a nose obviously broken a couple of times when he'd been younger, and which now sat a bit off-kilter. He and Delsey looked nearly the same age even though Delsey was six years his junior. According to her driver's license, Delsey had turned twenty-five the previous week.

She said quietly, "You know, Griffin, Dillon described you as the *real deal*. I'm glad you're here, for Delsey's sake."

Griffin arched a perfect eyebrow at Ruth and continued rubbing his sister's hand. He said, "Delsey told me she wanted to learn everything in the known universe about how to put together a multi-instrument score, and this was the place. She never wanted to go to Juilliard, said New York was too big, too noisy, too claustrophobic.

"I haven't seen Delsey since she moved here last September to attend graduate school. I didn't make it home for the holidays because there were three bank robberies right before Christmas that had the police chief and the mayor screaming at us, and so I volunteered to head it all up, since, unlike most of the other agents, I'm not married with kids whose stockings needed stuffing."

"Did you catch the bank robbers?"

Griffin nodded. "Two brothers, both two-time felons, neither very bright. We cuffed them while they were
sleeping off a drunk in a Napa Valley motel."

"I'll bet they bragged about their big score in a bar."

He gave her a grin that would smite female hearts
from twenty paces. "Yeah, something like that. The
bartender called us."

A tech appeared in the doorway. "Dr. Chesney said
to bring this to you right away, Agent Noble."

Griffin said, "The results from the blood in Delsey's
bathtub?"

"Looks like." Ruth took a piece of paper from him.

CHAPTER
4

Ruth sighed, handed Griffin the lab report. "All the results tell us so far is that we were right about the blood in the bathtub not being Delsey's. The blood on the floor, Delsey's blood, was AB positive, and the blood in the bathtub is the ever-popular type O. They've started the DNA typing, so we can still hope for some magic from the lab if they get a match in the DNA Index System." She eyed him. "A cold hit is not very likely, though, as you know."

Griffin said, "If she walked in on a burglary that morphed into a murder, or on someone putting a body in her bathtub, he would have killed her, not hit her on the head."

"Maybe he thought the blow did kill her. Maybe that's what he intended. Or maybe he panicked." How close had she been to dying? He tasted ashes in his mouth. What they needed was for Delsey to tell them what happened last night.

Ruth said, "Dix has already assigned a deputy to stand guard outside her room. If the perp does think he killed her and finds out she's alive, he might try again."

Griffin said, "Let's hope not, but thank you. If the person in the bathtub was dead, the killer took the body out of Delsey's apartment for a good reason. And what could the reason be? Someone could have seen him, no matter that it was well after midnight. He was taking a huge risk, carrying the body into her apartment, then carrying it out after Delsey screamed. Either Delsey's attacker walked out, was helped out, or his killer really didn't want us to know who he was, which would be the case no matter what else was involved. If it was a burglary, what were they after? I've thought about that but can't think of anything particularly valuable. Her guitar is, I suppose, but not her piano, so that adds to the questions. What did they want? What did they hope to find?"

Griffin looked back at Delsey. "I guess I should tell you we have a name for my sister in the family—Trouble Magnet—that's with capital letters, her official title. She drives our parents nuts." Griffin told her about Delsey's first newspaper route, when she delivered papers to a bank robber.

Ruth stared at him. "That's pretty funny, but only

since it turned out well. Does Delsey have anything to do with why you became an FBI agent?"

"Not really, but some of our instincts are the same. I have several more stories about Delsey that'll make your hair rise on your neck. If there's a wrong place and a wrong time, and the wrong guys, Delsey will find them or they'll find her. Maybe it's all mistaken identity. I wouldn't be surprised, given her history."

"I believe our patient moved a bit."

Delsey heard voices, one of them familiar, and the voice seemed to be talking about her. She slowly opened her eyes to see her brother not three feet from her nose. "Griffin?"

Her voice was a skinny thread of sound that scared him to his feet. "Yep, I'm here. How are you feeling, Dels?"

"Don't ask me that yet; I'm not sure. My brain seems to be floating up there somewhere near the ceiling. Maybe it's better if I let it hover up there for a while."

He patted her cheek. "Hovering is good. Gotta tell you, Dels, you look a little pathetic with the big white bandage around your head."

"So you're more beautiful than me right now?"

"Maybe, but you've got the win on drama points with that big honker bandage. Very impressive."

"I heard you talking. You didn't sound happy. Why?"

"Something happened to you," he said. "Again."

Delsey pulled her hand away from his and slowly raised it to touch her head. "What? Was I in an accident?"

"No, not an accident. You don't remember?"

She frowned, then shook her head and gasped. "I don't think I should move again. My head, Griffin—my head feels like it'll explode if I do. That would be an awful sight, even for you, Mr. Macho FBI Agent."

Griffin was on his feet. "I'm going to go find a nurse, get some meds for you, all right?"

"Yeah, that'd be good. Oh, no."

She lurched up, and Ruth managed to get a bedpan to her mouth in time. She fell back against the pillow, shut her eyes. "I'm sorry. I had too much to drink last night."

"Not a problem." Ruth wiped Delsey's mouth with a wet towelette. Not a good time for questions. She said, "Close your eyes and make your breathing light and shallow, that's right, relax." She began stroking the back of Delsey's hand as she said slowly, her voice as calm as a shallow summer river, "I'm Agent Ruth Noble. No, don't try to talk. Keep everything easy, Delsey, just listen, don't think. I'm married to the local sheriff, Dix Noble. He's a lovely man, all tall and dark and tough as a muscle truck. He actually saved my life last year. It turned into a real gnarly mess here in Maestro, as I'm sure you've heard, but we got it all straightened out. I have two stepsons now, Rob and Rafer, seventeen and fifteen. Both of them look like their father, and that means they're going to be heartbreakers. Well, Rob already is. I'm going to be working in Washington with your brother, at the Hoover Building.

"There, that's better, isn't it? I don't want you

to worry about anything. Keep still until your insides settle."

"Could I have a sip of water?"

Ruth set a plastic straw on her tongue. "Not too much, now; that's right."

Delsey took a single sip, felt her stomach twist, then, thank the Good Lord, it quieted down. "I've heard of you, Agent—"

"Call me Ruth."

"Okay, Ruth. Most everyone at Stanislaus has heard of you and your husband, Sheriff Noble. I heard a Stanislaus student was murdered, then the director's secretary."

"Yes. We got it sorted out."

"A lot of the women at Stanislaus think Sheriff Noble's hot—some of the guys do, too. It will get even worse now that Griffin's in town. When the women get a load of him, there'll be fistfights."

Ruth smiled and patted her hand. "You might be right. He's quite a package."

"Poor Griffin, he has to deal with females up to about eighty coming on to him. Maybe the older women want to mother him. Or not, hard to say."

Griffin came through the door with Nurse Morsi, who checked Delsey's pulse, put a stethoscope to her chest, and said "good" several times. Ruth told her about Delsey getting sick. Instead of a magic med, Nurse Morsi produced a saltine cracker. "Chew on this, Delsey. Go slow, that's right, a bit at a time. It will help with the nausea."

Delsey chewed on the cracker. Her stomach didn't complain. "Thanks. That's good."

"A flash of nausea is common with a concussion; nothing to worry about. It's already gone, right?"

Delsey took the last bite of cracker, waited for a moment, and nodded.

"Good. If the nausea comes back we can give you an injection to calm things down. You had quite a bit of alcohol last night that showed up on your blood tests. That can't be helping. Right now I want you to lie still, have some more water and saltines when you feel like it, and let your body reboot."

Nurse Morsi left after a long look at Griffin, one Delsey recognized as saying, *How about I buy you a drink?* Delsey focused on her brother. "Griffin, I don't understand. What are you doing here?"

"I was on my way to my new job in Washington and planned on stopping here to surprise you."

"Did you see Jennifer?"

"Yes, she's fine, made me the best waffles on the planet."

Delsey said to Ruth, "Jennifer is an incredible cook. Believe it or not, she's never wanted to be anything but Griffin's friend."

Griffin didn't have the heart to tell her Jennifer was gay.

Delsey said, "She owns Jenny's Café over in Gaffer's Ridge, an hour or so northwest of here. I visited her this past fall and put on three pounds."

Griffin knew she was being chatty; she always was when she was scared. It was a wonder she could manage it. He bent down and lightly laid his fingers over her mouth. "Don't worry about all this, Dels, I'll do all the worrying for you—or, better yet, we'll let Ruth carry the worry load."

"Not a problem," Ruth said and began rubbing the back of Delsey's hand again.

Delsey sighed. "It's probably just as well Jenny's gay. If she wanted to marry you, Griffin, you'd gain a hundred pounds."

So she knew, did she? "Nah, I've got more willpower than you."

"Do you know, Ruth," Delsey said, "whenever we were sick, our grandmother would rub our hands and she'd sing that beautiful aria from *Madame Butterfly*, 'Un Bel Dì,' to us. You don't have to sing, Griffin."

Griffin said, "No, I won't. Is the hand rubbing working?"

"It's a good distraction."

Ruth wanted to ask Delsey Freestone what had happened, but she decided Griffin should take the lead. She said only, "It's snowing, bunches of big flakes drifting down. I'll bet my two stepsons are sledding and snowboarding with half the kids in town at Breaker's Hill."

"I sledded at Breaker's Hill three days ago," Delsey said. She closed her eyes. Ruth thought her head must be really hurting.

Delsey turned very slightly to look at her brother.

"You've got to get married, Griffin, and have kids. Imagine how gorgeous they'll be. Maybe they'll be lucky and have some of my talent."

"Back at you. Maybe your kids will have some of my talent."

Even though her head hurt and she wished she had another saltine to keep her stomach off the ledge, Delsey smiled. "I've gotta admit, your talent's more interesting than mine. I mean, you've always simply *known* things no one else knew. I've always had to run into things, head-on, like the time that boy snatched Mrs. Garland's tote bag and ran right into me when I came around the corner." She closed her eyes again, but there was a small smile on her mouth. "At least Mrs. Garland got her tote back."

He said, his voice very precise, "I meant my talent for solving crimes."

"Yeah, yeah. Griffin never wants to talk about it, Ruth, but Miss Aladonna not only sang, she was psychic, and she swore that was her biggest talent and she passed it on to him."

Ruth said, "Did Miss Aladonna speak to spirits?"

"No, like Griffin, she simply knew stuff there was no way she could know. She—"

"Enough of that, Delsey. I told you, I was talking about my talent as a cop. I see patterns sometimes, that's all, look at puzzle pieces and can many times see how they all fit together. You're looking better, you're arguing with me, so let's get down to business here, if you can do it without throwing up again."

Delsey said to Ruth, "I told you he never wants to talk about it."

Ruth only smiled.

"That's enough, Delsey. You need to tell Ruth and me what happened. If you feel sick again, you stop talking, okay?"

Delsey felt a twist of nausea and swallowed. "Yeah, I can do this." She swallowed again. "I went to a party over at Professor Salazar's house." She stopped cold, and her breathing picked up, suddenly hard and fast.

Ruth leaned close. "No, don't panic, Delsey. Relax. What upset you?"

"I can't seem to remember anything after I parked my Spyder at Professor Salazar's house—there's nothing else until I was here with you."

Griffin said matter-of-factly, "Not remembering is common with a bad concussion. Now, you went to a party at this Professor Salazar's house? You mean Rafael Salazar? The classical guitarist? I've got a couple of his CDs. He's very good."

"That's him. He's better than good, he's brilliant. I've read he was a child prodigy."

"So why is he at Stanislaus?"

"He's a visiting professor, brought here by—this is really cool—his twin brother, who happens also to be the director of Stanislaus, Dr. Elliot Hayman."

"I didn't know he had a twin," Griffin said. "And it's Dr. Elliot Hayman? I also have some of his CDs playing Bach. Okay, I want to hear more about him, too, but first tell me more about Rafael Salazar."

Delsey said, "I've never seen technique like his on the classical guitar. His fingers are a blur. His students adore him, particularly the women, and it's not only his musical ability. He throws great parties and drinks his weight in vodka martinis, but what he excels at is dazzle and seduction, which he does with great regularity." She grinned. "He's with Gabrielle DuBois right now. She's a voice student. I think he made a mistake—he let it out he thought Gabrielle sings like Edith Piaf, and believe me, she doesn't let anyone forget it."

"Wait a second," Griffin said. "If he and Hayman are twin brothers, why do they have different last names?"

"All I know is they were separated as boys; Mom took one to Spain, married again, and changed his name to the new hubby's name, Salazar, and Dad kept the other one with him here in the States."

"Okay, back to the party at Salazar's house."

"I remember there were lots of people and cars and the music blaring out even though the windows were closed. Then it's a blank."

"Someone hit you on the head at your apartment, Delsey. We're trying to figure out who." Ruth stopped in her tracks when a woman rushed into the room, bundled up to her eyebrows, pulling off a wool cap and sending a long, thick dark braid flying down her back. It was Anna Castle, a Stanislaus student and part-time waitress at Maurie's Diner. Ruth liked Anna, who'd come to Stanislaus at the beginning of the semester in September. She was always smiling and welcoming to her customers, knew all their likes and dislikes, and always had time to chat with everyone. Ruth said quickly, "Hi, Anna, it's okay. Delsey's all right," but Ruth saw all her attention was focused on Delsey. Since they both attended Stanislaus, she supposed they'd know each other, but this was more, this was real caring, real concern.

Delsey tried to sit up but couldn't manage it. She held out her hand. "Anna, I'm okay."

Griffin was up, his hand on his gun. "How did you get in here? Anna who? Who are you?"

"Griffin, it's all right. This is Anna, a great violinist and my best friend."

Griffin eyed the woman bundled up in a bright green ski jacket and wearing black knee boots over tight black jeans. He saw she was staring at his hand resting on the SIG clipped to his belt. He started to back off a bit, but then she walked up to him and smiled, her hand out. "I know you've got to be Delsey's brother, since the two of you look like mirrors of each other. I'm Anna Castle, and like she told you, I'm her best friend. You're the FBI agent, right?"

He nodded, never taking his eyes off her face. Dark, dark eyes, nearly black, and that voice of hers dripped as slow and smooth and rich as the syrup he'd poured over his waffles at Jenny's.

"Yes, I'm FBI Agent Griffin Hammersmith, Delsey's brother. It appears you already know Ruth."

"Hi, Ruth. I think Delsey might be safe now, with two cops standin' over her bed." She stepped around him, and lightly laid her palm against Delsey's white cheek. "Sweetie, you don't look so hot. Can you tell me what happened?"

Griffin said, "There was a guard already outside her room when I came back in. How'd you get past him?"

Anna Castle turned, smiled at him. "Everybody eats at Maurie's Diner. Do you know, Ruth, that Deputy Claus likes mayonnaise on his hamburgers?"

Delsey said, "Griffin, it's okay, really, everybody knows and likes Anna."

Anna looked at Griffin. "May I speak to your sister?"

"Don't make her laugh," he said. "It might bust her head open."

"That might be tough," Delsey said. "Anna's funny."

"Okay, sweetie, here's the deal," Anna said. "Rumors are flyin' all over town ever since Henry started talkin' to people at the diner about how you were naked and the paramedics were all guys, about how there was blood in your bathtub and someone bein' there with you. That's only one of them, admittedly the most interestin'. Believe me, everybody was wild to hear the details. You never mentioned a lover. You didn't pick one up without tellin' me, did you?"

Delsey laughed, squeezed her eyes shut at the shaft of pain slicing through her head. "You weren't supposed to be funny, Anna."

"I'm sorry. Here, this will help." Anna smoothed out a dampened hand towel and lightly laid it on Delsey's forehead. She leaned close. "That better?"

"Yeah, it is. Now, listen, I may have picked up a lover last night for all I know. I don't remember. It's like hitting a blank wall. Why did Henry come down to my apartment?"

"He said it was really late and he was hearin' bumps and bangs, and then he heard you scream so he called 911. He stitched up his courage and went in your place and found you on your bathroom floor, lyin' naked—he always lowers his voice and whispers it." She shrugged, smiling. "You know Henry."

She turned to Griffin. "I'm very glad you're here. Your timin' in Maestro is like a miracle. You guys have different last names. Why?"

"She married a loser crook, kicked him to the curb, but kept his last name because she said it made the muses of music swarm into her head. Delsey said you play the violin?"

"Actually, since I grew up in the Louisiana boon-docks, bayou country, I played the fiddle first. I could still make you want to polka until you fall in a heap and shout yourself hoarse." She turned back to Delsey. "You need to get your brain back together and tell us what happened. Exactly."

CHAPTER
5

West Potomac Park
The Lincoln Memorial
Washington, D.C.
Saturday morning

"Keep everyone back!" Metro Detective Ben Raven yelled to the three WPD officers as he knelt beside Savich at the broken body of a young man. It was hard to tell how long he'd been dead because he was frozen stiff. There was a small black halo of frozen blood around his smashed head. Did that mean he hadn't died here?

It wasn't ten o'clock yet and had been snowing hard since early that morning, so there was barely a trickle of traffic. Yet there were already at least twenty gawkers bundled up in their coats looking in on them, attracted by the yellow crime tape and all the police activity.

Ben told Savich a Park Service employee had found the body only an hour before and called 911. When Ben had realized the body was on federal land, he'd gotten hold of Savich as he was babying his Porsche through the ice-covered streets from Georgetown to the Hoover Building.

Savich looked up at the solitary figure of Abraham Lincoln, felt a familiar awe and sadness for the man, wondering as he often did whether Lincoln would have managed to bring the country together again if he hadn't been assassinated. Savich looked away from the nineteen-foot marble statue and back down at the frozen, broken body. He was a boy, really, no more than twenty, Savich thought, lying close to Lincoln's statue, one frozen arm flung out toward Lincoln's chair. Savich knelt down beside him. Why was he naked? Why had his killer added this indignity? Savich found himself studying what remained of his young face. There was something about him that looked familiar. Who was he?

"No ID anywhere around him?" Savich asked.

Ben Raven shook his head. "Nothing, no clothes, no nothing at all."

His arms and legs were sprawled at odd angles, as if he'd been thrown or fallen from a great height. Savich looked up sixty feet to the grilled ceiling. "We've got to check with the Park Service, see about access." Had someone managed to haul the young man up sixty feet and throw him from the ceiling above Lincoln's head? He didn't see anything broken or unusual about the grills.

"Ben, does he look familiar to you?"

Detective Ben Raven studied the face. "Hard to tell, he's so messed up." He looked up quickly, said in a sharp voice, hard and clear as glass, "Hey, buddy, back off. No photos. This is a crime scene."

Savich wondered how many photos had already been snapped with cell phones or even with zoom lenses and uploaded to YouTube and Facebook, emailed to friends and family and *The National Enquirer*. Crime scenes in living color were everywhere now. It made their jobs harder.

"Ben," Savich said, "look again."

Ben again studied the young man's face. "No, I don't recognize him. I've got to say he wasn't dressed for the weather. Looks to me like most every bone in his body is broken. You think he was thrown from up there?" He jerked his head upward.

They both turned when the four-person FBI forensic team came up the steps of the memorial, with them Dr. Ambrose Hardy, the FBI medical examiner from Quantico.

Hardy was as skinny as his favorite fishing pole, his face covered with a thick black beard, like some underfed mountain man. The few patches of gray in his beard added to the effect.

"Savich," Dr. Hardy said, not looking at him but

down at the frozen body. "Not something I like to see on a beautiful Saturday morning." He knelt down beside the boy.

"Hey, Dillon, you look both hot and cold. Isn't it sad how that works?" He grinned up at Ms. Mary Lou Tyler, supervisor of the FBI forensic team. She was tough and smart, and though she was his mom's age, she was still a seasoned flirt. She knelt down beside Dr. Hardy. "Geez, this isn't how I planned to spend my Saturday morning, either, Ambrose."

"None of us did," Savich said, turned, and saw Sherlock running up the steps toward him. He said, "Ben, do you want to be in on this?"

Ben looked back at the thin shattered body. "Yeah," he said, "I do. Let me take you to the guy who found him. He's a longtime employee of the Park Service, name's Danny Franks. I told one of my guys to keep him warm in his squad car."

Sherlock had her creds out, so the cops in her path parted easily as she walked quickly to Savich and went down on her knees beside Mary Lou Tyler and Dr. Hardy. The two women spoke quietly. Savich watched her take in her surroundings, carefully, completely. It was her special gift, a kind of magic that happened when she re-created a crime scene in her mind. Sherlock said, "This was staged for effect, to focus public attention. Leaving him in front of Lincoln is a touch of drama to serve that purpose. A good choice, really.

"He was dead when his killer tossed him down here.

You already realized there's not enough blood with all his injuries for him to have died here." She looked up. "So how could this work? I can't see the killer climbing up access stairs sixty feet up, the boy over his shoulder. It had to be somewhere else. Actually, I doubt there's any access to the ceiling."

Dr. Hardy said, "I agree these look like massive deceleration injuries, Sherlock, such as a fall from several stories."

Sherlock rose and dusted off her hands on her pants. "Yeah, but not here, which means the killer carried him here, to this public stage, where he arranged him just so." She stared silently down at the broken body. "He's so young. This is such a waste, such a horrible, needless waste." She shivered, tucked a hank of curly hair back beneath her wool cap. "Dr. Hardy, can you tell us anything else about him?"

"Not a great deal. I'd say he was placed here within the last twelve hours; that's as close as I can get since he's frozen. He was alive when he suffered the visible injuries to his face and head. We'll know at autopsy whether any of his other injuries were postmortem. I'll have more for you this afternoon."

She said, "Thank you, Dr. Hardy. We'll leave him to you, then."

Savich said, "Ben, let's go see Danny Franks." As they carefully made their way through the heavy snow down the steps of the memorial, Savich asked her, "Sean's okay?"

"Sean's well occupied with Simon and Lilly. Computer games and popcorn at your sister's house." Sherlock shivered. "It's cold, Dillon; it's so very cold. What kind of monster would do this? And why?"

Savich said, "A monster wanting to make a statement, though it's not clear what it is. Picking the Lincoln Memorial was a sure way to make the international news very fast."

Sherlock said to Ben Raven, "I'll bet you Callie is already getting photos emailed to her at *The Washington Post*. I see the newspeople are setting up already."

Ben said, "I got a call from my wife a few minutes ago about the email she got along with a grainy photo shot from the sidewalk—impossible to see anything clearly through the snow. She wanted to know what was happening. Of course I couldn't tell her." He grinned. "It doesn't keep her from hammering at me, though." He looked up at the fat white flakes pelting down thick from the steel-gray clouds. "We'll find out who our victim is soon enough, no doubt about that." He paused, looked out over the Reflecting Pool. "Why are the weatherpeople always right when it comes to predicting the bad stuff?"

Savich looked one last time over his shoulder through the falling snow at the statue of Lincoln. What kind of statement did this horrific act mean to send? Would they be hearing from this killer again? Soon? He saw the media had arrived en masse despite the weather, newscasters speaking urgently into microphones as they stood on steps that began at the edge of the Reflecting Pool, probably leading off by describing the Lincoln Memorial with its thirty-six Doric columns and what it means to all of us. What else would they have to talk about until they learned something about the dead young man up there?

Ben eyed all the reporters. "Don't let it slip your mind, Savich, that we're standing on federal land, and that means you're in charge. And these guys are all yours." He gave Savich a huge grin and slithered off into a crowd of WPD officers.

Savich manned up and spoke to the reporters. It was nice to tell them he didn't know a thing yet, and not lie.

CHAPTER
6

Lincoln Memorial

"Makes me sick," Danny Franks said to Savich and Sherlock as they sat beside him in the Metro squad car. "Awful thing. I haven't ever seen anything like that, I mean, this poor young guy, frozen dead, and he looked like someone beat him to pieces." Franks's voice shook, and he sucked in a deep breath and focused his eyes on Sherlock's face. She'd pulled off her wool cap, sending a riot of red hair around her face. Mr. Franks didn't seem to be able to pull his eyes away from her hair. "I mean," Mr. Franks continued, "you see dead bodies all the time on TV, even see them medical examiners cutting them open, showing bloody organs, whatever, but it isn't real, you know it isn't real."

Danny looked back up to the memorial. "That young man was so young, barely starting his life."

"I know what a shock it was, Mr. Franks," Sherlock said, squeezing his gloved hands in hers. Even if she'd found his outpourings fascinating, she had to bring him back on track. "We need your help, sir. You seem like an insightful person, very visual. Can you tell us what you saw when you found the body?"

"My wife always says I'm clueless, thick as a brick. It's good to know an FBI agent thinks she's wrong. I already told a bunch of cops everything, but I know you're federal, so if the U.S. government wants to have another go, it's all right with me." He gave her a big smile. "You guys are at the top of the cop food chain."

Sherlock grinned back at him. "Start at the beginning, Mr. Franks, if you would."

He nodded. "It was almost nine o'clock when I climbed all those steps . . . Geez"—he looked down at his watch—"that was less than two hours ago. I didn't see him at first. I was whistling 'Yesterday,' you know, the Beatles? Anyways, I was making sure everything looked like it's supposed to when I nearly stepped on him." He swallowed. "I really did nearly step on him. I looked down and couldn't believe it. *It's a dead kid* was all I could think, and someone took all his clothes and left him lying beside Lincoln and he's frozen stiff."

"Did you see anyone?"

"Not a soul; no one was out yet in this miserable weather. It was real cold, I was huffing my breath into my gloves to keep my pipes from freezing up, and like I said, I nearly stumbled over him."

Sherlock squeezed Franks's hands again, kept all her attention on his ruddy face, seamed from years in the sun. He looked nearly sixty, a steady man, straightforward, and he was badly shaken. "It's all right, Mr. Franks. Take your time."

"Okay. Like I said, there wasn't anybody around except for the one guy I saw standing by himself by the Reflecting Pool, looking down at the water. I wondered if the guy was nuts. I mean, why stand there and freeze? I was thinking he wouldn't want to come trudging up here, not with the wind howling all around the columns and the blowing snow.

"As soon as I saw the kid, I called 911. It took a good five minutes for a couple of squad cars to arrive. I think the squad car we're in is one of them. Glad they've got the heat cranked up. The officers came running up and we all stood around the kid—the body. Nobody could believe it. I mean, the cops weren't as shocked as I was, but they were surprised, I could tell. One of them said to the other, 'Call Detective Raven, he's on.' And so they did. In twenty minutes or thereabouts, here comes this big young guy, and he looks down at the body and says, 'Federal land, FBI,' and he called you guys, then sent his men to interview anyone they could find."

"So it wasn't long until people started coming up to the memorial?"

"Folks seem to sniff out when something bad's happened. I'm sure you know that. They came by ones and twos, and the worst part of it was all of them wanted to rush in and freak themselves out. The cops pulled out crime scene tape, bright yellow, like on TV.

"There were about twenty people, all yapping to beat the band, wanted to know what was going on, and they were snapping photos like you wouldn't believe, until the cops managed to get them away again. I don't know if they got any of the kid, though. I sure hope not. You think about his mama seeing her son like that—"

Savich kept his voice slow and calm. "You said you saw a man standing by the Reflecting Pool, Mr. Franks. Did you see anyone else nearby? Anyone hurrying away? Running?"

"No, only that one guy standing by the Reflecting Pool. Like I said, I remember wondering why he was here, I mean, you could freeze your eyeballs early this morning."

Savich said, "Can you describe him, Mr. Franks?"

"He was all bundled up in a dark blue parka with the furred hood pulled up, nearly covered his face. I couldn't tell if he was fat or thin, he just looked bulky. I was too far away to even guess how tall or short he was, sorry. I'd guess he wasn't exactly fat; he gave me the impression he was strong, big, but I could be wrong."

Sherlock said, "Did you see this man anytime later? Could he still be here?"

"No, and I've looked for him. Haven't seen him anywhere since before the cops arrived."

Sherlock said, "Mr. Franks, when repairs are needed,

how do you access the area above the ceiling in the central chamber where Lincoln is sitting?"

"You don't; there's no access. If anything needs attention they've got to bring in those really big extension ladders, or put up scaffolding."

Savich said, "Did you look at the boy, Mr. Franks? At his face?"

Danny Franks lowered his own face to his hands, both his hands still clutching Sherlock's. "Yeah, I couldn't help myself. I looked at him good."

"Mr. Franks, did you think the young man looked familiar?"

Mr. Franks shook his head. "His face was such a mess, I don't have a clue who he is."

TWO HOURS LATER, Savich and Sherlock were at the Hoover Building when Palmer Cronin, the retired former chairman of the Federal Reserve Bank, called the FBI to identify the dead boy as his grandson, Tommy Cronin, still on his winter break from Magdalene College. His grandmother had made out her grandson's white frozen face in a photograph picked up by an Internet news site. Someone had posted it on YouTube.

CHAPTER
7

Maestro, Virginia
Early Saturday afternoon

Griffin had to pull over for half a dozen big SUVs on his prayer-filled drive through winding snow-drenched streets to Professor Salazar's house on Golden Meadow Terrace. He slid up as close as he could to the curb in front of Professor Salazar's ranch-style home. Its sloping roof and large front yard were covered with snow and flanked by snow-laden oak and pine trees. He counted four cars in the driveway. Was the party still going on?

The front door opened before he could raise his hand to knock.

A woman about his age, wearing pink shorts, of all

things—and in the winter and while it was snowing—a
nubby pink sweater, and black boots to her knees blinked
up at him. Her hair was long and black, parted in the
middle, hanging down on either side of her pale, striking face. She eyed him. "Oh, I thought it was Barbara
finally back from Starbucks, but no, you are a guy."

She sounded French. She'd spoken formally, but her
English seemed perfectly fluent. A student?

"How can you tell?" Griffin's face was covered up to
his eyebrows.

She said, "You are tall, and I can picture your legs
inside those nicely fitting jeans. Come on in; everyone
is in the living room and kitchen. Hurry, I am freezing.
Hang your coat on the rack."

No wonder she was freezing, Griffin thought, watching her hurry into the house, her hair streaming down
her back, straight as a board. He shut the door behind
him, shrugged out of his parka and wool scarf, pulled
off his ski cap and gloves, and hung everything on a coat
rack near the front door. She called over her shoulder,
"I am Gabrielle DuBois. I am Parisian, in case you are
wondering about my accent. I play the oboe. Rafael and
I make beautiful music together."

Guitar and oboe duets?

"I sing as well—in fact, better than I play the oboe."

"That's nice to know," Griffin said.

She turned to say something else and her mouth
snapped shut. She stopped in her tracks and stared at
him.

"*Mon Dieu*, if you had been at the party last night

every female would have wanted to leave with you. *C'est pas bon*—Rafael isn't going to like you at all. Who are you?"

Griffin thought she sounded both a bit alarmed and amused. Her French accent had thickened, and why was that? He fumbled pulling his creds out of his jeans pocket because her eyes were following his every move. He gritted his teeth, finally held up his shield. "Special Agent Griffin Hammersmith, FBI."

"Mais c'est impossible!" came out of her mouth. She cleared her throat and said, "But how can you be an FBI agent? I mean, you should be a movie star like Brad Pitt."

"Can't act," he said.

Gabrielle gave him a classic Gallic shrug. "Ah, but who would care if you can act, except for those idiot critics no one with a heart pays any attention to?"

A male voice heavy with the mellifluous cadence of Barcelona called out, "Gabrielle! Who is at the door? Is it Barbara? With my Starbucks nonfat mocha cinnamon latte?"

Griffin waved a hand toward the voice. "Professor Salazar, I presume?"

"Yes, that is he, and he is not going to like you, *pas du tout*." Gabrielle gave him a wicked smile, and sashayed away, hips at full throttle. Griffin smiled after her since he wasn't dead, and followed her mobile butt and swinging hair toward the noise. He'd hoped to find the professor alone, but that was not to be.

He stepped into a long, narrow living room to see a

half-dozen women, though none in shorts like Gabrielle, all chatting and laughing as they filled plastic tubs with dirty plates and glasses, emptied overflowing ashtrays, rearranged furniture. How did the good professor manage to pull off a cleaning crew like this? And in this weather? Griffin was impressed.

Professor Salazar was the only man in the room. Griffin hadn't taken the time to check up on Salazar before he came over. He wanted to get a sense of his character before knowing anything else about him. He was tall and dark, his black eyes heavily lidded—*smooth-looking* was the word that came to Griffin's mind. His haughty dark brows and high-bridged nose were set in a face that hadn't seen forty in a good long time. He had thick black hair, with distinguished flecks of gray at the temples, and beautiful hands, with long, tapered fingers. All in all, Griffin thought, he managed to carry off the European aristocrat look rather well, but sadly, he also reminded Griffin of a complacent lizard sunning on a rock, fully aware that his rock was the most important anywhere around. He was wearing dark slacks, moccasins, and of all things, he wore a smoking jacket. A cigarillo dangled between his fingers. Maybe he was trying for the Barcelona Bohemian look. Griffin wanted to tell him he was an idiot to smoke.

He was staring toward Griffin, not moving. He did not look happy. And why was that, since his house was getting cleaned for him?

"Oh, hi," said another young woman, stepping in front of him. She came to his armpit, a little fairy with long glossy light brown hair kept back from her face with a gold band. She was wearing sweats and sneakers. "I'm Gloria. I play the viola." She lowered her voice to a whisper, "My goodness, I can't believe Professor Salazar actually asked you here to help clean up. Why haven't I ever seen you before?"

"I just got into town."

She brightened. "What is your instrument?"

"Sorry, no instrument." He pulled out his creds again. "He didn't invite me. I'm from the FBI, here to see the professor."

Gloria blinked up at him as she quickly stepped back. "I swear we didn't smoke anything but a little weed last night, and Professor Salazar didn't know about it, well, maybe he did, but he didn't have any—I didn't see any cocaine or anything *really* illegal like that, really."

"I'm here because of Delsey Freestone." He'd raised his voice a bit and the room fell silent, every face fastened on his. "Have you heard what happened to her?"

Griffin saw Professor Salazar straighten when he said Delsey's name. He hurried over, introducing himself in midstride. Griffin showed him his creds and the good professor waved them away.

"What do you mean about Delsey? Something's happened to her? Is she all right? She left last night without telling me. I looked for her, but someone said she slipped out the back door. I tried calling her this morning to see if she wanted to come over, but there was no answer, only voice mail. Why is the FBI here?"

Griffin told them Delsey was in the hospital with a

concussion because she'd been struck down in her apartment late last night, assailant unknown. He said nothing about the blood in the bathtub. "No one called any of you? Apparently, it's all over town."

Salazar said, "Our little party ended rather late. I gather many of us have hardly been out. But she will be all right, will she not?"

Griffin nodded.

"I'm so sorry," another young woman said, this one thin as her black pigtails, and wearing six rings on her fingers. She reminded him of Abby on *NCIS*, but without the tattoos. "Delsey's a sweetheart. Was it a robbery?"

"We're not sure yet."

"Can we see her?"

"She has a concussion, so she's not up to visitors yet," Griffin said.

"Please tell her we're all hoping she gets well soon."

"Thank you."

"It's awfully cold out. Would you like some coffee?"

"No, thank you. I prefer to wait for Barbara and that Starbucks nonfat mocha cinnamon latte."

There were nervous laughs.

"This is terrible," Salazar said, stubbing out his cigarillo in an ashtray held out to him by another woman, this one about Delsey's age. Salazar's accent grew exponentially thicker as he said, flapping his hands, "My beautiful Delsey, how could such a thing happen here in Maestro? This is hardly New York, where robberies take place every second. Who would do this? She should have been safe here, but then again, this is America, and who knows what can happen anywhere in America? There is too much violence on your television. It is disgraceful.

"Poor Delsey would have stayed here if Elliot had left her alone, but no, he was all over her, getting her to drink his deadly margaritas—and that is why she went home and interrupted a robbery, is this correct? It is his fault this happened." Salazar caught himself when he realized every ear in the living room was wide open and receiving.

"We don't know yet whether or not it was a robbery."

Salazar shrugged that off. "Come with me, Agent Hammersmith. We will go to my study and I will answer all your questions." He gave a general nod to the women in his living room and walked out.

Griffin smiled at the women. "After I've spoken to the professor, I'd like to speak to each of you. Please don't leave."

"We cannot leave at all until we finish cleaning up this pigsty," Gabrielle said.

Skinny Black Pigtails said, "How did this stain get on the sofa?"

Gloria, the little fairy, sang out, "Who could even get in Delsey's apartment? She has a gazillion locks on the door."

She got that one right, Griffin thought. Delsey always locked up tight ever since a kid had broken into her apartment in Santa Monica, looking for dope. Delsey, of course, had walked in on him, belted him with a lamp, and called the cops. Last night she never realized the back door had been broken open.

Gabrielle said, "I know who you are now, Agent Hammersmith. You're Delsey's brother. She looks like you. She also talks about you all the time." She turned away, said to no one in particular, "Perhaps she was involved in something very bad, I think, knowing she has this beautiful FBI brother to protect her." He heard her add, a bit of venom lacing her words, "You know she is all about trying to steal other women's men. I wouldn't be surprised."

Sounds like you've got an enemy here, Delsey. Who is she jealous about?

CHAPTER
8

Griffin followed Salazar down a short hallway and through a soundproofed door on the right. It was a music room, not a study. Four different beautifully crafted antique classical guitars, all polished to high brilliance, were placed with obvious care by a loving hand throughout the room. A music stand with open music on it stood by a shining black baby grand piano, and folding chairs were lined up side by side against a wall, as if Salazar practiced for an audience. Probably the group in his living room.

Griffin walked to the small fireplace, leaned against the mantel, and crossed his arms over his chest. "Tell me what you know about Delsey. You said someone called Elliot was showing her too much attention at your party last night. Who is that, Professor Salazar?"

Salazar gave a Gallic shrug to rival Gabrielle's and walked to the grand piano. He paused a moment, pulled a white handkerchief out of his smoking jacket pocket, and lightly rubbed it over a small spot on the piano lid, then moved to stand behind a small, hypermodern ebony desk in the corner. "I am as sorry about Delsey as you are, Agent, believe me. You have my sympathy. As for Elliot, I suppose you will find out soon enough. I was speaking of Dr. Elliot Hayman. He is the director of Stanislaus and also my brother—my twin brother, to be exact. We are fraternal twins and so are not mirrors of each other."

"I understand the two of you grew up apart."

"That's right. I was a teenager before I saw him again, in Madrid, but we are brothers, and thus when he invited me to spend a year at Stanislaus, I accepted. Now, I will tell you that what happened last night is not unusual. This time Elliot focused on Delsey, gave her margaritas he made himself. I must say that Elliot is entirely too familiar with female students here, despite his position. I have told him as much, but he ignores me. As for the Stanislaus board, they pretend not to notice. You would think they'd be more watchful, since Dr. Gordon Holcombe, the former director of Stanislaus, left under, let us say, a very black cloud."

The pot and the kettle. "What cloud was this, Professor?"

"There were murders here at Stanislaus last year. It is believed Dr. Holcombe murdered his longtime secretary and lover. He fled. No one knows where he is. I doubt anyone is looking for him, since I was told there isn't enough evidence to send him to jail."

So this was the horrific trouble Ruth and Dr. Chesney had spoken about. He wanted to know more about it, but not now. Griffin asked, "So Dr. Hayman was asked to become the director of Stanislaus after Dr. Holcombe's departure?"

"Yes. He plays the piano rather well on the international stage, and that gives him the stature for his position, and a certain cachet, I suppose. But withal he has the soul of an administrator, so he was taken to be a good choice by the board."

Griffin said, "Your brother invited you here, yet you don't get along?"

Salazar drew up. "I am not criticizing my brother. I merely state facts."

"You mean it's a fact that Dr. Hayman seduces Stanislaus students?"

Salazar spared him a condescending glance. "I know it is difficult for you, but you must try to understand. It is not at all uncommon among musicians—these attempts to connect with those who share our passions, to keep our balance, and, shall I say it, to gain a certain release. It happens everywhere. Music is a haunting mistress that can consume the souls of the truly gifted."

And the Spanish lizard shrugged yet again. *As if that said it all,* Griffin thought, *and excused any behavior.* He said, "I see. So as long as one is careful and exercises a bit of discretion, these connections are overlooked, ignored?"

"It is the civilized thing to do."

"Then why were you so angry with Dr. Hayman for wanting to forge a connection to Delsey?"

"I suppose because she was hurt last night and because Elliot is not what she needs. She is an innocent, though she is a brilliant musician, more driven than most. It is unfortunate she continues to pursue a commercial path. I am endeavoring to guide her away from that profane choice." He lightly flicked a spot of lint from his smoking jacket. "Naturally, Delsey, like all gifted musicians, needs guidance."

"And you wish to be the one to provide this guidance?"

If Salazar suspected irony, he didn't show it. He merely nodded. "That is correct. We are like spirits, she and I."

Amazing.

"But tell me, Agent, what happened to her last night? What *really* happened to her, not the press version you gave out to those credulous girls in the living room."

Griffin smiled. "What happened was exactly what I said. I have nothing more to add for the moment." He realized he really wanted to punch out the lizard—not good, he had to get control of himself. He said, "I assume you're enjoying your year here at Stanislaus?"

"Yes, certainly. So many talented musicians, and the atmosphere here is intimate and congenial and conducive to study and performance. Not like all the distractions that plague Juilliard, for example."

"Professor Salazar, you said Delsey slipped out without anyone seeing her?"

"Hardly anyone. I went looking for her, but I could not find her. Clarice—she is one of our flautists—told me she saw Delsey slip out the back door. She saw her do this, so it is not supposition. I know she was escaping him. There is no doubt in my mind."

"Did you notice if anyone else left the party about the same time Delsey snuck out?"

This gave Salazar pause. He slowly shook his head. "Not that I can remember. One of the students demanded my attention, and I was occupied. Always the students need my attention."

"Was Delsey drunk from the margaritas Dr. Hayman gave her?"

"It is possible."

"Did you ever hear Delsey mention she was worried about someone? Another student, perhaps? Another professor here at Stanislaus?"

"No, certainly not. Well, the students—you must understand that competition is not only encouraged, it is necessary. There are few truly major orchestra seats available for talented musicians to win. For those students, like Delsey, who wish to gain success in composition, there are also many others vying for recognition. Talent is not enough. It is drive that gains the brass ring. Delsey's fingers could close on the ring, if she would fight for it."

"Could all that competition have led to violence? Out of jealousy, perhaps?"

"Surely not, but it is a thought that must intrude, is it not?" He frowned toward one of his guitars. "Drive and effort are what are needful in every worthwhile pursuit in life. Perhaps even in yours?" Again, a whiff of contempt.

"Perhaps you will be able to observe that for yourself, Professor," Griffin said.

When Griffin left Salazar's study, he heard him shout for Barbara to bring him his nonfat mocha cinnamon latte. Griffin returned to the living room, settled in on the sofa with the stain, and started asking questions.

Gabrielle DuBois said, "There was no earthly *raison* for Dr. Hayman to single her out, but Professor Salazar is right. He did last night, gave her drink after drink. And why, I ask you?" Her French accent was very pronounced, this time for dramatic effect, enough to make Griffin grin. "I mean, does she sing like Edith Piaf? *Non*, she does not. She has not the talent to achieve any sort of magnificent height." *Like mine*, he heard her add under her breath.

If Gabrielle was edgy and harsh in her dislike of Delsey, Griffin soon got the impression several of the other women also didn't appreciate Delsey's getting so much of Dr. Hayman's attention. Simple jealousy or ambition? He realized some of the women were frightened about the attack because it was too close to home. Others appeared to be worried about Delsey, but none of them admitted to anything strange or unusual having happened at the party the previous evening or to having any idea who might have hurt her.

Griffin asked the group, "Why do you think Professor Salazar and Dr. Hayman don't get along?"

Barbara of Starbucks fame, a full-bodied future opera singer with an incredibly rich speaking voice, said, "They're brothers, twins. I'll bet they've competed since they were kids, fought all the time. And now here they are together again at Stanislaus, both fishing in the same pond."

The little fairy, Gloria of viola fame, said, "Really, Barbara, I don't like to think of myself as a tuna. Professor Salazar and Dr. Hayman have made it into a fine art. But, you know, I can't recall ever hearing Dr. Hayman saying anything about Professor Salazar."

"Professor Salazar, on the other hand," Barbara said, "is always insulting, snipping, but only when Dr. Hayman isn't around."

Gloria said, "It is true, though many of the professors who aren't married or near death are the same way." She grinned at him. "But the professors aren't stupid. Most of them steer really clear of the undergraduate students."

Black Pigtails said, "No one wants to be lonely, do they? Everyone wants some attention and intimacy now and then, and what's wrong with that? I only wish Professor Salazar would pay for our gas to come here."

Gabrielle said, "Yes, but Professor Salazar is not like his brother. He is seeing me, only me."

Black Pigtails said matter-of-factly, "Yes, and since Professor Salazar told you you sing like Edith Piaf, you've practically had it tattooed on your butt."

There was one lone snigger.

Salazar strolled into the room, his Starbucks cup in one hand. He didn't look at Griffin, but told Gabrielle he was certain he'd seen a small sausage roll beneath the sofa. She was on her hands and knees in an instant, her butt in the air, and he stood behind her, smoking another cigarette.

Griffin had to admit it, he was shocked, though none of the other women seemed to find her display unusual.

Griffin left Salazar's rented house on Golden Meadow Terrace a thoughtful man. Would Delsey have ever told him about this soap opera?

CHAPTER
9

Henderson County Hospital
Saturday afternoon

The door to Delsey's memory wouldn't open even a crack. The more she shoved at the door, the more it made her head hurt.

Griffin strode into the hospital room, paused for a moment in the doorway to study her. "Stop it, Delsey, you're thinking too hard."

She flapped her hand at him. "It doesn't matter how hard I try, I still can't remember much. Where have you been? Nobody knew."

He walked to her bed, took her hand. "You were sleeping, so I went to see Professor Salazar. The snow's been coming down so hard again you can barely see a foot in front of you, but the good professor had managed to convince half a dozen students to drive to his house and clean up the mess from last night. The place was gossip central, once I told them what had happened to you."

"I'll bet they were all women, and Professor Salazar won't pay them a cent. There's not even any extra credit."

Griffin smiled. He told her about Gabrielle DuBois in her summer-pink shorts, on her hands and knees searching under the sofa and putting on a show for Professor Salazar.

"Gabrielle has been after him from the moment he stepped out of his brand-new Fiat in September. Then he made the mistake of paying attention to her. She's having an affair with him, but still, he likes to be among his musicians, especially the women. As you probably saw, this doesn't make Gabrielle happy. You know, even if he does play like a god and looks really good, he's still got too many notches on his belt—I wouldn't want to sleep with him."

Griffin said, "You've always been clear-sighted about people, and living in the melting pot of L.A., I imagine you've seen it all before. None of these personalities is new to you. True?"

"Yes, all right, but I sometimes think I saw too much in L.A." She brightened. "But at least in L.A. the guys on the beach were buff. Hey, did Gabrielle bring him his chilled glass of fresh-squeezed orange juice, the pulp removed?"

"That must have been before I arrived. He was obsessing about a latte. Oh, yes, Gloria sends her best wishes. Now, Salazar told me the director, Dr. Hayman—his twin brother—was all over you last night, plying you with too many margaritas. I think Salazar wants you to replace Gabrielle."

Delsey shook her head, regretted it, and held perfectly still. "Not me in particular." And Griffin laughed, since she'd echoed the other women at Salazar's house.

"Nope. Professor Salazar really wants Anna, not Gabrielle."

"Anna, as in your best friend?"

"Yep, but he better pray he doesn't get her, because Anna's tough, doesn't put up with any guff."

"Sort of like you?"

Delsey laughed. "Anna says Professor Salazar's a talented lush with a cool name and an exaggerated accent, but I know he wants her; I'm only a stray guppy, an afterthought. She's the one who told me she'd read he and his twin Dr. Hayman were separated as boys and it was Rafael the mom took back to Spain. He is always waxing eloquent about his upbringing in Barcelona and his training at Queen Sofía College of Music in Madrid, studying under the famous Natalia Bron."

She sighed. "I guess I was drunk."

"Sounds like it. That's weird for you, Ms. One Drink." He turned toward the door. "Ah, here he is, your friend and neighbor, Mr. Stoltzen. He asked if he could come see you." Griffin nodded to Henry. "Mr. Stoltzen."

Henry didn't quite meet his eyes. He whispered, "Please, Agent Hammersmith, call me Henry."

"All right," Griffin said, and watched Delsey smile with affection at him.

Henry was different, Delsey knew it when she'd first met him, and she really liked him—impossible not to. She took his hand, shook it. "Hey, dude. You found me and called the paramedics. Thank you."

Griffin had met music nerds before Henry, and when Stoltzen had stopped him in the lobby, Griffin knew he fit the bill nicely. He was on the short side, his shoulders stooped, his skin vampire-pale and soft-looking, like he'd never thrown anything heavier than a wadded-up piece of paper into a wastebasket. He wore a long goatee, blacker even than his shaggy hair, meaning he probably dyed it. Still, all six inches of it was a pure distraction, an excellent affectation for him. Even though Griffin had read the statement Dix took from Henry, he thought it was a good idea to let him visit with Delsey. Perhaps he would help her remember something.

He watched Henry slink to Delsey's bedside, and stand looking down at her knees, not her face, shifting his feet back and forth. "It was really bad, Delsey," he said, finally looking at her face. "I came by earlier to speak to Agent Noble. Then I wanted to see you, but the deputy outside your room wouldn't let me come in—"

"You didn't recognize Deputy Claus?"

"Sure, and he recognized me, too, but he said I still

needed permission, but Agent Noble was gone and there was no one to give it to me." He turned to Griffin. "Delsey talks about you a lot."

"Not all bad," Delsey said.

Griffin said, "Why didn't you go to the party, Mr. Stoltzen? Henry?"

"I wasn't invited. I'm not pretty enough."

Delsey said to her brother, "Professor Salazar's parties always have more women than men."

Both Griffin and Delsey heard spite in Henry's voice when he said, "According to what I've heard, Salazar doesn't like competition."

Then where's the harm in inviting you? Griffin said, "I know you already told your story to Sheriff Noble and Agent Noble, but please humor me and tell us both again, from the beginning, Mr. . . . Henry."

"Yeah, okay, I can do that." He looked down at Delsey. "I heard you pull in at about one o'clock and looked out the window, saw you unlock your door and walk in. I admit it, Delsey, I did wonder if you'd had too much fun at Salazar's party. You looked like you were weaving around a bit."

Delsey said, "And I'll never do that again for as long as I live, so help me God."

"Good," Griffin said, then turned to Henry again. "You said you heard something come from Delsey's apartment and it worried you? How long was this after she came in at one o'clock?"

"Maybe about ten minutes before she walked in. I thought I heard some bumping around, like there was someone in her apartment, a visitor maybe, but then I didn't hear anything else, and so I thought I imagined it. Until Delsey screamed. I banged on the floor and called 911, and then I listened some more, and then I walked down."

"Do you remember what time it was?" Griffin asked.

Henry's eyes darted to Griffin's face. He popped his knuckles. "You know, it took me a while to decide there really was a problem, Delsey. I didn't know for sure until you screamed. But I thought maybe you had a guy staying with you, and I didn't want to intrude."

Was that a hint of jealousy in his voice?

Delsey snorted. "Come on, Henry, when was the last time I had a guy over for the night?"

"Well, now that I think about it, maybe never."

"It's sad," Delsey said. "Anna's always telling me to get rid of the bushel."

"Bushel?" Henry asked.

"As in hiding your light under—"

"Hey, that's funny, Delsey." Henry beamed at her.

Griffin said smoothly, "How long did you wait after you called 911 before you went downstairs and through Delsey's front door, Henry?"

"I heard some more noises, and I banged on the floor again. I was going to wait for the cops to arrive, but after a couple of minutes I didn't hear anything, and like I said, I went downstairs."

Griffin said, "Better you waited a bit, Henry, or you might have been hurt. You didn't see anyone? Hear anyone or anything other than the bumping sounds?"

Henry shook his head. "Nope, not a thing—well, I did hear a car engine when I was already on my way to check on Delsey, but that's it. I was thinking about her."

"Did you happen to glance out a window, see the car?"

"No, sir, I'm sorry, but I didn't."

"What did you do next?"

"Your front door wasn't locked, Delsey, so I stuck my head in and called your name. When you didn't answer, I went on in."

CHAPTER
10

Griffin asked, "Was anything out of place, Henry?"

Henry said to Delsey, "Yeah, that little Persian carpet you're so proud of was all crumpled against the table you have for your mail."

Like someone had dragged a body over it or was in a big hurry.

"I can't remember anything else out of place. When I looked in your bathroom, there you were lying on the floor, on your side, your clothes in a pile beside you. You weren't moving, and I thought you were dead at first. It scared the crap out of me, Delsey. It looked like you'd slipped and fallen, hit your head, maybe, because there was blood in your hair and on the floor. I didn't see the blood in the bathtub until a paramedic pointed it out, said it was way too much to all be yours. I guess one of the paramedics called Sheriff Noble, because he came right away and asked me about it. He let me follow the ambulance to the hospital, but they wouldn't let me near you since I wasn't family, so I finally went home.

"I did go to bed, but I couldn't sleep, not a wink, so I spent most of the night listening to Anton Rubinstein's Cello Concerto in A Minor. You know, the piece I'm going to perform in February. What I really wanted was to actually practice it, but I know Mr. McGibbs would be pissed since it was the middle of the night—" Henry shrugged. "Mr. McGibbs lives a good fifty feet away from us but he still bitches if I play too late. I guess I finally fell asleep, since I didn't wake up until about nine o'clock this morning. I called the hospital, but nobody would tell me anything, so I went to Maurie's Diner for breakfast. Anna was there. Since she's your best friend, I told her what happened. She was really upset. I saw her walk over to the restrooms and make a call on her cell phone. When she came back with my bacon and eggs, she spilled coffee on me."

Who did she call? Griffin wondered.

"Henry, did you tell someone I found my lover dead in the bathtub? Why ever did you say such a thing?"

Henry flushed, looked agonized, and popped his knuckles again. "Well, that blood the paramedics saw in the tub and what I heard meant someone else was there—and, well, I didn't know who, Delsey, that's all, I said something about your maybe knowing him; it made it a little less scary, you know?"

Griffin let it go. "Is that all you remember, Henry?"

"Yes, sir."

Griffin nearly laughed at all the "sirring," since Henry Stoltzen looked to be a couple of years older than he was. He'd seen it before. It was the power of the FBI shield.

Griffin said, "Delsey, since I taught you well, I know you locked your front door when you left for Salazar's party. Whoever was in your place jimmied open the back door."

She stared at him. "I didn't know. I must not have noticed when I went in. I still don't remember anything."

They heard Claus say, "Sir, you can't go in there—"

Henry said, "Oh my, it's Dr. Hayman."

Griffin raised his hand. "It's okay, Claus. Thank you." He watched Dr. Elliot Hayman, director of Stanislaus, walk—no, stroll—into the room.

So this was Professor Salazar's brother. Dr. Hayman was a bit taller than his twin, a bit leaner, and even more the fashion plate in a fur-lined suede jacket, perfectly pleated black slacks, white shirt, tie, and Italian loafers he'd obviously protected since they had a high shine and no sign of snow or mud. Apart from a certain Mediterranean look, there wasn't much physical resemblance between them. There were no slashes of gray at Dr. Hayman's temples. He looked younger than his brother, and, Griffin thought, he appeared more thoughtful. Dr. Hayman's eyes rested on Griffin; his dark brows went up. He didn't look through Griffin, as his brother had. He met his eyes and nodded. "So I'm told you are Delsey's brother, Agent Griffin Hammersmith of the FBI?"

"Yes, I am." He shook Dr. Hayman's hand, a fine hand with long, thin fingers, like his brother's. Griffin had to admit Dr. Hayman looked more a convincing aristocrat than his smooth lizard twin. He had more gravitas, had the look of a man in charge of his kingdom.

"I am glad to meet you, Agent Hammersmith. I have come because I was quite worried when I heard Delsey had been hurt. She is one of our finest students. No one could tell me what happened. Ah, here is Mr. Stoltzen. How are you today, Henry? How is the Rubinstein cello concerto coming along?"

Henry beamed. "I'll be ready, sir."

"Yes, of course you will."

Henry darted Delsey a glance. "I, ah, I've got to go, Delsey, all right?"

She nodded, waited for Henry to leave, then said to Dr. Hayman, "Thank you for coming, sir."

"Of course. You and your brother, you have different last names. Why is this?"

Delsey smiled up at him. "Freestone was my married name. Even though I'm no longer married, I liked the name because it sang to me, and so I kept it." She left unspoken *even though it belonged to a real loser.* "How did you know Griffin is my brother?"

"Ah, your brother has already been around town,

asking Rafael, and many of your well-wishers, about you. I heard he was here at the same time I learned of your injury." He walked regally to Delsey's bedside and took her hand. "My poor child, whatever has happened? Are you all right?"

With the way he'd recognized and treated Henry, the concern he was showing for Delsey, Griffin thought Dr. Hayman had all the charm and charisma his twin lacked.

"Could you please tell me what happened?"

Griffin gave him the general outline, but no more than he needed to know. "Dr. Hayman, I understand my sister had a bit too much to drink at your brother's party last night. Something to do with your special margaritas?"

Dr. Hayman nodded toward Delsey. "If that had anything to do with what happened to you, I am very sorry." He smiled down at her. "The party gave me an opportunity to speak to you, since there is so little opportunity at school. But then you disappeared and no one knew where you were. What happened?"

"I decided to go home, Dr. Hayman, and someone hit me on the head in my apartment."

Dr. Hayman waited for her to say more, but she didn't.

Griffin said, "Sir, have you noticed anyone recently who didn't seem to belong on campus? Someone you found not quite right?"

Dr. Hayman seemed to give this thought, stroking his chin with his beautiful long, thin fingers. "I'm sorry, but no. I am quite busy in my position, Agent Hammersmith. There is so much to do each day, so many students demanding my attention, not to mention the faculty and the board of directors. It sometimes seems a whirlwind, and I see so many people. It's rare that I'm able to simply enjoy the company of a student as I did last night. But then you were gone, Delsey, simply gone, and I must say, I was a bit worried." He gave her a warm smile.

"They tell me I will be fine, probably back to school in a couple of days. Please don't worry about me. Thank you for coming to see me."

"It is my responsibility to worry about my students," he said, but gave Delsey a warmer smile than Griffin thought was necessary or appropriate. "Such a shock, someone in your apartment, striking you down. I certainly hope our law enforcement officers will get to the bottom of this quickly and put an end to it. We cannot have such things happening to our students; the board will not stand for it." He added to Griffin, "I am glad you're here to help them, Agent Hammersmith."

Griffin nodded.

Dr. Hayman said to Delsey, "You will call me if there is anything you require? And you, Agent Hammersmith? If there is anything we can do to sort this all out, we are at your service."

Griffin followed Dr. Hayman out of Delsey's hospital room, impressed with how well he wore the mantle of director of Stanislaus, like a well-picked actor from central casting. Unlike his brother, Dr. Hayman was one to quiet troubled waters, not stir them up.

There was nothing Griffin liked better than to stir troubled waters. He said without preamble, "Why are you so interested in my sister, Dr. Hayman?"

Dr. Hayman said, "I am interested in all my students, Agent Hammersmith. Delsey reminds me of your incredible grandmother Aladonna Hammersmith. She was an immensely talented woman, both witty and charming. I can still remember her incomparable voice, her artistry. I consider it a privilege to mentor her granddaughter and perhaps change her mind about continuing in a commercial direction with her compositions. She should be developing her talent to create something lasting with her music."

"Thank you for those nice words about my grandmother, Dr. Hayman. As for Delsey, she has never been at a loss about what direction to take her life. I met your brother this morning. Why is it you invited him here as a visiting professor?"

Dr. Hayman blinked, taken off guard for a moment, but clearly understanding why Griffin was asking. "Rafael is a fine musician, and, more important, he has the ability and the temperament to teach, which many talented musicians do not. He was more than qualified to join the Stanislaus faculty." He looked back at Griffin as if daring him to express an opinion.

"I wish you a good day, Agent Hammersmith, and hope you will solve this nasty business. If you would be so kind as to keep me informed? And of Delsey's progress as well."

Griffin nodded. Dr. Hayman shook his hand again, and walked away.

When Griffin returned to Delsey's room, she said, "I remember now. I remember seeing a dead man in my bathtub."

CHAPTER
11

Savich's house
Georgetown, Washington, D.C.
Saturday evening

Since a record snowfall had brought Washington to a
standstill, Savich Skyped his agents and Mr. Maitland
from home. He looked at each of them arrayed in front
of him on MAX's new twenty-three-inch monitor. He
could see Mr. Maitland's wife moving around in the
background, carrying what looked like a huge bowl
of guacamole and chips for her four sons, whose eyes were
probably fixed on the play-off game the agents were missing. In smaller boxes were the faces of agents Ollie
Hamish, Lucy Carlyle, and Coop McKnight. Ollie rocked
his infant daughter in his arms.

Savich said, "Thomas Malcolm Cronin was twenty years old, a student at Magdalene College in Boonton, Virginia, about an hour's drive from the Beltway. As you probably know, Magdalene is a small, prestigious liberal-arts school with an outstanding academic reputation. Most of its endowments come from its wealthy alumni, leaders in both the business world and in politics, in roughly the same percentage as Harvard or Yale. It's very private and very expensive.

"Thomas declared a business major at the beginning of the fall semester, junior year, with an emphasis in international banking."

"Like his granddaddy," Agent Lucy Carlyle said, "following in the steps of the Big Buddha."

Jimmy Maitland shook his head. "Not anymore, sadly. That nickname, though, it sure fits Cronin, even though he's skinny as a bicycle spoke. It's that placid all-knowing smile, the way he sits with his hands folded in front of him. Too bad he wasn't enlightened enough to try to head off a worldwide banking collapse."

Savich said, "Coop, tell us about Palmer Cronin's son and wife."

Coop said, "Cronin's only son, Palmer Cronin Jr., was a big muckety-muck partner at Pearlman Lock. I'm sure some of you remember he was killed last year when his Ferrari skidded off an embankment, through a railing, and into the Potomac. His wife, Barbara, died two years ago, a purported suicide with a bottle of pills."

Lucy said, "I remember the son's death was huge news. It was ruled an accident."

Coop said, "Yes, it was. You know his son's tragic death had to hit Cronin Senior hard. First Barbara, his daughter-in-law, then his son, both dead within two years."

Savich said, "Cronin Junior left three children, two daughters and a son, Tommy. Barbara Cronin's sister, Marian Lodge, had moved in with the family after her sister's death to take over the care of the kids. After Cronin Junior's death, she applied for guardianship, and it was made official a couple of months ago."

Lucy said, "So much tragedy in one family, and now this."

Savich thought of Sean, and closed it off.

He said, "Okay, that's the background. Now let's get back to the grandson. Thomas Malcolm Cronin—Tommy—had a three-point-eight GPA, quite an achievement at Magdalene. His father and his grandfather were both alumni, and both were big contributors. There's a big new business administration building on campus called Cronin Hall, after the grandfather, who, as you know, retired as chairman of the Federal Reserve Banking System right after the investment banking debacle came to light."

Ollie Hamish snorted. "Talk about a retirement coming way too late. It still frosts me that Palmer Cronin claimed he never expected the bankers' shenanigans, that his philosophy of self-regulation turned out to be simply wrong. How incompetent does that make him?"

Coop said, "I think you're expressing only one side of the anger and frustration that's out there, Ollie. What about the politicians who said they were willing to take the risk and then pressed the banks to finance home loans for people who obviously couldn't pay the mortgage?"

Mr. Maitland said, "There was predatory lending, for sure, but don't forget the people determined to cash in on the real estate bubble, willing to sign anything to get their share of the pie. There's surely enough blame to go around."

"Maybe so," Ollie said, "but most of the anger out there is at the bankers and Wall Street. That's where it all started, with their packaging crap derivatives and worthless home loans and selling them to pension funds and municipalities and other banks—hey, to anyone who trusted them."

As if to agree, Ollie's small daughter burped in her sleep, making everyone laugh.

Ollie patted her small head. "I wonder if she'll agree with me when she's a teenager. So there's rage out there, and there's been some violence. There may even be justification for thinking some of the bloody bankers and some of our precious lawmakers ought to be in a criminal institution. Where does that leave us?"

Lucy and Coop were sitting side by side on the sofa, both in sweats. She said, "It leaves us with the fact that Palmer Cronin wasn't the one who was murdered. It was Tommy, a twenty-year-old, who for all we know never did anything wrong in his short life. If Tommy was targeted by some kind of deluded out-there anarchist to make a statement, that isn't a reflection of any justified anger still circulating in society, it's a Timothy McVeigh kind of insanity."

Savich said, "That's assuming the crime was a political act, Lucy, but that's not a trail I'm ready to commit to unless the investigation points us that way. All right, we've all had a chance to vent. Let's move along to the photos of Tommy uploaded to YouTube. We're going to treat the photos as part of the crime scene, since anyone close enough to upload a photo of Tommy may have been a witness, and we've been tracking those uploads to find those witnesses. Mr. Maitland?"

He saw Mr. Maitland turn around at the shouts and groans coming from his sons, who were glued to the play-off game, then back again. He said, "Ben Raven has been handling that. Most of the photos that have been uploaded aren't relevant; they're from around Magdalene College, yearbook photos, or photos with friends horsing around. We've found several photos of the crime scene, though, most showing no real detail because of the snow or because the cops had already established a solid perimeter around the Lincoln Memorial by the time they were taken. There was one, though, that was very close and very clear."

"This is the photo," Savich said, and brought it up onto the screen. "It's the one Mrs. Cronin saw on the Internet that led Mr. Cronin to call us. It's a close-up, straight-on view of Tommy's face. Was it taken by Tommy's killer or an accomplice, as a way of assuming credit and publicizing his killing? Or by someone who happened by at the right time and thought it would be cool to post it? There were no comments posted with it."

Ollie said, "Or maybe even a cop."

Savich said, "No one wants a cop to be the source. Believe me, Ben Raven is all over it. We're dealing with all the photos by tracking down the IP addresses they were posted from. We have all of them already, except for this one."

"What's the holdup?" Coop asked.

Savich said, "Our techs have run into a roadblock, because whoever posted this photo used a bogus YouTube account and a proxy server to hide his tracks. We're up against a computer nerd who knew we'd be trying to track his posting and knew how to protect himself. It's the strongest reason we have to believe the killer or killers posted this picture, and not someone who happened by."

Mr. Maitland said, "So why not get Spooner in on this? You've said yourself, Savich, it takes one to catch one."

"You're right," Savich said.

Ollie said, "We've all heard about surfing the Web anonymously, using what they call anonymizers. What do they do exactly, Savich?"

"They're a sort of privacy shield between a client computer and the rest of the Web, so you can protect your personal information by hiding your computer's identity."

Lucy said, "I read that a lot of the child pornography on the Internet is accessed through anonymizers."

Savich said, "Like a lot of tools, anonymizers can be used for good or bad. If you lived in Iran or China, for example, where the Internet is severely restricted, using an anonymizer could save your life unless you make a mistake, and believe me, you've got to know what you're doing. It gets even more complicated when you're posting something—like a photograph. Then you need your own software to create a Web proxy and establish connections between chains of servers to hide your tracks. We've got a shot, though. I'll get Spooner on it right away."

Mr. Maitland said, "Spooner has liaised with the NSA for us in the past. If there's a way to find this guy, Spooner will do it. Of course, there are new articles and postings about the Cronins all over the Web now—photos of the family, comments by Tommy's friends at Magdalene College, as well as blogs and forums with theories about why he was murdered in such a public way. It's a hodgepodge, though some of them are cruel. There's even talk of a family curse, what with the death of both Tommy Cronin's parents in the last two years, and now their only son."

Ollie said, "All the Internet hype—I'm thinking it's what the killer wanted. Savich, do we have anything else going besides Spooner tracing that upload to YouTube?"

"Not much. Ben has already spoken by telephone to two men and one woman he tracked down who'd uploaded what they could see of the crime scene on social networks. They told him they didn't see anyone get close to the body because the police were keeping everyone at a distance by the time they arrived.

"Needless to say, we'd know a lot more about Tommy's whereabouts last night by now if the weather hadn't shut down the power and the roads, making it a no-go today.

"Sherlock and I will drive to Chevy Chase to visit Tommy Cronin's grandparents tomorrow morning. Then we'll go on to see Marian Lodge, Tommy's aunt, who lives in Potomac Village in Montgomery County, Maryland. I've already spoken to them, and they'll be expecting us."

Maitland said, "The snow's supposed to stop during the night, and then it'll warm up again. Director Mueller called Palmer Cronin and has assured him and his wife that we will find whoever murdered his grandson. Guys, I don't want to make a liar out of the director."

Sean came dashing into the living room, Sherlock racing to catch him. Sean shouted, "Papa, I bet Marty my next allowance the Patriots are going to win the Super Bowl!"

There were some boos, some laughter, some "Hey, Sean, how's it going?" To which his boy grinned and waved wildly at all the faces displayed on MAX's monitor.

After Savich gave out assignments, Mr. Maitland ended the conference call and everyone went to catch the rest of the play-off game. Savich shut MAX down. Sherlock went to the kitchen to make Sean hot chocolate. Savich and Sean walked to the front window and looked out at the deserted street blanketed deep with snow. Savich could barely make out Mr. MacPherson's house across the street through a veil of soft fluid white snow, with no end in sight for the moment. No way would he make his Porsche dig its way through that mess tomorrow morning. It would have to be Sherlock's stalwart Volvo to make the trip to the Cronins' and to Marian Lodge. He said to his son, "Hey, kiddo, you're going to hang out with your Aunt Lilly and Uncle Simon tomorrow while your mama and I take a field trip."

"Aunt Lilly's going to have a baby," Sean said, and he didn't sound very happy about it, because Lilly's and Simon's attention wouldn't be focused on their one and only precious nephew.

"These things happen, Sean," Savich said, and he lifted Sean in his arms and hugged him. "Sometimes you've got to suck it up."

"Marty's mom is really fat now. Marty says she's going to have a little brother in March, and I should want a sister so I'd be balanced out like her. I told her I didn't want to be balanced. I told her I like being the only kid here."

Now, that, Savich thought, was something to think about.

CHAPTER
12

Henderson County Hospital
Early Saturday evening

"I got here as soon as I could," Sheriff Dix Noble said, shaking off his leather coat as he came into Delsey's room. "Ms. Freestone, you're looking much better than the last time I saw you." He studied her face for a moment. "I'm Sheriff Noble."

She smiled up at the hard-faced man with heart-melting dark eyes. "Everyone in town knows who you are, Sheriff Noble. I met your wife, Ruth, today as well. You're kind of local heroes."

Dix waved that off. "Griffin said you remembered what you saw in your bathtub?"

"Yes, it was a dead man. I lost it and screamed my head off. Then something hard hit my head."

"Did you see who hit you?"

"No, I don't think so. I mean, I don't remember. Sorry."

"Are you quite sure the man in the bathtub was dead?"

Delsey shuddered. "Oh, yes, his eyes were staring straight up, and there was blood all over his chest."

"Had you ever seen him before?"

"Yes, but I don't know who he was. I saw him around town during the past week or so. Once on the Stanislaus campus, maybe three or four more times here in Maestro."

"Where?"

"On the sidewalk once near the Holcombe Bank, and a couple of times at Maurie's Diner, sitting in the back, where you'd walk past him to get to the restrooms. He always smiled at me and nodded; once he even asked me how I was doing and we chatted for a few minutes. He seemed like a nice man. No, he never came on to me, nothing like that, and we never really visited, if you know what I mean."

Griffin asked, "Did you see him speaking to anyone in particular?"

"No, not really. He seemed quiet, like he was marking time, maybe waiting for someone, but he was always alone. He spoke to Anna, of course, since she was his waitress. I heard her laugh once, I guess at something he said to her."

Dix said, "Did you ever think he was 'off' somehow? Maybe paying too much attention to you, watching you?"

Delsey shook her head. "I didn't get any vibe like that. He never told me what his name was or why he was here, but I did wonder what he was doing on campus that time I saw him going into the administration building."

"We don't have a police artist on staff," Dix said, "but we do have Miss Mavis. She'll do a sketch with you, and then we can show his photo around town, find out where he was staying, who he was, and what he was doing here. It's only logical, Ms. Freestone, that he has to be somehow connected to you, or else why would his body have been in your bathtub?"

Delsey shook her head. "I'm sorry, Sheriff, I can't think of any connection between us other than those few times I saw him. Maybe if you can tell me who he was I can make some sense of it." Her breathing hitched. She again felt the punch of shock at seeing him lying there when she'd whipped back the shower curtain, and the terror that had screams ripping out of her throat. Griffin took her hand. "It's okay, Delsey, now it's okay."

"Why would he have broken into my apartment? Who would have killed him?"

Dix wondered for a moment how he would have reacted had he been in her shoes.

Delsey got herself together. "Like I told you, Anna had waited on him several times at Maurie's Diner. Maybe she knows his name. She's really friendly to everyone, plus she's way more visual than I am, too. She's done some drawing herself. She should be the one you do the sketch with."

Dix nodded and turned away to call his wife.

After he slipped his cell back into his shirt, Dix looked from Agent Griffin Hammersmith to his sister. "You two really do look a lot alike, almost like twins."

"Nah," Delsey said. "Griffin's better-looking."

Griffin said, "Even if you're right, it's only because you're still in your twenties. I'm hoping you'll improve once you hit thirty."

Dix smiled, brought it back. "Does anyone else know you've remembered the dead man, Ms. Freestone?"

"Dr. Hayman left before I remembered anything."

Griffin saw the shock and fear still mirrored in her eyes. He took her hand again. "Why don't you tell the sheriff why you're Freestone and not Hammersmith?"

Dix said, "Yeah, I was wondering that."

Hadn't she already told someone about why she had a different last name? She couldn't remember. Freestone— Delsey had all sorts of memories of that wild time, but now they didn't even piss her off, particularly. "I was married to a creep for longer than I should have been after I graduated from UCLA. He'd just gotten a master's degree in civil engineering. He was smart and awesomely ripped, and I fell hard for him. I really liked his cool name—Alexander Freestone. Sorry, Griffin, but I was tired of being saddled with Hammersmith."

Dix said, "Seems to me *Freestone* is just as much of a mouthful as *Hammersmith*."

"*Freestone*'s more a musician's name, at least it is to me," Delsey said, then laughed at herself. "So I kept it, no matter that Alex turned out to be something I didn't see coming at all."

"What, did the fool cheat on you?"

"No, not that. He wasn't a horn dog. He was a jewel thief. Two different women called me out of the blue after the wedding to tell me they'd had jewelry go missing after he'd broken up with them. I told both of them he hadn't broken up with me, he'd married me, and besides, the only good jewelry I had was the wedding ring he gave me." A laugh spurted out. "I'd forgotten about Grandmother Aladonna's jewelry, all very expensive, all very beautiful. Since I hadn't let him move in with me, he had to marry me if he wanted to explore Grandmother's jewelry box. Yeah, yeah, I guess I told him about the pieces and it was enough to make him see himself drinking rum cocktails on a beach somewhere. I reported him when I discovered my grandmother's diamond brooch gone, the same day I filed for divorce. I think he served maybe eighteen months."

"Did you get your grandmother's diamond brooch back?"

"The cops tracked it down and the pawnbroker had to cough it up. It's once again snug in my jewelry box. I'm sure Alex returned to his light-fingered ways after he got out of prison, only in a different city or state. Poor women." She laughed. "The wedding ring he gave me belonged to one of the women who'd called me. I gladly returned it to her."

"I don't think I'd want to keep the jerk's name," Dix said, "not after all that."

"I did go back and forth for a while," Delsey said, "but then I decided to think of Freestone as his parents' name, with Alex an unfortunate offshoot, and they were nice people."

Dix shook his head at her. "Do you have her jewelry box in your apartment?"

She nodded. "Oh, no. What if that was their target?"

"Let me check that out right now." Dix turned to call one of his deputies. "We'll know in a few minutes. I wish we had more to go on, Ms. Freestone. If the jewelry box is missing, that would mean the break-in was a burglary and one of the thieves came to a very bad end right there. I think I'll also see if Mr. Freestone is still in prison. Who knows?"

"Nah, even though Alex was ripped and looked all sorts of heroic, he was a wuss. He'd take on any jewelry box, but not a person who could hurt him." She sighed. "Freestone—such a lovely name."

Dix said, "I'll send Miss Mavis to see Anna, but I'd like to hear how you describe the dead man first."

"He was older than you, Sheriff Noble, somewhere in his early forties. He was stocky, dark and swarthy, I remember. It was such a shock to see him there, and I was screaming—I can't seem to focus on his features. It was horrible. Why ever would someone put him in my bathtub?"

Griffin said, "If the jewelry box is missing, then the thieves could have been in Maestro this past week looking for targets for break-ins. This party at Dr. Salazar's would have presented the ideal opportunity. On the other hand, why pick a graduate student's place rather than a well-to-do faculty member's? And why didn't they trash your place?"

Delsey said, "I haven't advertised my grandmother's jewelry, not after Alex. Anna and I are the only ones here who even know about it, as far as I know."

Dix's cell phone buzzed. When he punched off a moment later, he said, "Grandma's jewelry box was sitting on top of your dresser, still locked, didn't look to have been touched."

"That's a relief." Delsey squeezed her eyes shut. "But if not robbery, then why was the dead man there? I wish I could think of another reason why someone would do this. Do you know, it's dumb, but it's even worse to think the man might have been killed in my bathtub."

The amount of blood, Dix thought, he very likely was killed right there. He said, "Did you plan on getting home about one o'clock, Ms. Freestone?"

"I would have been a lot later if I hadn't gotten sick."

"Which means you surprised them," Griffin said. "Whoever was there probably wanted to be long gone by the time you got home."

Delsey said, "Goodness, I write music, sing, and play the piano and guitar and not much else. I'm boring and predictable, everyone knows that."

Dix pulled out a notebook from his jacket pocket. "Tell me about this party you went to last night. They had to find out from someone that you weren't home."

"Dr. Salazar's secretary emailed me a couple of weeks ago, said I'd been invited to his lovely new-semester get-together. I didn't want to go, so I told her I had a long-standing date with my best friend, Anna, to go ice-skating here in Henderson. Before I knew it the great man himself called me and didn't leave me any graceful way I could get out of going.

"I'd already heard what his parties were like—booze-laden, bawdy Spanish fiestas. Henry Stoltzen, you know, the cellist and my upstairs neighbor, was right. Most of the students there were women, with a few straight and gay men sprinkled in along with some faculty. And, of course, Dr. Hayman, Professor Salazar's brother. Yeah, I know, more different last names. That's because the mom took Professor Salazar to Spain and left Dr. Hayman behind with the dad. New name for one brother when she remarried, and the dad's name for the other."

Dix said, "I'll need a list of all the faculty you remember being there, Ms. Freestone."

She grinned up at him. "Since your wife and my brother are colleagues, please call me Delsey."

"Delsey, not a problem." He eyed her for a moment. "Call me Dix. A booze-laden Spanish fiesta with the students? Stanislaus is a world-renowned institution. What is wrong with these people?"

"Well, the fact is the students at the party were older, graduate students, anywhere from, say, my age— twenty-five—to Marjorie Hendricks, an incredible flautist, who's in her forties. Stanislaus is a rather isolated environment, and Maestro is a small town, so I suppose it's more accepted here that, ah, friendships spring up between some of the faculty and the older students."

"Maybe so, Delsey," Griffin said, "but what I saw at Salazar's this morning was something different."

"Not so different. The reality of it is, Griffin, that a small group of women enjoy being groupies to the great Professor Rafael Salazar himself. He's visiting Stanislaus for a year, he's in the boondocks, hardly knows a soul, and he wants companionship, so he finds it where he can—namely, at Stanislaus. Why are you smiling, Dix?"

"My uncle-in-law, Dr. Gordon Holcombe, who was director at Stanislaus until circumstances forced him to leave last year, would agree completely with you. I remember he called some of the undergraduate students he slept with his muses."

"I've heard some stories about Dr. Holcombe," Delsey said. "Usually with whispers and rolled eyes."

"Whatever their age," Griffin said, "the faculty is in a position of power over all of them. Salazar pressured you into coming to his party, for example."

"And why, I wonder? I remember thinking—before I got so drunk I couldn't see straight—that Professor Salazar didn't seem all that involved. I mean, as the host, he made the rounds, gave students and faculty drinks and munchies, but he seemed sort of set apart from his own party. I remember thinking it must be driving Gabrielle DuBois mad. The drunker she got, the more she stuck next to him, trying to get him to dance, but—"

"But what?" Dix asked.

"I just remembered. Professor Salazar was watching me, and I wondered why. Here I was, trying to fend off Dr. Hayman, and I remember seeing Professor Salazar standing across the room, his very expensive cashmered back leaning against the fireplace mantel, a drink in his hand, looking my way."

CHAPTER
13

Saturday evening

Griffin hunkered down in Delsey's room, alternately
studying her face while she dozed, reading a biography
online about Stanislaus, and keeping half an eye on
the national news on TV. When he heard Savich's
voice, he jerked around, then realized his new boss
was on TV, not in the room with him. Savich was standing in front of the Lincoln Memorial, thick swirling
snow piling white on his black hair, talking about the
murder of a young man. He spoke briefly, went into
no detail. The clip looked to have been recorded that
morning.

Griffin's cell phone buzzed. He looked down at a
message from Ruth.

Body found at Lincoln Memorial this a.m.—grandson of Palmer Cronin, ex-chairman of Fed, body staged for max effect—see YouTube.

Griffin stared at the message, then back to the TV, where a bundled-up Washington correspondent stood, mike in hand, in front of the Lincoln Memorial, finishing up his story about the murder victim found at Lincoln's feet. The coverage switched back to the newsroom, where the anchor, trying to look properly somber but looking excited instead, gave the "just in" update that the dead young man had been identified as Thomas Malcolm Cronin, age twenty, the grandson of Palmer Cronin, retired chairman of the Federal Reserve Bank. The scene switched to a view of Palmer Cronin's tall iron fence and gate in Chevy Chase, Maryland, where another reporter, her face under an umbrella in the heavy snow, spoke of the victim's illustrious family.

Suddenly Delsey said clearly, "No, shut up! You can't be, you can't!"

He was at her side in an instant, saw horror on her face. "Delsey, wake up, you've having a nightmare. Wake up."

But the nightmare didn't let her go. She jerked straight up in bed and screamed in his face, "No!"

"Delsey!" He took her shoulders in his hands and shook her hard as her eyes flew open, blind and wild. She was panting, still terrified.

He sat beside her and drew her up in his arms and rubbed her back. "It's all right, Dels. Hold on to me, you'll be okay."

He felt her slowly get herself together. Her arms fell away, and she leaned back in his arms.

"Tell me," Griffin said.

He saw it was tough for her, and waited. Finally she whispered, "I dreamed I was in a small room—about the size of my bathroom—no windows, only white walls, but they weren't plain white, Griffin, they were splattered with blood from the men lying dead on the floor. Then they all sat straight up and stared at me and I know they blamed me, and then they started screaming at me, but it wasn't words, only sounds that didn't make any sense. There was so much blood, fountains of blood—and it was thick and red and I was naked and I felt the blood splashing on me, streaking down the front of me. The blood was so hot, Griffin, and it was like the blood wanted to burn through me."

Griffin thought her subconscious had torqued the truth of what had happened to her into a crazy dream, and he wondered whether what her subconscious had dished up might have a kernel of truth lurking in the craziness. He said, "It's possible when the dead men sat up and looked at you, started screaming at you, that it was your dream trying to tell you that you'd seen or heard something more, Delsey. Get your brain together. Think about this."

But she couldn't reason yet, her brain was still frozen. "All those dead men in my dream, Griffin, all of them looked exactly like him, they were all the dead man in my bathtub. Who is the dead man, Griffin?"

"We'll find out. Now, close your eyes a moment. Think—no, picture—your bathroom in your mind. Do you see or hear anything else?"

She was breathing fast, and he smoothed her hands to calm her. "That's right, steady yourself."

"Yes, now I realize there are two other guys there and one of them is yelling in Spanish, words, curses, I don't know, but not jumbled sounds like from all the dead guys. Wait, I see one of them, Griffin—only a glimpse, really—a young Hispanic guy. And then something hits my head and I'm gone."

"So one of the Hispanic guys struck you down. Were any of the dead men Hispanic?"

"No. Like I told you, they were all like him, Caucasian."

He squeezed her hands. "It shouldn't be much longer before we know the dead man's identity."

"So Anna didn't know who he was?"

"Anna told Ruth she'd spoken to him only a couple of times, said he was friendly, but she didn't know his name, or anything about him, only that he was new in town."

"Where is Anna? Why hasn't she come back to see me?"

"She'll show up when she can. Tell me more about the men in your dream."

"His face is here in front of my eyes, Griffin, all their faces, really, plaster white, like they aren't real, but I can see dark whiskers on their cheeks. They won't go away."

"Tell me about their faces."

"Their faces are full—well fed, I'd guess you'd say—boyish, and their eyes are open like his were. They look surprised, Griffin, their mouths open, too, showing their front teeth. But the blood, so much blood." She fell silent, looking inward, then, "I told the sheriff I'd seen the dead man near Holcombe's Bank and in Maurie's Diner, but I remember now I might also have seen him on Breaker's Hill, Griffin, three days ago, when Anna and I were snowboarding. Anna took a wild turn and went skidding toward the trees and fell on her butt. I was yelling at her and laughing, and I saw a man standing in the maple trees beside the trail and I remember wondering what he was doing there, since I didn't see him holding a sled or a snowboard. He moved back, really fast, like he didn't want anyone to see him. But Griffin, I think it could have been the dead man in my bathtub."

Now, this was interesting. "In your dream, all of the dead men screamed something at you—think about this, Delsey. Can you now make sense of any of the sounds?"

She eyed him for a moment. "No, it's just jumbled noise. You're thinking the dream was a sort of message to me? You think they were telling me it was my fault the man was murdered?" She looked beyond him, at the drifting snow outside her window. How beautiful the scene outside looked from inside the warm hospital room. But the man in her bathtub wasn't warm, not any longer.

He felt her corrosive fear and dropped it. "Nah," he

said, and gave her a final squeeze. He'd bet his favorite Rossignol skis the dead man in her bathtub had been the same man she'd seen in the woods on Breaker's Hill. Was he following her? Surveilling her? It sure sounded like it. But why, for heaven's sake? *Because she saw something she wasn't supposed to see, or overheard something she wasn't supposed to hear?*

Griffin eased her back down, patted her cheek. "You did good. Now, for a reward I'm going to get you pistachio-pineapple ice cream. Used to be the only flavor you'd eat. Can you get it in Maestro?"

"Look, Griffin, I'm being crazy, I mean, look at what my mind conjured up—a whole bunch of dead men. Why would I deserve a reward for that?"

"You're not crazy, your mind's trying to sort things out and make sense of them. You've got a great brain, Delsey. Hey, your brain and mine, together we could rule the world."

"I don't want to rule the world. I wouldn't mind winning an Oscar for best musical score, though. That pistachio-pineapple ice cream sounds nice, too."

CHAPTER
14

Saturday evening

It was Anna Castle who showed up with Delsey's pistachio-pineapple ice cream after Delsey had Griffin call her. It was Anna who'd convinced Maurie of Maurie's Diner fame to put pistachio-pineapple on the menu, since the local grocery stores didn't carry it. Anna grinned. "Maurie bitched and moaned, but Delsey gives him a good profit on every servin', not to mention all the other converts she's brought in. I think it tastes weird, myself, but there's no accountin' for taste, now, is there? At least Maurie's a happy camper."

Griffin watched Anna's mouth while she spoke—*A very nice mouth,* he thought—and enjoyed her drawl coming out of that mouth, enjoyed the way she dropped *g*'s. It was unconsciously charming. He found himself smiling back at her. He watched Delsey dig a spoonful out of the small carton, lick it slowly, and run her tongue along it to get every last bit off the spoon. Griffin had to laugh, because she looked like a happy little kid on her birthday.

Anna said, "One of the regulars, Ray Dunlap, saw her eatin' the ice cream like that. I thought the poor guy was gonna hyperventilate and I got a paper bag ready, in case."

"Maurie gets anything Anna asks him to," Delsey said. "He's got gumbo and boudin on the menu now, and bottles of Slap Ya Mama spice set out next to the salt and pepper shakers. Has he asked you to marry him yet, Anna?"

Anna peeled off her leather gloves and lightly patted Delsey's arm. "Maurie loves his mama too much to ever consider sharin' himself with any other woman, so not in this lifetime, sweetie."

Delsey licked another spoonful of ice cream, then said, "I figure you say half as many words as I do, since it takes you so long to finish a sentence. It's like you worship each syllable and want to stretch it out to infinity."

Anna patted her arm again. "Don't be jealous, Delsey. Since you weren't born in Louisiana, the land of the happy vowels, then you gotta sound like you're sawing wood, no hope for it."

Sawing wood? Griffin laughed.

Delsey said, "Anna, I'm so glad you're here."

"I'm glad to be here, too." Anna turned to Griffin.

"Hey, Mr. FBI, you got word on the dead guy's name? And who clobbered Delsey?"

He shook his head.

"I had a horrible dream, Anna. I think I saw the man who hit me. He was very young and Hispanic, and there was another young Hispanic there, too, yelling, in Spanish, so I didn't understand what he was saying."

Griffin thought he saw a flash of something hard and angry in Anna's eyes. What was that all about? He saw her pull back the anger. Well, he was mad, too. "That sure sounds scary, Delsey. I hope they find those guys. I'm so glad you're lookin' better." She looked at Griffin. "Thanks for clearin' me in to see my favorite songwriter."

Griffin said, "Not a problem. You've got a nice full voice. Do you sing?"

"Well, I did sing once to Maurie, thought he'd stick his head in the oven to escape it."

"He'd try to escape me, too," Griffin said. "Do you have a favorite? Song of Delsey's, I mean."

"Now, that's a toughie, but the one about racin' toward love and death on the 405, I love to sing that one in the shower."

Delsey said, "I remember I started it sitting in a traffic jam with a new boyfriend. Anna, I asked Griffin to get you clear anytime you can come."

"Great. There are a good dozen or so other folk, mostly Stanislaus students, who've asked about seeing you."

"Not a problem. I'm going home tomorrow."

"But isn't your apartment still a crime scene?"

Delsey said. "Is it still a crime scene, Griffin?"

"Yep. Regardless, there's no way you're going back there, Delsey. Remember, there's no working lock on your back door. For all we know you could still be in danger. I'm at Bud Bailey's B&B on High Street. I want you to stay with me when you get out of here. I want to keep you close."

Delsey rose up on her elbows. "Griffin, you know very well the Hispanic guy could have killed me if he'd wanted to, which means he didn't want me dead. That's good, isn't it? Henry can get the lock fixed on my back door."

Griffin said, "There's no way we can know what the killer intended, who that second man was, or if they'll start to worry that you're a witness. You're staying with me, subject closed."

Griffin didn't much expect for her to cave, since he could picture her going toe-to-toe with him when she'd been five years old and so he wasn't surprised when she said, "You're going to be out and about, Griffin. I doubt you'll want to take me with you, so how about I stay with Anna? I'll be plenty safe with her. Do you mind, Anna?"

Griffin saw something flicker over Anna Castle's face. Alarm? Then her expression was smooth and easy again, and she leaned toward Delsey, smiling, her dark hair loose, curtaining her face. This musician/waitress, with her beautiful drawl and very nice mouth, could protect his sister? Sarcasm slipped right out of his mouth. "What did you say your instrument is—the violin? Are you going to hit these guys over the head with your fiddle?"

Anna swiveled about to look up at him. "Do you know, Agent Hammersmith, I might have to belt out a nice song with full vibrato for that bit of snark."

Griffin hated being a jerk, hated having it slap him back in the chops. "Sorry for the comment. Please, not full vibrato."

Anna turned back to Delsey. "I think your brother's right, sweetie; it's better you stay with him. I have to work, too, and he's the big bad Fed with a gun."

"But you've got a gun, too, Anna," Delsey said. "She's got a Smith and Wesson .44 Magnum, Griffin. I saw it when I happened to barge in on her and she was cleaning it. When I asked her what she did with that sucker, she said she liked to shoot cones off the pine on Lone Tree Hill."

Griffin laughed. "What are you doing with a .44 Magnum, and not a small handgun?"

Anna said, "It belongs to my mom. She insisted I take it since I was moving here to the boondocks. Like her, I also believe in self-protection, and yes, I can use it. I won't shoot myself in the foot. And yes, I have a license for it. But, Delsey, that's not the point. Despite his snark, I agree with your brother. We have no clue what the killer's intentions toward you are. Those two men—they could have thought you were dead and simply left you on your bathroom floor. Tell me again, Delsey, you're sure the man who struck you down was a young Hispanic? Do you remember enough about him to help give them a sketch?"

"I told Griffin I only got a quick look. He was young, younger than me, but I was terrified, Anna. It was so fast, it was really only an impression. As for the other man, I didn't even get a glimpse of him, only heard him yelling."

Anna turned to Griffin to see him staring at her, and stopped asking questions. Her voice became quiet and calm as the falling snow outside the window. "I know Bud's B&B has a two-bedroom suite that's usually available."

The gun-toting violinist who served up boudin and Slap Ya Mama spice at Maurie's Diner agreed with him? She thought Delsey could still be in danger? She never seemed to say what he expected, and it had nothing to do with her accent.

"You from New Orleans?" he asked her.

"Nope, but nearby. Bosard is only about thirty miles from New Orleans. It's a little flyspeck, even on a good map."

Delsey said, "I remember once, when I told her about falling out of a tree when I was ten and landing on you, she told me how she shot her first alligator when she was nine. I couldn't top that one, Griffin. We didn't have anything cool like that in our childhood."

Nurse Cotton appeared in the doorway. "Are you all right, Ms. Freestone?" From her look, it was obvious she'd overheard some of what they were saying. Griffin thought she'd probably like to see the back of all of them, including the guard outside the door.

Delsey smiled at her. "I'm fine."

Nurse Cotton said, "That's good, but I need to check your vitals." She stepped right over, took Delsey's blood pressure, checked her pulse, and took her temperature. "You have any dizziness when you went to the bathroom? No? That's good. How about nausea? Headache? Okay, seems to me you may be good to go, but let's see what Dr. Chesney has to say tomorrow morning."

"Would you like the rest of my pistachio-pineapple ice cream? It's wonderful."

This offer got a smile and a raised eyebrow from Nurse Cotton. "You go ahead and finish it, you like it so much." She looked at Griffin. "When Maurie added pistachio-pineapple ice cream to the menu, I thought it sounded strange, but after I tried it, I was a convert. Okay, guys, she's had a big day. No more upsets for her. She needs a good solid sleep tonight. Hey, you really shot an alligator, Anna? When you were only nine years old?"

"Sure enough. I thought I was a goner. I was out lazin' around where I shouldn't have been. Good thing for me I had my brother's shotgun. I said enough prayers to hold me in good stead until I was eighteen."

Ruth appeared in the doorway. "Hey, Delsey, you look pretty good. How's your head feeling?"

"Fine, Ruth, I'm fine."

Nurse Cotton pursed her lips but didn't say anything even though Griffin knew she wanted them out so

Delsey could hang it up for the night. She nodded to them, a warning in her eyes, and left.

Ruth said to Griffin, "I wanted you to know Dix is getting Bertie—he's an old hound who drools a lot—out tomorrow morning to see if he can track where they took that man's body. I've rubbed a bit of blood from Delsey's bathtub on a cloth to give him the scent. Hopefully there'll be a trail for him. We'll turn Bertie loose right outside Delsey's apartment, both at the front and the back entrance."

Griffin said, "There's so much snow, if Bertie doesn't find him, he could be buried until there's a thaw."

"The snow's supposed to stop during the night; then, of all things," Ruth said, "the sun's supposed to come out tomorrow and warm us up to forty degrees."

"Good luck to Bertie, then," Anna said.

CHAPTER
15

Breaker's Hill
Maestro, Virginia
Sunday morning

Billy Boynton, third baseman on Maestro's high school team and a good friend of Dix Noble's older son, Rob, was on his knees, clutching his belly, still dry-heaving, since his stomach was empty. "He barfed his guts out," his friend Jonah said. Jonah was green, his voice thin as a thread.

For once the weatherman was right. The snow had stopped in the middle of the night, and now the sun shone brightly, warming both land and people. If it weren't for the dead man at his feet, Dix might have admired the postcard beauty all around him, the trees and rolling hills covered with pristine white as far as the eye could see. He'd already examined the body and stepped back for Griffin and Ruth.

Dix went down on his knee in front of Billy. "Tell me," he said.

"I-I touched him," Billy said, raising tear-filled eyes to Dix. He was still shuddering, his face pale against the white of the snow. "I didn't know what it was; I mean, it looked like a dark patch covered mostly with snow. I saw lots of animal prints and figured something had tried to uncover him, and so I leaned down, and I touched him. When I realized, I yelled for Jonah to stay back. I knew it was the guy everyone's looking for. I saw the sketch of him Miss Mavis did. And I knew I'd found him."

Jonah said, "We were snowboarding down the hill, and Billy tried a backward flip and lost control, headed off-trail into the woods. I saw him bounce off a tree, and his snowboard whacked against a rock. Billy was lucky he landed in a pile of snow."

Well, not so lucky, Dix thought. He helped Billy to his feet, hugged him against his side. There was no need for Old Bertie now. "You did good, Billy. Listen to me now. It will take you a while to forget this and put it behind you, but I promise you, it'll fade over time. Remember, you found him for us, and that makes you a hero. Now, the two of you get your snowboards and head on home. I'll call your folks, tell them you were a big help to us."

Griffin saw Billy was torn. He'd been terrified, but

he was getting hold of himself now, not sure he wanted to leave. The dead guy was his find, and the dead guy's gross arm lying on top of the snow wasn't making him sick anymore. He wanted to keep talking about it.

Having two sons nearly the same age, Dix held to his patience. Limelight like this didn't come along every day for a teenage boy. "Billy, Deputy Claus is down on the road. You hook up with him and he'll take you home. If I have more questions, I'll come see you, all right? We've got to take care of him now. Go home." Billy knew when an adult meant it, and so he hung it up. He and Jonah carried their snowboards down the hill, Billy talking a mile a minute about how the dead guy's fingers curled around his hand when he fell on him—*I heard the finger bones snap*—Dix knew it was a story that would glitter with epic detail by nightfall.

The bright yellow crime scene tape his deputies had placed marked off the man's body. At least there was no more snow in the forecast. Processing the scene with snow pelting down on them would have been a nightmare.

When the forensic team was finally through, the ME's van slogging through the hard-packed snow to the road at the base of Breaker's Hill, Ruth turned to her husband. "If animals hadn't disturbed the site, if Billy hadn't fallen in the woods, maybe not even Bertie would have found him."

True enough, Dix thought. He'd brought the portable fingerprinter and wondered what the chances were the man's prints would be in AFIS. He said, "It's still too cold. Let's get ourselves out of this weather.

"Now that we have his body, we'll find out who he was. Maybe then we'll know why he was here in Maestro, and what he was doing in Delsey's bathtub."

Ruth looked up into the brilliant sun. It was odd, still feeling so cold with the sun so bright overhead. She counted the steps to Dix's Range Rover.

Dr. Hayman's house
Deer Ridge Lane
Maestro, Virginia
Sunday morning

Griffin pulled his Camry into Dr. Hayman's driveway, the first tire tracks of the day. He'd read that Stanislaus had provided Dr. Hayman with a director's residence for the duration of his contract, an old shingled bungalow set in the middle of an expansive tree-filled lawn. He saw the information wasn't exactly accurate. Calling it a bungalow was a misnomer. The original house had been enlarged and modernized. After his initial take on Dr. Hayman, Griffin thought the new version of the house suited him pretty well. Two more perks he'd read about—a gardener and a housekeeper. *No cook?* Griffin grinned as he walked up the six front steps to press the doorbell.

Dr. Hayman answered the door himself. He looked the part of a Euro-aristocrat even on Sunday, Griffin thought, all duded up in *GQ*-casual running-suit elegance, down to expensive sneakers that, Griffin thought, hadn't ever slammed their soles on a road top. Was he trying to emulate Professor Salazar after all?

"You are late, Agent Hammersmith."

Griffin said, "I was held up unexpectedly at Breaker's Hill. A couple of kids with their snowboards strapped to the roof of their car skidded into a snowdrift, and I helped get them out."

"You should have called me."

Maybe so, but more fun to see you go all haughty and pissed off. Griffin nodded and stepped forward, forcing Dr. Hayman to take a quick step back.

There was no bungalow coziness on the inside, either. Inside was all aggressive and ultramodern. It struck Griffin between the eyes. All high style and dash, but no particular charm. He said, "Did you redecorate?"

"Yes, I had to. Though they kept the house nicely on the outside, the inside was a disgrace. I'm told an eighty-year-old spinster with a dozen cats originally lived here. When she died, she donated the house to Stanislaus.

"What I have done suits me now. I must admit to being pleasantly surprised by the workmanship here in Maestro. Come into the living room, Agent Hammersmith."

Hayman waved him into a large square room with wide windows that gave onto the front yard. He pointed to a deep burgundy sofa and moved to stand beside the fireplace. He crossed his arms over his chest, then crossed his feet. Too bad Griffin wasn't a photographer; this was a pose for posterity, and again, it reminded him of Professor Salazar, only Dr. Hayman did it better, with more natural grace.

"How is Delsey?"

"She is better."

"I look forward to seeing her back with us. Now, what can I do for you, Agent Hammersmith? I'm afraid I've already told you everything I know that might be helpful. As I think we all told you, Delsey left the party without telling anyone." He looked down at his watch. Who was he expecting?

"Tell me what special ingredients you put in the margaritas Delsey drank Friday night."

If Hayman thought that an odd question, he didn't show it, and answered readily, "It was a very fine tequila— Patrón Silver—that should not have made her ill. Naturally, I used an excellent Cointreau, lime juice, and a bit of additional triple sec."

"What was your special ingredient?"

"Nothing more than a dash of Tabasco sauce."

Not very original at all. "She was sick enough to leave. How many drinks did she have?"

"I did not count. Three, I believe. Although the Patrón Silver is an excellent tequila, it is potent."

Probably enough alcohol to flatten an elephant. "Do

you think someone could have added something to her drinks, Dr. Hayman? Something to make her ill?"

"There is no reason for anyone to do that, Agent."

"And what about your brother, Dr. Salazar? Whatever your own intentions toward Delsey, I got the impression the man is far more a hedonist than an ascetic. He uses his students, particularly the women, treats them like his own personal servants."

"A hedonist? Because he enjoys life and takes advantage of what life offers to him? Well, yes, he does take advantage, and that isn't something I admire, but still, Rafael is a fine musician, no matter his small character flaws. He is both admired and respected. Have you ever seen him perform onstage?"

"I didn't ask you about his musical abilities, Dr. Hayman," Griffin said. "You don't seem to care for him much, and since he is your brother, you certainly know him. You are the director here, responsible for the behavior of faculty at an academic institution. Why would you bring someone with such flaws in his personal life, someone who is something of a predator, to Stanislaus? Why would you take that risk?"

"Perhaps he has not behaved quite as I expected. At any rate, whatever his habits, his questionable behavior, this will be his last semester here."

"Why do both of you appear to want to get close to my sister? Is there some sort of competition between you?"

"I am not at all like Rafael, and I do not compete with him."

"Did he pressure you into inviting him to Stanislaus for the year? Or did someone else?"

"He is my brother, Agent Hammersmith. I was not pressured, but perhaps it is true that I listened too kindly to our mother. She is never reticent about what she feels and wants. But Maria Rosa is a lovely lady who perhaps cares too much for Rafael. Perhaps she has indulged him too much over the years. After my parents divorced when we were boys, she took Rafael with her to Spain, her homeland, where she married a rich Spanish industrialist, Carlo Salazar, now happily passed on."

"Why did she leave you behind?"

"It was my father's condition for a divorce, and so I grew up in New Jersey. If you wish to know more about Rafael or Maria Rosa's family, you can ask my brother. I expect him shortly."

He called his mother by her first name? Well, Griffin supposed it could be natural, given he didn't grow up with her.

"And why is Professor Salazar coming here this fine morning?"

"His lifestyle does not relieve him of his responsibilities here at Stanislaus. He is a colleague, Agent. We are to discuss the scheduling of his students' recitals for the coming semester."

Griffin pulled out his smartphone, scrolled to a photo of the dead man on Breaker's Hill, and held it up. "Have you ever seen this man before, Dr. Hayman?"

Hayman studied the photo. "No, I can't say that I have. Is this man involved with what happened to Delsey?"

"Perhaps," Griffin said. "We also know the man who struck Delsey was a young Hispanic. Were there any Hispanic men at the party?"

Hayman blinked. "There are perhaps a dozen Hispanic musicians at Stanislaus, though I don't recall seeing any of them at the party. Surely it was not one of them. They are all accomplished musicians, here to study and improve themselves, not rob houses. And perhaps that is what it was—a simple robbery, after all."

"Dr. Hayman, there is nothing at all simple about what happened to Delsey."

They heard the front doorbell ring.

"It is my brother, I believe."

Griffin said, "Do you have a music room, sir? Could you take me there, then send Professor Salazar in to see me?"

Hayman shrugged and walked out of the living room, Griffin on his heels. He opened a door on his right, motioned to Griffin. Griffin stepped into a small room filled with books, a huge grand piano, and a wall of shoulder-high mirrors set against it, all with ornate antique frames.

"I will ask Rafael if he wishes to speak to you," Hayman said and walked out. Griffin heard his footfalls toward the front door. Would Salazar agree to speak to him?

The music room was good sized, with nothing out of place. Sheet music sat atop a small desk, neat and tidy. The concert-size Steinway was bare. And what about all those mirrors, some so old the glass was distorted and shadowed? Did Hayman stare at himself while he played the piano? Why? To perfect some special demeanor for his audiences?

He moved to the door, opened it a crack, and listened. He heard voices, but they were speaking too quietly for him to make out what they were saying. *Too bad.*

Professor Rafael Salazar strolled into the small study, walked to the piano, and leaned against it—no, he lounged against it. He was wearing gray cashmere today, and looked very sharp indeed.

He said, "Agent Hammersmith, I understand you are concerned for your sister, but I have been more than generous with my time with you already. I have learned nothing more since we last spoke. I have a great deal to accomplish today, even on Sunday, and I ask that if you or the sheriff wish to speak with me again, you make an appointment through my office. From what my brother tells me, you have already formed an opinion of me. A hedonist, sir?"

Griffin smiled at him. "Tell me, Professor Salazar, do you dislike your brother as much as he appears to dislike you?"

Salazar blinked at him, then smiled with genuine amusement. It changed him, made him seem real, but only for an instant. "Dislike my brother? He is a brilliant pianist, naturally, but he carries the burden of being a bourgeois—after all, he was raised here in the United States—who could expect him to simply appreciate some of the splendid diversions life offers? Ah, like a certain measure of hedonism."

"Unlike in Spain?"

"Very possibly. In Europe, the artist and his needs are better appreciated and valued, his needs for diversions understood and accepted."

"Is that what your mother, Maria Rosa, does? Understand you? She taught you to enjoy life's diversions?"

Salazar's mouth seamed. "My mother is a woman of infinite good taste and judgment. She certainly understands me. I will say, too, she has the good judgment to never interfere in my personal life, Agent. My brother should never have spoken of her to you. I do not understand why you wish to discuss such things."

"I ask because you appear to have no shortage of perceived self-worth, and I wondered how it was nurtured in you."

"You mock me, Agent? The truth is I have been blessed, but I also work incredibly hard. My life is not all pleasurable amusement, you know." Salazar shrugged. "So why pretend I am like everyone else when I am clearly not? As much as I've enjoyed this chat, Agent Hammersmith, if there is nothing truly pressing, I will ask you to excuse me."

Griffin showed Salazar the photo of the dead man, and after the expected demur, asked him, "Do you know any Hispanic males who might have hurt Delsey?"

Of all things, Salazar hummed. "Hurt her? Why? No, I'm afraid no name springs to mind."

"Why do you think Delsey was attacked in her apartment?"

"I do not know. It maddens and taunts me."

When Griffin left Dr. Hayman's lovely bungalow he looked back to see Professor Salazar and Dr. Hayman standing together in the open doorway; they appeared to be arguing. His interviews with the two men had been informative, but not particularly helpful. He found them strangely alien; he'd met many kinds of people, but none as self-absorbed as these two. Could he believe what either of them had said? And why this fascination with his sister?

CHAPTER
17

Maestro, Virginia
Sunday afternoon

When Dix pulled his SUV into his driveway early that afternoon, he heard Brewster—his four-pound toy poodle—barking his head off. He opened the front door and quickly grabbed him up and held him away from him when he walked into the house so Brewster wouldn't pee on him in his excitement. As it was, he, Ruth, and the boys were supporting the dry cleaner.

"Yeah, yeah, fluffball, I'm home, and yes, I'll take you outside, but you're not going to like it."

"No need," Ruth said, coming out to see him, a big spoon in her hand. "Rafe took him out a few minutes ago, laughing his head off when Brewster sank into the snow over his head. Turned into a game. Soup's on." She pushed through a half-dozen licks from Brewster when she tried to kiss her husband. "I invited Griffin to stop over to get something to eat and take some of your yummy chili—if there's any left—back to Delsey. She's probably really tired of hospital food. He says she's seen the photo, Dix, and confirms it's the same man."

She took Brewster, let him lick her some more, and shouted to her boys, who were watching a recording of the football play-off game from last night in the living room. She made them promise to wash essence of Brewster off their hands before lunch.

"I'm glad the photos have been of some use," Dix said as he took off his thick jacket and leaned over to pull off his boots. "We've been showing them around town, and we've heard everything from his being a salesman from Henderson to a basketball scout visiting the high school. The guy was friendly, like Delsey and Anna told us, visited with everyone, but no one knew his name."

"Maybe Dillon's facial-recognition program could help," Ruth said.

"Maybe. Is it halftime yet? I missed the game last night, too, you know."

"Nope, in a few minutes, depending on the number of time-outs the coaches take. We can watch the game if you like while we chow down on your chili and corn bread, made from—who was it? Oh, yes, your grand-dad's favorite recipe. And I made the mandatory salad I expect everyone to eat."

As they set up trays to take to the living room, Ruth said, "I spoke to Dillon, told him what was going on here. He's tied up with his own case, that Tommy Cronin murder. He asked me to stay here and save your bacon and figure this all out for you."

Dix laughed. "What a nice guy. That's quite a case he's got. Why murder a twenty-year-old and set him up on the world stage like that?" But Dix didn't expect an answer. His eyes were locked on the TV and the game.

"What do you mean?"

Thankfully, there was a time-out, and she got his attention. "If it was payback, it's like killing the messenger. I mean, why kill the boy when he wasn't responsible for any of the mess himself? He's not his grandfather."

Ruth said slowly, "Unless it was some kind of message. 'You all hurt me, so I'm taking one of yours'?"

"If that's so, it's a stranger world than I thought," Dix said.

CHAPTER 18

Chevy Chase, Maryland
Sunday morning

FBI Special Agent Ted Atkinson, a former college football tackle with a neck the size of Sherlock's waist, met
Savich and Sherlock at the oversized oak front door of
the Cronin estate. "I'm glad to see you guys. It's quiet
as a tomb around here." He cracked his knuckles. "What
a terrible business."

"Amen to that," Sherlock said.

"Some of the media were here when I arrived early
this morning." He waved past the postcard-beautiful
lawn with snow blanketing the maple and oak trees
toward the three TV vans hunkered down at the distant
curb. "Those gates you drove through have helped keep

the vultures out, but they're still sitting out there. Why? Do they think someone will welcome them in, tell them how they feel, offer them a latte? I take a stroll around the perimeter every once in a while, show them how big and mean I look. Did they hassle you?"

"Not really," Sherlock said. "We smiled at them and gave them a little wave. I thought one of the guys was going to try to sneak through the gate, but better heads prevailed at the last minute. I do believe, though, he had some comments about Dillon's antecedents."

"Give me the nod and I'll go speak to him." Atkinson gave a ferocious grin. "Come on in before you freeze to death. It's beautiful with the sun shining on all the snow, but it's still cold enough to see your breath.

"Mr. and Mrs. Cronin are in the living room, have been for the past three hours, huddled together, not talking much. Enduring, I'd guess you'd say. It's been a terrible blow for those poor old folks." Atkinson shut the front door behind them, paused for a moment, then locked it and shrugged as if to say, *You never know, now, do you?*

"This old place dates back to 1910," Atkinson said. "Can you imagine the heating bills?"

They stepped through a large Art Deco entrance hall with signature black and white floor tiles. A kidney-shaped Art Deco table that looked to be an Émile-Jacques Ruhlmann original sat against one long wall. Savich's mom loved Ruhlmann, had bought a small table designed by the man himself.

Centered on the wall over the table hung a painting

of a small barefoot girl in pink shorts running on a beach, hanging on for dear life to a kite string, the tail of a vivid red dragon nearly slapping her face as it whipped and whirled about in the wind. You could feel the young girl's excitement and the absolute perfection of that single moment, feel the beating wind stinging your face, tearing your eyes. You could smell the brine. Savich stared at the painting, couldn't help himself. It was one of his grandmother's, titled *The Child*.

He said quietly to Sherlock, "There are only three of my grandmother's paintings I haven't seen since I was her age." He pointed to the little girl. "This is one of them. The Cronins have owned it for a very long time."

Atkinson nodded at the painting. "You like that painting? I think it's kind of pretty."

Sherlock smiled at him. "The artist is Sarah Elliott, Dillon's grandmother. Most of her paintings are in museums."

Atkinson said, "My wife tells me I'm going to get shot for my big mouth one day, since I'm too big to bother beating on."

Savich waved it away. They followed Atkinson into the living room on their right, a barn of a room that was, surprisingly, toasty warm, the fire in the old brick fireplace blasting out heat like a bellows. Palmer and Avilla Cronin sat pressed together on a sofa, silent, their eyes moving to the three agents walking toward them into the room. Even their eyes looked flattened, Sherlock thought, and no wonder.

Their deadening pain was palpable in the very air,

bowing the Cronins under the weight of it. Sherlock knew the pain would morph into rage and blame; it was the only way to survive such devastation. The Cronins would blame the monster who murdered their grandson, yes, but she knew they would blame the world at large and the FBI as well, for not somehow preventing Tommy's murder from happening in the first place. It was human nature, and she'd seen it far too many times, and was prepared for it.

Palmer Cronin was seventy-seven, once a compact and solid man, with swarthy skin and lots of hair, and looking more in keeping with his moniker, Big Buddha. Now he was thin, his shoulders stooped, his hair a tonsure of gray around his large head. He looked, Savich thought, ten years older than the last time Savich had seen him on the cover of *The Economist* six months before. Inside the covers was a smoothly ironic review of Cronin's decisions and where they'd led, with photos of mortgage, banking, and investment-firm villains sprinkling the pages.

Cronin was wearing ancient leather bedroom slippers, old brown wool pants, a faded plain brown shirt, and, oddly, a lovely new pale blue cashmere cardigan. A Christmas present?

He got slowly to his feet, shuffled more than walked across to them, and looked up at Savich. He seemed folded in on himself, Savich thought, his face pale and drawn, but those dark eyes of his were deep and hard, with an intelligence that looked beyond every word uttered to him to the consequences of his reply. Odd,

Savich thought, that such formidable intelligence had gone so awry in what had been his undisputed area of expertise.

And now this. This man whose daughter-in-law had died two years before, and his only son last year, had now seen his only grandson brutally murdered yesterday. His name would die with him. He looked, Savich thought, like he'd reached the end of his road and didn't care.

Cronin said, his voice flat, "You're the FBI agents Director Mueller told me he was sending."

Savich nodded, introduced both himself and Sherlock to Mr. and Mrs. Cronin, and out of habit, they showed them their shields. He said, "Please accept our condolences, though they aren't enough, we know that; nothing could be. We are very sorry to intrude on you at this time, but we have to move quickly, and we lost a day because of the blizzard."

"We have heard of both of you," Cronin said. "Avilla and I saw you Saturday morning, Agent Savich, speaking in front of the Lincoln Memorial. The news stations have been showing that clip all weekend. You didn't know then that the victim was my grandson. We watched you like every other benighted human being, shocked and horrified, of course, at the finding of a frozen dead body at Lincoln's feet. It doesn't say much for the human race, does it, our rapt attention at our safe distance to a violent death displayed for the world to see? Neither Avilla nor I thought you wanted to be standing there speaking to the media. You looked . . . angry, Agent Savich."

"No, sir, I didn't want to speak about it," Savich said, "and yes, I was very angry."

Avilla Cronin said from beside her husband, "Tell me now, Agents, do you honestly believe you will find the monster who murdered our grandson?"

"Yes, Mrs. Cronin, we do," Sherlock said.

Palmer Cronin gave Sherlock a brief dismissive look and continued as if she hadn't spoken. "Despite that revolting photo and where that poor boy was left, is the FBI considering the possibility that Tommy was murdered for personal reasons?"

Savich said, "It's possible, sir. That's one of the reasons we're here, to find out more about him."

Cronin studied Savich's face for a moment. "But of course you know it's a waste of time. Sit down, both of you." He waved at two Art Deco chairs sitting opposite the rounded sofa. Savich watched him take his wife's thin hand in his, but he didn't squeeze it. Their two limp hands simply rested against each other.

Cronin asked, "Do you know yet who posted that horrific photo of Tommy? Has anyone claimed responsibility?"

"Not yet, sir; we're working on it."

"Avilla and I have talked of nothing else, of course, and it seems obvious that a quiet, studious boy like Tommy would not have had an enemy who would go to such lengths to kill him and add the final humiliation of placing him at Lincoln's feet. I do not wish to accept it, but Avilla tells me I must. He was killed because I am his grandfather, as revenge against me.

"What kind of insane person would hold Tommy accountable for my actions, any mistakes I may have made, even if he held me responsible for his financial misfortunes?"

"We will return to that, sir," Savich said. "Bear with us."

Avilla Cronin sat forward and said, her voice filled with the authority of someone who expects to be listened to, "No, answer him. My husband is correct. Tommy was too young to have such crazed enemies. The killer has made it obvious, has he not? A malcontent or a radical or an anarchist murdered Tommy, spurred on by all the media frenzy about those people in Zuccotti Park, or perhaps because he lost everything in the banking crisis. He wanted to make someone pay, and he selected Palmer, the most important and well-known face of banking in the world. He wanted to show the world he was getting revenge. Will he try to murder us next?"

Avilla was seventy-six years old, a year younger than her husband, the daughter of Boston shipping wealth and for nearly fifty years the wife of the powerful Palmer Cronin. In her early years she'd been outspoken, involved in the civil rights protests, and spent a few nights in jail. Later, she'd been managing director of MIS—Make It Stop—a charity organization that awarded antipoverty grants for economic development in the third world.

"We don't know what he will try to do," Savich said. "Until we make an arrest, we will do our best to protect you."

She nodded. "Yes, Director Mueller said we would have an FBI agent to guard us. For that, at least, we are grateful." Her strong face collapsed, but she didn't cry, she sat there frozen, her hand now clutching her husband's.

"What I find difficult to understand," Mr. Cronin said, "is why anyone would wait so many years after I resigned my position as the Federal Reserve chairman."

Savich nodded in agreement. "Mr. Cronin, your staff has forwarded to us the file of threatening letters you've received in the past two years. If need be, we will look back all the way to 2008. Have you personally received any threats, sir?"

"Nothing in my personal mail at the house, or in my private email. But of course no one would be able to get my private email."

"Do you know if Tommy received any such threats?" Savich asked.

"Not that he mentioned. You know, Agent Savich, I have never paid too much attention to protests in the street or to random threatening letters. It would seem to me that you in the FBI always know more about such people, and such matters, than I do."

"Indeed we do, Mr. Cronin," Savich said. "And so that would bring us back to information you can help us with, more personal matters."

Mrs. Cronin said in a deep, strong voice, "Very well, Agent Savich, ask your questions."

"Let's begin with Tommy," Sherlock said. "Do either

of you know where Tommy was Friday night or what he would usually be doing on Friday nights?"

"Tommy was our beloved grandchild, Agent Sherlock," Mrs. Cronin said, "but since he got busy at college, we saw him far less than we would have liked. You will have to ask his friends at school."

"Agents are interviewing his friends at Magdalene right now, Mrs. Cronin. Did you meet any of Tommy's college friends?"

Mr. Cronin said, "Tommy has brought a number of college friends here upon occasion, as well as his friends from childhood. I remember when he brought his girlfriend here for Thanksgiving. He was proud of that girl, besotted."

Mrs. Cronin said, "We were distressed because she was a very unfortunate choice, but Tommy is—was—young and experimenting, and we thought he would get over her, given time and experience."

"Why did you think she was an unfortunate choice, Mrs. Cronin?" Sherlock asked.

"It became obvious to us she was using Tommy to gain entrée to our world, probably sleeping with him to keep him interested. I even saw her making notes while they were here, saw her messaging on her phone. She was doubtless writing down what Palmer said to post on a blog, or some such thing.

"Her name is Melissa Ivy, and she is a sophomore at George Washington, a communications major."

Mr. Cronin said, "When we asked her what she intended to do with her communications degree, she told us she wanted to become a TV news anchor. Many things fell into place. It should have been clear to Tommy as well, but it didn't appear to be. He was so young. We asked how they'd met. We were not surprised to learn she had sought Tommy out. I even chanced to see them kissing. I know, I know, they are young, but still—we had no wish to see her here after that."

"Tommy called me in early December," Mrs. Cronin said. "He wanted her to come over on Christmas Eve, when all the family gathers here. He was upset when we told him we did not wish to have her in our home again." Mrs. Cronin sighed. "He was angry, demanded to know why we didn't like her. I was honest, told him she was using him, that she was even taking notes during her visit here, that it wouldn't surprise me if she'd tried to sell her 'exclusive' with us to the tabloids.

"Tommy didn't come Christmas Eve. We never saw him again after Thanksgiving. We regretted his absence, as did his Aunt Marian and his sisters, but what I told him was honestly what we thought; it was the truth."

He was twenty years old and in love, for heaven's sake, Sherlock thought, and wondered how the Avilla Cronin she'd read about had become so rigid and judgmental. She could only imagine the intense and never-ending scrutiny that had colored their every interaction because of Mr. Cronin's position over the years, particularly after the world's economies had almost imploded.

Mrs. Cronin said, "I imagine she broke off with him when she realized we'd seen through her. If only I'd been able to see Tommy again, before he—" She swallowed. "Tommy was such a bright boy, a very high GPA, higher even than yours, Palmer, or his father's, at Magdalene. He'd laugh when we asked him what he was doing besides studying. He didn't have all that much time to socialize, he told us; he had to study too hard."

Mr. Cronin said, "So you see, don't you, Agent Savich, that Tommy simply didn't have the time to stir up a lot of enmity from anyone. I'm sure some students were jealous of him because of his grades, but surely not because of his connections. After all, most of the students at Magdalene come from families of position and wealth."

"He tended to be a loner," Mrs. Cronin said, "not very big on parties or drinking. That's not to say he wasn't popular, because he was, maybe not in high school, but he was admired and rewarded at Magdalene for his fine mind and his hard work.

"We always found him levelheaded, and respectful to us. The only time he gave us cause for worry was when he brought that Melissa Ivy girl here with her notebook, and her fingers flying on her phone." She fanned her thin veined hands in front of her. "What else is there to say about him? He gave Palmer the lovely cashmere sweater for Christmas." Avilla Cronin's fingers lightly stroked her husband's arm, feeling the soft material. She blinked and licked her lips, so white they disappeared into her parchment face.

Sherlock said, "If we could discuss some of Tommy's other friends, perhaps. Of course we will be speaking about that with Tommy's aunt, Marian Lodge, and Tommy's two sisters as well."

Cronin's old mouth seamed and twisted. "Marian—she will mourn the boy with us as if she were his mother, though she showed no such courtesy to my own son, Palmer Junior, when he died. But that is a family matter." He fell silent for a moment. "Avilla and I couldn't take the children, simply couldn't, so we stepped back when she sought their guardianship.

"You asked about other friends. One of the boys Tommy brought here regularly was Peter Biaggini—I remember I didn't care for him. He was a handsome boy, but too polite, a bootlicker, that's what you called him, Avilla. Nor did I like the way he tried to dominate Tommy, treated him as if Tommy were his acolyte or his boy Friday. Why Tommy put up with that, I can't say.

"There was Stony Hart—his real name is Walter. His father, Wakefield Hart, was at one time a colleague of mine, one of the senior accounting officers at Fannie Mae during the accounting irregularities that led to the whole senior staff resigning some eight years ago. When he was forced to resign that position, he reinvented himself as a financial consultant and a public speaker. Perhaps you've heard of him. He earns most of his money now denouncing his erstwhile colleagues, calling for decentralization and regulations, and warning of financial Armageddon. We no longer speak.

"His son, Stony, though, has always seemed a fine boy, though he, too, seemed too much under Peter

Biaggini's thumb. Actually, all of them were. Stony—Walter—is another smart young man who attended MIT, one of those very logical people who used to write software programs for fun, and now— I really don't know what he is doing now." Mr. Cronin stopped talking, as if it were simply too much effort to continue.

Avilla said abruptly, "When will we be able to bury Tommy?"

Savich said, "We will notify you as soon as we know."

CHAPTER
19

Henderson County Hospital
Sunday morning

When Griffin left the elevator on the hospital's third floor, he stopped to speak with Maestro Deputy Tuck Warner, stationed outside Delsey's room. There'd been a lot of people wanting to see Delsey, Tuck told him. He'd let Henry Stoltzen in again since Delsey had called out when she'd heard his voice. Anna was still with Delsey. He said Anna's name with a good deal of affection. Griffin didn't know if Deputy Warner was married, but if he was, Griffin hoped he curbed his enthusiasm at home.

Warner said, "We all know Anna. She's not snooty like some of the students at Stanislaus. She's always nice, always ready with some fresh coffee and a big smile when you sit down at the diner. She even invited some of us to one of the concerts at Stanislaus last fall, to hear her play a violin solo."

Anna was sitting beside Delsey's bed, her head down, her long hair falling along her face, looking over some papers on her lap. All her winter gear was on the floor beside her chair. She was wearing jeans and a blue turtleneck, boots on her feet. He heard Delsey in the bathroom taking a shower. She was set on leaving the hospital once she was cleaned up. Griffin knew she'd walk over him to get out of here.

"Hello again, Ms. Castle."

Her head jerked up, and she shuffled the papers she was reading and slipped them back inside a notebook. He held out his hand to her, showing her the photo of the dead man's body on his cell. He saw something in her eyes, something hard, maybe a flash of anger, and then it was gone. "I understand you never knew his name, Ms. Castle?"

She looked up at him, her eyes clear, and when she spoke, her words came out so slowly as to be nearly frozen. "No, he never mentioned his name. I didn't want to be rude and ask. As I told Agent Noble, what I remember about him is that he usually sat alone in the back, and he was always a good tipper."

"Do you remember any of your conversations with him?"

"We only spoke about everyday things as I took his order. He was friendly."

"You never asked him what he was doing in Maestro?"

"From your incredulous voice, Agent Hammersmith, I gather you think I'm best buds with every customer. Actually, I assumed at the time he was a local. There are bunches of locals I can identify but can't tell you anythin' about."

Griffin knew from her first reaction to the photo there was something more, something she hadn't wanted him to see—he was good at reading people. Why wouldn't the woman level with him? Wouldn't his sister's best friend want to get this crime solved?

Griffin slipped his cell back into his jacket pocket. "We should know who he is when we hear from AFIS."

"If AFIS has his fingerprints."

Griffin stilled. "What do you know about AFIS?"

"I watch TV." *You schmuck* was clearly written on her face.

They both turned when Ruth appeared in the doorway, looking hyped.

"What's happened, Ruth?"

Ruth looked over at Anna, and back at Griffin.

Griffin said, "Would you excuse me, Ms. Castle? We have some FBI business to conduct. I'll ask Delsey to give you a call later."

Anna gave each of them a long look, shrugged, and gathered up her winter gear. "You do that, Agent Hammersmith." She looked toward the bathroom, heard the shower and Delsey singing, her voice like an angel's, high and clear. She said, "Delsey wrote that song. It's about a rich guy who gambled with the devil and won."

Griffin heard her speak to Deputy Warner, then heard the clip of her boots down the corridor.

"So what do you have, Ruth?"

"Mrs. Maude Simpson, who rents out rooms in Henderson, identified our dead guy when one of Dix's deputies canvassing the motels and B&Bs showed it to her. He was registered as Ernest Weathers, checked in six days ago, but Mrs. Simpson hadn't seen him or his car since Friday, said maybe he was away visiting a cousin of his at Stanislaus for the weekend. She thought he had a local job, but didn't know where, which would have been nice to know. All his things were still in his room, so Mrs. Simpson thought he'd be back. She said Mr. Weathers was polite but they hadn't had the chance to socialize or visit. If there was a relative at Stanislaus, we still haven't found the name. She said Mr. Weathers didn't brag on the cousin being at such a prestigious school or mention the name or an instrument, which Mrs. Simpson found odd. He stayed to himself when he wasn't working, and he came and went at odd hours, since he catered parties. He drove a tan Ford Focus, and she hadn't seen it since Friday, and no, she hadn't taken down the plate."

"So what's wrong with this picture?" Griffin asked, knowing a setup when he heard it.

Ruth gave him a maniacal grin. "Funny you should ask. Let me back up: the fingerprints we took off the dead man are indeed in the AFIS system, but access to the ID is classified. I called Dillon and asked for help. He made some phone calls and found out it was the

DEA who put in the block. Dillon told me it's going to take someone with muscle to pry the man's identity out of the DEA. He said Mr. Maitland was going to speak to his counterpart, Mac Brannon, explain the situation, drop the name Ernest Weathers, and see what he had to say. Dillon laughed, said if the guy's real name is Ernest Weathers, he'd eat Sean's soggy Cheerios. He'll get back to us as soon as he finds out what's going on."

Griffin said, "Well, now, where does that leave us? Our dead guy was working undercover. Undercover, Ruth? That couldn't have been about some rural gun dealer breaking some rules. What was it? Arms shipments, drugs? Here in Maestro?"

"Got to be, don't you think? I've talked with Dix about this. There's gang activity spreading all over the country now, you know that, Griffin," Ruth said, "though I wouldn't have imagined it in Maestro, either. Maybe that's why they picked this route to move whatever the DEA is after.

"Did you read about the DEA and the metro cops taking down fourteen gang members in Nashville last year? Almost the entire local gang. They were members of a violent El Salvadoran *mara*, La Mara Salvatrucha, or MS-13."

"Sure," Griffin said. "MS-13 is big, maybe ten thousand members now in the U.S., in cities from Los Angeles to New York. They're scary dudes, over-the-top violent."

"That's right. They love their tattoos and their code of absolute loyalty to the gang. Anyone acting against them is dealt with quickly and with extreme violence, as you said. The Sinolas Cartel recruited them in the drug wars south of the border. Most of them grew up with violence as a part of their lives."

"So you and Dix think someone working with them, or some other gang, is shipping drugs, or guns, through rural Virginia?" Griffin asked.

"Well, the I-95 is one of the main corridors in the east for running drugs and guns up from South America to Miami, and the number of weapons and drugs coming east from the southwest increases by the day. The DEA has been working to infiltrate the gangs, and they've stepped up their surveillance along the interstate. The gangs, unfortunately, have almost limitless motivation because of the huge amounts of money they can make shipping drugs for sale up to the U.S., and the guns and money are going back south. It's a nightmare."

"So you're thinking that Maestro, Virginia, might be a perfect route, or even a place to stash or distribute, to avoid that attention?"

Ruth nodded. "Maybe. Only an hour away from I-95 and you're in a different world. We don't know what attracted the DEA, but why else would an agent— Weathers—be here undercover if not to find out how they're coordinating things locally?

"I'm thinking there's got to be somebody who can help them disguise the operation, someone who fits right in and doesn't look like a gang member, someone who knows his way around."

"Maybe someone at Stanislaus, since there are new faces there all the time, so no one would notice?"

"Hopefully we'll find out, if the DEA comes clean with us," Ruth said.

Griffin said, "Okay, let's say whoever's in charge found out about Weathers and had him killed. That would mean Weathers only lasted six days. I wonder what happened to trigger them, how they outed the agent's real identity."

"Don't know yet. We searched Mr. Weathers's room, found nondescript clothes—three pairs of jeans, three sweaters, underwear, and a pair of size-twelve boots, and absolutely nothing else. Gotta admit, I find that odd."

Griffin nodded. "Yes, I do, too."

Ruth said, "Maybe his murderer went to his apartment, scooped up his laptop and his papers. If so, his murderer now knows details of the DEA operation here. Did he have stuff stashed in the tan Ford? Even if Dix's deputies find the Ford, I can't see it'll be much good unless he was struck down in his car and it's part of the crime scene. I wouldn't be surprised if the DEA already has the tan Ford."

Griffin said, "Ruth, it's hard to believe Maestro is the epicenter of a gun and/or drug stash. Where? Somewhere on the Stanislaus campus? In a secret room off the auditorium? Has Dix heard any rumors at all?"

"No, but we're a small, tight community here that keeps to itself, a gun dealer's wet dream, when you think about it."

"Since Delsey's a student at Stanislaus," Griffin said slowly, "she could have accidentally stumbled over something she shouldn't have, more likely there than in town. But Delsey actually never met Weathers. She probably saw him at Salazar's party Friday night, but so what? Why place the agent's body in her bathtub and haul it away? What kind of warning is that?"

Ruth said, "Maybe they thought she was DEA, too, but if they killed her to make a statement, the DEA would come back in assault helicopters. They wouldn't want that to happen."

Delsey opened the bathroom door. She looked shell-shocked. "If I hadn't seen that the man was Latino, then you'd never have guessed it might be this MS-13 gang, right?"

Ruth said, "Not really, Delsey, even MS-13 members come in all races now. It fits, though. Finding out the man in your tub was DEA, though, that should blow things open."

Delsey said, "You're thinking the dealers believed I was working with Mr. Weathers?"

Griffin said, "I don't know. I mean, we can come up with all sorts of scenarios." Delsey smiled at Ruth and watched Griffin frown as he paced, thinking, that wonderful brain of his focused entirely on the problem. He turned. "And none of them really tie everything together. Mr. Weathers wasn't tortured, he took a knife in the chest, so they weren't interested or didn't have the time to try to make him talk about what the DEA knows."

"Who was the other man whose voice I heard?" Delsey asked.

Griffin said, "No clue. But I promise, Dels, whatever the DEA knows, they're going to tell us." He stopped, stared at her. "That small bandage is lots better, but you're looking a bit on the peaked side. How about we get you to the B&B and tuck you in?"

Delsey waved that away. "What did you learn from Dr. Hayman?"

"Not a whole lot. Professor Salazar dropped by as well. The two of them are different in a lot of ways. But they both want you, sis, and that I find very curious."

CHAPTER
20

Potomac Village
Potomac, Maryland
Sunday afternoon

The countryside was pristine white, tree branches bowed low from the weight of snow, houses domed under six-foot-deep white hats. Savich was thankful the roads were clear and he could rocket his Porsche toward Potomac, Maryland, his light bar flashing on the roof. There were no harried commuters on the road this beautiful Sunday morning, and the few cars in their way pulled over to let the Porsche speed by.

Savich felt it to his gut—if they didn't move fast, something else bad was going to happen. Then he thought it might not matter if they moved at the speed of light, something bad was still going to happen. He hated the feeling of helplessness, of inevitability.

Sherlock settled sunglasses on her nose to cut the glare. "I wonder what all the pulled-over drivers are thinking about a red Porsche cop car."

"They probably think we're yuppie idiots who paid someone to steal the flasher for us. We'll fit in better once we get to Potomac Village. Did you know the place is one of the best-educated small towns in America? Lots of money, too, and not far from Washington.

"I forgot to tell you, I got a voice mail from Bo Horsley. You remember him, don't you? Partnered with my dad on a lot of cases in the New York field office? He was the SAC until he retired a couple of months ago and opened his own security business."

"Did he say what he wanted?"

Savich shook his head. "Something about the *Jewel of the Lion* exhibit in New York City in a couple of weeks. You know, that exhibit at the Met. I haven't had time to call him back since we've been moving so quickly on this case. It didn't sound all that urgent, so I'll get to him when we come up for air."

The Porsche slowed as they left the highway and cruised to the intersection of Falls Road and River Road.

"Nice place." Sherlock nodded toward the clusters of upscale shops and businesses.

Savich turned the Porsche onto Rock Creek Court, checked his GPS, and after another half block, turned into the driveway of a two-story white Colonial with black window frames. Lush, snow-heavy pine and oak trees dotted the sloping grounds. Like its neighbors, Marian Lodge's house had a big front yard, a sturdy white fence on two sides, and a three-car garage. It looked welcoming and particularly charming with the Christmas lights still up, turned on, and shining brightly under the midday sun.

Marian Lodge was expecting them. When she opened the front door, they heard the sounds of the *Titanic* movie theme song playing faintly in the background.

Sherlock had seen Marian Lodge's photo, but the woman in the flesh was far more striking. She was nearly as tall as Dillon, built like an Amazon, her dark hair pulled back with a careless hand and fastened with a clip. She wore black yoga pants and an oversized white shirt that hung off one shoulder, showing a black bra strap. She was barefoot.

"Come in, come in—don't want all the heat to whoosh out of here."

Marian Lodge waved them into the entrance hall and quickly closed the black front door. After introductions, Ms. Lodge checked their creds and waved them straight ahead into the living room.

The house's pure Colonial exterior gave way to American country inside, with big overstuffed furniture, cozy and without pretense. It looked lived-in and welcoming. Half the back living room wall was glass, and a deep backyard beyond that sloped down to a frozen creek. Like the front, the back was filled with motionless white trees and dozens of hibernating rosebushes you could barely make out in all the snow.

Marian Lodge faced them, her arms crossed over her chest. "My nieces are upstairs watching *Titanic* for about the tenth time. At least it's a distraction. I'll bring them down later if you wish to speak to them, though I hope you don't. They would be of little help. Come into the kitchen. We'll have coffee at the table."

It was a worn wooden table, with scars and scratches, a family table that had seen gossip, arguments, laughter. Tommy Cronin had eaten at that table, Sherlock thought, maybe spread his books out, yelled at his sisters—she shook it off, anger at what had happened to him wouldn't help.

Her coffee was good, though not as good as Dillon's. Sherlock listened as Dillon expressed their condolences.

Lodge said abruptly, "Yes, everyone is very sorry. Who wouldn't be? Tommy was only twenty years old, and now he's dead, killed by some maniac who could only find Palmer Cronin's face to connect to the anonymous banks that screwed him over. So he took his revenge, not by killing Palmer, since he's an old man, his life nearly over, so why not make him suffer to his dying day by taking his only grandson?

"And so he did. He brutally murdered Tommy for the world to see. I'll bet he walked away smiling, the monster, and now he's enjoying all the media outrage at him. If Tommy had at least been one of the bankers who'd worked with Palmer, I'd bet there would be some chortling behind people's hands, some jokes that he probably deserved it.

"But not with Tommy. They can't chortle, since it was Tommy."

She started to say more, but she seemed tired of talking. She sat with her head down, staring into the coffee and letting its hot scent waft up into her face. A lone tear streaked down her cheek, but she didn't make a sound. Sherlock stretched out her hand and lightly placed it on her forearm. "We don't yet know if Tommy's murder was an act of revenge, but we will find out, I promise you that."

Her head came up fast. She dashed away the tear. "Not if I catch this monster before you do. I'd disembowel him and hang him naked by his ankles from the front gate at Palmer Cronin's house, with a sign around his neck—I WISH I'D KILLED YOU—see what the media thinks of that."

Whoa. How raw was that pain?

Sherlock said smoothly, "In that case, Ms. Lodge, we'd best keep any information we have from you. I certainly don't want to have to arrest you for murder."

Lodge gave a bitter laugh. "Tommy's girlfriend, Melissa Ivy, called me yesterday, bawling her eyes out, wanting to come over. Real tears? Maybe, since she saw Tommy as her meal ticket. She told me, stuttering through her tears, that she had to talk to someone and I was closest to Tommy. I told her I didn't want to see her. I told her she was a user, a little social climber, and that's what I'd told Tommy about her." She paused, frowned at a fingernail and began picking at it. "When she heard that she hung up on me. Dreadful girl.

"I did tell Tommy what I thought of her shortly before Christmas, when he wanted me to be on his side and against his grandparents. But I agreed with them. He was really angry at me, yelled I was just like the old relics—that's what he called his grandparents when they made him angry, which was nearly every time he saw them. I remember he walked out, drove back to Magdalene, he told me, but I'll bet he went to see Melissa.

"He didn't come to his grandparents' house on Christmas Eve. He stopped by here on Christmas Day, but he stayed only ten minutes, long enough to give presents to his sisters and give me a nasty look. He ignored the presents I got him and left, told me he was going to spend Christmas with someone he loved and who understood him."

Marian Lodge raised pain-filled eyes. "I never saw him again. The entire month before he died was filled with his anger toward me."

She was breathing hard by the time she got that all out. Sherlock and Savich waited to see if she would say anything more, but she didn't. She picked up her coffee mug and sipped, staring out the back kitchen windows at the white backyard with the sun glistening down on the white trees. She said, "I had Christmas lights in the backyard trees, too. I took them down early this morning, couldn't bear to look at them any longer."

Savich said, "You said you disapproved of Melissa Ivy as much as the Cronins."

"Yes, it surprised me to agree with them, my step-in-laws, I guess you'd call them now that I'm their granddaughters' legal guardian. After Barbara's—my sister's—funeral, I saw what a mess her kids were, saw their father was next to useless, and I moved here to take care of them. I remember it was a couple of weeks after that before the Cronins finally let me know, all benign and condescending, that I could call them Palmer and Avilla.

"Well, they're not condescending now. With Tommy's murder they're even more devastated than they were when their own son, my sister's husband, Palmer Junior, died in that bloody ridiculous Ferrari of his last year."

"I take it you didn't care for your brother-in-law, Ms. Lodge?" Sherlock asked her, studying her mobile face and thinking that Marian Lodge would always lose at poker.

"I called him JP—Junior Palmer. As you can imagine, he really didn't like that. He'd say he wasn't like his father. But the fact is Junior and Senior Palmer were like two peas in a pod, completely consumed by their careers. Only JP was deep in the financial muck his father was supposed to be regulating, a king of the junk bond world. I know he was always talking to his father, sawing away not to change anything, not to question the wonderful boom, to keep everything on track. As I said, father and son were very much alike, so why would Palmer Senior change anything?

"*Junior* didn't like me any more than I liked him. He didn't want me around until Barbara died. Then he swallowed his bile, and when I offered he was glad to have me move in to take care of the kids."

Savich said, "Your sister, Barbara, committed suicide, didn't she, Ms. Lodge? What was it, two and a half years ago?"

Marian raised a face fierce with warrior rage. "If it *was* suicide! The coroner called it that, and Barbara's shrink agreed she was suicidal. But what else would he say when they were feeding her so many drugs, both JP and that damned shrink?"

Talk about a fountain of black suspicion—this woman was Niagara Falls. Sherlock said slowly, "You believe your brother-in-law was responsible for your sister's death? He fed her drugs that drove her to kill herself?"

"I can't prove it, but he might as well have. He kept me from seeing her, helping her. She didn't have a lover in the wings, or any friends to speak to, because JP liked her under his thumb, the ultimate hausfrau. But none of that is important now; both of them are gone and buried. But so is Tommy, isn't he? He's dead, too." She slammed her hand on the kitchen table, her mug teetering before it righted itself again. "He was twenty years old! How can any of us live with that? How can his sisters not have nightmares for the rest of their lives after seeing his dead face on YouTube? How can the Cronins survive this?"

Sherlock wondered if she wasn't right. Her last thought about the Cronins when she and Dillon had followed Agent Ted Atkinson out of their living room was that they were props of themselves, that the only thing keeping them going at all was the promise of catching Tommy's killer. What would happen to them once they did catch Tommy's killer? They'd have no focus, no reason to continue.

Savich said quietly, "We'd like to ask you a few questions about Tommy, Ms. Lodge. Apart from his girlfriend, Melissa, was there anything else recently that caused you to worry about Tommy? Any change in his behavior or grades, any sign he was in trouble?"

She shrugged. "As I said, I barely saw him the last month he was alive. Did his friends at school tell you something like that?"

"We're talking with his dorm mates, his professors, checking his room and his computer, but no, they have not, Ms. Lodge. What can you tell us yourself about Tommy's friends?"

She cocked her head at them. "But I thought this was a domestic terrorist act committed by someone who'd been crushed by the banking collapse and blamed Palmer."

"We are looking at all the possibilities," Sherlock said.

"Tommy had two main friends, together since they were kids—I used to call them little jerk faces, even after Tommy turned twenty last October. They'd come by with him after classes at Magdalene sometimes, try to kiss up to me or try to hit on Marla. She's seventeen, the older of Tommy's two sisters, and a looker, like her mom. Joanie is only fifteen, so she was safe from Tommy's friends, only giggled a lot around them. Most of them were geeks, trying to grow out of it, like Tommy, and like most geeks that age, they had a long way to go. I mean, they'd play at speaking Klingon, but try to carry on an adult conversation with them in English?—Good luck. Except for Peter Biaggini—now, he's a piece of work. Peter's really smart, not a geek bone in his body. Sometimes I wanted to quash him like a bug."

"The Cronins felt he dominated Tommy," Sherlock said. "What did you think?"

"Peter was something like the Fonzie of the group. The one with some social graces as well as brains, and they all seemed to let him take the lead. Peter didn't talk to me or the girls too much, like he was too busy handling the controls to waste time talking to the underlings. I remember asking him if he was like his father. He gave me an angry look—it was gone real fast. Then he said his dad was dead. I asked Tommy about Peter's father, and he told me he wasn't dead, he ran a beauty-supply company with franchise stores all over the country. He said Peter didn't like to talk about his father, that he was ashamed of him for being so ordinary, for selling cosmetics—the Hair Spray King, he called him. But Tommy really liked Mr. Biaggini, said he was a great guy, always doing stuff for the kids."

She went on to tell them of how thoughtful Tommy Cronin had been to her and his sisters, until Melissa Ivy had come into his life.

"Do you know what Tommy's aspirations were, Ms. Lodge?"

"He was already studying banking and finance, like

his father and grandfather, and he was ambitious, too, like both of them. He joked about running Deutsche Bank by the time he was thirty.

"He spoke German after spending a year in Cologne. He had an internship at the Deutsche Bank Washington office this past summer. He wanted a chance to work directly at the Deutsche Bank Frankfurt headquarters." Her voice hitched, and her hand clutched the coffee cup.

Sherlock gave Marian a moment to collect herself. "The Cronins mentioned a Stony Hart."

"Stony was Tommy's other main friend, and the oldest of the three of them. As I told you, they've all been friends since childhood. I think Stony was Tommy's very best friend. His dad, Wakefield Hart, was a big deal in investment banking, and that's how Stony and Tommy met, through Tommy's grandfather Palmer.

"I remember my sister, Barbara, telling me that Stony's father, Wakefield, had hung on every word out of Palmer Cronin's mouth when he was chairman of the Fed. I don't know what Palmer thought about the man when Hart had to resign his job at Fannie Mae along with most of their senior executives when they were caught cooking the books. Wouldn't it be something if even one of those yahoos had the honesty to apologize for what they did?

"Anyway, it was something Tommy and Stony shared, dominant fathers who were bankers, burned by their own greed. I think they both wanted a chance to do better."

Savich and Sherlock met Tommy's two sisters, Marla

and Joanie, on their way out. The girls seemed as blank and frightened as Marian Lodge said they were. It was not the time to talk with them. Savich arranged for an agent to stay with them, since they were also grand-children of Palmer Cronin.

Their last view of Marian Lodge was of her holding the sisters against her, her cheek pressed against Joanie's head.

They'd just pulled back into Rock Creek Court when Jimmy Maitland called to tell them Spooner had found the computer used to post the photo of Tommy's body at the Lincoln Memorial.

CHAPTER
21

The Hoover Building
Sunday afternoon

Agent Lucy Carlyle gave Savich and Sherlock a big smile as they walked into the CAU. "You'll love this. Walter Hart—Stony—opened his apartment door, took one look at our creds stuck in his face, and turned white as Coop's boxers. First thing out of his mouth was, 'I didn't do anything illegal.'"

Coop laughed. "Talk about an open book; his face was a lovely mixture of guilt and fear. I asked him what he did do, and he said, 'Nothing, I didn't do anything.' Who could forget a classic like that? I gave him my *nailed you* look, told him we had a warrant to seize his computers and routers and that he was coming with us to the Hoover Building. He hemmed and hawed until I told him we'd arrest him if we had to. I patted him down while Lucy slapped cuffs on him. He said his girlfriend, Janelle Eckles, was coming to see him, and could he at least call her? We said no.

"He was nearly in tears he was so scared. He kept babbling in the backseat about how everything he had on his computer was legal, or if it wasn't, it should be, and why wouldn't we tell him what he'd supposedly done? We ignored him, told him you'd be answering his questions. Made you and Sherlock sound as mean as the Hulk on a green day and his sidekick Cruella, who scared him even more."

"Good. You've got him all set up," Savich said. "You got a background check yet?"

"So far, not much more than a Google search. His name is Walter Hart, goes by Stony. His apartment is right off Dupont Circle. He really is a computer nerd, had quite a setup in his apartment, several boxes and monitors. He graduated with honors last year from MIT, started work after that as a junior securities analyst at the UBS office here in D.C. Just started to make a name for himself, I would guess. Spooner says he's got the IP address dead to rights. There's no chance he's wrong. It was the kid's computer."

Savich said, "At least we know now this wasn't a domestic terrorist act committed by some disenfranchised victim of the banking scandal."

"Nope," Sherlock said. "What we've got is something very close to home. Where is Stony, Coop?"

"We stashed him inside the interview room, where he's been sitting by himself. I took him to the men's room a little while ago. Strangest thing, he acted scared, of me, yes, but it was more. He seemed terrified, as if his life was over and someone was going to come up to his urinal and pop him. For uploading that photo on YouTube or because he'd gotten caught? He asked me if he should get a lawyer, and I said he should talk to you about it. Then I left him alone to do his business, because, frankly, he was too scared to get it done. I marched him back to the interview room and left him snuffling into his shirtsleeve."

Sherlock said, "You want to hear something interesting? It turns out Stony and Tommy Cronin and Peter Biaggini have known each other all their lives. We know that Stony and Tommy were best friends."

Lucy went nearly bug-eyed. "You've got to be kidding. I mean, he uploaded a photo of his murdered *friend*? But that would make him—what? The murderer? At least an accomplice?"

Coop shook his head. "I don't see him murdering Tommy Cronin."

"Why?" Savich asked him.

Coop was thoughtful for a moment. "He doesn't have the fire in the belly for it—he's a nice kid, Savich, that's the long and short of it."

Lucy said, "But he was willing to upload the photo of a dead friend, which means if he didn't kill Tommy, he has to know who did. That's pretty slimy."

"We're about to see," Savich said. "Why don't you

guys come in and stand against the wall looking grim while Sherlock and I speak with Stony. From what you say, he responds to that."

Coop grinned. "I like the Gestapo look—arms crossed over the chest, eyes mean and slitted."

Lucy poked him in the ribs. "Good thing you took him to the bathroom, Coop."

Savich and Sherlock walked down the hallway to the interview room, Coop and Lucy behind them. They paused to listen at the door, then Savich unlocked it and went in. Savich could practically see waves of despair rolling off Stony Hart. Coop was right, whatever else this young man was, he wasn't a murderer. But then what was he? Given what he'd done, it was hard to believe he was really Tommy Cronin's best friend.

"Good afternoon, Mr. Hart. Everyone calls you Stony, right?"

The young man's eyes met theirs and froze like a deer in the headlights. He looked terrified down to his pocket protector, and painfully young, though Savich knew he'd turned twenty-three last week. His eyes slid to Coop and Lucy, standing with their backs against the door, ready to leap on him. He ran his tongue over his bottom lip and managed a hoarse whisper, "Yes, I'm Stony. I already told those agents I haven't done anything wrong. I didn't call a lawyer because I'm not a criminal, and I understand I haven't been arrested. It's very important if I'm going to keep my job that I not be arrested."

Savich said, "You're not a criminal? I'm glad to hear

it, because that means you'll tell us the truth." Savich leaned in close. "I always know when someone is lying to me, Stony, always, so save us all time and don't try it. I want you to tell us what you meant when you told these agents you didn't do anything illegal. What is it you did, exactly?"

"Look. You took all my computers, though I don't see how you have the right. Sure, I have some file-sharing stuff—music and videos, mostly—and that might not be strictly legal, but they can sue me, can't they? Some of it's a little embarrassing, maybe. But I don't have a clue why you brought me here like this"—he swallowed—"in handcuffs." His eyes darted to where Lucy had left the handcuffs on the edge of the table.

Savich asked, "So is that why you use anonymizers? So you won't be embarrassed?"

"Sure, I have the software to do that. It's the best, I vetted it myself, even made adjustments to make it better. It's best to have the option of keeping out of sight on the Internet. Sometimes I cruise underground sites in China, Iran, and no one ever knows who I am. Why do you care about my anonymizer? What do you think I've done?"

Savich backed off, let him wait. "Tell me first, how'd you get the nickname Stony?"

Stony flexed and unflexed his fingers. "What? You want to know that? My mom and dad said I kept looking at stones when I was a kid; I had kind of a compulsion that way, had to see what was under every rock. Now I'm an adult I see it has a different meaning, but

I'm still Stony. My folks thought it was funny. My friends picked it up from my folks. Look, I tried to get past some firewalls, but nothing dangerous—" His face drained of what color was left. "No, I mean, nothing illegal. Just fooling around."

Sherlock said, "Then why don't you tell us why you used your anonymizer to upload the photo of your best friend's dead body on YouTube."

Stony sputtered, put his face in his hands, and shook his head back and forth. "What are you talking about? This is about Tommy? That photo? You think I did that? No, never, it was horrible."

Savich leaned forward. "The thing is, Stony, the commercial proxy you used is secure enough, highly sophisticated with your tweaks, but not for someone committing a cybercrime linked to what might be an act of terrorism."

"That would be impossible with my software, Agent Savich. You'd seriously have no way."

"The NSA has access to more of those servers than you'll ever know. We nailed you, Stony. We can prove the photo was sent from one of your computers."

Stony Hart sat frozen, his eyes fixed, still shaking his head back and forth. "One of my computers? No, that's not possible, it's not."

Sherlock said, "We know Tommy was dropped from a great height, and not at the Lincoln Memorial. Whoever took that picture probably carried him there and arranged him at Lincoln's feet for a public display. Was it you?"

"No! I couldn't do that; I wouldn't."

Now, that's the truth, Savich thought. "But you know who did? You posted that picture for someone else, didn't you?"

Stony put his face in his hands and began to sob.

Savich sat forward, grabbed Stony's bony wrist, hauled him close. "Stop crying; it only makes me mad. We've got you cold, Stony, so you might as well own up to the contemptible thing you did, posting that picture. Stop being a pitiful coward. If you don't tell us exactly what you know, that makes you the murderer's accomplice. You could spend the rest of your life in jail."

Stony nearly rose straight out of his chair. "Listen, I couldn't believe Tommy was dead, couldn't believe someone would kill him and put him in the Lincoln Memorial. It was horrible. I'm not a monster, I'm not! I would never post that photo, not for anyone. You've got to believe me, I don't know anything about it. I want my dad. I want a lawyer."

Savich drummed his fingertips on the table. "I doubt Wakefield Hart or a lawyer can help you, unless you tell us what we want to know."

"How do you know my dad's name?"

"There's no hiding anything from us," Savich said, his eyes hard, "even what you did on your supposedly foolproof anonymizer software. It's about time you realized that."

"No, no, listen, I told you, I don't know anything about it. And my dad, he's smart, and he knows people, important people, people who could stop you from saying these things to me. Where is he?"

"Your dad might as well crawl on the ground and root up worms," Sherlock said. "What are you trying to do, moron, make us madder with your silly mean-daddy threats?"

Savich turned to look at Lucy and Coop. "Stony's right about his dad being smart. Did you guys know Daddy—Wakefield Hart—makes his money by giving speeches now, blasting Palmer Cronin for 'facilitating' the banking crisis when he was the chairman of the Fed? Quite an accusation for Wakefield to make, especially since he was one of the major players in the screw-the-world game while it lasted. Are you proud of your dad, Stony?"

Wakefield Hart's son stuck his chin in the air. "Hey, I am proud of him. Sure he made some mistakes, but it was business, and there were a lot of events no one anticipated." Stony fell silent, stared at them.

Sherlock said, "Yeah, yeah, I see. How can it be wrong if everyone's doing it, is that your dad's defense? It helps if you've got no moral compass, and I'd say that's a profound lesson for a son to learn at his daddy's knee. I got the impression from the Cronin family that you're not like that, and neither was Tommy. Are we wrong? Is that why you didn't flinch at uploading a photo of your brutally murdered friend on YouTube? That you were involved in killing him?"

"You've got to believe me. I don't know anything about it, I swear."

"Then why did you try to hide behind an anony-mizer?"

Sherlock stood, leaned over the table, and got right in his face. "Why did you do it, Stony? What did Tommy ever do to you to make you hate him so much? To humiliate him even in death?"

Stony sat frozen.

CHAPTER
22

"You've got to believe me. I wouldn't do that. I loved Tommy. I can't believe he's dead, just can't believe it. I mean, why? And you think I'd upload that horrible photo?" At their stone-cold faces, his eyes rolled back in his head and he slid out of his chair and landed in a heap on the interview room floor.

Savich and Coop hauled him up, sat him back down in the chair. Savich slapped his face until his eyelashes fluttered and he opened his eyes.

"Better now?" Sherlock asked him. She poured him a glass of water, and he studied it closely but didn't drink.

"All right, Stony," Sherlock said, "if you didn't upload that photo from your computer, that means somebody else did. Where were you Friday night and Saturday morning?"

"I spent the night with my girlfriend, Janelle Eckles. We met three and a half weeks ago. She works at State."

Savich said, "Who could have had access to your computers, or used your IP address?"

"Anyone, if they were in my apartment and knew how. Or someone could have hacked through my router, I guess."

Sherlock asked, "And who could that be?"

"I know a lot of people—at work, from school, friends—though I'm better at it than most of them."

Savich said, "Let's begin with a friend. How about Peter Biaggini? Did he have an apartment key, know your passwords?"

"Peter doesn't have a key, and yes, he may know some of my passwords. I'm not that careful with them."

"Have you ever known Peter to be involved with anything illegal?"

Stony thought about this. "Only teenage stuff, a long time ago. When he was in the eighth grade, he wanted me to ruin another kid's science project so he would win. I told him I wouldn't do it, so he slashed my mom's tires. It was her new car, a Prius, and she loved driving it around. He denied it, but I knew. When we were growing up, Peter made sure we all knew there'd be payback if we didn't do what he wanted."

"And now?"

"We're grown up now; it's not like that."

"You deny you posted Tommy's photo. Did anyone else ask you to post it for him? Like Peter?"

"No, no, I swear." Stony shook his head. "It's all so

terrible," he said, and he lowered his face into his hands again.

Savich said, "You may go, Stony."

Stony's face jerked up, hope blooming bright through the tearstains on his face. "Really? You're not going to arrest me?"

"Not at the moment," Sherlock said, her eyes on Dillon, "but we'll be talking again. And if you've lied to us, you're in more trouble than you know."

Savich handed Stony a card. "If you find anything or think of anything that could help, call me. I'm sorry you lost your friend, Stony. We're keeping your computers for the time being. I'm calling a guard to take you home."

"Thank you, sir."

Savich said, "I suggest you don't speak with anyone else who might be involved in this, including Peter Biaggini, all right?"

"But how can anyone I know have done this? I mean, we're all friends, especially Peter, now that Tommy's gone. Well, sometimes Peter—well, he likes to run the herd, that's what he calls his friends, but he wouldn't have anything to do with this." He paused, shook his head, and went silent.

Sherlock leaned in close to him. "What do you want to say, Stony? Is it about Peter?"

Stony's face was white and set. "No. I don't know how or why Tommy was murdered, why anyone used my computer to upload that photo. I didn't mean anything in particular. Really."

Stony looked up at the guard who came to escort him out of the Hoover Building, then he looked down at his sneakered feet and never looked up again; he was misery walking.

Coop said, "Whatever it is Stony's not telling us, the kid's going to live with this for a lifetime."

Lucy said, "Why wouldn't he tell us what he was thinking? Was it about Peter?"

Coop said, "Or maybe he's protecting someone else. Someone close."

Savich said, "We'll speak to him again after he's had time to think things over. Right now I want to speak to Peter Biaggini and his father. I've got this feeling we'll get more out of them if they're together." Savich called Ben Raven, WPD, and asked him to send two uniforms to pick up Peter Biaggini and bring him to the FBI building in the oldest squad car he had. "Shake him up a little, too, this leader of the herd. I want him cuffed if he gives your officers any lip, and sitting behind the wire mesh, smelling that old car."

Savich telephoned Mr. Biaggini from his office, asked him to come to the Hoover Building to speak to them about Tommy Cronin's murder. Mr. Biaggini wasn't happy, couldn't understand why they would want to speak to him, but agreed. Yes, he would be there in an hour.

Not a minute later, Savich's cell sang out "Sweet Home, Alabama." When he punched off his cell, he said, "Stony's dad is here. Mr. Wakefield Hart, in the flesh."

CHAPTER
23

The first impression Sherlock had on seeing Wakefield Hart was that he had the look of gravitas down cold. He was a good dresser, too, and he looked confident, in charge of his world. He also looked royally pissed, and that gave her a warm glow.

He walked straight through the unit to Savich's office, ignored her, and planted a fist on Savich's desk. "Where is my son? What have you done with him?"

Sherlock noticed his voice was carefully modulated, a perfect blend of protectiveness and outrage. She wasn't surprised, because he was a public speaker now, relying for his bread on his audiences believing he was speaking to them from a redeemed heart, no matter how much he'd mucked about in the viper pit with the rest of the bankers, the unrepentant ones. Sherlock always found it fascinating that no matter how heinous the crime, some people with a knack for it—televangelists, politicians, financiers, whoever—had but to humble themselves and admit their wrongdoings before their flock to be granted forgiveness. She supposed anyone taking responsibility for a bad decision was so rare that forgiveness poured in, beginning with the media.

Savich didn't rise or answer him. He merely motioned Mr. Hart to a seat beside Sherlock. Hart sat, but it was obvious what he wanted to do was tell Savich he was a bully and a moron and he was going to get him fired.

Savich said in a deliberate, slow voice, "Though he denies it, Mr. Hart, your son may have uploaded the photo of Tommy Cronin's body onto the Internet using an anonymizer. Do you know what that is?"

"Not really, but I do know they have legitimate uses. And they're untraceable, aren't they? But who cares? Even if Stony uses them—"

Savich simply spoke over him. "He wasn't careful enough to keep us from finding him. When did he call you, Mr. Hart?"

"He called me from the bathroom here. He was crying." Hart Senior was clearly disgusted. "He couldn't tell me anything except that your agents had seized his computers and he could lose his job and his career if you arrested him."

Sherlock said, "Mr. Hart, we try very hard not to harm people's lives when we bring them in to interview, even if they're not entirely up front with us."

"I told him not to admit to anything illegal. But he

wouldn't lie, nor would he have any part of uploading Tommy's photo, he—" Hart jumped to his feet and paced Savich's office, a few short steps in each direction. "All right, very well. Let's say he did upload the photo. Who cares? It's not a crime. Perhaps he had reasons he can't tell you about. I demand you release my son to me or I'll speak to Director Mueller myself. Where is my son? What have you done with him?"

"He's on his way back to his apartment," Savich said. "Sit down, Mr. Hart." Savich's voice was deeper, and clipped. Hart gave him a look and sat.

"What will happen to my son because of this? Will his employers know? The press?"

Savich said, "Mr. Hart, did you know Tommy Cronin?"

"What? Of course. He was one of a small group of boys who've been friends since they were children. Tommy was in and out of my house for years."

"Tell us your impressions of Tommy Cronin, Mr. Hart."

Hart paused. "Tommy was a smart boy, a bit conceited, actually, because of who his grandfather was—understandable, I guess. A tragedy he was killed. Wait, what does this have to do with your persecution of my son?"

"And what about Peter Biaggini?"

No hesitation: "A right proper little shite."

Savich said, "How would you describe your son's relationship with Peter Biaggini?"

They saw it: Hart wanted to snarl and curse, not at

them, but at Peter, but he got hold of himself. "What does— All right, Peter is a leader, always has been. My son is not. It sometimes seemed when they were growing up that if Peter had told him to eat oatmeal, he'd have dived into a tub of the stuff and eaten his way out. And Stony hates oatmeal."

"Did you think Peter may have asked your son to upload that photo of Tommy?"

Hart cursed under his breath. "That sniveling little—"

Sherlock wondered who he was talking about, his son or Peter Biaggini. Hart plowed his fingers through his beautifully styled black hair with its glossy wings of silver at the temples. "I'm not surprised, but Stony would never do something so despicable unless he had a good reason. No, there's no way he would. I mean, what reason could he have? Maybe you're right. Maybe it's on Peter's head. Maybe he uploaded the photo." There was more he would have said. Both Savich and Sherlock saw it, but he held back.

Savich said, "We'll be talking to Stony again, and to Peter as well."

"Yes, you do that. It's obvious my son had nothing to do with Tommy Cronin's death." Now he let contempt and anger flow out. "I've noticed on every TV station that Tommy has achieved sainthood—crackerjack student at Magdalene, brilliant mind, well liked by his peers, a bright future—well, that's quite an appealing story, isn't it? What about my boy—is he going to be cast as the villain now?" His cell rang. Hart ignored it, but then he looked down. "Excuse me." He rose and walked to the door of Savich's office. They heard his impatient voice, then he punched off his cell and turned back to them. "That was my son. He is—distraught." Hart turned on his heel and walked out of the CAU, not another word.

Savich said, "I wonder what else Mr. Hart was going to say about Tommy Cronin."

Sherlock rose. "You know, it's the oddest thing, but I got the impression that Mr. Hart was relieved about something."

"That we didn't arrest his son?"

"No, something else."

"We'll never find out from Hart Senior. My money's on Stony telling us."

CHAPTER
24

Bud Bailey's B&B
Maestro, Virginia
Sunday afternoon

Griffin punched off his cell. "That was Savich. The DEA is stonewalling us. They say the dead man's ID and what he was doing here in Maestro is part of an investigation that's too sensitive to discuss. They told Savich to keep even that information under his hat." He paused, shook his head. "Amazing, isn't it? All of us are supposed to be working together."

Dix snorted. "It doesn't make much sense to me, either, Griffin. I mean, their agent is dead; the drug dealers he was after know that we know. I'm the freaking law; why won't they trust us?"

Griffin said matter-of-factly, "The DEA couldn't deny outright he was their agent; we already knew that, thanks to Savich. He didn't have a shield or any ID, so we know he was undercover. If they're holding us off and they're not here in force, their operation is still in play. They've got to have at least one more undercover agent here in Maestro they don't want to put at risk."

Dix said, "Makes sense. But who? No new faces in town or I'd have noticed."

Griffin suddenly knew exactly who the other undercover DEA agent was. "Dix, could you leave a deputy here to guard Delsey? I've got to speak to someone, and I don't want to wake her up and haul her with me. She needs to rest."

Dix gave him a long look. "You want to discuss anything with me, Griffin? Like who this person is you need to speak to, for example?"

"Not yet. I'll tell you as soon as I'm sure."

"You're FBI; why should I be surprised? You're mad at the DEA one minute, and the next minute you're as tight-lipped with me as all the *Federales*." Dix would have busted more chops, but he saw something in Griffin Hammersmith's face and realized he was really serious about this. So be it, he'd give Griffin a few hours to sniff out what he needed to.

After Griffin saw Deputy Penny Loomis settled in the charming early-American living room of Bud Bailey's only two-bedroom suite, he headed for Wolf Trap Road, his cell's GPS and its sweet female voice guiding his way.

The bright sun had melted most of the ice and was pockmarking the snow, leaving slush wherever humans drove and walked. Griffin found the small, detached 1950s cottage ten minutes later, set back from the street in the middle of a beautiful snow-filled yard. The sun glistened off the oak and maple trees, and clumps of snow occasionally thudded to the ground.

It was picture-postcard perfect.

The only sign of human habitation was the small dark blue Kia Rio, fresh tire tracks in the driveway, and the double set of footsteps on the snow-covered sidewalk to the front door.

Griffin rang the doorbell as he breathed in the cold air. He felt anger rise in his gut as he waited, wondering what would happen when the door opened.

"Who is it?" Her voice was calm and serious, with no hint of fear or grief or rage, though he knew she had to be feeling all three.

"Special Agent Griffin Hammersmith, FBI. I'd like to speak to you."

There was a moment of silence, and then a dead bolt slid back, a chain unhooked, and a lock unclicked. As the door opened, he heard a violin solo playing in the background.

She was wearing thick white socks, no shoes. Her dark hair was hooked behind her ears, her face clean of makeup. If he weren't so mad, he'd take another look at her mouth, but since his gut was churning, he looked her straight in the eye instead. "You're being careful.

That's smart, given what happened to your partner. And to my sister."

She stiffened all over, but she didn't blink, didn't look away from his face. She was good.

Griffin saw she had a Glock pressed against her leg, and he wondered if she'd had it clipped to her waistband beneath her blue and gray oversized Stanislaus sweatshirt before pulling it out at his unexpected knock at her door.

"Glock 22, I see. Forty-caliber, no doubt, standard-issue service weapon. Couldn't you get your daddy's .44 Magnum qualified for duty, Anna? By the way, is that your real name?"

Her chin went up. "It's my mom's .44. What's this all about, Agent Hammersmith?"

He walked toward her, forcing her to take a step back or hold still and shoot him. She stepped back. He turned and closed the door, clicked the dead bolt. He saw her eyes were shadowed, as if she hadn't slept well, and she was pale. It made him madder, and his voice came out stone cold. "If I hadn't realized it had to be someone Delsey knew, I might believe you, Anna, but I do know. You're an undercover DEA agent, like the man who died."

She didn't change expression, didn't say a word.

"Anna—excuse me, Agent Castle—my sister could easily have been killed Friday night, no thanks to you and your operation. Your own agent died at her place. It's past time you leveled with me."

She met his eyes directly, didn't falter. "I'm a music student at Stanislaus and a part-time waitress payin' my own way. What do you want from me? Why are you even here?"

He stepped right up to her face. "This is my sister we're talking about, and I'll do anything I need to in order to protect her. I thought Delsey was your friend, that you cared for her. But you don't have any friends, do you? You're only an operative trying to get information.

"Whatever you're after is the DEA's business, I accept that. But Delsey is mine. You were onto something, weren't you, and that's why your partner was killed. What was it? What happened? What was your partner doing in Delsey's apartment? And the big question— what does Delsey have to do with any of this?"

She was shaking her head back and forth, but now he saw her eyes were sheened with tears. Or maybe rage over what had happened to Delsey. Still, she repeated, her mouth hard, "I don't know what you're talkin' about, and I want you to leave, Agent Hammersmith. Now."

He took her shoulders in his hands and shook her. He let her see his own anger now. "Tell me the truth. I know you care about your murdered agent, but think of what could still happen to Delsey. Your partner's killers now know she identified him and they could start to worry she might have seen them, too. They wouldn't want a possible witness breathing, would they? Talk to me. Don't you owe Delsey that much? She could have been killed because of you."

"Agent Hammersmith, you have no right to question me," Anna said. "You're guessing at somethin' you shouldn't, do you hear me?"

"Guilty as charged. Here I have the gall to interfere with a federal investigation. So why not take that up with your DEA boss? We could work together, help each other if you'd level with me. Otherwise, Sheriff Noble and the FBI might blow your whole investigation without even meaning to. Does that give you a different slant on things now, Agent Castle?"

She cursed him, nice full-bodied curses, then whirled around, and said over her shoulder, "Stay here, I mean it. I need to make a call."

He watched her walk on stockinged feet down the hallway and into another room, heard her speaking on her cell, though he couldn't make out the words. Five minutes passed; he timed it. When she came back, she walked right up to him, and her look was both angry and resigned. "You win. I spoke to my boss in Washington, Mac Brannon. He's calling Mr. Maitland, bringing the FBI in with us. You're right, I'm DEA, Special Agent Lilyanna Remie Parrish. You've embarrassed me, made me look incompetent to my boss. How did you know?"

She was so close he could feel her warm breath on his face. And her mouth was too close. He stepped back. "You obviously didn't realize you were sending out clues."

"I sent out clues? I'm very good. I never send out clues. What clues?"

He smiled down at her and counted off on his fingers.

"You knew quite a bit about guns, you knew about fingerprints, and the biggie—you disappeared all day Saturday. It takes a cop to know a cop, don't you agree?"

"That's not much at all, not a single real clue at all. All a guess."

Griffin shook his head, pointed to her Glock. "Smart of you to be really careful. You went out this morning. Where did you go?"

"How'd you know that?"

"I'm psychic." At her startled look, he said, "Would you believe I saw the double footsteps to and from your front door to your car?"

She said, "I went to Bridy's Market for some bagels and cream cheese."

He walked past her into a small living room that looked like a clone of his grandparents' lake cottage, old and faded and a bit saggy, neither place updated since the day the front doors opened circa 1950. There was an ancient chintz sofa across from two overstuffed flowery chairs, scattered rag rugs over a banged-up oak floor, and an old fireplace belching a bit of smoke and little heat.

Music soared, and he recognized Itzhak Perlman. "Turn off the music, please. We need to get a lot of things straight."

There was suddenly a loud yowl. Griffin whirled around to see a fat black tail disappear under the sofa. He turned to her, an eyebrow arched.

"That's Monk. He adopted me right after I moved in. He's still scared of people." She switched off the music, turned to face him, her Glock still in her hand. "I don't know if he'll come out while you're here."

"What's your real name again?"

"Lilyanna Remie Parrish."

"Lilyanna. Such a sweet, romantic name. I'll bet you're called Anna, right? I see you're still holding your gun."

She looked blank, then whooshed out a breath and stuffed the Glock back under her jeans waistband. "My mom's maiden name is Castle, so it's worked well. It's a precept in undercover work—you stick as close to the truth as possible. And yeah, you're right, everyone calls me Anna."

Griffin said, "So you've done undercover before?"

She nodded. "A couple of times. No, no one guessed what or who I was."

"Let's get to it. What are you doing here in Maestro?"

She turned slowly. "First of all, Agent Hammer-smith—"

"Griffin. Don't go all stiff and formal on me now."

"You called me Agent Castle and looked like you wanted to punch me."

"I did until I looked at you and realized you were not only scared, you were hurting because of your part-ner's murder."

That was true enough. "Yes, all right, Griffin. Listen to me, I do care for Delsey—a lot. I wouldn't do any-thing to put her at risk, and I haven't. I was horrified— and very angry—when she was hurt." She punched her fist against her palm. "My partner—his name was Arnold Racker—he was a fifteen-year DEA veteran who taught a lot of us what we know. Arnie had three grown daughters. His wife's name—widow's name—is Janice. He'd just become a grandfather." The dam broke. She lowered her face and let tears roll down her checks.

He made no move toward her, although he wanted to, but he knew it wouldn't be smart. He simply waited.

She got herself together, scrubbed her hands over her face, and walked to the fireplace to warm her hands. *Good luck with that.*

He said, "I'm very sorry, Anna."

"Yeah, I'm sorry, too," she said. "About all of it. About Delsey gettin' involved, about her seein' Arnie dead, about Arnie bein' dead."

"We're going to work together now to get these bastards. Tell me how all this started."

"All right. You've heard of the Transnational Threat Alliance? It involves collaboration at all levels of law enforcement, even international, to bring down criminal organizations moving drugs across borders.

"Our own National Drug Intelligence Center picked up on a flood of marijuana and very pure cocaine comin' into the D.C. metro area startin' last summer. And not only D.C., but other cities in the area—Baltimore, Richmond, even Philadelphia.

"We traced its source to this general area with a new technology I'm sure you know about, the National License Plate Reader program. Customs and Border Protection have installed handheld license plate readers at all our land ports of entry. They can't catch everythin' because there's a lot of commerce and travel they can't disrupt. You've heard how the cartels started concealin' drugs in car transmissions, truck manifolds, gas tanks, even produce, and it's tough for them. But they record all the license plates.

"We've expanded that program with established fixed locations inside the U.S. Police cruisers, municipalities— even private companies—now have automated readers. We mine that data and cross-reference it with known and suspected gang members and drug traffickers. You want to hear the kicker? Turns out there was simply too much of that kind of traffic in and out of this area for it to be a coincidence."

Griffin nodded. "And since Maestro is only an hour away from I-95, it makes a good drop-off and distribution center? Is that what you think is happening? In the perfect cover of a peaceful small town?"

"That's right. But there's more. The drug trade within a few hundred miles of here has some new players. The Mara Salvatrucha, a gang of mostly Central Americans, was always a threat, but they were mostly a loose aggregate of local gangs, more of an association than an organized cartel. You probably know them better as MS-13. Now they've established a major smugglin' center in Mexico, and they've become major local players in drugs, money launderin', even arms dealin' into and out of Mexico. Someone is makin' them into a force in this area, someone with the money, muscle, and guile to do it."

"And that person is here in Maestro?"

"We think so. We think that person is Rafael Salazar."

Griffin felt the shock of surprise. Surely not possible. But—"We'll get into that in a minute. Start at the beginning again. What do you know about him?"

"We heard last summer from the Spanish National Police—the Cuerpo Nacional de Policía—that Rafael Salazar was a person of interest to them. He's part of a powerful Salvadoran family, the Lozanos, involved in guns and the drug trade. They spread their business into Spain, primarily through North Africa some two generations back, and now they could be branching into the U.S. The Spanish police alerted us Salazar was on his way here, to Stanislaus, for at least a year. That jibed closely with our own investigation, and it rang big alarm bells."

"You thought that Salazar's coming to Stanislaus meant the Lozano family was widening their influence to the local Maras?"

She nodded. "And the establishment of new sources for them from Mexico and South America."

Griffin was shaking his head. "Salazar is a world-famous classical guitarist. You believe he's a drug trafficker, too? It sounds nuts. Why would he do it? It makes him a criminal, and surely he's got to realize if caught he'd be playing guitar to prisoners for the rest of his natural life. No more fame, adoration from fans, no more money in his pockets. You're saying he's also involved with his family in drugs? He's the one running organization MS-13 here at Stanislaus? I can't get my brain around it."

"Neither could I, at least for a while, but our information was solid. Salazar's mother, Maria Rosa, belongs to the Lozano crime family, originally out of San Salvador, as I said. At least three generations of extortion, weapons, drugs, prostitution, you name it. Several of the cousins are high up in the Mara Salvatrucha in El Salvador. The Spanish police told us they didn't believe Maria Rosa had any involvement with the criminal part of the family enterprise, and that like her sons, she was a fine musician.

"But Salazar—we discovered he spent a good deal of his time with his mother's brother, Mercado Lozano, when he was growing up. His mother sent him there every summer from Spain. Mercado is now the kingpin of the Lozano operation in El Salvador. So the Spanish police have watched him for years now. But nothin' has stuck yet."

"I understand Salazar's brother invited him here," Griffin said. "Is Hayman involved, too?"

She shook her head. "To the best of our knowledge, Dr. Hayman has never dealt with the Lozano family, except, of course, his mother, Maria Rosa. She seems to have kept him out of the family business. Don't forget, he never lived with his mother, has never met any of his relatives in San Salvador, so far as we know."

Griffin nodded. "Twins, separated as boys. Look what happened to the two of them."

"Very different upbringings, but the same deep well of talent."

"Don't you think it's strange Dr. Hayman has no clue who and what his twin brother is? And his mother?"

"Yes, I agree with you, and so do my bosses. I've been keeping an eye on Dr. Hayman, but in six months I've seen nothing suspicious at all, and his name hasn't appeared anywhere it shouldn't. And so, Griffin, this is why I was sent here undercover. No one outside the DEA knew I was here, not even local law enforcement."

Griffin spoke his fear aloud. "Anna, he wants Delsey very badly."

"It bothered me as well until I realized she was probably only his obsession du jour. Since his arrival in September I've seen him focus on other graduate students, and after a while, he moves on."

He prayed she was right. "How did the DEA get Stanislaus to let you in?"

"Three of us agents applied, with the help of some imaginative letters of recommendation supplied by the Agency, but I was the only one to pass the audition."

He gave her a long look, nodded slowly. "What were you supposed to do exactly, search Salazar's house, his office? Or lie low and listen?"

"Maurie's Diner is gossip central, the perfect place to pick up random information and news. I know about every extramarital affair in Maestro. Now, as for Salazar's house, he's got a state-of-the-art alarm system, no gettin' around that, and I did try. But I did have occasional access, since he invites students to his house. But I could rarely look around alone; he'd have noticed.

"Finally in December I got into his office long enough to find a hidden drawer in his desk with records of large foreign bank transactions, and this was enough to get a federal warrant for electronic surveillance.

"Then about a week ago we got word from an informant in Baltimore that the MS-13 gang there was expectin' a large shipment from this area. With the federal warrant, we were set to move, so Arnie was sent in to set up surveillance in Salazar's house. He took a job with the Golden Goose Catering Company in Henderson because we knew Salazar would call them for the party Friday night. It gave him the opportunity to set up during the party."

"You never saw him after that," he said. It wasn't a question.

She shook her head, misery shining out of her eyes. "Someone got onto him, I don't know who. It's the only thing that makes sense." She swallowed. "When I didn't hear from Arnie Saturday morning, I called him on his throwaway cell phone several times, but there was no answer. I called the Golden Goose, and they told me he hadn't helped with the cleanup at the party; they were really angry about it. That's when I knew for sure somethin' had happened to him. I went to his apartment house in Henderson and waited for Mrs. Simpson to go out so she wouldn't see me. I went to his apartment and cleaned it out before someone else did. I took his files and his computer but left his clothes."

Griffin said, "And that's why there were only the basics there by the time Dix's people arrived at his apartment. At least you got the stuff out before the drug dealers did."

"A good thing, since I was in those files. They would have found me."

Monk meowed, pressed his face against her leg. She reached down and picked him up. He was a behemoth, at least twenty pounds, and she had to brace herself. Then she stood rocking the cat, shifting from one foot to the other. He could hear Monk's manic purrs from six feet. She pressed her face against his thick black fur.

"What do you think happened Friday night?"

CHAPTER
25

"Arnie called me that night, about six o'clock, as usual, told me he'd arrived with the other caterers at Salazar's house. I remember he told me how easy it would be, said since he was one of the crew he'd be able to move easily around the house without bein' noticed. He said the house would soon be filled with people, so he'd have all the cover he needed.

"I remember when I told him to be careful, I swear I could see his smile over the phone. He told me it was a bummer I'd had to be here for six months with nothing more to do than serve hamburgers and play my fiddle. I could tell from his voice how wired he was."

She swallowed, looked at the wisp of smoke drifting out of the fireplace. "But it didn't work out that way." She paused. "I never spoke to him again."

"But even if Salazar or someone who works for him caught Arnie wiring the place," Griffin said, "why would Salazar have a federal officer killed? They had to know it would bring the wrath of God down on them. How was that worth it?"

"If Mac Brannon had thought Arnie's life was at risk, he'd have never sent him in there. The gang—MS-13— most of them are anything but smart; they're street thugs. One of them might have panicked, or gone into a rage. Or Arnie might have seen something or someone that was too threatening to let him go. We don't know yet."

"So why not pull the trigger? Bust in there, clap the handcuffs on Salazar, interview all the guests and caterers to see if someone saw something?"

"That's what I wanted to do on Saturday as soon as I saw that sketch of Arnie," she said. "Mr. Brannon was hot to do it, too, but he got orders to lay back and keep me undercover. We could have arrested Salazar and all the gang members within three counties, but we'd have had nothing firm to hold them on, and you can bet we'd never have found where they stashed the drugs. And since Arnie wasn't killed in Salazar's house, there wouldn't be any trace evidence there, nothing to tie him to Arnie's murder.

"I wanted to tell you everything I knew, but there

was too much riding on taking down Salazar entirely. Mr. Brannon told me to lie low and wait. We all know there has to be panic, even chaos, behind that scene Salazar staged for you at his house on Saturday. They have to know we'll be there at any minute, and people who are panicked make mistakes.

"Everyone in our local office is out in the field. If Salazar and the gang make the mistake of trying to move the drugs away too soon, the chances are good we'll get them."

"And what's to keep Salazar from getting on a plane back to Madrid?"

"If either Salazar or Dr. Hayman, for that matter, buys a plane ticket or tries to leave the country, we'll know, and we'll arrest him."

"How does Delsey fit in?"

He saw her flinch, saw a flash of guilt in her eyes. "All right, I realized Salazar was interested in her, not his obsessive sort of interest, and I thought it would be smart to get close to her. But listen, that was only at the start. I really came to care for Delsey, and she for me. I didn't want to use her, all I ever wanted to do was protect her.

"When Professor Salazar guilted her into coming to his party, it never occurred to me there'd be any problem, and there shouldn't have been. Who knew Dr. Hayman's margaritas would make her sick and she'd leave early?"

"Early enough to see a dead man in her bathtub

and get bashed on the head. How in the world did that happen?"

"I was as shocked as you were. Even though Arnie spoke to Delsey a couple of times at the diner, they were never introduced. But he knew where she lived. The only way I can put it together is that they got a couple of gang members to haul him back to his apartment to search it and see what he had on them."

She drew a deep breath, picked up Monk again, and began to stroke him really hard. He reared back and nearly toppled her over as he struggled to get out of her arms. "All right, all right." She set him down. "Arnie knew he couldn't take the thugs to his apartment. There was too much for them to find there. He had to decide fast where to take them. He knew Delsey was at the party. He also knew she lived alone—and that's the biggie—so I'm thinking he directed them to her place instead. They broke in the back door, realized soon enough it wasn't his apartment. I'm betting he made a run for it, but they forced him into the bathroom and killed him there."

"But then Delsey came in unexpectedly."

"Yes. They had to be gang members, violent thugs, and they probably hadn't been told to kill anyone else. I'm thinking one of them hit her on the head before they hauled Arnie away and ended up dumping him beside Breaker's Hill in the thick snow and trees.

"Of course, that's a guess, but one that makes sense.

If I've got it right, then Arnie saved my life. But he never thought Delsey would be in danger. And now the gang members who killed him know that Delsey saw Arnie well enough to describe him. They've got to be wonderin' if she saw them, too, and if so, she was a witness against a gang of killers. I didn't know what to do, what to say, or how to protect her until I realized you were worried for her safety as well, and put a guard on her door. We have to continue to protect her."

He looked at Monk, who was washing himself in front of the fireplace, looked back at her, standing stiff and so contained that if she moved, she might break apart. He rose. "We're now in this together. Why don't you come back to the B&B with me? You can spend some time with Delsey. Anything's better than being stuck out here alone with a gun pressed against your leg."

"I can't. I've got Monk, and Bud Bailey would have a hissy fit if he saw this big boy come through his front door. I know him well. Trust me. Besides, I've got to start my shift at Maurie's soon. Remember, Griffin, I'm still undercover, still plain Anna Castle." She fidgeted for a moment. "Are you going to tell Delsey who I am?"

"No. When that time comes, you'll tell her. And good luck with that."

He gave her a long look, patted her cheek, and started to leave. "Be careful."

"Okay. You, too."

He looked back to see her standing at the front

door, her arms around herself against the cold, that Glock of hers still settled in the back of her waistband, watching him, and Griffin knew he not only admired her greatly, he wanted more from her and wanted it badly.

CHAPTER
26

The Hoover Building
Washington, D.C.
Late Sunday afternoon

Savich looked down at his cell to see another missed call from Bo Horsley. He listened to the message. *I know you're up to your neck in alligators, but give a passing thought to coming up to New York for the* Jewel of the Lion *exhibit. I'm heading private security for the exhibit for the Met—quite a job, let me tell you. Call me when you get a chance.*

Savich was on the point of returning Bo Horsley's call when he looked up to see Mr. August Biaggini walk into the CAU. He looked so much like Savich's father that for a moment he couldn't speak. Like Buck Savich,

August Biaggini was tall and fit, with thick salt-and-pepper hair, comfortably in his mid-fifties. But when Mr. Biaggini spoke, the spell was broken. His voice was quiet and lilting, with a whisper of Italy, not the clipped, edged cadence of Savich's dad.

"Special Agent Savich," he said and stuck out his hand.

"Mr. Biaggini, thank you for coming to us. This is Agent Sherlock."

Biaggini turned his dark eyes on her, and Sherlock found a smile blooming naturally. He reminded her a bit of the photo of Dillon's dad on their mantel. She shook his hand.

"Please sit down, sir."

Biaggini sat. "My son is not here yet, I see."

Savich said, "He's waiting in the interview room down the hall. Before we join him, I wanted to hear your thoughts about Tommy Cronin's murder."

Biaggini's expressive face turned hard, and Savich saw grief etched in the lines beside his mouth. "I have called poor Marian to give her my family's condolences. She is inconsolable, as are Tommy's grandparents and his sisters. I keep thinking it simply cannot be real, but no, it happened, some monster actually did this to Tommy. Neither my wife nor I can begin to understand the callous brutality, much less what sadistic message the murderer meant to send. Was there any sort of actual message found, Agent Savich?"

"Not yet, sir."

Sherlock said, "Mr. Biaggini, do you believe Tommy's

murder had something to do with his grandfather and his role in the banking scandal?"

Mr. Biaggini said, "As you undoubtedly know, revenge against Palmer Cronin seemed to be the consensus among all the talking heads on television both yesterday and today. The single member of the Federal Reserve Board I saw interviewed said he believed it had been a personal matter. All others interviewed implied he was whistling in the wind, trying to deflect any blame from himself and the board.

"It's a much more titillating news story, isn't it, to imagine some poor soul stripped of his livelihood and his self-respect in the banking collapse lashing out at Palmer Cronin through his grandson?"

"Yes, but what do *you* think, sir?" Savich asked him.

Biaggini waved a hand, an artist's hand, Sherlock thought, like Dillon's. "I find myself agreeing with the one lone opinion. Unless the man was insane, I can't understand killing Tommy to exact some sort of belated revenge on his grandfather. Palmer Cronin didn't mean for the banking collapse to happen; he wasn't involved in anything unethical during his watch himself. His guilt lay in holding the wrong economic philosophy and, I suppose, a stubborn blindness to what was happening. But again, he did not actually dirty his hands. If someone wanted revenge, why not kill the CEO of one of those big banking or investment firms who actually were responsible for leaving their investors dangling in the wind because they cared more about their golden parachutes than about morality, or ethics, or responsibility?

"I have thought about this and am forced to conclude that even though Tommy was only twenty, he must have made a violent enemy. A classmate, perhaps, though it chills me to think someone that young could have murdered Tommy so brutally."

Sherlock said, "Do you know of anyone capable of doing this?"

"No, I do not. From what I know about Tommy over the years, he never seemed to venture far out of his circle. He had a comfort zone, and he stayed well within it. If he enraged someone, it would seem likely to have been one of his intimate group, but I know that isn't possible. We're talking three young people—Tommy, Stony, and Peter—who've known each other most of their lives. Of course there are other friends as well, but none so close as those three.

"And yes, Peter is one of the three." He gave her a charming smile. "But of course Peter wouldn't be capable of such a thing, and certainly not Stony."

Savich said, "Naturally, Tommy's circle enlarged significantly when he entered Magdalene."

"Yes, of course. I imagine he initially had difficulty adapting, but adapt he did. Tommy was always liked well enough, but even more so at Magdalene, so my son Peter told me." The charming smile bloomed again. "My son Peter will graduate from Magdalene himself in the spring, with a degree in international business. He has already accepted a position with Caruthers and Milton here in Washington. After a year of training and exposure to all the Washington clients, they may transfer him to the New York headquarters." Mr. Biaggini radiated a father's pride, and no wonder, Sherlock thought. Caruthers & Milton certainly was a big deal, one of the large investment banks that had taken its share of the billions of dollars coughed up by American taxpayers so they could stay in business, chastened, at least in the short term. Last she'd heard, C&M was flourishing. She couldn't imagine anyone ever again handing their money over to any of the investment banks, but evidently there were many who hadn't learned their lesson.

Savich said, "Have you spoken to your son about Tommy's murder, Mr. Biaggini?"

"No, I have not seen him since Thursday evening, when he came over to the house for dinner. Spaghetti, always spaghetti. Peter loves his mother's meat sauce. My son is very popular, always in demand. Although he spends much of his time on campus, he also has his own apartment over on Willard Avenue."

"Peter has three residences? One of them an apartment? Why?" Sherlock asked. "I understand you live with the rest of your family—Peter's mom and his two younger brothers—nearby in Hillsborough?"

"His mother and I gave it to him as a gift for his senior year, to give the young man some privacy. We can always let the lease go when he moves to New York for Caruthers and Milton."

Savich already knew about Mr. Biaggini's extravagant gift to his eldest son—not too surprising, perhaps, for a successful owner of a chain of cosmetics stores. But he also knew about Peter's country club membership, and the two troublesome DUIs he'd gotten in Virginia. No consequences for Peter, thanks to his father's intervention.

Savich said, "How is your son doing in his senior classes at Magdalene?"

"Why, he's doing very well. He's a brilliant young man. Even though Peter is—was—Tommy's senior by nearly two years, they were still close growing up; our families spent time together."

Sherlock said, "Did you like Tommy, as a person?"

Mr. Biaggini thought about this for a moment. "Tommy was usually well mannered, respectful. But I remember thinking that as a teenager Tommy saw people as they really were and took advantage when he could. The word *sly* comes to mind, though it pains me to say such a thing now that he's dead."

Sherlock said, "Could you give us an example?"

Mr. Biaggini looked thoughtful. "I remember hearing him bait his aunt, Marian Lodge, about not preventing his mother's suicide. I will admit, I was appalled and thought that was very unlike him, since he had to know that was very painful for her." He shrugged. "Then his father died and Tommy seemed to change; he looked out for his younger sisters, became more thoughtful, more mature, rather than a spoiled teenage boy spewing out hormones and attitude. I guess you could say he became the man of the house, and Marian seemed pleased to let him assume that role."

Sherlock said, "Did Tommy defer too often to Peter?"

Mr. Biaggini blinked. "That's quite a question to ask a father, Agent Sherlock, and it is difficult to answer because Peter and Tommy were so different from each other. What I mean is, my son is a natural leader, and Tommy, well, wasn't. Tommy tended to hang back, as did Stony, to see what direction Peter wanted to go." Mr. Biaggini looked away for a moment, shook his head. "Who knows what Tommy would have done with his life if he'd been allowed to keep it."

She said, "And what do you know about Stony Hart, sir?"

"Stony? The second major member of Tommy's circle, and Peter's good friend as well, I might add. The three of them together since childhood. Unfortunately, Walter—Stony—lacks maturity, something common at his young age, I suppose, but with Stony I always wondered if he was ever going to grow up. He seems much younger than Peter in his behavior, in how he views the world and his place in it, even though he's a year older. Even his father, a rather authoritarian man, still treats him like a teenager in some ways.

"Of the three friends, Stony was the shyest, and the hardest to pry away from his computers. I remember when he was only eleven years old he was caught trying to hack into a local bank." Mr. Biaggini smiled at the memory. "The FBI, if I remember correctly, made it a point to scare the socks off him.

"Stony is a kind soul, though; he seems to feel things more than most others. I've noticed over the years that his father thinks Stony's kindness is a weakness, makes him less a man. But he's wrong."

Sherlock said, "You don't care for Mr. Hart, sir?"

"No, I don't," Mr. Biaggini said. He paused for a long moment, studied his thumbnail, then added, "Wakefield Hart wants Stony to be a chip off the proverbial old block, but he isn't, and never will be."

Savich rose and motioned Mr. Biaggini down the hall. He opened the door to the same interview room Stony had occupied not two hours before.

As with Stony, Coop and Lucy stood silent and grim, their backs against the wall, arms crossed over their chests. Unlike Stony, though, Peter Biaggini was sprawled in his chair, looking loose and bored, his fingers tapping a smart tattoo on the tabletop. He was whistling under his breath and texting on his cell with racing fingers. Sherlock's first thought was that he could be Dillon's younger brother—handsome as sin, dark eyed like his father—surely strong enough to haul Tommy Cronin over his shoulder and drop him at Lincoln's feet.

Her second thought was that he looked as though he didn't have a care in the world.

CHAPTER
27

When Peter saw his father flanked by two agents, Savich saw surprise and wariness register on his face before he caught himself and smoothed it out. Savich was impressed that a twenty-two-year-old could adjust the controls so quickly. His surprise and wariness were soon replaced by thinly veiled impatience and contempt in the look he sent his father—the Hair Spray King, isn't that what he called him? Savich wanted to haul him out of his lizard pose, but he merely nodded to the young man. His father didn't seem to notice anything out of the ordinary. Didn't Biaggini Senior see what was written so clearly on the son's face?

". . . And Mr. Biaggini, this is Agent McKnight and Agent Carlyle."

After nods and handshakes, Savich pointed to a chair

at the end of the table. Before he sat, Mr. Biaggini reached out his hand to his son. "You haven't returned your mother's calls, Peter. Your mother and I are so very sorry about Tommy. Are you all right?"

Peter Biaggini stared at his dad, stared at his hand, darted a fast look at Savich, and gave his father's hand a quick shake.

What are you like when you're alone with him? Savich wondered.

Peter nodded. "I'm all right, though of course I'm upset; none of Tommy's friends can believe it." He nodded toward Coop and Lucy. "Those agents over there told me the cops brought me here to be questioned about his murder. I asked them why, but they wouldn't answer me. I guess they didn't know because they're pretty low on the food chain around here."

Lucy bit her lip to keep from grinning. *Good shot, kid.*

Peter continued to his father, "They must think we have something to do with it. I know I didn't. Did you have him killed, Dad?"

Savich watched Biaggini Senior literally recoil from the flippant words out of his eldest son's mouth. Then he drew himself up again, and his voice was austere. "That is not amusing, Peter. The agents do not believe that either you or I had anything to do with this tragedy; they simply want to know about Tommy."

Peter never changed his lizard sprawl, and now an ugly sneer marred his mouth. "Tragedy, Dad? Tommy was *murdered*. Tragedy would be if he died of leukemia. That's like calling 9/11 a tragedy when it was mass murder. You really think these agents only want our thoughts and advice? I don't think so. I think they're looking for someone to blame. So what happens when they find out you hated Tommy's grandfather, called him a dangerous buffoon? I remember all your harangues about him, about practically the whole financial industry. Looks like somebody finally struck a blow against all the greed you hate so much. Tell me, Dad, are you really sorry?"

Peter Biaggini's contempt seared the air. Sherlock saw Coop and Lucy exchange glances, their thoughts clear on their faces—*Why doesn't Biaggini slam that idiot son of his to the floor and kick him a couple of times?*

Savich hoped they'd get back to their poker faces quickly, because he'd been watching Peter as he spoke and seen him preen when he got the reaction he'd wanted.

Mr. Biaggini was pale and still. It was obvious to Savich he was used to his son's abusiveness. When he finally spoke, his voice was a model of tolerance, probably used for so long with his son it was an ingrained habit. "I doubt Palmer Cronin would agree anyone deserves what happened to Tommy. He's devastated, Peter; so is Tommy's grandmother. I imagine he would gladly have taken Tommy's place if he'd been given the choice."

Savich said, "I'm sure you're quite upset, Peter. After all, Tommy Cronin was one of your best friends since when? You met when you were six years old and he was four, right?"

Peter Biaggini shrugged. "Tommy was lame as a kid, and he never really changed, but he was part of our group, right?"

Sherlock said, "So you're saying you're not upset that Tommy was murdered?"

Peter Biaggini turned dark eyes to her, very close to the color of Sean's eyes, she thought, and it scared her that she'd noticed that. Could the malignancy that brimmed in Peter Biaggini possibly be lurking in Sean? Did a parent ever really know what would develop in her young child's mind? Could a parent ever do more than guess and hope that her child would grow up to be honorable?

Peter's fingers stopped their tapping, and he leaned toward Sherlock. "Of course I am upset. Even if you didn't admire a person you grew up with, it would still leave a hole, don't you think? A very deep hole. I'll miss him." They kept staring at each other, and Savich wondered, *What is Sherlock seeing in him?*

Savich asked, "Peter, you knew Tommy's father? His mother?"

Savich watched a sneer mar his mouth again. It made him look common and mean. "Of course I did. Both of them liked to show off their money, but I've got to say they always treated Tommy's friends well, took us all to Redskins games, sailing on the Potomac, clamming and big bonfires on the beach. When Tommy's mom killed herself, I remember Mr. Cronin brought in Tommy's Aunt Marian, and everything continued on as it always had—barbecues and parties, whatever his dad and aunt could come up with—only with a change in moms."

Savich said, "It sounds to me like you don't think Mr. Cronin missed his wife that much."

Peter Biaggini's cell buzzed a text message. For a moment, it seemed he would answer, but he only touched the phone, then let his fingers drop away. "How would I know? It was weird, though, what happened. A year later, Tommy's dad dies in his kick-ass red Ferrari. Who could see that coming? But I'll tell you, good old Aunt Marian kept going, like neither of Tommy's parents had ever really been all that important. I mean, the house kept going, everyone kept hanging out there, and Tommy got all into himself since he saw himself as the new boss man of the house. Aunt Marian smiled behind her hand, let him strut around and act all serious about the electric bill."

Mr. Biaggini looked both embarrassed and pained. He cleared his throat, bringing Savich's and Sherlock's attention back to him. "It was a dreadful time. Barbara Cronin was a lovely woman, an excellent mother to Tommy and his sisters. I was shocked and frankly surprised she would kill herself. I knew of no reason for her to do such a thing."

"She was shacking up with the guy who remodeled the kitchen," Peter Biaggini said, slouching down farther in his chair. "All the kids knew about it; we thought it was funny."

Sherlock said, "Did Tommy think it was funny?"

"No, he'd leave whenever anyone said anything." He said to his father, "Come on, Dad, don't go all righteous and disapproving. Since all the kids knew it, surely you and Mom did, too."

"There is always gossip," Mr. Biaggini said, his body as stiff as his voice, "but if one has any sense and maturity at all, one discounts it. I do not believe and never believed Tommy's mother was unfaithful to his father. What does any of this have to do with Tommy's murder?"

Peter rolled his eyes and began tapping his fingers again. Another message came in on his cell and he began quickly pressing keys. Savich reached over, took the cell from his hand, and tossed it to Coop, who turned it off and slipped it into his pocket. Peter Biaggini froze. He started to say something but thought better of it.

Savich knew Barbara Cronin wasn't the point here, but her suicide bothered him, Sherlock, too, and so he said to Mr. Biaggini, "Indulge me. Now, something must have triggered her suicide. Do you remember anything out of the ordinary happening at the time, sir?"

Mr. Biaggini shook his head. "I was very busy with my business around that time, with expansion, new franchises going up throughout Maryland and Virginia. My wife and I hadn't seen the Cronins in some time."

Peter gave an ugly laugh. "Yeah, you had to get all the rich old ladies more *beauty products*, right, Dad?"

Savich was pleased when Mr. Biaggini slowly rose to his feet, spread his hands on the tabletop, and leaned toward his son. "You mock me for the fine house you've lived in all your life? You mock that your mother and I care for you, that we have provided for you, given you the best education possible?"

But not a new car? Savich knew Peter drove a five-year-old Honda, which meant Mr. Biaggini did have some limits, probably because of his son's DUIs.

Peter looked his father up and down. "Yeah, thanks for the Cheerios, Dad. But you didn't give me my education. I worked for it. I would have been valedictorian at Columbia High School if that jerk Noah Horton hadn't kissed up to all his teachers. And I could have gotten scholarships to college if you hadn't coughed up the tuition for Magdalene. I even earned that job with Caruthers and Milton on my own." Again, he shrugged, looked at Sherlock, then back to his father. "Have you ever thought you should have spent more time with us, Dad, rather than making hair spray?"

Mr. Biaggini had heard this before, too many times, Sherlock thought. He stared at his son, his hands working, but he did nothing, said nothing more, his look stoic. *The story of Peter's life growing up? A brief show of indignation, then nothing?* Sherlock wanted to leap over the interview table and plant her fist in Peter Biaggini's sneering mouth. She said, her voice as sharp as glass shards, "Tell us, Peter, about how you and Stony Hart tried to anonymously upload that photo of Tommy's dead body at the Lincoln Memorial on YouTube? That photo we tracked to Stony's computer?"

The lizard disappeared. Peter Biaggini snapped to, straightened and swallowed, one hand clenched into a fist. For the first time, he looked scared. "Wh-what?"

Scared now, Peter? Or do you not know anything about it?

Unfortunately, his protective father jumped in. Mr. Biaggini's face was red as he shouted at Sherlock, "What are you talking about? What do you mean my son and Stony were involved? Surely not that photo that ended up on YouTube—that's ridiculous. What sort of ploy is this?"

CHAPTER
28

Sherlock said matter-of-factly, "Mr. Biaggini, we know the YouTube photo was posted from Stony's computer, and we know Peter has a lifelong habit of driving the bus for his friends, that if they don't do what he wants, he sets them straight. Stony told us about Peter's slashing Stony's mom's tires on her new Prius. How old were you then, Peter? Twelve? Do you happen to remember what order of yours Stony refused to carry out?"

Mr. Biaggini surged to his feet. "You will stop this now! Do you hear me, stop this or I will have my lawyers in here to stop it for you."

"I didn't slash his bitch mother's tires."

Sherlock kept her eyes locked on Peter Biaggini's face. "Sure you did, and you really enjoyed doing it. Tell us about the death photo you got Stony to upload."

"Sorry, I don't know anything about a photo. If Stony did that, I don't know anything about that, either. I've got to say, I'm surprised. Even though Stony's a computer whiz, he's a wuss; say boo to him and he withers like a weed. He never wanted to do anything that was the least bit risky. Until now. I can't believe he did that, and I can't believe he got caught, either."

Sherlock said, "Mr. Biaggini, you've seen the photo, haven't you?"

Mr. Biaggini said, "Even the rebels in Rwanda have seen that horrible photo, but it has nothing at all to do with my son. He has no reason to lie to you. Regardless, uploading such a thing on the Internet is despicable. Peter would not have been a part of it."

That was all he was going to say? Then Sherlock looked at his eyes; Biaggini didn't believe what he'd just said. He looked devastated, but not surprised, because he knew his son.

Peter shot his father a look of pure disgust, but underlying that look was something else entirely. Had he seen the look of doubt in his father's face? Had he seen the devastation that the recognition of that doubt had cost him? Did he care?

Peter's voice climbed an octave. "He's right, I told you the truth. Stony's a dodging little nothing. His only talent is the computer. He's a liar; he's always looking out for number one. That story about his mom's Prius, I mean, how lame is that?"

Sherlock smiled at Peter Biaggini. "Why do you think he would lie, Peter?"

Peter was nearly panting now, words spewing fast and hard. "I see now, you scared him so bad he had to make something up, and he did. No one would believe it for a second. I mean, about the only thing Stony does well is hack NASA. And he did it without any help from me. I never even saw Tommy's photo!"

"Peter—"

Peter didn't look at his father. He leaned forward, his eyes dark and hard. "You want a scapegoat and you don't have squat, so you singled me out. I don't know what Stony did or didn't do, but I do know he couldn't have uploaded Tommy's photo."

He flung himself back in the chair, crossed his arms over his chest.

Savich's eyebrow went up. "And why is that?"

"Stony doesn't make mistakes on computers. If he didn't want you to know he'd posted something, you'd have never found out about it."

Time to test the waters. Savich said, "Sorry, Peter, Stony did make a mistake, and we caught him with the help of the NSA. Even Stony can't deny Tommy's photo was posted from his computer."

Sherlock picked it up fast. "Why don't you tell us about what drove you to do this, Peter? What did Tommy do to you to make you hate him so much?"

August Biaggini roared to his feet again. He slammed his fist on the table. "You will stop this now! My son couldn't have done this, for the simple reason that it's monstrous. Sure, he was the leader of his group of friends, there always is one. Everyone knows that. Peter had no motive to kill Tommy Cronin. No motive!

"Listen, about Stony. I told you he always sought the easiest path and that's why he blames Peter, to save himself. What's perjury to him now? It's obvious Stony is the guilty one here."

"And what would his motive be, Mr. Biaggini?" Sherlock asked him.

"I don't know. I don't know of a single motive to attach to any of Tommy's friends. No, Peter, don't say anything more, you don't have to defend yourself any further."

Mr. Biaggini sat down, leaned over the table, his eyes locked on Savich's face. "The next time we see you, Agent, we're bringing a lawyer. We're leaving now."

Savich said, "So we're clear before you leave, if you choose to, Mr. Biaggini, we never said Stony accused Peter of any involvement in posting that photo. We raised that question with you. Stony denies any knowledge of the photo, just as Peter does."

"Then how can you accuse my son of these crimes? Of being a liar? You people should all be fired."

"You may not have deserved to hear that, sir, but we're trying to find a murderer. Now, we won't keep either of you from leaving, but if Peter is willing to stay and answer a few more questions, it will save both of you a great deal of time and trouble later."

"It's all right, Dad," Peter said, suddenly cocky again. "I'll answer a few questions. What is it you want to know?" And he sat back in his chair, his arms crossed over his chest.

"Do you know where Tommy was Friday night, Peter?"

"No. I hadn't seen him in a while. He was usually studying late, or sleeping."

"When did you last see him?"

"Nearly a week ago, maybe last Monday. We had some pizza, then he said he had to study, and we split up."

"Did you notice if he was disturbed about something? Did he mention anything he was involved with?"

"Sorry, Agent. Tommy seemed fine to me. I told you, he was a serious go-getter since his father died, working hard at school, looking to fill his grandfather's shoes, I guess."

Savich said, "Now tell us where you were on Friday night, Peter."

Peter Biaggini raised his hand before his father could interrupt. He grinned, and Savich knew for sure that Peter had agreed to stay because he wanted to be asked that very question. He was preening now, no other word for it, and it wasn't a sham. He looked directly at Savich as he said, "I was at the Raleigh Gallery in George-town at a showing of modern American paintings, part of an assignment for my art history class.

"Oh, yeah, Tommy's former girlfriend, Melissa Ivy, was there with me." He smirked at them. "So much for Stony's photo. There's no way I could have taken a photo of Tommy dead. I wasn't anywhere close to the Lincoln Memorial Friday night."

"Where did you go after you left the gallery?" Sherlock asked.

"Mel and I went to her apartment and tangled the sheets all night. So I couldn't have killed Tommy. As for that stupid photo, who cares? No crime there anyway, now, is there?" He turned to his father. "See, Dad, no reason to get an ulcer. Can I leave now, Agents?"

Savich stood. "You may leave, but we will see you again soon."

As he walked to the door and opened it for them, Sherlock said, "Peter, don't leave Washington."

"I love Washington. Why would I leave?"

They heard Mr. Biaggini's harsh breathing as they walked away, and then his low, angry voice. "Why didn't you tell them right away where you were Friday night? Why drag this lunacy out?"

They heard Peter speak but couldn't make out his words.

They watched from the CAU doorway as Peter whistled his way along the wide corridor to the elevator. He turned right before he got on, and gave them a little finger wave. Mr. Biaggini followed behind him, his head down. He never looked at them.

"That kid should have been left on a Greek mountainside at birth," Coop said.

"I want to meet Melissa Ivy," Sherlock said.

"Peter's got to believe she'll lock in his alibi," Coop said.

Sherlock said, "I'm willing to bet my Pink Panther socks she'll not only swear they spent the night together, she'll also swear she made him breakfast Saturday morning, didn't just toss him a box of cornflakes, either. Melissa will tell us she made him scrambled eggs, with blueberry pancakes on the side."

"After she broke up with Tommy," Lucy said, "she sure hooked up with Peter Biaggini real fast."

Savich said, "Mr. Biaggini isn't a thing like my father."

CHAPTER
29

Ward Place, N.W.
Close to George Washington campus
Early Sunday evening

It was near dinnertime when Savich parked his Porsche
a half block from Melissa Ivy's 1970s three-story redbrick apartment building.

"Place looks tired," Sherlock said. "Probably not a
lot of upkeep, since it's mostly students. Look at how
they've trashed that little yard. What were they doing,
throwing rocks at snowmen?"

The lobby was narrow and pedestrian, with a lino-
leum floor and a triple row of black mailboxes. They
walked to the third floor, down a bare-floored wooden

hallway that creaked. The lighting, though, was bright, even glaring. They stopped at apartment 3B.

Melissa Ivy answered their knock fast, as if she'd been standing by the door, her eyes plastered to the keyhole.

Gorgeous was Savich's first thought, staring at the small Venus standing in front of them, biting her bottom lip and twisting her hands, even as she tried to look grown-up and confident.

After Melissa looked at their creds and they introduced themselves, she led them into a small living room, its white walls covered with oversized prints of media legends going back to Edward R. Murrow and a young Barbara Walters, all dozen or so in stark black and white. You didn't even notice the Goodwill furniture until you sat down on her living room sofa and were immediately aware that the springs were too close to the surface.

Melissa was wearing tight jeans, a short pink crop top that left her white midriff bare, even though it was thirty-three degrees outside, and pink UGGs on her small feet. Her figure was well nigh perfect. Her hair was long, blond, and straight as a stick, falling to the middle of her back. Savich imagined the camera would love her heart-shaped face, with its impossibly high cheekbones.

He said without preamble, "Ms. Ivy, you're twenty years old, a sophomore at George Washington, majoring in communications. Is that correct?"

She nodded, still chewing on her bottom lip.

Savich waved at the photos on the walls. "So you want to be a newscaster?"

She beamed, nodding. "It's always been a dream of mine to be an anchor on a major network. I'd really like to be on FOX News. They have the highest ratings, you know."

Sherlock smiled at her. "Who knows who'll have the ratings when you're ready to anchor a desk? It might be something not even on TV yet, like Amazon World News or something."

Melissa blinked—beautiful long lashes—and nodded thoughtfully toward Sherlock, as if grateful for this insight from an older woman.

Savich said, "We'd like to record our conversation. Is that all right with you, Ms. Ivy?"

She straightened like a shot, looked alarmed, her eyes darting to his cell phone, then to his face.

"It's for your protection, Ms. Ivy."

"I didn't do anything bad. Do I need a lawyer?"

She sounded for all the world like a teenager busted for pot. Savich assured her she didn't, identified the three of them, gave the date and time, then said, "Ms. Ivy, where were you Friday evening?"

As if by rote, which it undoubtedly was, since he was sure Peter had called her, Melissa told them she was with Peter Biaggini. "It hadn't started snowing yet, but everyone knew the storm was coming, and so Mr. Raleigh closed the gallery at ten o'clock, and that's when we left. Peter and I had a late dinner at Pocco's near Dupont Circle, then he drove me home when the storm was just beginning."

"Then what happened, Ms. Ivy?" Sherlock asked her.

Melissa's very pretty eyes lowered to her hands, and her voice fell to a whisper. "Please don't tell my parents, but Peter didn't leave until late Saturday morning. We—we were eating a late breakfast when we heard about Tommy on TV. Peter was very upset; I mean, we were both upset. Tommy and I—well, maybe you know we dated for a while, and he was one of Peter's best friends."

"We're very sorry for your loss. I'm sure you want to find out who murdered Tommy Cronin as much as anyone."

"Oh, yes, of course. It's horrible, the way Tommy died."

"We know you were Tommy's girlfriend until, what, three weeks ago?"

"Certainly I dated Tommy, but—" She raised blurred eyes to Sherlock's face. "Of course I was upset—devastated, really. Tommy was a really nice person, even if our relationship didn't work out. But you know Peter had known Tommy nearly all his life."

"Since Peter knew you were upset, did he stay to comfort you?"

"No, he couldn't stay. He said he had things to see to. When he left I cried and cried."

"What did you have for breakfast, Ms. Ivy?" Sherlock asked her.

"Breakfast?"

"Yes, before you found out about Tommy, when you were still smiling."

"I-I scrambled some eggs—Peter loves scrambled

eggs. He had three of them, but he told me only one yolk, and wheat toast with two pats of butter on the side."

Sherlock said, "So no pancakes?"

"Oh, no," Melissa said. "I've got to watch my figure."

"You said Peter spent the night?"

Her mouth opened, then snapped closed.

Savich said, "Peter told us how he tore up the sheets Friday night with you."

They watched Melissa dart a look at Savich's cell, recording every word, and thought she would scream. But she held herself perfectly still instead and drew several deep breaths. She said finally, "I know you probably won't believe me, but I'm not lying. I really don't remember."

Sherlock said, "The way Peter tells it, he might never forget Friday. But you say you don't remember?"

"I had too much to drink. I don't usually drink more than a glass or two of wine, I really don't, I swear."

"Was that when you came back to your apartment Friday night?" Savich asked her.

She gave him that marvelous blink again, very effective, the way her lashes swept over her eyes. "Well, we had some wine at dinner, too. Peter brought a lovely chardonnay with him from Frog's Leap Vineyards in Napa Valley. He made a big deal out of it, told me it was the best he'd found, that he'd been saving it for me, for us together."

"Did the wine taste good to you?" Sherlock asked her.

"I thought it tasted only so-so, but Peter was so excited, I lied and told him I really liked it, and he poured more into my glass. I guess the second and third glasses were too much for me.

"It was weird, though. Even if I ever happened to drink more than I should, I've never had a hangover. But when I woke up Saturday morning, I did. My head really hurt. Peter brought me a cup of coffee and some aspirin, told me how sorry he was that his wine had made me feel bad. Please don't tell my parents."

"But you felt well enough to fix Peter breakfast? One yolk?"

Melissa smiled. "The aspirin helped."

And Sherlock wondered: Had Peter drugged her wine? She considered asking Melissa's permission for a blood test, but decided not to risk it as long as Melissa was answering their questions. Instead, Sherlock asked, "Did Peter call you this afternoon after we spoke with him at the Hoover Building, Ms. Ivy?"

Melissa nodded, and Sherlock was pleased she didn't lie. "He was very angry, said he was glad we were together that night. I can't believe you really suspect Peter of killing poor Tommy."

"We haven't charged him with any crime at all, Ms. Ivy," Sherlock said. "We're simply establishing where Tommy and all his friends were on Friday night."

"Tell us about your visit with Tommy to his grandparents' on Thanksgiving," Savich said.

"Oh goodness, was that ever something. Do you know they had a chef prepare the dinner? It was amazing."

Savich, who knew she'd been raised in Kentucky by two barely middle-class parents, also knew she'd probably been blown away that day. There was something else, too—it was envy, and it was clear in her young voice.

"But he didn't take you back to their home on Christmas Eve?"

"By that time we weren't nearly as good friends anymore."

Now, why was that? Sherlock said, "Tommy's grandparents spoke of you, Ms. Ivy."

Sherlock paused, stared closely to see Melissa's thoughts were written clearly on her beautiful face. *Of course they'd talk about me, I'm beautiful and not a stuck-up debutante like they expected.*

"They were very nice to me," Melissa said, "and Thanksgiving was very nice, too, but it was only one afternoon. Why would they talk about me to you?"

Savich cut in. "They told us you were using Tommy, Ms. Ivy, to gain entrance into their world, that you'd searched him out because you knew who he was. They even saw you writing in your notebook. They thought you were a social climber who was seeing Tommy because you knew Mr. Cronin was famous and had money and a lot of very important friends."

"Not anymore he doesn't, not for a long time now," came out of Melissa's mouth before she could stop herself, but it was too late, her words hung stark and mean in the silent air. She said, "Oh, I really didn't mean that. Really, Tommy and I were only dating, we were friends, and they were nice to me. I wonder if they misunderstood, saw more to it than that because they're older. I mean, how could they have seen the notebook when I didn't have one?" And her lashes swept down again to excellent effect. When she raised her head again, she looked trusting, honest, guileless.

"They saw you and Tommy kissing, Ms. Ivy," Sherlock said, speaking in perfect rhythm with Dillon, "more than a friendly kiss, an all-out French deal, and it bothered them. I know that sounds prudish, but the Cronins are of a different generation."

She watched Melissa's lovely mouth quiver, then firm up. "So I kissed Tommy. It was a thank-you kiss, really, nothing more. I thought they liked me." The wistfulness in her voice was well done.

"But you knew they didn't like you because they told Tommy they didn't want him to bring you to their house Christmas Eve," Sherlock said. "Did it bother you to find out they were merely being polite to a girl they believed was an opportunistic gold digger?"

"They should have liked me, because I'm not an opportunist. I'm a good student, I study hard, and I have lots of friends, too, more than that evil, crooked old man!"

Savich said, "So what did you and Tommy do on Christmas Eve?"

"We had our own private Christmas. Tommy said he'd drop by his aunt's house in Potomac Village on Christmas Day, then he'd come right back to me, and he did."

Sherlock picked it up. "Did Tommy give you those lovely pearl earrings?"

Melissa's fingers touched one exquisite pearl drop. She wanted to say no, but realized it wouldn't be smart, saw it in Sherlock's eyes. Melissa cleared her throat. "Yes. They're beautiful, aren't they? I'm wearing them today to honor Tommy. There's nothing more I can do, is there? It's all so horrible."

"Why did you break up with Tommy?" Savich asked.

Melissa looked down at her UGGs, then shrugged. "We just sort of drifted apart, but I still really liked him."

"You call it drifting in only three weeks?"

"Well, yes, sort of, I guess."

Sherlock said, "All right. Did you do most of the drifting or did Tommy?"

"Well, I suppose I was the one to break it off."

"Was Tommy upset about this?" Sherlock asked her.

"No, I don't think so, not really."

"Was Tommy upset when you hooked up with Peter, one of his best friends?" Sherlock asked her.

"He never said he was. I think he was ready to date someone else, too." She was lying on that one, Sherlock thought, but let it go for the moment.

"I find that odd, Ms. Ivy," Savich said. "He took you to meet his grandparents on Thanksgiving, and he wanted you to be with his family on Christmas. It doesn't sound to me like he wanted to drift at all, like the furthest thing from his mind was to date another girl. It sounds like Tommy was very serious in his feelings for you; maybe he was in love with you."

"No, Tommy didn't love me. I mean, we only dated, and he was very sweet, but—"

"Was Peter upset that you'd been with one of his friends, Ms. Ivy?" Savich asked.

"Oh, no, Peter always knew Tommy and I were only friends." She stared straight at Savich as she spoke, and he could feel the pull to believe her.

"But you didn't hook up with Peter until after you broke up with Tommy?" Savich asked.

"No, of course not." Big nose on that one. Sherlock leaned toward her, sympathy brimming. "I'll bet you were very concerned that your turning to Peter might affect their friendship."

"Yes, of course, but I don't think it did. I mean, they've known each other forever."

Savich asked abruptly, "Where are you from, Ms. Ivy?"

"From Cincinnati—well, from a suburb on the Kentucky side."

"Are your parents paying your tuition at George Washington? Are they paying for your apartment?"

"No. My dad lost his job and all his money after the banking crash. He and my mom lost their house last year. I have to work, Agent Savich, to pay my tuition at GW." He saw she finally realized where he was going, and added quickly, "I waitress over in Foggy Bottom. A lot of lobbyists and politicians. I get really big tips."

Savich said, "Ms. Ivy, your income from your part-time waitressing brings in about half what it costs to pay the rent on your apartment. Then there's your tuition, food, those new UGGs on your feet. Did Tommy help you out with rent money, with your bills?"

She wanted to say no—it hovered—but again, she proved she wasn't stupid. She stuck up her chin. "Yes, he did, because he knew I couldn't pay all my tuition last September and he offered to help me out. As I told you, Tommy was my friend. He knew I'd pay him back."

Savich said, "When exactly did you stop seeing Tommy and start up with Peter Biaggini?"

"Weeks ago, really, right after Christmas."

"And Peter then took over Tommy's assistance with your bills?"

"No! Well—a little bit."

Savich said, "You've been making healthy cash deposits since around the first of the year, right? All from Peter?"

She hadn't expected that question and stumbled out a reply. "What of it? Peter's a really nice guy—"

And you're so beautiful you drop boys in their tracks at twenty feet, a perfect damsel in distress. "Like Tommy?" Sherlock asked. "How many other boys have helped you out since you arrived in Washington, Ms. Ivy?"

"I know you're federal officers, but you shouldn't be able to look at my bank account. It's not right. It's none of your business how much money my friends lend me."

"I agree," Savich said, rising. "A cop would never do that without a warrant."

She looked at him, realized she'd emptied her bucket without a whimper and looked furious. She jumped to her feet. "I didn't have anything to do with Tommy's awful murder, I didn't! Peter said you'd come here and threaten me, but I couldn't imagine why you would. Peter was with me, he really was. Yes, I remember now, we did make love. He didn't snore; he never does. He didn't have anything to do with Tommy's death; he didn't."

Sherlock said, "Ms. Ivy, I really hope you're not lying to us. But I've got to tell you, I do wonder if you're telling us the whole truth about Friday night. I'd hate to see you in a federal penitentiary for a couple of years. It wouldn't be a pretty sight."

"I'm not lying; I'm not."

Sherlock smiled. "I think you might do very well in TV someday if you guard your reputation, your looks. Oh, yes, if you're not lying, then I suggest you be careful around Peter Biaggini. I would wager my Super Bowl ticket that if he drugged your wine he might have killed Tommy, too." She shrugged. "I fear you could be a loose end, Ms. Ivy."

"There's no reason for Peter to kill Tommy. I mean, why would he? I left Tommy for him. He knows that. He won! I don't know if he made fun of Tommy about it, I don't, but why would he? They were friends forever!"

At last the truth, Sherlock thought.

Savich said, "Ms. Ivy, a tech could be here in a half hour to draw your blood, and we could find out."

She stared at Savich as though he'd grown an extra head. "Draw my blood? No! My mom would never allow that, never. Peter's not bad, really, he's—"

"Very generous, I know," Sherlock said. She handed

Melissa a card. "Wouldn't you like to know what really happened on Friday night, Ms. Ivy? Perhaps you owe it to Tommy to try to find out the truth."

Melissa stared at the card but said nothing more. Savich turned at the doorway. "Ms. Ivy, like Agent Sherlock, I caution you not to speak to Peter Biaggini. If you tell him you don't remember spending the whole night with him, if you can't really give him an alibi, you could be a danger to him."

Sherlock's last sight of Melissa Ivy was her chewing on her lower lip, her pink UGGs bright on the banged-up hardwood entrance hall.

CHAPTER 30

Maurie's Diner
Maestro, Virginia
Sunday evening

Griffin eyed Anna, the kick-butt waitress wearing a
Maurie's red apron, and decided her full name, Lilyanna,
brought to a man's mind a vision of a flowy-dressed
Southern woman with long loose hair lifting romanti-
cally in a summer breeze while she served sweet tea on
the front porch. Nope, this was a solid Anna with a
Glock 22 stuck in her jeans. He realized he'd like to get
into it with her, let her wrestle him down. Griffin shook
his head. He was losing it. He watched her, always
friendly to the customers, always a smile in place. She
was moving closer to their booth.

He'd brought Delsey here for dinner after she'd awakened; showered all the hospital off her again, she'd told him, since once wasn't enough; and managed to cover the sutures with a small bandage, a hank of hair covering it.

A ketchup-drenched french fry paused on the way to her mouth. "Hey, whatever are you thinking about, Griffin?" She smiled over at Anna, watched her wave a menu at them, then start over.

She saw her brother's eyes follow. "Hmm. Maybe you don't have to tell me. She's something, isn't she?"

"What? Who? What did you say, Delsey?"

"Anna. She's very cool, isn't she? And here she comes, and would you look at that, her eyes are locked right on you, like a laser. Hmmm again."

Griffin eyed his spoonful of mushroom soup. "Shut up."

"Have I been missing something since I got my brain addled?"

"No more than usual. Eat your salad."

She forked up some lettuce with Maurie's signature dressing. "So if you're not checking out Anna, what are you thinking about? That DEA agent? I'll tell you, Griffin, I can't get over that. Every time I think about him, I get cold and want to cry. I wish I knew why he was in my apartment in the first place."

Griffin was silent as a post and spooned up some more soup.

"Hi, Anna." Delsey popped another french fry into

her mouth. "Tell Maurie his fries are still the best, and the salad—I'll eat the salad if you put a gun to my head."

"I'll tell him, but he knows it. He always eats two fries out of every order, for quality-control purposes, he tells me. And would you look at him, skinny as a fence post. Hey, Mr. FBI, how's your soup?"

"It's great."

Anna looked down at the nearly full bowl. "Great, huh? You on a diet, Griffin? Nope, not even a shadow of flab on you. You're not eating because you're still worried about Delsey, aren't you? Well, stop it. Look at her, she looks ready to salsa on Main Street."

"Maybe tomorrow, Anna," Delsey said, and Griffin saw his sister look from Anna back to him. "We were talking about that poor DEA agent. I overheard Griffin and Ruth talking about him at the hospital and why he was here in Maestro." She drew a deep breath. "And I heard them talk about maybe Professor Salazar being the drug czar, or whatever you'd call it."

Griffin said, "Do you ever remember seeing anyone hinky at Stanislaus, Delsey? Anyone who didn't look right being there?"

"There are always so many people visiting Stanislaus—that's why it's such a great place. Musicians performing from out of state and their entourages, critics, writers, so yes, lots of strangers. I'd have to say Professor Salazar has more strangers than anyone cruising around him. I've asked who they were and was told they were visiting friends, from Europe, from New York, classical guitarists from all over the country here to worship at his Gucci-clad feet. All of them looked like they fit right in."

Griffin said, "When I met Salazar at his house yesterday morning, he was wearing moccasins."

"I'll bet they were Gucci," Delsey said.

"Dels, did you ever see any Hispanic guys hanging around him?"

Delsey shook her head. "No, and I already told you, I never saw the man who hit me before, only heard two men's voices. Anna, have you ever noticed any young Hispanic guys in the diner before?"

Anna shook her head.

Griffin watched his sister's forehead knit, a sure sign she was thinking. She leaned close. "What about Mrs. Carlene?"

Griffin went on alert. "Who's Mrs. Carlene?"

Anna said, "She's Professor Salazar's secretary. She came with him when he arrived at Stanislaus this past September."

Griffin said, "Mrs. Carlene sounds very Southern. How would a musician from Madrid hook up with a Mrs. Carlene?"

Delsey said, "I don't know, never thought about it, really. I overheard her."

Griffin would find out all about Mrs. Carlene. "So what did you overhear?"

"It was last November, and I'd left a theory class with Professor Coffman in Brackford Hall, and I heard

Gloria Brichoux Stanford—she's a famous violinist, retired—"

"I don't live off the planet, Delsey. I've heard her play. Go on."

"She was speaking with another professor, I don't remember who it was, woodwinds, I think, and he was telling her that Mrs. Carlene guarded Dr. Salazar like a lioness with her only cub. I heard Ms. Stanford say she was so secretive she wouldn't even let anyone hear her speak on the telephone. She said Mrs. Carlene noticed her standing close by and clammed right up, didn't say another word, punched off her cell. I remember the woodwinds professor shook his head like, who cares? I didn't hear anything more. But I didn't forget it, it was too weird."

Delsey shook her head. "I can't get over you believing Professor Salazar might be a drug kingpin. I can't fathom it." She paused for a moment. "What I mean is he's got everything, more than everything, he's at the very top, but to sell drugs to teenagers? I know you guys think the same thing.

"So enough. Anna, what do you think of my gorgeous brother?"

Anna cocked her head to one side, looked him over. "This baboon? I've got to say I like the guy; it's probably the Jane Goodall in me. Now I've got to get back to work before Maurie comes out here yelling."

CHAPTER
31

Wolf Trap Road
Maestro, Virginia
Late Sunday

Griffin didn't call ahead. He was content to wait for Anna in his car a half block from her cottage. He knew she helped close the diner at ten o'clock, Maurie usually trailing along after her with a happy buzz on if the day's receipts were good.

He watched Anna pull her Kia into her driveway, climb out, and trudge to the cottage's front door. She looked tired, he thought, one job too many between trudging around with food and worrying about her cover.

Before he raised his hand to knock, the door opened

and there stood the DEA agent, her Glock pointed at his chest.

"Griffin! I'm glad it's you and not some—well, I don't need this." She slid her Glock back in her purse, still on her shoulder. "Why are you here? Is Delsey all right? I didn't see your car."

"It was parked up the street. Delsey's asleep. I asked Penny to keep watch. I'd like to talk to you some more, make some plans, if we can."

Griffin followed her down the hallway to her kitchen. It was like the *Julia Child's Kitchen* exhibit at the Smithsonian, with an antique stove that still looked ready to take on a roast, and what looked like an ancient dishwasher, with its door cracked open, ready for business.

He watched her pull down two big mugs from an ugly mud-brown wooden cabinet, and sat down as she made coffee.

"It's decaf," she said over her shoulder. "It won't taste wonderful, but it might fool our brains into stayin' alert a bit longer. Did Delsey tell you anything else useful?"

He watched her shove her hair behind her ear. "You already know about Mrs. Carlene, don't you? Tell me about her."

"She cleared our background check. I've met her, of course. She's originally from Savannah, Georgia, but spent some ten years living in Madrid—her home away from home, I've heard her call it—and that's where she met Salazar. Word is they once had a relationship, remained friends, and never really split up. She's been schedulin' his appearances and appointments for years now. Maybe it's workin' for Salazar for so long that makes her seem like she's more involved with this business than she is. We'll check again."

Anna gave him a small smile as she poured coffee into his mug. "You like plain black?"

"Yes, thank you."

He took a sip, watched her take a couple of bagels from the toaster and put them on a plate along with a fresh tub of cream cheese.

"Same bagels from this morning?"

"Yep. Toast them and you never know how ancient they are. Would you like one?"

He shook his head. He watched her smear cream cheese on the bagel. "If it's not Mrs. Carlene and you don't suspect Hayman, do you have any ideas who Salazar's working with—other than the Maras, of course? He's got to have someone close by. I didn't see any men at his house at all Saturday morning, and no one but Delsey has seen any gang members that I know of."

She shook her head, chewed. "I've never seen anyone around him I didn't expect to see, other than his visitors."

"Sounds odd, doesn't it? Who does he work with in Madrid?"

"Their police sent us a compete dossier on him. You can borrow it if you like. When he's in Madrid, he likes to spend most of his time with his mother, Maria Rosa, and her longtime friends, all of them older and male, in her lovely big home on the Paseo del Prado. Mother and

son play for each other at a small flamenco club. As you
know, she's quite a classical pianist. Bottom line, we
haven't seen any of his mother's associates here, only
Salazar."

"Has he visited El Salvador and his Uncle Mercado
recently?"

"No. His last visit was when he was in his mid-
twenties. Mercado was killed in a firefight with author-
ities some ten years ago. Another Lozano cousin took
his place. How did you meet your boss?"

He smiled at her. "I worked with Savich and Sherlock
in San Francisco a couple of weeks ago. Did you read
about Judge Dredd getting shot?"

"The whole planet has. You were involved with that?
You must have really impressed him to ask you to transfer to Washington to work for him after, what, a week
of knowin' you?"

Griffin nodded. "Everything worked out. I'll tell you
though, I had to think long and hard about the transfer.
I really like San Francisco, enjoyed my life there. But
Savich and his unit are usually in the eye of the storm,
and, I gotta admit it, I like the rush, the challenge."

"The danger, right?"

"Maybe there's something else—I called lots of people, and all of them told me you can trust Savich; he's
always got your back."

He began tapping his fingers on the tabletop. "In the
morning I'm going to start talking with everyone who
was at the party, including everyone from that catering

company. No one will wonder why, since everyone knows we're conducting a murder investigation."

"If you can, talk to Salazar again. I'd like to know your impressions of where his mind is at now. Again, I think he's got to be panicked. All of them must be."

She took the last bite of the bagel, sighed, and sat back in her chair. "I was raised on bagels. My grandma made them for me the first time when I was maybe four years old. 'Succor for the soul,' she'd say when she spread cream cheese on one for me."

"There were bagels in the South when your grandmother was a girl?"

She grinned at him. "I think the first bagel maker arrived in Louisiana with the carpetbaggers after the war. What's your favorite eat?"

"I'm a guy. Give me burgers and hot dogs and a grill and I'm a happy camper."

"Where'd you grow up, Griffin?"

"In Colorado, near Aspen. Yes, I've skied all my life, competed throughout high school and college."

"Olympics?"

"Not in this lifetime. I enjoy skiing whenever I have the chance. I don't guess you've ever done much skiing in Louisiana?"

"I always wanted to learn, usually for a solid three months after watchin' the winter Olympics on TV." She grinned. "I'm a water-skier. Now, that's fun."

He took another drink of coffee. It was pretty bad. The night was quiet, the air still and calm. He looked at her, wanted to run his finger over her mouth. He wanted to taste her. But not now, worst luck. He said, "Maybe we could teach each other."

"Yeah," she said after a moment, her dark eyes on his face, "maybe we could."

CHAPTER
32

Bud Bailey's B&B
Maestro, Virginia

Delsey dreamed she was skydiving into the very heart of Santiago, tourists and natives alike all staring up at her and pointing. She wondered why all the people were pointing at her when she realized she felt the parachute straps digging into her shoulders and her shoulders were bare. Then she noticed she was wearing only knee-high boots, nothing else. The wind danced wildly in her hair, and she was cold, freezing. Suddenly, she felt something coming close and she tried to move out of the way, jerk on the parachute straps, but she couldn't move. Something cast a shadow over her face and it was coming at her—not making any noise, but she could feel it, and it was a him, and she felt his breath on her cheek. She couldn't move, couldn't—

Delsey jerked awake. She stared up into the face of the man she hadn't until this moment realized she'd seen just before he'd smashed something down against her head. He was straddling her, holding her down, her arms by her sides under the covers, and his hand was over her mouth. He whispered above her mouth, "You bounced right back, didn't you, *pequeña niña*? You were lucky, but not tonight. You recognized me, didn't you? Can't let you stay around. Hey, you scared?" He laughed. "Don't worry, I'll just slip it in, it'll sink right into your heart and you'll hardly even notice."

The glimpse she'd gotten of him—she hadn't realized he was so very young, and his eyes were dead. She couldn't move. Griffin was across the living room in the other bedroom, sound asleep. She made a sound in her throat and stared at the glittering silver knife coming down.

Three shots rang out, loud as cannons. The man slammed forward on top of her. She opened her mouth to scream and tasted his blood. His blood was everywhere, hot and sticky, on her face, her neck—"

"Delsey, are you okay?"

It was Griffin.

She was frantic, out of control, but her voice came out in a hoarse whisper. "Get him off me!"

Griffin quickly shoved him off, let him land on the floor on his side, fall slowly onto his back. Griffin switched on the bedside lamp as he sat down to hold her. He saw blood splattered on her face. Then he felt the blast of cold air from the open window.

He dropped Delsey and ran to the window. Delsey was behind him, her blood-splattered nightgown flapping at her ankles.

They looked at a man standing at the base of a tall ladder leaned against the B&B wall in the alley below the window. He stared up at them, and they saw his face clearly. A split second later, the man turned and ran down the alley away from them and disappeared around a corner.

"Give me a second, Delsey, I've got to call Dix." He grabbed her cell out of its charger on the bedside table, since his was in his bedroom.

A moment later, he laid the cell on the bedside table and turned to see Delsey standing in the middle of the small bedroom, blood splattered, pale as death, trying not to look at the dead man on the floor beside the bed. He shoved the window down.

"You okay?"

"Yes," but she could hear herself wheezing for breath. "I'm cold, Griffin, I'm so cold I'm going to crack like ice. You're okay, right?"

"Don't worry about me."

"I'll bet the other man was the second man in my apartment." She raised shocked eyes to his face. "He was waiting for his partner to kill me and then what? They'd go have a beer?" She knew her voice sounded weak, thin as a thread, but she couldn't help it. She looked again at the dead man. "He's so young. Thank you for saving my life, Griffin. How did you know?"

Griffin shrugged. "I guess I woke up and I heard him."

"But how could you hear him? He was whispering and he had his hand over my mouth so I couldn't make a sound. I couldn't scream or anything."

"Well, whatever, we're both okay."

He'd somehow known, and for that, she was more grateful than she'd ever been in her life. She felt a punch of nausea and swallowed convulsively when she looked down at herself. Her old soft-as-butter white granny nightgown wasn't soft or white now. "May I go take a shower, Griffin?"

"Make it nice and hot, okay?"

She nodded, took one more look at the dead man. "He's so young, Griffin, maybe not even twenty. The other man, he knows we saw him. He knows."

"Maybe so, but we don't have to worry anymore about this one. Go take your shower."

When he heard the water turn on in the bathroom, he went down on his haunches beside the dead man. He studied his face. Delsey was right, he was so damned young. He'd shot him three times in the chest, center mass. His eyes and his mouth were both open, his mouth in silent surprise. He saw something on the side of his neck. It was a tattoo. He gently turned his head to the side. There in Gothic script were *MS* and the number *13* right below.

CHAPTER
33

Washington, D.C.
Sunday, midnight

When his cell belted out "Tequila," Savich was sleeping beside Sherlock, dreaming for some reason about Sister Maria's song in *The Sound of Music*, the movie Sean had watched for the umpteenth time before bed. He awoke instantly. "Savich."

"Savich, Agent Sparks here. Stony Hart's dead, dammit, and I swear I never saw anyone go in. The girlfriend came running out of the building screaming. I called 911, and Metro is on their way. I calmed her down, took her back upstairs, told her to stay in the kitchen. I looked in the bedroom. It looks like Hart committed suicide."

"We'll be there in fifteen minutes."

The early-morning hours in Washington were like
an entirely different city for Savich and his Porsche.
The only traffic was mostly young professionals trying
to get themselves home safely before the workweek
started again in a few hours. Moonlight reflected off the
white snow and helped light their way. The streets were
free of ice, the temperature still hovering above freezing.
The heater started to blast out hot air as the engine
warmed.

While Savich drove, Sherlock called Agent Sparks to
get more details. When she punched off her cell, she
said, "Bill said Stony never left his apartment. There was
a pizza delivery at eight. Bill checked with the pizza guy,
verified he delivered the pizza to Hart's apartment, said
a young woman paid him. Her name's Janelle Eckles,
his girlfriend. She left about nine o'clock, got into a car
with two other young women. Bill said Stony's lights
were the last to go off in the building, about eleven. He
saw the girlfriend come back before midnight, let herself
in. The apartment lights went on, and she came out
screaming. No wonder."

Savich was frowning. "Suicide?"

"I suppose someone could have gotten in through
the rear entrance of the building without Bill seeing
him, but Bill says we'll see for ourselves." Sherlock
looked at the GPS, then shot a look at a street sign. "Not
much farther. Turn left here on Green Leaf Avenue,
Dillon. And I know you're already blaming yourself, so
stop it, or you're going to piss me off. This is not your
fault."

He looked at her quickly and only shook his head.

"Bill said a Detective Moffett of the WPD just drove up."

They found themselves in a not-quite-gentrified neighborhood of mid- to low-end apartments that left very few trees to soften the scene. Instead, there were stuffed garbage cans lining the street, and piles of filthy snow packed back against buildings. Four cop cars blocked the street. Officers were already out canvassing the neighborhood wherever they saw a light.

"I hate this," she said.

Detective Lorenzo Moffett, a fireplug topped with a short halo of hair hugging his head, and eyes that had seen too much, met them at Stony Hart's apartment door on the second floor, waved them in. "So you're Agent Savich. There's a lot of talk at the Daly Building about that poor kid found at the Lincoln Memorial. I'd say this one is a suicide, first glance, but given the circumstances, we'll see. Hart's in here."

"Our forensic team and the FBI ME will be here soon, Detective Moffett," Sherlock said.

"My Loo's got no problem with you guys taking over the forensics once he heard it's connected to Tommy Cronin's murder. I've got officers out speaking to the neighborhood, and I want to be kept in the loop. I've got the girlfriend in the kitchen. She was pretty drunk when we got here, since she'd been out partying with girlfriends. She told Agent Sparks she decided to surprise him with a return visit, all unplanned, according to her, and this is what she found. Needless to say, she's stone-cold sober now. Naturally, she didn't know about an FBI agent sitting in front of the building. Did Hart know?"

Savich shook his head. "I assigned Agent Sparks to keep watch here."

Moffett didn't say a word about that, although they could tell he wanted to. "I ran a check on the girlfriend while I waited for you guys," Moffett said. "Janelle Eckles is twenty-two; she's a clerk at State part-time and finishing up her senior year at George Washington, majoring in history. Parents live in Independence, Iowa, work in Cedar Rapids, both engineers in a biotech company."

As Moffett spoke, he led them into the good-sized living room that had a lovely view of an alley. The living room furniture looked to be college dorm seconds Stony had gathered over the years, from a fifties-modern coffee table to a beat-up early-American sofa. Stacks of CDs covered an entire side of the sofa, and there was a bowl filled to the brim with shrink-wrapped flash drives on the coffee table. Along one wall was a long cafeteria-style table, mostly empty except for a lonely keyboard, a printer, and a beehive of computer wiring. Layers of dust in geometric patterns were scattered around the table, where Stony's computers and routers had stood before Spooner and his crew had removed them all that afternoon.

Moffett waved his hand around. "You can see Hart was really into his computers. Agent Sparks told me the FBI hauled away his stuff. I'd like to know what

that was about. First let's see if you agree this is a suicide."

He ushered them into a long, narrow bedroom that
held only a single dresser, a leather chair, and a king-size
bed. No computer paraphernalia in here, maybe on orders from his girlfriend, only a big flat-screen TV hung
on the wall opposite the bed.

Walter Stony Hart was lying on the bed on his back
with his arms at his sides, dressed in old jeans, a blue-
and-white Magdalene sweatshirt, and black Nikes on his
feet, his arms at his sides. His eyes were open and staring at the ceiling. Beside him on the bedside table stood
two empty pill bottles. Savich looked closely at the
bottles, saw the prescription labels had been ripped off
so no one would know where he'd got them? Or because
he didn't want to be saved if the pills didn't kill him?
Next to the bottle was a piece of white paper.

"Ms. Eckles said she read it," Moffett said. "She said
it was neatly set beneath the bottles.

"We didn't touch it again," Moffett said. Sherlock
leaned down, read aloud, *I can't live like this. I'm sorry.*"
It was signed "Stony Hart."

Sherlock studied the scene, studied Stony's face.
"Where is the pad this sheet of paper came from?"

"It's here, on the floor beside the bed."

"And the pen?"

Moffett said, "It's on top of the pad of paper. It's
really a journal sort of notebook, but funny thing is,
there's nothing written in it."

Sherlock took the journal, thumbed through the pages. "It still smells new," she said, and gave it back to Detective Moffett.

"Devil's advocate here. It's suicide; look at him, he didn't struggle, he's all peaceful, like he came to a decision and followed through, even left a note. Hard to fake all that."

Sherlock lightly touched her fingers to Stony's gray cheek. "Poor boy, you should have told us the truth, but maybe in the end it didn't matter."

Savich was studying the pill bottles. "Since he ripped off the prescription labels, it will take a few hours to know what they were. From the size of the bottles, I'd say maybe narcotic pain relievers, like oxycodone, and some kind of sleeping pills or tranquilizers. Either Stony stole them or someone else did."

Sherlock said to Moffett, "If it turns out it's not suicide, we'll have a suspect. Peter Biaggini, and that would mean Peter killed one of his best friends and danced out all pleased with himself for stage-setting a perfect suicide scene."

"Talk to me," Detective Moffett said. "Tell me who this Peter is."

Savich saw no reason not to tell him. By the time he finished speaking, Moffett was shaking his head. "But you don't know yet."

"No," Sherlock said. "We don't. Something I do know, though, is that Peter Biaggini will be alibied up to his tonsils if he had anything to do with this. We'd appreciate it if you'd keep this all close to the vest, Detective Moffett. We don't want it to get out to the media."

Detective Moffett said, "Not a problem."

Savich lightly touched his hand to Stony Hart's flaccid hand. Another life gone, simply snuffed out. The waste of it all made him want to weep. He said, "Murder or suicide, the ME can tell us for certain."

CHAPTER
34

Ten minutes later FBI crime scene techs swarmed into the bedroom. Savich and Sherlock walked with Detective Moffett to the small kitchen that smelled faintly of day-old garbage and unwashed dishes, with an occasional whiff of lemon.

An untouched pizza with congealed cheese, still in its box, looked ready to topple off the kitchen counter. Janelle Eckles sat in one of the two cane-backed chairs at a small laminated green table with salt and pepper shakers shaped like kittens sitting on top of a pile of napkins. A gift from her to Stony, Sherlock thought, and felt her throat close. A WPD officer sat silently with her.

Janelle wasn't crying. She was sitting tall, her face and her eyes blank, and Sherlock realized the only thing tethering her here was her body. She nodded to Dillon, and he and Moffett and the officer left the kitchen.

Sherlock sat beside the young woman. "Janelle Eckles? Did I pronounce your name correctly?"

"Yes." She didn't look at Sherlock, but continued to stare blankly toward the sink filled with dirty dishes. "Some people say it Eck-less, not Eckels, like I do." She waved a hand. "I was going to clean up this mess before I left because Stony was so upset all weekend after Tommy died. But then Stony acted like a jerk this afternoon. He hardly talked to me, so I told him he could be a pig on his own time. I called some friends and we went to a rave at the DC Star on Queens Chapel Road, you know, in the warehouse district. I guess I got really drunk." She raised blank eyes to Sherlock's face. "I'm not drunk now."

A rave at the DC Star, Sherlock thought, down and dirty, so not the shy, conservative girl she'd expect to be with Stony. Either that or she was so angry she was out experimenting.

Sherlock took Janelle's hand in hers, held it firmly when Janelle resisted, then felt her slowly ease. "What time did you leave, Janelle?"

"About nine o'clock. Stony was pacing around, groaning, pulling on his hair. He was obviously upset about something. I kept asking him what was wrong, asking him where he was this afternoon, who'd upset him like this. I'm not blind, I saw all his computers were gone. And I asked him what happened to them, but he shook his head and wouldn't tell me, muttered something about getting them replaced. It was like he didn't think it was any of my business to ask him. And that was after I spent most of the weekend with him to show him how sorry I was about Tommy. Finally I told him it was time he talked to me or I was going to leave. You know what he did? He punched a wall with his fist and walked out of the room. I called my two girlfriends to come pick me up right after that.

"You know he was always on one of his computers—have you seen the living room, imagine what it looked like? He wouldn't put any of that crap out of sight. I swear all that junk would breed from one week to the next; there was always more. He spent all day at work in front of a screen, and then he came home and didn't want to do anything else." Her voice broke, but still she didn't cry, merely swallowed, and was still again.

She doesn't know anything about Stony coming to the Hoover Building, doesn't know anything about the anonymizer or Stony's involvement with Tommy's death.

Sherlock asked her, "Did you know Tommy Cronin?"

"Sure. Tommy was over here whenever he could get away from Magdalene, maybe once a week. I liked him a lot. For a while he was thick with one of my girlfriends, Melissa Ivy, and it was Melissa who introduced me to Stony. She said we might as well go out with guys who had a future rather than those jocks and losers at school who were only out to score. I remember she was so pleased when Tommy invited her to Thanksgiving dinner at his grandparents' house—well, mansion, really, she told me. But that didn't work out. I'm sorry, Agent, I got off track."

"That's fine," Sherlock said. "Tell me whatever you wish."

"Well, Melissa was with us at the rave, went home as drunk as I did. I think she was mad at Peter—Peter Biaggini; he's another of Stony's friends—but she wouldn't say anything about it, said she wanted to forget about it and him. I wondered if he was as upset as Stony and shutting her out.

"They're both gone now, both Tommy and Stony. And they were so young. Isn't that strange?"

Sherlock lightly touched her fingertips to Janelle's sweater sleeve to bring her back. "Were you surprised when Melissa left Tommy and went with Peter?"

"Melissa said Tommy was too uptight, said he wanted to study all the time instead of be with her. She took up with Peter then; I don't remember exactly when."

"That's all right. Now, I know this is hard, Janelle, but we really need your help. When you left Stony tonight, did he tell you he expected anybody?"

"I don't know, because we weren't speaking. He didn't even say good-bye to me. I didn't say good-bye to him, either. I slammed out." Tears were falling down her face. She didn't make a noise, just let the tears fall. "When I got back I was too drunk to fight with him. I went in the bedroom to say something snarky to him and I saw him lying there. I thought he'd fallen asleep with his clothes on, and I touched him, but then I saw his eyes and they were staring at me." She gulped, sat stone still.

"I picked up his note and read it. I know now I shouldn't have touched it, but I did. I don't understand what he meant—*I can't live like this. I'm sorry.* Did it have anything to do with Tommy dying? Do you know what he meant?"

Sherlock shook her head.

Janelle looked down at her clasped hands. "I looked at the bottles. He must have stolen some of his mom's pills. Can you imagine how she'll feel when she finds out he used her pills to kill himself?"

"Did you see the pills here before tonight?"

She shook her head. "Stony hated to ever take pills. I'd have to beg him to take an aspirin when he had a headache. He was weird that way. I can't imagine when he stole them. Did he visit his parents this weekend? But to steal his own mother's pills? Why would he do that? Do you think she knows yet?"

She raised her white face to Sherlock. "Do you think Stony had anything to do with Tommy's death? Is that what he couldn't live with? Was he feeling guilty about something he did? When we heard that Tommy was dead, I saw him crying in the bathroom, and that's why I stayed with him almost all day Saturday. Then he was gone most of today and I left, too, but I came back. But when I got here, and ordered his favorite pizza, he wouldn't even talk to me, wouldn't say a thing, just cried and got angry at me. Why would he kill himself?"

She fell silent again. She was a pretty girl, Sherlock thought, gold-streaked hair, nice figure, but too much makeup that was all smeared now. All the eye shadow made her look older than she was. Sherlock supposed she wanted to look like a grown-up at the rave.

Sherlock said, "I promise you, Janelle, we will find out why."

CHAPTER
35

Judge Hardesty's Airfield
Near Maestro, Virginia
Monday, dawn

The early morning was freezing cold, the snow shiny with an ice crust. The trio of pine trees next to the small hangar stood tall like white sentinels, straight and still in the cold air. Griffin, Delsey, and Anna stood huddled against a clapboard wall of the still-locked hangar, their breaths making white puffs of vapor as they waited for the plane. Griffin and Delsey were running on fumes after a night of recorded interviews about the crime scene and discussions with Sheriff Noble, who'd had no luck finding the man they'd seen running away in the alley last night. Worse for Griffin than the cold was that his sister had been arguing with him since he woke her up in her new bed in their adjoining rooms at the B&B to tell her she was leaving Maestro. Not even Anna's being there with him had helped convince her, and now she opened her mouth and started up again. "Look, Griffin, I know last night was scary, I mean, it was terrifying, but—"

Her brother put his fingers over her mouth. "There's no reason to go through all this again, Delsey. The Mara came after you at the B&B while I was close, in the next bedroom, and that's too close to home.

"You know Maestro hasn't been your friend since Friday night. Anna and Ruth and Dix, all of us, want you out of here and safe in Washington with Savich. I told him what happened—namely, our gun runners are desperate enough to lean a ladder on the side of the B&B, climb in through your window, and attempt to stick a knife in your heart. The MS-13 gang member wanted you dead, Delsey, because you were a witness." Saying the words made his throat clog. He swallowed. "Look, if I hadn't—"

Hadn't what? Delsey wondered.

"—if I hadn't heard you and come in time—" He couldn't get out the words. "Let me say Anna and Ruth and Dix all want you out of here as well."

Delsey didn't bother pointing out yet again that the man had had his hand pressed over her mouth and she hadn't made a sound, yet Griffin had somehow known. She looked off toward the hills at the low rumble of an incoming airplane. "Look, I'll be really careful, and I can help. I can be bait; maybe I can—"

Griffin pulled out his killer argument. "Listen, if you stayed, we'd have to protect you, and that could scatter our focus, maybe endanger all of us. You don't want that, do you? We don't have the resources to protect you, and there's no reason to risk your life here. It's best for all of us if you leave."

Delsey sighed. "I guess I don't want to get a knife in my heart." She shuddered.

"I don't want you to, either," Griffin said.

"This wasn't what I expected to have happen when I decided to study music composition at Stanislaus." She gave Griffin a crooked grin. "How can I have such sucky luck? But you know, what about my classes? And I've got to compose. What if I lie really low, so no one—"

Anna interrupted her, placed her hands on Delsey's shoulders. "You can compose anywhere on the planet. Your professors can email your assignments. Your brother's right, you don't want to be here. I'd be so worried about you all the time that I'd get all my customers' orders wrong and lose all my tips and maybe even my job. Then how could I afford to practice my violin?

"Listen, Delsey, bottom line, if something happened to you, I'd never forgive myself, and no one else would, either. I'd end up in Nepal, where I'd become a monk and shave my head. A Louisiana girl shouldn't have to do that. Don't make me show off my bone-white bald head, Delsey."

"How do you know it's bone white? Oh, never mind. All right, you guys win. Now, there's something that's been bothering me, so I'm going to spit it out. I understand my BFF would want to be here to see me off and maybe help my brother talk me into going, but I'm not blind. There's something more going on here that neither of you has told me. It's like you're both guarding defenseless little Delsey for her own good, little brain-dead Delsey, who wouldn't understand something only you grown-ups would know. And no, this isn't about the thing you guys have between you—that's okay, I think it's great. Maybe you don't even see it yet yourselves, but you will. Nope, it's something else, way something else."

She studied their closed faces a moment. "Anna, you and Ruth behave differently, too, when you're together. I'm asking you, Anna, because Griffin can stare me right in the eye and lie clean. So talk."

Delsey saw Anna shoot a look to her brother, saw Griffin start to shake his head, then pause, shrug. "It's up to you. She'll be out of Maestro, out of harm's way, and safe in Washington, and so will whatever you tell her."

Anna thought for a few seconds, drew a deep breath, and prayed. "Okay, here it is. I'm a DEA agent, Delsey, undercover here in Maestro since last September, because we believe some people at Stanislaus, including Professor Salazar, are involved in large-scale drug smuggling. I enrolled at Stanislaus to find out more about it."

Delsey stared at her like she'd grown a third ear. "*What*? You, Anna, a DEA agent? My best friend here at Stanislaus, my girl from Louisiana who's working her way through music school and shot an alligator when she was nine years old, you're really a federal cop like my brother? *A DEA agent?*" She was shaking her head back and forth, trying to come to grips with a new reality. "But you and I are friends, we've been friends since last fall—but wait—" Delsey smacked the side of her head. "I'm an idiot. That's not true at all, is it? All I've ever been to you is a source of information." Delsey's voice had raised a good octave and had begun to shake, with anger, with hurt.

"I don't believe this, no, it can't be true. Tell me, Anna, tell me."

"Listen to me, Delsey, I simply couldn't tell you earlier. That's what undercover means. You can't tell a soul what you're really doing. It's my job, my assignment. Telling anyone, even you, would only have put you and all of us at risk."

Delsey gave her a full-blown sneer. "Turns out I was at risk anyway, doesn't it?"

Anna hated Delsey's anger, but there was nothing she could do about it. She slowly nodded. "That's true enough."

"Like that dead agent or partner of yours I found in my apartment, the night I was almost killed? Did that have anything to do with you, Anna?"

"I would never have put you at risk, Delsey, not knowingly. I didn't know about it until after it happened. That's why I'm here to see you safely out of Maestro now."

Delsey wheeled on Griffin. "And you, brother, how long have you known? And Ruth, Dix, everyone else that Anna simply *couldn't* tell, since she was here *undercover*?"

Griffin took her hands, since he couldn't be sure she wouldn't belt him, or Anna. "Stop being so pissed off. Like Anna said, she's only been doing her job."

"Yeah, and part of it was to play me."

Anna said, "Yes, it started out that way, but Delsey, I'm not lying to you, I came to like you a whole lot. You're my BFF. Please. I don't want to ruin our friendship."

Griffin said, "Listen, Dels, she's so closemouthed I only got it out of her yesterday afternoon. She didn't want to tell me, but I forced her hand. I'd figured it out, you see."

"Here you figured it out in two days and I didn't because I'm a blind idiot, and here I've known her for months and months."

"I've seen you be an idiot, Delsey, but not about this. As for Griffin figuring it out, so much has happened since he got here. We've been in a pressure cooker, and it's ready to pop.

"Please understand, Delsey, I was sent here because I needed to get something concrete on Salazar, get some idea of the operation, where they're stashing the drug shipments locally. He's been very careful. But things are moving really fast now; plus, we have the MS-13 gang members to deal with."

To Griffin's relief, he saw Delsey had calmed down. She was chewing this over. She said slowly, "Two people are dead. Won't Salazar realize it's all a sham, that you're onto him, and run? Take the drugs with him?"

She'd nailed it. Anna said, "He might run. We're waiting for him to pull the trigger now and try to move the drugs to D.C., to Baltimore, Richmond, wherever he has clients. We think he's got a fortune in drugs stashed out here somewhere, ready to go to his buyers."

"Salazar, a drug runner. It blows my mind. I mean, here he is a world-famous classical guitarist. And a drug kingpin?"

"It would seem so," Anna said.

Griffin shaded his eyes at the blur of cloud-covered sun climbing above the mountain line in the distance. The small search-and-rescue plane he'd heard was clearing the foothills to the east and lining up with the runway. "That should be Agent Davis Sullivan," he said, pointing. "He's flying you back to Washington, Delsey, in *Marauder Two*."

"Griffin, what in heaven's name will I do in Washington?"

You'll stay alive.

"Hey, where will I stay? What happened to *Marauder One*?"

"You're staying with my boss, Dillon Savich. As for practicing your music, I know Agent Sherlock has a beautiful Steinway, and she'll love to listen to you.

"I've heard Sherlock play, by the way. I was told she

was on her way to Juilliard when she changed her mind. Maybe you can compose an FBI movie theme song together."

"I don't want to fly on *Marauder Two* until I find out what happened to *Marauder One*."

"Maybe they've got a fleet of *Marauder*s. You can ask Agent Sullivan. See, that was a good landing, wings level, no bounce or skid at all."

The plane slowed after it touched down and taxied slowly toward them. A tall, whip-lean man wearing a Redskins cap climbed out. He looked up at the snow-laden clouds and frowned, zipped up his brown leather jacket, and walked toward them—no, he didn't walk, he moseyed, Delsey thought, like a loose-limbed cowboy.

Griffin stepped forward. "Agent Sullivan?"

Off came the ball cap to show mussed dark hair. "Yep. It looks like snow's coming in pretty fast, so we'd better take off now. You Agent Hammersmith?"

"Yes." The two men shook hands. Griffin said, "This is my sister, Delsey Freestone, your passenger. This is Anna Castle, DEA."

Agent Sullivan gave Anna a long look. "Didn't I beat your socks off on the firing range at Quantico? Or was that one of your spastic bros?"

"It must have been Agent Hammersmith here. I doubt either of you would give me any competition worth mentioning."

"Good answer," Sullivan said, smiled, and gave her a salute.

Delsey said, "Before I put my life in this stranger's

hands and get in that tiny little flying box with him, I want him to tell me what happened to *Marauder One*."

Sullivan laughed. "Agent Jack Crowne had a small bomb problem a while back. He survived, but *Marauder One* bit the dust. Good plane, held together long enough for Jack to bring her down. Look at those black clouds hovering like bad dreams. Not much time; let's get going."

He took Delsey's hand and began pulling her away.

"I'll speak to you later today, Delsey," Anna called. "Don't worry. I'll take care of your pretty brother here, keep him out of trouble."

Griffin and Anna stood side by side, listening to Delsey and Agent Sullivan argue as they walked toward the plane. They watched him pick her up and heave her in, climb in after her, and pull the door shut.

Anna smiled. "I'm glad Agent Sullivan wasn't nice to Delsey; she'd have run all over him."

"I'm not pretty."

Anna patted his arm. "You keep telling yourself that. Hey, you've got some boss at the FBI to pull this off, and so fast."

"Yep, I'd say he is." A snowflake hit Griffin's nose, and he pulled his parka up over his head. "Thanks for coming out here with me. And for trusting Delsey with your cover. I have one less worry since she got on that plane. Want to drive back to Sheriff Noble with me and talk strategy?"

Anna pulled him up. "Agent Hammersmith, I'm here undercover. The whole point is nobody knows who and what I am. Now look at me. Sheriff Noble and Ruth and even Delsey know. I wouldn't be surprised if it's scrawled in the men's room at Maurie's pretty soon."

"Nah, it's way too early, but I'll check next time I'm in. No one who knows is going to give you up."

"I don't want anyone to see me in your company, since they know you're FBI. I only came with you this morning to say good-bye to Delsey, and, well, you thought she'd kick up a fuss about leaving even after MS-13 tried to kill her last night. It was the least I could do for her after what she'd been through. I took a risk no one would follow us this lovely morning. I've got to get back to my next shift soon, back to being sweet Anna at Maurie's Diner until my boss, Mac Brannon, tells me otherwise."

Griffin patted her face, pulled her parka together, and zipped it to her chin. "Listen, being out and about is lots safer than being alone in your house. If anyone notices you're with me they'll think we're talking about my sister. Everyone knows you guys are close." He paused a moment. "You know it'll be all over town by noon that the same guy who struck Delsey down in her apartment Friday night was shot trying to kill her last night."

They both turned to watch the plane clear the mountains and disappear in the morning mist.

Anna hated that he made even a bit of sense, remembered she'd been relieved to pull her Kia out and away from her house that morning, away from the quiet of Wolf Trap Road and its thick trees and her old house that creaked and groaned with wind at night, scaring the bejesus out of her. She now carried her Glock in a clip on her belt even during work.

She kicked a pebble out of her path and jerked the Camry's passenger door open. She looked at him over the roof. "You've got your hands full—two homicides, banging some of the gang members' heads together if you can even find one hanging somewhere, and finding that guy in the alley. I wish I could help."

"I know, but you've got to stay in character. By the way, if we ever compete on the firing range, you don't have a chance, not in this lifetime."

The thought of his having the last word frosted her, and it wasn't going to happen on her watch. She said, "Maybe not, but you'd still be pretty."

CHAPTER
36

The Hoover Building
Monday morning, three hours later

Savich said to Agent Sullivan, "Thanks for picking Ms. Freestone up in Maestro, Davis, and delivering her to us in one piece."

"Not a problem. Always a pleasure to be flying." He turned to Delsey. "It was fun spending some time with you, Ms. Freestone, but you've gotta suck this one up—you're way off base about Vincent and the Onepotts. And if you don't like Big Escape, you're an enemy of rock 'n' roll. Hey, what's not to like about tattoos and huge doses of punk attitude?"

Before Delsey could jerk out his tonsils, he added, "I was out surfing with my brother in L.A. last June. He took me to hear them play in Santa Monica at the One-Up Club. He actually called it a little retro for his taste. It takes all kinds, right? So, I'll pick you up tomorrow evening at seven o'clock, at Agent Savich's house. Any problems, there, Savich?"

"Not a one."

Davis Sullivan gave them a general salute and was out the door.

One of Sherlock's brows shot up. "Davis is a fast worker. Be careful, Delsey, that man's got a reputation that would make Mama's hair turn white."

"I used to," Delsey said sadly.

Savich said, "As long as he doesn't wear a dog collar like Vincent, I'm fine with it."

"Sounds like it's his brother I want to meet," Delsey said.

Savich grinned, and Delsey found herself smiling back at the big man with the hard face. "Sherlock, before you take her home and settle her in, we need to speak a moment."

"I'm really staying with you? You don't mind?"

"Not a problem," Sherlock said, and patted her arm. "It will be our pleasure."

Delsey fretted her thumbnail. She suddenly felt like she was being tossed around like so much flotsam, sleeping in yet another strange bed, intruding on strangers, like she didn't belong anywhere, and she hated that. "I've never been to Washington before. Davis said you live in Georgetown."

Sherlock nodded. "Your room is across from Sean's.

He's our five-year-old son, and a live wire. Sometimes he talks in his sleep. You can either join in and discuss Flying Monks, one of his gazillion video games, or ignore him.

"Since you're not only talented but also beautiful, I have a feeling Sean might ask you to marry him. If you accept, you'll be his fourth wife and the oldest. So he might ask you to help support his other wives." She laughed, and Delsey thought she was the most beautiful woman she'd ever seen. And she was married to Mr. Hard and Tough.

Then she remembered exactly who Sean was. "Goodness, Sean is *the* Sean Savich? Like half the planet, I saw him on YouTube at Emma Hunt's performance in San Francisco."

"Hopefully all the hype and media attention is about over," Sherlock said. "A five-year-old on a two-week sugar high isn't any fun."

Savich took the time to introduce Delsey Freestone to all the agents in the CAU, tell them all she was the sister of Griffin Hammersmith, the new agent coming from San Francisco to join the unit. Then he guided her into his office, nodding for Sherlock to follow.

Savich looked Delsey over. "You look like Griffin's twin."

Delsey grinned. "Isn't that something? Griffin told me that you, Sherlock, play like a dream. I can't wait to hear you. Does Sean play?"

"After a fashion," Savich said. He studied her, then his voice dropped and she realized it was time to get down to business. "Griffin tells me you're a trouble magnet, that two people have died around you in the past three days, one of them a gang member who tried to kill you."

What to say to that? Nothing but the truth. She said, "I'm pretty scared, all right," and leaned toward this man who looked like he ate knuckles for breakfast. "I'm sorry I'm a trouble magnet, but things always sort of happen when I'm close by. It started when I was a teenager, but listen, there wasn't any trouble at Stanislaus until I opened my shower curtain to see a dead man in my bathtub and got smacked on the head. Really, it wasn't my fault."

Sherlock said. "Are you having any concussion symptoms?"

Delsey shook her head. "I feel fine, no more dizziness or feeling like someone hit a home run off my head. I got my memory back really fast, so I could tell Griffin what happened."

Sherlock studied her as her husband had. "Maybe it's a good thing Griffin is so intuitive."

"Oh, you mean how he simply knows sometimes what someone's going to do or where they are? Yeah, he's done that all his life." Her eyes lit up and Savich thought, *Uh-oh.*

She leaned in close. "Agent Savich, I've got some ideas about what happened to poor Tommy Cronin. I don't want to be a burden, I'd like to do something. Really, tell me what you need and I'll do it."

She was as eager as Sean with a new basketball. Sher-

lock was right, he thought, Sean was sure to ask her to
marry him. She was dealing with a horrific experience
in Maestro, she'd had to leave her brother behind, and
she was worrying about being a burden. It must be driving her nuts. Not a bad idea to keep her busy. "You're
part of the family here, Delsey, but we can't have you
working for us; there are rules about that. You'll be no
burden, believe me. We're looking forward to having
you stay with us."

Rats on Rafts belted out "Orangeorangutan." He
picked up his cell off the desk. "Savich." He listened,
then punched off.

He walked to the door and called out to Ollie, "I
have someone here who's dying to see your photos of
Sarah, right, Delsey?"

Something had happened and he wanted to get rid
of her. Delsey smiled and met Ollie Hamish at the door.
He'd been smooth about it, she'd give him that. What
had happened?

When they were alone again, Savich said to Sherlock,
"Dr. Hardy said Stony had enough oxycodone and lor-
azepam to kill him, with plenty left over in his stomach.
They call it edible heroin, and an overdose is just as
deadly. He said other than being dead, Stony was in
perfect health. No signs of anyone forcing those pills
down Stony's throat, no bruising or any other signs of
any violence or coercion. He's going to rule it a suicide.

"And since Dr. Hardy's rarely wrong, it's time to go
see the Harts. It's going to be hard, but we're going to
have to find out when Stony stole his mother's pills.

Probably yesterday after the interview." He sighed, hating to have to ask Stony's mother that, knowing it would add more pain, more devastation. And guilt.

Sherlock said, "I keep thinking about what Stony said when we spoke to him yesterday—*But how can that be? I mean*—like he knew something wasn't right. What was it? Did whatever it was drive him to kill himself? What was he holding back?"

He cupped her face in his big hand. "We'll find out. But first we'll have to deal with their grief."

"I hate this," Sherlock said.

CHAPTER
37

Tunney Wells, Virginia
Late Monday morning

Savich turned his Porsche onto Cotswold Lane in the
Metterling section of Tunney Wells, home of Wakefield
Hart; his wife, Carolyn; and their two surviving daughters. It was a cul-de-sac in a high-end community of
large houses on big lots with so many pine and oak trees
covering the grounds it had to drive the fire department
nuts. Though the snow was no longer as thick on the
ground, the pristine yards still glistened like diamond
facets under the noonday sun. He pulled into the three-
car driveway behind a Mercedes and an Audi beside a
house that looked like an in-your-face modern painting.

The Hart manse was mostly glass held together with steel and a couple planks of redwood and little else. Maybe a third of the other houses on Cotswold Lane were various versions of extreme modern sitting next to Federal-style houses and a few big sprawling Colonials. A mishmash of styles, every one with its own spin on the American dream.

Sherlock said, "The setting's incredible, and I'll admit it, the house is a marvel, but I wouldn't want to live in it. Couldn't run around in my undies. Hey, idea—I could let you stroll around in your boxers and charge admission."

And Savich thought, *Nope, it would be you strolling around in your hair rollers.*

Before he could offer up that thought, she turned sober and grim as a judge, and so he leaned over and kissed her instead. He held her for a moment. "This is going to be tough. The Harts are going to be a mess. Their twenty-two-year-old son was alive one day and dead the next. He killed himself and that's horrible enough, but to know he did it because he felt guilty about something, couldn't live with it. How devastating to a parent not even to know what it was that pushed him over the edge, and that he didn't even talk to them about it."

"It's got to have something to do with Peter Biaggini, Dillon. I wish I could figure out what. If only Stony had written more in his suicide note, made things clearer."

That in itself was odd, Savich thought, as he looked toward a raven hopping up and down on a low-hanging oak tree branch, sending puffs of snow into the air. Most suicide notes he'd ever seen laid things out in detail. "If Peter's responsible, we'll get him," he said.

Mrs. Hart wasn't at home, Regina, the maid, told them in a charming thick Polish accent, but Beth and Lisa were upstairs. Regina was small and slight, her light hair a near skullcap around her head. She was dressed entirely in black. They saw she'd been crying. They showed her their creds.

"Mr. Hart is here, alone in his study, but they leave soon now for funeral dealing. It is sad thing, very sad thing. Little Miss Lisa tells me Mr. Walter was here Saturday and Sunday, and he was so sad because his friend was dead. But I know Mr. Walter. For him to take his own life, he was beyond sad, and I do not know why." Regina shook her head and turned away. She led them through an immense angled entry hall that soared high, giving directly onto the blue sky through spotlessly clean skylights two stories up.

They followed her into a huge room with two glass walls filled with high-gloss black lacquered furniture, beautiful stuff that reflected your face back at you. Sherlock wondered how Regina kept it so spotless. They didn't sit—couldn't, really—it felt too much like they were on a stage, an unseen audience watching their every move.

Nearly five minutes passed before the door opened

and Wakefield Hart came in. They'd been with him not twenty-four hours earlier. Yesterday he'd radiated an air of supreme confidence and a healthy dollop of arrogance. But not this Wakefield Hart. This man, the grieving father, looked haggard and pale and almost insubstantial, his bespoke English suit no longer flat against his sagging shoulders. The powerhouse man was awash in shadows, grief bleeding the life from him.

"You two again. Why are you here? To tell me my son is dead? I know my son is dead. Director Mueller gave me the courtesy of calling me himself. Did he send you here?"

Savich nodded. "We are very sorry about Stony. As you know, we must work very quickly, and that is why we're here, to speak to you. We need your help, Mr. Hart."

"Help for what? My son killed himself. If there is blame here, it is on you sadists. If not for you, my son would still be alive. You pushed him to this, treating him like a criminal, making him feel guilty over Tommy's death. This is your fault. You should be brought up on murder charges."

He eyed them for a brief instant, his hands fists at his sides.

Savich's eyes held pity and infinite calm and patience. "Mr. Hart, we understand Stony was here Saturday morning."

"Yes, he'd heard Tommy was dead. He drove here in that blizzard, nearly killed himself. He was distraught, as we all were. My son was broken; he was a mess. I tried to comfort him, but he was inconsolable."

Sherlock said, "Mr. Hart, was Stony also here Friday?"

"Why? What does that have to do with anything?"

"Please answer, sir."

"Yes, he was here, for a little while."

"And what about Sunday after the interview at the CAU, after he called you?"

"Yes again. My wife and I asked him to come over, to talk with us about what happened. He was frightened and bewildered, said he knew nothing about Tommy's death, or about that picture."

Savich said, "We're trying to pinpoint when Stony took your wife's prescription pills, sir, whether he planned this before or after we brought him in to interview. It would help us all understand Stony's death better, and maybe something more about why he did this."

They looked up to see Regina standing in the doorway, wringing her hands. "It's Mrs. Hart, sir, she cry. Please come now. She say *cas-ket* over and over, and she cry."

Hart's face was a study in contradictions: he wanted his wife to keep her awful grief away from him, he wanted to escape these FBI agents or, better yet, shoot them, and he wanted to be left alone in a corner somewhere, all his thoughts passing like movie frames across his face.

He said, "Forgive me, but my wife is distressed, as

you can well imagine. At least one likes to believe you can imagine her pain," and Hart walked quickly from the living room, and closed the door behind him.

Savich said, "Hart wants to blame anyone but the person who murdered Tommy. His lashing out at us is his way of dealing."

"He deserves to be allowed whatever works for him for now. At least he's talking with us." Sherlock paused, rubbed her hands over her arms. "I'm cold. It's this room, not the temperature."

Savich agreed. "I wonder what it costs to keep these windows sparkling. It's like being out of doors inside this room." He turned directly to her, and his voice dropped to a whisper. "There's a camera focused on us, over my left shoulder, molding height. Probably mikes, too."

Sherlock took only a glancing look at the camera, then waved her hand toward the fireplace, built like a funnel of smoked glass. She said, "They use the fireplace often; look at how black it is on the inside."

Savich nodded, felt his cell vibrate in his pocket. He answered, listened, and said after a moment, "Griffin, yes, Delsey's at our house, safe and sound. Have you got your sketch of that dead gangbanger posted? And the one who ran down the alley?"

Sherlock listened to one-half of the conversation, her attention on Dillon, trying not to look at that camera until Mr. Hart walked back into the living room.

Savich looked up over at Hart, said something to Griffin, and punched off. "Mr. Hart, do you know whether Mrs. Hart noticed her prescription medication was missing? May we speak with her?"

"My wife is not well enough to speak to anyone. Director Mueller did not, naturally, ask about her prescriptions. It's more than likely the pills were hers; where else would Stony have gotten them?

"Listen, Carolyn is not well. She has a great many prescriptions to help her deal with her chronic pain and an anxiety problem. I doubt she would have noticed a missing bottle or two, and I'm certainly not going to ask her now. What difference does it make, except to try to absolve the FBI from being responsible for his death?"

Sherlock didn't let that indictment hang in the air for long. "Mr. Hart, when Stony came yesterday, did he have an argument with anyone while he was here? On the phone, or with you or Mrs. Hart?"

"I told you, we talked about Tommy's death and your accusations against him. It was an emotional day for all of us, but of course we didn't argue. What in heaven's name would we argue about? As for phone calls, he only had two that I remember, and they made him cry. Is that enough for you?"

Savich said, "You told us Peter Biaggini wielded great influence over Stony."

"Yes, that's true. I asked Stony if he thought Peter might have posted that picture, since my son certainly didn't post it. Stony said he didn't know who did."

Sherlock remembered Hart's veiled contempt toward

his son yesterday about how Peter treated him. She said, "Stony told us yesterday he and his friends usually did what Peter wanted. He said Peter slashed the tires on your wife's new Prius years ago because he'd refused to do something Peter wanted him to do. Do you remember that?"

Mr. Hart began pacing the living room, all the way to the huge floor-to-ceiling windows and back, his hands clenched at his sides. She saw him take a quick glance up at the camera, then away. "I don't want to believe that, but the thing is, I do. Carolyn was livid. Stony didn't tell us it was Peter who'd done it, but I knew. I knew."

Savich said, "Sir, you told us Sunday you thought Peter Biaggini was a little shite. I neglected to ask you why you believe that."

"Peter's as arrogant as only a young man who's smart and knows he's smart can be. I don't understand why this isn't clear to you. Peter must have uploaded Tommy's photo on Stony's computer because it has the anonymizer software and he believed no one could ever trace it. There's simply no other reason I can think of for any of this. So why don't you go arrest him and make him tell you who it was who viciously murdered his friend, and why he uploaded that photo, thus putting blame on my son."

Savich wished he believed Peter had murdered Tommy, but deep down he knew he didn't believe it at all, despite Peter's asinine behavior in interview, despite his just-so alibi. Had he uploaded the photo? If he had, then—"Was there any reason you know of for Peter Biaggini to kill Tommy Cronin?"

That brought Hart up short. "Well, no, not really. And listen to me, as much as I dislike Peter Biaggini, I don't believe he did murder Tommy Cronin; why would he? If he uploaded the photo, then where did he get it? I have no idea, but still, where's the motive for him to do such a heinous thing? It had to be someone striking out against the old man, against Palmer Cronin. If the fool hadn't turned a deaf ear to all the warnings bombarding him, if those imbeciles in Congress hadn't kept encouraging the banks to continue writing unpayable mortgages, let them develop and market derivatives no one understood, the collapse wouldn't have happened. It's that simple. But no, they all kept going on, a triumph of greed and stupidity."

Savich had already heard about a more flamboyant version of the same diatribe delivered by Hart to the Commonwealth Club two weeks before. He'd probably been paid a princely sum for it. Savich said, his voice precise and cold, "I understand, Mr. Hart, that you sold quite a few of those bonds yourself before the crash. Wasn't it after they went under that you decided to turn against your own compatriots and join the talk circuit?"

Hart looked like he wanted to punch Savich in the face, but he was smart enough not to try it. He turned away and walked quickly toward the windows, to get control of himself. He said over his shoulder, "What we did, we did because it seemed smart, it seemed simply good business that made money for the banks and a good return for our investors. None of us guessed some of the biggest banks in the world could totter toward collapse in a few short weeks. Impossible, most thought, but happen it did.

"I am on the talk circuit now, as you call it, to encourage the Fed, the SEC, Congress, all interested parties, to move forward with the regulations I suggest."

Another quote from Hart's speech, and a question he had fielded many times. Not defensive, not all that remorseful, either, but look at the new man, the new *wise* man with a plan of action. Savich thought he did it well.

"If you're right, Mr. Hart, about Tommy's murder being revenge against Palmer Cronin, then how do you explain the photo uploaded on Stony's computer? Why did Stony kill himself?"

They watched Hart deflate, no other word for it, his son's suicide once again front and center in his mind. He said, his voice hoarse with pain, "An innocent boy was brutally killed, and my poor son killed himself. I can't explain any of it, but I know it had to be revenge on Cronin, had to be. Peter Biaggini didn't do it. It was someone you don't even have on your radar."

"Mr. Hart, why do you have cameras in this room?"

"What—oh, the cameras. When I bought the house the former owner had an elaborate security system installed because he had an expensive art collection. I thought it interesting, and so I kept it. Easier than ripping it out.

"I need to be with my wife now, Agents. Regina will show you out."

Savich was aware of Hart's bleak eyes following them as Regina led them from the living room.

CHAPTER
38

Maestro, Virginia
Monday afternoon

Anna was surprised when Dr. Elliot Hayman walked
into Maurie's Diner well after the lunch crowd would
normally have thinned. It was still crowded today here
at gossip central, what with all the buzz about the shooting at the B&B last night. She'd heard many hairy tales
about what had happened, but few that remotely resembled reality. And Delsey didn't star in any of them,
a lucky thing indeed.

He sent her a warm smile, maybe too warm, she never
really knew with Dr. Hayman, and he waved. It had been
at least a month since she'd seen him in here, too pedes-

trian for him, too blue collar, she'd always assumed. Why today? He walked straight to a back table where three female Stanislaus graduate students Anna had already been serving were gossiping, not about the shooting but about Gabrielle DuBois. "I wonder if she'll go after Dr. Hayman now that Professor Salazar's cooled off," and, "Well, she's French, isn't she?"

Musicians, cops, waitresses, Anna thought, listening to them. Jealousy and gossip were always the same. She followed Dr. Hayman to the table, where the three women gladly welcomed him to join them. Anna gave him a big smile after he'd settled in. "I believe you like sweet tea, don't you, Dr. Hayman?"

He smiled back at her, that too-warm smile, and nodded. "Yes, thank you. I'm told Ms. Freestone didn't attend classes this morning. Is she not feeling well?"

"I'm not sure, Dr. Hayman, but I know she would have been there if she could."

"Do you know where she is now, Anna?"

"Can't say, Dr. Hayman."

"Our campus police chief told me there was another break-in and a shooting at the B&B. He said he couldn't find out more because Sheriff Noble was keeping a tight lid on it. Have you heard anything about it, Anna?"

"People have been talking about it, but like you said, the sheriff isn't letting out any of the details." It was a relief to all of them that the gang member had tried to kill Delsey in the middle of the night when no one was around. And luckily the forensic team and the ME and his team weren't from Maestro and not around to be grilled over scrambled eggs.

Anna poured Dr. Hayman's sweet tea, took more orders, and delivered them to the kitchen window—most medium-rare hamburgers, Maurie's specialty, and orders of his stiff-as-soldiers-at-attention french fries. It didn't feel right to her that Dr. Hayman was in here today asking questions about Delsey and the shooting. A local shooting was unusual, it was exciting fodder for the gossip mill, but for Dr. Hayman?

He wasn't drinking his tea. She was also aware he was watching her. Did he disbelieve her? Did he think she was holding something back, since she and Delsey were best friends? No matter. She had no choice, she had to keep working and lying through her teeth.

She delivered late lunches, refilled glasses, and smiled and said cheery things and passed more orders through the kitchen window to Maurie, who was sweating in a thick, fat-filled heat, whistling softly as he flipped hamburger patties and barked at Mickey Cross for another order of tuna salad. Mickey was an aging Desert Storm vet who never paid Maurie much mind, having survived an Iraqi prison.

And she had a growing premonition that trouble was going to walk through the door at any minute.

She took a bathroom break, walked back to the ladies' room, thankfully empty, locked the door, and called Griffin.

"Griffin, it's Anna. As you can imagine, this place is

buzzing about the shooting, but nothing's gotten out yet. Dr. Hayman's here, and I know his main reason for coming was to ask me why Delsey hadn't been in class today. Please tell me she's safe in Washington."

"She's fine, all moved in at Savich's house."

"I'm so glad she's away from here. As you can imagine, everyone is talking about the shooting, and you wouldn't believe some of the stories."

"I've heard some myself. Thank you for allowing me to tell Dix and Ruth that you were DEA and here undercover. Dix called your boss, told him what had happened. Brannon asked him to keep the details quiet, if possible, and so Dix threatened physical damage if anyone leaked anything about the gang member being shot to anyone, spouses included. Your boss wants to keep the gangs out of it for as long as possible."

She wondered if Mac Brannon had cursed loud and long when he got a dawn call from the sheriff of Maestro. "Do you know who the dead guy is?"

Griffin said, "Yeah, thanks to the MS-13 neck tattoo, it wasn't hard. His name was Raul Alvarez, out of Fairfax County. Low-level drug conviction, assault, two murder charges that didn't stick. He had a hard-as-nails rep, took care of business. Turns out Brannon called Savich after he found out what happened here to tell him they've rounded up half of Raul's homeboys for questioning, see if they can lead us to the accomplice we saw running down the alley at the B&B last night. It seems likely whoever was with Raul last night was also involved in killing your partner. With all the attention they're getting, I can't see anybody in that gang trying to move drugs anytime soon."

"Yes, that's what Mr. Brannon told me. So there's no break on where the drugs are yet?"

"As you know, DEA agents are all over this area, a good thirty-mile radius, checking out private farms and questioning locals who live outside of town. Nothing solid yet."

"And Salazar?"

"Haven't gotten to him yet."

"Griffin? I don't want to be a wuss or an alarmist, but I know to my gut that something's going to happen and I'm going to be outed."

He was silent a moment. "Respect your gut. Leave now, Anna. Call your boss."

"No, no, I'll wait to call him from home. My shift's over soon."

She sensed he wanted to argue, but he didn't. "Okay, then, I'll meet you when you get off."

She was picking up orders again when Henry Stoltzen waved to her. He slid into a booth across from a front window. He sat alone and silent, and fingered his long goatee.

She delivered an order and went to his table. He looked tired, she thought, and sad. "Hey, Henry, you okay?"

"Delsey's gone," he said. There was sudden silence in the diner. "She's gone, and she didn't even say good-bye. And she could have gotten killed last night."

Dr. Hayman turned slightly on his burgundy vinyl

seat. He asked in his deep voice, "Do you know where Ms. Freestone went, Mr. Stoltzen?"

Henry said, "Old Man Chivers told me she flew out from Judge Hardesty's Airfield early this morning in a small search-and-rescue plane. He said you and Agent Hammersmith were waiting there with her, Anna, and you saw her off."

Her heart dropped to her sneakers, and both of them were hovering over the edge of the abyss. Chigger Chivers—where had the old coot been hiding? She and Griffin hadn't seen a soul. Why hadn't he come out to talk to them? Had he overheard them talking? Oh, yes, for sure, no doubt in her mind. He'd heard every single thing out of their mouths.

She was fully aware of Dr. Hayman staring at her. Would he pin her on the lie? If he did, what would she say?

She knew everyone was staring at her now, whispering behind their hands, and Dr. Hayman sat there drumming his fingers on the table, simply looking at her, his expression curiously blank. The three women with him at the table were also silent, their eyes on her, along with everyone else's in the diner who'd heard her lie.

She ignored all of them, stopped to take an order from the elderly bookkeeper at the Holcombe bank who played Santa Claus at the hardware store.

To her surprise and relief, Dr. Hayman left with the gaggle of graduate students without touching his sweet tea. He paused for a moment at the door and looked back at her, shook his head, and left. She served Henry a glass of soda and watched him run his fingers down the outside of the glass. Finally, he let out a dramatic sigh.

"Henry, what's wrong?" As if she didn't know.

"Are you going to tell me about Delsey, Anna, where she went?"

"Delsey went to Washington, like Mr. Chivers told you. Wouldn't you be afraid to stay if you found a dead man in your bathtub?"

"Well, yeah, I guess, but she should have told me."

"Henry, did Mr. Chivers tell you anything else?"

"Nope. He started whistling, you know how he is, and strolled away, hitching up those ratty old wool pants of his, snapping his suspenders. I called after him, but he kept whistling, wouldn't say anything else."

"Where did you see him?"

"He was sitting outside the hardware store, shooting the breeze, as usual. Why were you out there with Delsey, Anna?"

"Because I'm her best friend. I was glad to see her off because it still might not be safe for her here in Maestro. You know she would have said good-bye to you if she'd had time."

"Well, tell her hi for me if you talk to her."

Anna watched him walk out, stroking his goatee. She realized she was exhausted, too little sleep, running her feet off, but more than that was the fear. Fear drained you faster than hauling a wet carpet. She hated to be afraid, hated she had to own up to it. She wasn't going to stay till the end of her shift. It was time to leave.

Maurie didn't mind, since there were only a dozen

customers left. She was bundled up in her winter togs and out the door and into her Kia within five minutes, on her way to Wolf Trap Road to pack. She knew Mr. Chivers had told everyone who'd come into his orbit about seeing her, no doubt in her mind, and if he had overheard them talking, he'd probably said a great deal more to many of them. Dr. Hayman knew she'd lied to him. Who would he tell? His brother? Did it matter? She didn't know, but she knew she couldn't take a chance.

She took a corner too fast and the car tipped for one terrifying second before she got traction again. She felt as though she'd jump out of her seat if the steering wheel wasn't in the way. *Pay attention*. She was about to fish her cell out of her pocket to call Griffin when it gave its familiar ring, a worn-out razor buzz.

"Are you home yet?"

"Not yet. Another seven minutes."

"I forgot to ask you when your shift ended."

"I should have called you, but all I could think about was getting away. My gut was right. I'm busted."

"I'm five minutes behind you." And Griffin punched off before she could even say Mr. Chivers's name.

She was spooked, a premonition again. She passed two cars with single men driving them, their faces indistinct in the dull late-afternoon light. She watched until she saw them turn off.

She mentally packed a few things in her duffel. She'd be ready to leave the instant Griffin pulled in. She looked in her rearview mirror at a black SUV, but it was way back. When she turned onto Wolf Trap Road she realized she didn't want to go near her charming cottage in the lovely dense woods, not when it would be dark in an hour, not with the winter wind whipping the tree branches into a mad frenzy. She hated that she was afraid.

She pulled into her driveway, cut the engine, and the world became quiet as a tomb. Even the wind seemed dead now. She locked her hands on the steering wheel and stared out the car window at the trees, huddled together like dark monoliths, brooding and waiting, the dark clouds weighing down on everything.

She didn't want to open the car door, didn't want to walk the twenty or so steps to her front entrance, out in the open, for anyone hiding in the woods to see her, and what? Shoot her? No, there was no one there. Anna calmed herself and her breathing. She was a strong, smart, well-trained DEA agent. There was no reason for her to let her imagination run away with her, no reason to get freaked out. If there were bad men out to get her, she'd shoot them first, no problem. She'd face things head-on and not feel terrified at what could be hiding behind all those heavy shadows that cloaked the trees. And there wasn't anything there. There wasn't.

Everything was as it should be, even if the shapeless low-hanging clouds made everything seem otherworldly, like the devil himself was nearby, counting souls.

Don't run in the house to pack; don't get out of your car. Stay locked in and safe. No, don't wait for Griffin, leave now. Who needs clean underwear?

A laugh spurted out. That last thought was too much

for her to stand. She opened the car door and eased out, her Glock clutched at her side in one hand, her keys fisted in the other hand. She could kill with a gun or with her keys, didn't matter, she was ready.

You're an idiot to come back. Who cares if you're wearing jeans and a sweater that smell like hamburgers and fries? You'll be back in Washington soon enough.

This was nuts. *I'm smart and I'm fast, so shut up!* Anna pressed her Glock against her leg and refused to sweep it around her as she walked to her front door.

She heard something, something like a branch dragging on the ground, and froze in her tracks. Then nothing. She didn't fumble with the keys, in and open, and she had her back pressed against the wall next to the door, her breath coming fast, and for a crystalline instant, she was back in the abandoned warehouse in New Orleans that was really a meth lab where she'd seen her first and only firefight. *You came through that, didn't you? You stayed focused, didn't lose your nerve, even though, admit it, your hands were clammy with sweat and fear, and your heart was beating a mad tattoo. You did okay; you did great.*

She'd never before been so spooked, so close to having her control shatter. It was humiliating.

Would Griffin be scared?

No, he wouldn't. She wouldn't, either. She'd get a grip.

Sure enough, no one was hiding behind the mop in the kitchen pantry. Nothing had disturbed the meager lineup of shoes in her closet, and she heard no quiet breathing that wasn't her own. She opened the bath-room door and turned on the light, the white tile glar-ing back at her. Her heart skipped as she remembered Delsey finding Arnie's body behind her shower curtain, his blood trailing into her bathtub. She stared into the bathroom mirror at the pasty white face of a woman running too close to the edge. She stood there and changed that woman's face into her own, strong and sure and ready to kick big butt. She heard a car engine, heard fast footfalls coming toward the front door.

Griffin was here. There was a loud knock on the door, and his steady, sane voice: "Anna?"

CHAPTER
39

Washington, D.C.
Monday evening

It was way past Sean's bedtime, but since Delsey was a new chapter in Sean's life, they'd let him stay up, even microwaved a bag of popcorn. Savich watched Delsey clean the butter off Sean's fingers as he confided in her how his future wife, Emma Hunt, could play the piano nearly as well as his mama. He was going to make sure Emma had a big grand piano so she wouldn't regret marrying him, and maybe Delsey wouldn't mind playing it, too?

Savich grinned as he leaned down to pick up stray popcorn from the kitchen floor. He liked Griffin's sister, the Trouble Magnet, and so did his son.

Jimmy Buffett sang out "The Piña Colada Song" on Savich's cell. Savich met Sherlock's eyes. They both hated late calls because a lot of the time it meant bad things had happened, that their night with Sean was over. He was aware that Delsey was staring hard at him.

"Savich."

He listened to a hysterical Melissa Ivy screaming at him: "He's dead! Oh, dear God, Peter's dead!"

"Where are you, Melissa?"

"I'm in Peter's apartment. I just walked in and he's dead, do you hear me? He's dead!"

"Listen to me now, Melissa, I want you to call 911 and do as they say. Wait for the police. Tell them you called me. We'll be there as quickly as we can."

"What?" Sherlock said.

Savich punched in Detective Moffett's cell number as he said to Sherlock, "Peter Biaggini's dead. That was Melissa Ivy. She found him; she's at his apartment."

"Stony and now Peter? What's going on here? Oh, Delsey, this is about the Tommy Cronin murder. We've got another"—she gave a quick glance at Sean, who was all ears—"incident."

Delsey felt bile rise in her throat, gulped. "I'll take care of Sean." She looked down at the little boy, who was still staring at his parents. "Do you mind staying with me, Sean, while your parents go out and take care of some business?"

Sean thought about this as he watched his father punch in a number on his cell.

"Do I have to go to bed?"

"Not yet. Let's play some Hot Dogger. I'm good, really good at skateboarding, Sean. I can skateboard with the best of them." Hot Dogger, Sean had told her, was like the real thing.

"We only got Hot Dogger a week ago, but Daddy said I'm already a champion at it."

"We'll see. You ready to put your thumbs where your mouth is, Sean?"

"I want to play until Mommy and Daddy get home."

Delsey smiled back at Savich and Sherlock, nodding.

On the third ring, Savich heard a low pissed-off voice. "Yeah? Moffett here. I'm not on call."

"Sorry, Detective, but I need you."

IT TOOK THE PORSCHE only seven minutes to reach Peter Biaggini's upscale apartment building at 322 Willard Avenue. Sherlock had put Mr. Maitland on speakerphone on the way, and he'd nearly flatlined at the news, and finally said he would notify Mr. August Biaggini. "Keep him away from his son's apartment, sir, please," Sherlock said.

"Yes, I will. I'll call Director Mueller, too. Guys, this can't be happening. Three kids are dead, three promising young men. Three! And here I thought Peter Biaggini was behind Tommy Cronin's death, that you were looking hard at him. Who's responsible for this? We've got to put a stop to it, Savich."

There were four cop cars with their running lights

on in front of the apartment building, and two plain Crown Vics. A dozen people were already milling around in the street, wondering what was going on. Savich pulled in behind Detective Moffett's big black SUV. He must live close to be here so quickly.

Savich's first thought upon entering Peter Biaggini's apartment was that Daddy must have laid out a bundle for this place—it was spacious, lots of windows. There was a single posh brass number spelled out on the door—*Three*. When you walked through it, you entered a large entryway that seemed to boast of space by wasting it. Large windows that had to mean lots of light and gorgeous wooden floors led your eyes to a kitchen out of the next century.

They heard sobbing from the living room, but didn't stop there. They walked to the master bedroom at the end of a wide hallway. The three cops near the doorway stepped aside. Detective Moffett said, "Not a pretty sight."

Peter Biaggini, twenty-two years old, lay sprawled on the floor at the foot of his king-size bed, on his back, his head and face a mess of gore. Blood splattered the pale gray bedspread, the gray leather easy chair, had even spewed in an arc high on the bedroom wall. His green cashmere sweater was soaked in his own blood, his blue jeans streaked with it, even down to his black sneakers. His bloodied cell phone lay on the rug next to his arm. And beside his cell lay a highly polished old Bren Ten.

She looked up at Moffett. "The murder weapon, and

the killer left it beside him. Just walked over and dropped it. Leaving it here smacks of a professional, but the chances of that are highly unlikely."

Moffett said, "You'd better believe the killer wiped off the prints, and you can bet there'll be no registration. It looks old, maybe 1970s. We'll check it out."

Savich said, "I wonder why the killer didn't take the pistol and dump it in the Potomac."

Sherlock went down on her knees beside Peter Biaggini's body, fighting sadness and regret, trying to focus. She felt a moment of nausea, swallowed several times. She would have laid her hand against his cheek or his forehead to see how warm he was, but he didn't have a cheek. There was so much blood in a human body. She touched her hand to his throat instead, feeling the sticky wet of his blood. She said, trying her best to keep her voice flat, "He's still quite warm. I'd say he'd been dead only minutes before Melissa got here. When the doorbell buzzed I'll bet Peter thought it was Melissa, so he opened the door without checking, or else he knew the person who killed him. When he saw the gun, I'm thinking he turned and ran, but his killer was right behind him. He would have slammed the bedroom door, locked it? Dillon, could you see if the door's been damaged?"

Savich said, "There's no lock on the bedroom door, no need to shoot it open or slam into it. The killer opened it, and Peter turned to face him, his cell phone in his hand, only he didn't have time to call 911." Savich leaned down, carefully picked up the black cell phone beside Peter Biaggini's right hand to check his calls.

Sherlock sat back on her heels, careful not to touch anything else. She looked around her. "When the door flew open, Peter looked at his killer, maybe he was begging for his life, but it didn't matter, his killer shot him twice in the head from no more than six feet away."

Sherlock got to her feet, stared down at Peter Biaggini. "What a waste, what a horrible waste." And she thought, *Peter, you poked at the wrong lion this time. This lion wasn't twenty years old. He didn't run away; no, this lion ate you.*

Savich said, "His last call was to Melissa Ivy forty-five minutes ago. I'll get Ollie started on the rest of this call history."

Sherlock stared around the room. "Peter's death—it makes no sense. We have to start fresh, Dillon, look at all our assumptions. Tommy, Stony, and Peter—they were friends most of their short lives. They had to be involved in something more dangerous than they knew, with people they shouldn't have been." She looked down once more at the ruin of Peter Biaggini. "They were in over their heads."

"Let's see what Melissa knows," Savich said.

CHAPTER
40

Melissa Ivy was rocking back and forth on the expensive burgundy leather sofa, her beautiful face slack, her eyes vague, unfocused. A female officer held a cup of no doubt very sweet tea in her hand, encouraging her to drink, then holding the cup to her mouth as she sipped, all the while speaking quietly to her, telling her to breathe.

Melissa was wrapped up in two afghans that looked to be hand-knit, Sherlock thought, probably by Peter's mother. It was odd that she was sitting in a living room as modern as Wakefield Hart's house in Tunney Wells.

The female officer moved aside, and Savich sat beside Melissa, took her limp hand. "Melissa? Do you remember you called me? I'm Agent Savich. I need to speak with you, all right? I need your help."

There was no sign of life from Melissa, not a sound, not a blink, only her relentless rocking back and forth. It always surprised him at how quickly shock could leach the life out of a person. Even Melissa's hair looked dull under the cold light of the fluorescent lamps scattered around the living room.

Sherlock sat down on the sofa on Melissa's other side, slipped her hand beneath the brilliant blue afghan, and lightly stroked her forearm. "Someone killed Peter, Melissa. Do you know who it was?"

Melissa slowly turned her head to look at Sherlock, looked through her, really, Sherlock thought. "Did you see someone, Melissa? We want to catch the person who killed Peter. Can you help us?"

Melissa licked her lips, leaned toward Sherlock, and whispered, "I didn't know who you were until yesterday. Isn't that strange? And now you're stroking my arm because Peter's dead. Three days—Tommy and Peter are both dead. Stony, too. How can that be?"

"Talk to me, Melissa. Did you see anyone? Hear Peter speak to anyone?"

Her voice was so thin Sherlock imagined she could see through it. "I talked to Janelle, Stony's girlfriend. It was horrible she found Stony's body. Just like I found Peter."

"Yes, I know."

"I wanted her to know how sorry I was. She . . . she

couldn't stop crying. She was waiting for her parents to drive in from Delaware to take her home." She turned deadened eyes to Sherlock. "There isn't anyone for me to go home to."

"Do you want me to call your folks?"

"No, they're in Kentucky, and they really wouldn't want to come here. Do you know, I was thinking that Peter probably did drug me, even if he wasn't using me for an alibi. I didn't tell you, but I was real sore Saturday morning, like he'd done things to me he shouldn't have. Peter was like that; he was cruel, he used people. Peter didn't love me, not like Tommy did."

Her voice fell into a pit. She lowered her face in her hands, but she didn't cry.

Sherlock met Dillon's eyes over Melissa's head. His eyes were cold and flat, but he didn't know what to say to this girl who'd gotten together with the wrong boy, a boy craven enough to give his girlfriend a roofie in her wine. In their first meeting with her, she'd lied through her perfect white teeth, but not now, she was too shocked, too strung out. She was only twenty years old, young enough to have believed even a week ago the world's doors would be flung open for her. She was beautiful enough, surely, to attract boys with money to help her with her bills and tuition. But she'd never counted on a Peter Biaggini, and now her world was in tatters. She would have nightmares for a very long time, maybe for the rest of her life.

Sherlock pulled Melissa into her arms and rocked her. Still, Melissa didn't weep, didn't move. Sherlock stroked her long, straight hair, then said against her cheek, "Why did you come over to Peter's apartment, Melissa?"

Silence, then a whisper: "He begged me to come over, said he needed me. I thought he wanted to apologize after our fight yesterday, wanted to make up. Now I'll never know what he wanted to say to me."

Sherlock said, "Let's go back a minute. You spent some of Saturday with Peter because both you and he were upset about Tommy?"

"I think I was more upset than Peter was. He was quiet for a long time on Saturday, like he had a lot on his mind, like he was really worried rather than sad, or maybe he was scared of something."

Sherlock said, "Did you ask him what was wrong? If he was scared and why?"

"He wouldn't tell me anything. I started crying, not about how cold he was being, but about Tommy. I told Peter Tommy had really been a nice guy, and Peter gave this ugly laugh and said I was wrong about that. He said Tommy was no saint.

"That was so weird, and I asked him why he'd say that, now that Tommy was dead, but he wouldn't tell me. Then he got this look on his face like he'd come to some decision, nodding and talking to himself. He acted nervous, jumpy, you know what I mean?"

"You don't know what he was nervous about?"

Melissa shook her head. "Since he was being such a jerk, I left. The snow had lightened up, so I hooked a ride on a motorcycle."

"Did you see Peter yesterday?"

She nodded. "He called me after you interviewed him and his dad. He sounded really pleased with himself, said how he rubbed your noses in it since we were together in Georgetown Friday night, at that gallery."

Savich said, "Do you know if he spoke to Stony yesterday?"

"I don't know." She raised her eyes to Savich's face. "Stony killed himself. Why did he kill himself? I don't understand it. All three of them are dead, just dead. Why?"

"We have to find out," Sherlock said. "Melissa, what exactly did you and Peter fight about last night before you went to the rave with Janelle?"

"I finally accused him of drugging my wine. He denied it, of course, grinned at me. Do you know he said I should have some more of that wine, since it made me so wild? He thought he had the right, you know? Because he was helping me pay some bills. He didn't have the right."

"No, he didn't," Sherlock said. "No one has that right."

Savich said, "You got here at what time, Melissa?"

She blinked at him, as if she couldn't quite understand what he'd said. She looked at Sherlock, who said, "Was it about nine o'clock when you knocked on his door?"

"Closer to nine-fifteen, maybe."

Sherlock said. "Now, Melissa, I want you to think about when you arrived here at the apartment building tonight. Did you see anyone you didn't recognize?

Maybe someone running or walking very quickly here in the building or outside when you drove up?"

She paused to think, and that was good, Savich thought; she was focusing her brain. Finally, she shook her head. "No, I didn't see anybody."

Savich brought up hypnosis. Melissa said, "Do you think I could really remember more?"

"Yes," he said, "I do."

"Then I'll think about it, I promise, Agent Savich," she said, and turned back to stare down at her pink UGGs.

CHAPTER
41

Maestro, Virginia
Monday evening

Rolling clouds scuttled over the black sky again, threatening snow before morning. It was only nine o'clock, but already the temperature had dived so low it was too cold to breathe comfortably without a wool scarf covering your mouth.

Griffin looked at Anna's taillights, a couple dozen feet ahead. It seemed they were the only two people on the winding roads in Maestro. He knew she didn't want to go back to her cottage, since she'd packed and locked her duffel in the trunk, but she hadn't found Monk and she'd looked in all his hiding places. They'd find Monk together. When she'd said it was her fault because she'd spooked the cat, acted like a madwoman, he got in her face and told her not to be an idiot. He took her seriously when she'd told him if anyone at the B&B said anything about pets, she'd draw her gun and shoot them.

She hadn't wanted to have dinner at the Nobles' house, but Griffin had known she needed the distraction, needed contact with the real world again. He'd talked about Dix's barbecued ribs and potato salad and Ruth's green salad she always made for show until he'd swear Anna was salivating.

Anna wasn't salivating now. She felt jumpy and worried, not only about Monk but about everything that was happening so fast she couldn't get her mind around it.

When she'd backed out of her driveway to follow Griffin to the Nobles' house, she was wondering if she'd ever see her cottage again after today. No, it was all over for her here in Maestro, and it was all on her record— she'd failed here, miserably. Arnie Racker had been murdered under her nose, and she'd learned nothing of value except that being in Salazar's house had gotten him killed—that, and her vastly improved violin technique. Six months wasted, along with the taxpayers' money and her time. All of it made her want to scream and cry at the same time.

Still, she thought now, Dix and Ruth had made her glad she'd come. It felt safe and warm in the Nobles' house, and she'd felt herself relax with each passing minute. She'd packed away nearly as many ribs as the

Nobles' two sons, Rafe and Rob, good-looking teenagers who'd wanted to know everything about the shootings in Maestro. They groused and complained at the dinner table when their father cut short their questions, but they'd left happily enough to study, since that meant they wouldn't have to help clean up.

Dix sat back in his chair when he was sure they were out of hearing and folded his arms over his chest, now dead serious. "Claus couldn't locate Chigger Chivers, even went out to that fleabag shack he lives in. He's probably okay; he can be hard to track down sometimes. But I agree with you, Anna, Chigger heard every word you guys said. Don't know if he understood it all, since his brain's been pickled for decades from all the moonshine he's cooked over the years."

They were distracted when they heard Brewster yipping madly, and heard the boys talking and laughing as the front door closed behind them. Ruth said, "Brewster likes to dance in the snow, catch snowflakes in his mouth. Unfortunately, he never remembers he always sinks like a stone.". She paused and looked at Anna. "We'll plan something out first thing tomorrow morning, Anna. Are you sure you don't want to stay here tonight?"

Anna carefully set down her coffee mug with MAESTRO COUGARS written in bold red across it. "Thank you, Ruth, but I'll be fine with Griffin." She looked at each of them. "I can't stand that I'm afraid of those monsters. They can't do this, guys. Not here, not to us."

Griffin lightly laid his hand over hers. "We'll get it done."

She stood up. "I need to get back to my house and find Monk. Then I'll follow Griffin to the B&B."

Griffin rose to stand beside her as she said her good-byes and walked beside her out to her Kia, his hand cupped around her neck.

Yes, Griffin thought, they would get it done. His brain clicked back to the here and now and the casket-black darkness as he watched Anna pull her car into the driveway. He pulled in behind her. It boggled his brain when he realized he'd met her for the first time less than three days ago. He was thinking that over, starting to open his car door, when he realized something wasn't right.

The streetlight was out.

He sat on his horn, shoved open the car door, and rolled out onto the driveway just as an automatic weapon opened up into his Camry, shredding the metal, shattering the windows, so many so fast the car seemed to lift and sway on the asphalt. He rolled behind the rear tire and was relieved to see Anna on her belly not ten feet from him, one arm covering her head, the other holding her Glock.

His ears were ringing, adrenaline pumping so wildly Griffin felt he could shoot Superman out of the sky, but his training took over, and he focused. He counted three separate weapons, firing at will, grouped in the woods on the driver's side of the cars.

He saw she was still pressed against the asphalt, waiting. He yelled, "Anna, stay down!"

Then he heard it, a whistling sound, and he jumped

to his feet, firing as he ran. He slammed down beside Anna, then pulled her beneath him as his car exploded into flames. He saw the car roof fly into the air. The backseat and the steering wheel crashed to the ground. He covered her head as hot debris fell down around them. One tire rolled into the street, and another was ripped to pieces, flinging scraps of burning rubber everywhere. He grunted when something struck him, and when she looked up at him, he said against her cheek, "We've got to move; your car's next."

He rolled off her, and together they backed away on their hands and knees as fast as they could, only twenty feet to a row of trees behind them. Bullets sprayed randomly around them, mostly over their heads.

Despite the billowing black smoke, Griffin knew they could be seen because of the mad orange flames firecracking into the sky, light so brilliant the shards of glass from his car's windshield glittered like slivers of sun.

It happened fast. Two grenades struck Anna's car, lifting it off the ground. The explosion sucked up the air, the force of it hurling them back. He saw a tire jack fly outward over them like a boomerang, and thick burning smoke clogged their throats. Then they heard a shout, a curse, then more gunfire. It was all around them, a rock splitting apart not a foot from Griffin's arm, peppering the hard ground, sending frozen clots of earth exploding into the air. Then the spray of bullets moved away, toward the cottage. They were firing blind.

When they pressed behind a pine tree, Griffin knew

they had a chance. He grabbed her hand and they raced another thirty feet into the forest. They stopped, panting, sucking in the clean air, and turned toward the light of their burning cars through the trees. They listened as the gunfire slowly died away. They heard men cursing in a mixture of English and Spanish. Someone was moaning.

Griffin said against her ear, "I must have hit one of them when I was laying down fire to get to you."

They heard another man's voice. "They're dead. No way could they survive that."

The best words Anna had ever heard in her life.

Griffin said, his voice a whisper, "Three different voices. They'll wait, stay hidden and quiet, and see what happens. If they have a brain, they won't step into the open, won't take the chance either of us survived. Keep moving back, quiet and slow."

They slithered back as quietly as they could, and heard the blessed sound of sirens in the distance. "Okay, this is good." Griffin pulled out his cell and punched in Ruth's number.

Ruth's frantic voice blasted out of his cell. "Griffin? What's happening? Dix got a call from 911. What's going on? Tell me the two of you are all right. We'll be there inside three minutes."

She punched off before Griffin could say a word. He slipped his cell back into his coat pocket. "That smell—you forget what burning rubber smells like. Did you hear an engine revving? The second they heard the sirens they were out of here. Too bad my car is history."

Anna stared at him. She grabbed his face between her hands and kissed him hard.

He kissed her back, his hands in her filthy hair, stroking down her back, bringing her hard against him.

Between kisses, she said, "Who cares about a freaking car? I don't care about mine, do you? We're alive. That's a miracle," and she continued to kiss him.

Finally she leaned back in his arms. "Were you hurt?"

The instant Griffin heard the words he felt a burning pain in his left thigh. He grunted in surprise, and then his leg collapsed and down he went. He lay on his back, staring up at her, his hand pressed hard against his leg. "Your mouth—I didn't realize how much I liked the taste of smoke."

"Yeah, yeah," she said, on her knees beside him, pressing down hard on his leg. Siren lights cut through the trees. They heard voices shouting, back where the cars burned, billowing up thick black smoke into the night. They saw a flashlight, heard a woman's voice yelling their names. It was Ruth. When the flashlight landed on Anna, Griffin said, "You've got blood all over your face."

Anna touched her cheek, felt the trickle of oozing blood, then the sting of a glass cut. "Not bad, and I don't think your leg's gonna fall off, either." She grinned at him, leaned down, kissed him again, then jumped to her feet. "Apply pressure. I've got to find Monk."

CHAPTER
42

Henderson County Hospital
Late Monday night

It was strange to see Griffin in the very same hospital,
lying in the same kind of bed Delsey had occupied.
There was a drip in his arm, and his eyes were veiled
with drugs, but he was thrumming his fingers on the
light hospital coverlet. "Is that museum print a Monet?"

"Yep. Glad you can see it."

"Only an impression."

"Ha ha." She leaned over him, covered his hand with
hers. "But we made it. Guess what? You managed to
draw the same doctor as Delsey—Dr. Chesney. She says
you're lucky to have the war wound everyone used to
hope for: some stitches, a little soreness, and a sexy limp

for a while, and best of all, some feel-good drugs and a bed for the night. She said you'll be out tomorrow."

He gave her a lopsided grin, took her hand in his, and pulled her down to him. He kissed her, hard and fast, and laughed. "You still taste like smoke. Tomorrow's good. We've got lots to do. You're really pretty, you know that? And the smoke, it really does taste fine."

"Griffin, you do know you kissed me and not Dr. Chesney, right? I mean, how drugged up are you?"

"Maybe more than I'd like, but who cares?"

But I'm not drugged up at all, and a girl's gotta take her chance when she gets one.

She leaned down and kissed him just as hard, just as fast, and thought, *What a great decision that was.* She cupped his cheek in her palm. "You taste pretty fine yourself."

She started to straighten, but he grabbed her arm, kept her close. "Why'd you do that, Anna?"

She studied his drop-dead gorgeous face. Truth was, what she really wanted was to burrow right into the man behind those incredible eyes to learn every single thing about him. Even after only a few days, she recognized rare and special when she saw it. "What did you say?"

"I want to know why you kissed me."

"I figured one good turn and all that."

"Yeah? That's it?"

"Okay, I wanted to."

He nodded slowly. "Good. So did I. Did I mention I like your smoke taste?"

"Which time?"

His eyes were on her mouth. He gave her a grin that could lead a girl astray if she weren't chained to the path. "I'll take the first. No, wait, the second, when you kissed me. I gotta think about this." And from one moment to the next, his eyes closed, his head fell to the side, and he was out.

She stood over him a long time, studying his face. That something special she saw in him—she was thinking part of it was pure grit. She had to admit she didn't mind the pretty face, surely a treat to see across the breakfast table every single morning, but she knew if the Fairy Godmother of Good Looks hadn't perched on his crib railing, she would still fly to him like a buzzed moth. As she'd journeyed through her twenties, she'd come to see herself as the consummate kick-butt DEA agent until—until what? Until she ran the Agency? Now, there was a thought—all alone at the top? Maybe there could be something else in her life now.

"Anna?"

She jumped, turned to see Ruth in the doorway.

"Sorry I startled you. How's Griffin?"

"He's out, but before he cashed in his chips, he thought he was winning the jackpot." Well, she felt like she'd surely won.

The silly look on Anna's face gave Ruth a very clear picture of what had happened. *Very nice,* she thought. *Very nice indeed.* "Nothing like anesthesia and drugs," Ruth said. "Dr. Chesney said he'd be smiling and sleepy for a good eight hours. Then he'd hurt a bit, but he'll heal quickly, and that's all that counts. All the rest fades into the past over time."

"He wants to be out of here tomorrow."

"He'll probably be good to go. We'll see how he feels in the morning. We've got all our people out, federal and local, manning checkpoints and looking for those morons who attacked you. No luck yet."

"What about Salazar?"

"Everyone's agreed now, no more waiting. We're serving a federal search warrant on Salazar's place in the morning and bringing him in for questioning. In fact, we're bringing in every MS-13 thug we can find in three counties. They've started a war by attacking you and Griffin, and they're going to lose it."

"Griffin's gonna want to be in on all of it."

"Sure thing, if he's up to it."

Anna looked down again at Griffin, saw he was breathing easily, deeply. "I think I'll stay here with him tonight. Did you find Monk?"

"I finally found him under your bed. He'd ripped open the bottom of the mattress and burrowed up inside. I pulled him out with an EMT's help, stuffed him into his traveling case, and took him home along with cat food and his litter box. He's calmed down now."

"What did Brewster think of a cat who could eat him for breakfast? Monk weighs a good twenty pounds."

"It was Brewster who got him to come out of his carrying case. The boys were ready to hurl themselves in front of Brewster if Monk attacked him. The funny thing is, after the two of them stared each other down, sniffed, growled, and hissed, they decided to have a nap together. The boys are still hovering, in case. Don't worry. When I left to come here, Monk was washing himself on the sofa, Brewster standing guard." Ruth patted her arm. "Griffin's okay, cat's okay, all of you are safe." Ruth looked at the Band-Aid on Anna's cheek. Both of them were very lucky. She started to ask her if she'd rather come home with her, but kept silent. It was probably safer here, both for her and for Griffin, especially with the guard posted outside the door.

"You do need to rest, Anna; even if you didn't get shot or burned, you'll feel it tomorrow." And because she knew Anna needed it, Ruth gave her a hug and said against her hair, "This will be over soon. It can't be long now."

WHEN GRIFFIN CAME TO at three o'clock in the morning, he knew where he was immediately, and that was good. He queried his leg. Surprisingly, he didn't feel a lick of pain. The nurses had propped his leg up on two skinny hospital pillows and he was toasty warm, his brain still buzzed with sleep and drugs. He heard breathing and froze, reached out his hand to flip on the directional lamp fastened to the side of his bed. He saw Anna not six feet from him, sound asleep on a narrow hospital cot, covers pulled up to her nose. Her face was turned toward him, and her dark hair hung over the side of the cot nearly to the floor. He hadn't realized her hair was so long, since she usually wore it braided or up in a pony-tail. He knew her face well now, and after only a few days. Amazing. He also knew how she tasted, how she felt against him, how she was so brave it scared him. He decided then and there that he wanted to visit Bosard, Louisiana, with her, wanted to look out at the bayou with her, and have her show him alligators. He wanted to meet her family and see if she resembled the mother who'd named her Lilyanna.

He'd met her Saturday, not Saturday six months ago, but Saturday only days before. Objectively, he should think wanting this woman in his life for the next fifty years, maybe more, was nuts. But now, in the middle of the night, with everything quiet and the air warm, and that long hair of hers hanging over the side of the cot, it seemed eminently reasonable. His brain snapped awake at that thought, and he chewed it over, decided it was an excellent thought, one of the best he'd ever had. What was even better, he was thinking in a straight line.

She moaned in her sleep, flopped onto her back. Was she dreaming about her car exploding, feeling that she couldn't breathe, that death was an instant away? He remembered how time had almost stopped until he'd pulled her under him as his car exploded. He turned off the lamp and closed his eyes, content that his SIG was in his bedside drawer and a deputy was outside his door.

Why didn't they blow up our cars at the same time? We'd be dead, gone. Why blow up my car before Anna's?

Because I saw the man running away in the alley last night? Because I was a witness, like Delsey is still a witness? She still wasn't safe, he knew it, but there was nothing to do tonight.

He heard Anna make a small yipping sound in her sleep as his brain tottered on the edge of oblivion, and he smiled before he fell asleep.

CHAPTER
43

The house alarm screeched, waking them as the hall clock struck three o'clock. Savich leapt out of bed, grabbed his SIG, and ran to the flashing alarm display on his bedroom wall. The outside floodlights came on as he read the LED: *Motion detected, bedroom 2 window.*

He raced across the hall, Sherlock behind him, with the alarm still blasting. Delsey was standing in the middle of the hall, Sean plastered against her, Astro dancing and barking around Sean's legs. "You guys are fast," Savich said. "Don't worry, it's okay." He and Sherlock disappeared into Delsey's bedroom and ran to the window. They looked down. An aluminum extension ladder teetered on its edge on the bushes below them, but no one was in sight. The ladder had tripped the alarm before the intruder could even climb up. He had to be running from the lights, long gone. Savich said to Sherlock, "Check all the upstairs windows; I'll take downstairs."

"You guys sure got out of bed fast," Sherlock said, pressing her SIG down along her leg as she patted Sean's shoulder. "Everything's okay. Sean, you and Delsey stay right here. Astro the Mighty Dog will protect you. I'm going to check the windows. Routine, not to worry. It's probably a battery out." She was aware Delsey was staring at her, and she smiled at her, nodding. She was glad Sean couldn't hear how heavy and fast her heart was pumping.

"I'll be right back." She didn't raise her SIG until she was out of sight again.

Of course, Delsey knew the story about the battery was meant for Sean's ears. She calmed herself; she was the adult, she had to calm Sean. She knelt down beside him and said in a chatty voice as she patted Astro's head, "Alarms malfunction all the time, Sean, don't worry."

"It's never gone off before," Sean said.

"Well, there's always a first time. We'll stay here with Astro until your mom and dad turn it off, then we can get back to sleep, okay?"

Sherlock walked back into the hallway to see Sean

talking to Delsey, not a shadow of fear on his small face, bless her. She smiled at them. "It's okay," she said, and at that moment, Dillon switched the alarm off and the sudden dead silence seemed more frightening than the blasting noise.

Delsey knew by Sherlock's face that something was happening, that it was no malfunction, and that Sherlock was still frightened for Sean. But there was nothing she could do, nothing at all. She kept stroking Sean's shoulder, petting Astro.

Sherlock called out, "Dillon, we're clear up here. Everything's shut and locked."

"Here, too," Savich shouted back.

Delsey stepped back into her bedroom, her eyes on her window, and she knew her window alarm had gone off, and that meant someone had wanted to come in and kill her, like the gang thug in Maestro. She swallowed convulsively. She hadn't realized Sean had followed her until she felt his small hand on her arm.

"I wonder who wanted to come in your room, Delsey."

"I don't know, Sean. Maybe the postman with a special delivery, you think?"

He thought about this. "I don't think so, Delsey, not at night. Don't worry, Mommy and Daddy will find out if the postman came to your window. They always find out everything."

They walked back into the hall to see Sean's mommy and daddy meet at the head of the stairs and speak quietly to each other, Sherlock wearing cat pajamas and

Savich in a tee and boxers. They came over together, and Savich took Sean from her. Sherlock rubbed Sean's back, and Astro started barking wildly again, and so she picked him up. He licked any part of her he could reach. "Yeah, yeah, Astro, stop eating my hair. Sean, did the alarm wake you up from a neat dream?"

Sean pulled back in his father's arms. "Who wanted to get in Delsey's room? She said it was the postman with a special delivery, but that's silly."

Maybe so, but you're not scared out of your head. Savich kissed his forehead. "We'll find that out first thing in the morning, okay? I don't think it was the postman, either. He's too old to climb up to her window."

"You'd have bashed him, Papa."

"Yeah, there's that. You ready to go back to dreamland?"

Sean nodded, looked over at Delsey. "You'll take good care of her, won't you, Papa?"

Sherlock gave him a smacking wet kiss. "We will, Sean, we both will. Now, we have a couple of patrol guys coming over. You and Delsey go back to bed, and your papa and I will speak to them. Sean, take Astro and give him lots of hugs; he's still scared."

The doorbell rang a minute later as they walked down the front stairs, Savich in sweatpants and Sherlock in a robe. Savich said, "I think the Trouble Magnet has landed in Georgetown. Amazing they'd come after her here. She knew, of course, and she's scared. She doesn't know yet that Griffin was hurt last night. I'll let him tell her himself in the morning."

"Have you checked your cell lately, Dillon?"

"It didn't even cross my radar."

"We got a text from forensics. They traced the serial number on the gun in Peter's bedroom, the gun that killed him. You won't believe this."

CHAPTER
44

Tuesday morning

Savich had half an eye on Sean as he ate a mini English muffin with turkey bacon and mayonnaise, his miniature BLT. Sean didn't look at all upset, Savich thought, as if he'd already forgotten about all the excitement in the middle of the night. Astro was sitting at his feet, waiting for another piece of bacon Sean was sure to slip him. He pulled out his cell to call Griffin and saw that this time Bo Horsley had texted him and he simply hadn't heard the buzz. *I know you're still up to your ears in bad guys. Call me when you can.*

Savich started to punch in Bo's number, realized Bo was right—he was up to his ears. Whatever was going on in New York, it could wait a bit longer. He looked

over at Delsey as he tapped Griffin's number. She was
sipping black coffee out of a Redskins mug, trying not
to look scared for Sean's sake, maybe for her own sake,
too. Her head snapped up when she heard him say her
brother's name.

Savich gave her a quick smile and walked out of the
kitchen into the dining room. He didn't want Sean
to hear him—didn't want to worry about Delsey, either, for that matter. He told Griffin concisely what had
happened. ". . . Two officers were here within minutes,
and the three of us checked out the neighborhood.
There was nothing but the brand-new ladder." He
paused for a moment, listened. "No, Delsey's all right,
but she's scared. You'll need to tell her yourself what
shape you're in."

"Yeah, I will. Got to assume he was after Delsey,
maybe that gangbanger we saw in the alley outside the
B&B, but in your own home? The same night they came
at Anna and me in Maestro? Has whoever's in charge in
that gang totally flipped?"

Savich said, "These people are organized, but they
appear to have more muscle and commitment than
brains. They came at an alarmed house of armed FBI
agents without even thinking it through. There are
easier ways to take out a witness."

Griffin said, "They must have been in a hurry. They
had to be watching the house, watching you through
the windows, if they picked the right bedroom."

Savich said, "They're crude and they're acting desperate, and that makes them dangerous. I'll take steps now,

Griffin. Trust me, I'll protect her. What's happening there? How are you feeling?"

"My leg's a little sore," Griffin said. "The doc wants me to hang around until this afternoon, but we're serving Salazar with a search warrant this morning, taking him into custody for questioning. No way I'm missing that.

"Savich, there's something I've been thinking about. This gang has struck in Maestro three times now, always at night, and last night with a lot of firepower. But no one has ever seen a gang presence in town, or around Stanislaus. They've disappeared every time, around our checkpoints and everyone out looking for them. They've been moving drugs in and through the area, and the DEA hasn't found them, either. I'm thinking they've got to have some local hideout somewhere near town they can get to by back roads."

Savich agreed. "The DEA has been checking property records, deeds, leases, even going door to door, Griffin. I put MAX to work on it yesterday. I'll see what we've got, check with Dix to see if he can help us narrow the search."

WHEN GRIFFIN RANG off the phone with Delsey a few minutes later, he looked over at Anna's nicely made cot, and then up at the clock. He felt a little pulse of pain when he put weight on his leg, but it wasn't bad. He limped to the bathroom. He was pulling on his wrecked pants from last night's firefight when Nurse Morsi came in, a tray of instruments in her hand. She stared at him zipping up his trousers. She sputtered, then said, "Agent Hammersmith, you get back in bed this instant. Dr. Chesney wants to check your leg before you leave, and I need—"

Griffin said over her, "If you could give me some aspirin for the road, I'd appreciate it. And maybe help me get my boots on."

CHAPTER
45

Tunney Wells, Virginia
Tuesday morning

Savich hadn't called ahead because he'd thought it better to surprise Wakefield Hart than to give him time to prepare for them with a lawyer at his side and, most important, get rid of evidence. He wanted to see Hart's face when he told him about Peter Biaggini's murder. How good an actor was he? He and Sherlock nodded to the agents and the CSI team holding back, with their vehicles parked a good half block from the Harts' house, pulled into the driveway, and walked to the front door.

"We're here to see Mr. and Mrs. Hart, Regina."

She looked them up and down silently, nodded, and

led them through the tall entryway, with its modern glass-block partitions and sculptures, to the glass living room.

Savich's eyes passed from the artfully recessed web-cam in the molding above them and down to Wakefield and Carolyn Hart. They were sitting side by side on the stark white sofa, a Meissen coffeepot and cups arranged beside a creamer and sugar bowl on a tray on the glass coffee table in front of them. It appeared they hadn't touched any of it. They weren't looking at each other; both were silent, as if sitting alone, their faces vacant with grief. Both looked up when Savich and Sherlock stepped into the living room. Savich saw a flicker of alarm in Wakefield Hart's dark eyes, but Mrs. Hart's eyes were unfocused, disinterested. Savich wondered how many sedatives she'd taken this morning, and if this was how she dealt with life in general. They hadn't met her formally, but he didn't want to take time for intro-ductions. He said from the doorway, "We came to tell you that Peter Biaggini was murdered last night."

Hart didn't shrink back, didn't feign confusion or ignorance. He rose straight up, his face tight, his eyes hard. "That worthless piece of scum is dead? He took our boy away from us, drove him to kill himself. Who did it? Who else did he hurt?"

What to make of this? *But not unexpected,* Savich thought. *No, not at all unexpected.* As for Mrs. Hart, she didn't move, didn't even blink. She seemed frozen, apart from all of them, except for her pale eyes. They were fastened on her husband's red face.

Savich said, "I need to know where you were last night, Mr. Hart."

There was a moment of stunned silence, and then Mrs. Hart said in a loud, clear voice, "Wakefield was here with me. He did not go anywhere. We had friends over to help with Stony's funeral arrangements. The wake is on Wednesday night, the funeral on Thursday at noon at the First Presbyterian Church of Tunney Wells. We had to wait because Wakefield's parents are flying in from Montana." Her voice broke and she turned her head away, holding herself stiff, her arms wrapped around herself, rocking, silent again.

Hart said, "When our friends left, neither of us felt like going anywhere. I know what I said was harsh. We are both truly sorry for Peter's parents, both nice people who will suffer for this. But what they loosed on the earth in Peter is—was—an abomination. Peter didn't love anyone, particularly them. He felt nothing but contempt for his father and indifference for his mother. He thought she was useless. I heard him say once that her only expertise was opening cans, in that dismissive, arrogant voice he had."

Mrs. Hart slowly rose. She tried to stand ramrod straight, though she swayed a bit, as if unsteady from too many drugs. Her face, Sherlock saw, was leached of color, but hard and set, as if she were trying to mask her pain from them.

Sherlock had seen several photos of Mrs. Hart and thought her a handsome woman, probably quite spectacular-looking when she'd been younger, a woman who seemed at home in her moneyed world and knew how to conduct herself on all its occasions. Now, Sherlock thought, she looked as though she'd been knocked sideways, loose from all the familiar moorings. Her hair was dull and limp, and still, deep lines scored the flesh around her mouth. The pants and sweater she was wearing looked too big for her. She looked as if death had touched her on the shoulder, caressed her cheek, then passed over her to take her only son, Stony, and her own soul with it.

She had to be a strong woman, Sherlock imagined, to have spent her life with a husband like Wakefield Hart. What did she think of him, this man who'd been up to his ears in joyous greed, and then profited again from the banking collapse by attacking the very people he'd once shared his bed with? Like Palmer Cronin. Did she not care? Whatever she thought of Wakefield Hart, whatever she'd suffered, she had stood up as tall as she could, and given her husband an alibi.

Sherlock said, "I'm sure we are all sorry for the Biagginis, Mr. Hart. What they will want from the FBI is to find his murderer. There are three young people dead by violence now. Tommy Cronin brutally murdered and left at the Lincoln Memorial, your son's suicide, and now Peter. We don't know yet who killed Tommy, Mr. Hart, but you have the motive to have killed Peter, you have told us so yourself. You could easily have slipped out of here last night and driven to Peter's apartment."

Savich picked it up. "When he answered your knock, did he see his death in your eyes? I'm betting you had the gun pointed at him and he ran into his bedroom, only there was no lock. And when you caught him, you shot him twice in the head. Did you imagine what it would be like, Mr. Hart, to have Peter's brain matter and blood splattered over you? Did his blood soak into your clothes, feel sticky and wet against your skin?"

Wakefield Hart raised his fisted hand and screamed at them, "I did not kill that puking little bastard! I never left home last night! Listen to my wife, she's not lying. Ask our friends, we were here."

Savich said. "You own a gun, do you not, Mr. Hart? Your father's Bren Ten, a gun he gave you?"

"My father did give me a gun when I turned sixteen, but I haven't seen that old Bren Ten in years. It may be in the attic somewhere, I don't know."

"It isn't in your attic, Mr. Hart. We have it. It was the gun used to kill Peter last night."

Hart reared back, opened his mouth, closed it, and seamed his lips. He looked confused, Savich thought, perhaps bewildered, but why? Then he looked down, as if studying the tassels on his Italian loafers. He shook his head, his hands clenching and unclenching at his sides. When he finally looked again at Savich, he'd wiped all expression from his face.

Savich waited, but Hart said nothing.

Sherlock stepped forward. "Mr. Hart, this is a warrant to search your house without restriction. Our forensic team is already waiting outside." Sherlock handed him the warrant, watching his face.

Mrs. Hart looked toward her husband, whirled back

around, and shouted, "You're saying my husband killed Peter with that ancient, ugly weapon? That's a horrible thing to say; it's ridiculous. He was here with me, all evening and all night! I have told you so. He did not leave. He did not kill Peter. He's right, neither of us have seen that gun in decades. It could have been stolen years ago, do you hear me? We haven't seen it! Are you accusing me of lying?"

Sherlock said. "Not yet, ma'am."

Savich had already texted the CSI team outside, and Tom Leads showed his face in the glass living room. Mrs. Hart yelled at him, "Our daughters are upstairs in their rooms. Will you at least leave them alone to grieve for their brother? Or are you going to tell them you believe their father killed someone?"

Tom Leads, father of six, said, "No, ma'am, we will respect your daughters' privacy. However, it might be better for you to arrange for them to go elsewhere. If you wish to go up to them, it's quite all right."

Savich saw Mrs. Hart look at her husband and slowly shake her head. "I must stay here. You will be respectful," she added fiercely, and Tom nodded.

Savich's cell rang. He walked into the hallway, saw Regina was there, her eyes red from crying. Naturally, she'd been listening.

He heard Hart yelling through the door at Sherlock, "My wife has sworn to you I was here last night. I'm calling my lawyer, to put an end to this harassment. We're going to bury our son on Thursday. Does that mean nothing to you?"

"Yes, Mr. Hart, it means a lot to me," Sherlock said. "It breaks my heart. For your family's sake, you should have waited to kill Peter until after you buried Stony."

That drew Hart up, but only for a moment. Savich heard him mutter something, but couldn't make out the words because he was trying to listen to Ollie on his cell. "While we were out interviewing your neighbors about the alarm last night, Delsey spotted an SUV cruising your neighborhood in Georgetown. She's got eagle eyes, Savich, and she tagged the car. The SUV was reported stolen right out of a garage in Mount Perse, Maryland. We'll go check that out. As you know, Coop is staying with Delsey. You know he'll keep her safe."

They'd taken Sean to spend the day with his grandmother, so he was out of harm's way, his short-term future bright with the promise of a half a dozen chocolate-chip cookies. Savich looked up when one forensic team leader, Ray Voss, called out, "Agent Savich, could you come over here, please? Bring Agent Sherlock."

CHAPTER
46

They followed Ray into a laundry room behind a large, painfully modern kitchen with stainless-steel appliances so highly polished they looked brand-new. The laundry was large and utilitarian, lined with shelves filled with detergents, softeners, cleaning liquids, and stain removers, no doubt for Regina's use.

Ray pointed to piles of freshly washed and folded clothes. "We'll start out with pictures of everything in here before we start looking for blood on those clothes. As you know, even washing can't get out all the blood. Nothing can. We'll go over the interior of the washer and drier with Luminol. If anyone washed bloody clothes in this washer, we'll find a trace. I'll tell you, I've got a feeling about this."

Savich did, too. "We'll have to hope he didn't burn the clothes or dump them."

Ray said, "We'll check the clothes hampers, spray all the sinks and showers, see if anyone washed blood off themselves last night. If you really think he was stupid enough to bury the clothes in the backyard, or even farther out in the woods, we can get that bloodhound, Bitsy, from the Washington Field Office out here. She can find anything."

"Good, Ray. I'll leave you to it."

"Wait a minute, guys; this was just my opening prelude. Now let's get to it. Come take a look at this."

Ray led them through another door to a large storage area with more shelves and bins holding luggage, ski paraphernalia, and golf equipment. He opened a smaller door, flipped a light switch, and ushered them in.

"Would you take a look at this."

They were in the control room for what once had been the complex and highly sophisticated surveillance system. Now it was a jumbled mess of ripped-out wires and connections, all the system guts strewn on the tiled floor.

Sherlock said, "Torn to shreds by very angry hands, not neatly uninstalled. Look, there's no dust where the computer sat. This was done recently."

Savich said, "Systems like this one are typically motion activated and store their audio and video on rewritable DVDs. I don't see any."

"They're all gone," Ray said, "and I've looked.

Maybe they're hidden in the house; if so, we'll find them. If they've been tossed, well—" He shrugged.

Savich knew in his gut the disks weren't here in the house. What was on them?

He and Sherlock returned to the living room, where the Harts stood silent and still at opposite ends of the room. Because Mrs. Hart had finally realized her husband was a murderer? He said, "Mr. Hart, where else in this house do you have cameras installed for your surveillance system?"

"What? You still think I spy on people who visit my house? That's insulting, Agent. I told you when you were here before, the cameras are simply left over from the past owner. When will your people be out of here?"

Savich said, "You seem to have torn the control center out pretty recently. The room is a shambles. What brought on such rage to push you to destroy your own system, Mr. Hart? What did you do with the recordings? Where are the disks?"

Hart's face suffused with color. "I destroyed nothing! I know nothing about any recordings, any disks! My lawyer advised me not to talk to you until he arrives, so the last thing I'll say is this. As I told you, the cameras were simply here. They do not work. There are no recordings. I have never recorded anything. Indeed, I have not been in the control room for a very long time. There was no reason for me to go there."

Savich didn't believe him for a minute. He knew Hart had ripped out the surveillance system. What had happened to enrage him so much to do it? His son had killed himself, that's what. The disks, he thought; it had to do with what was on the missing disks.

He'd thought to arrest Hart then and there, but he realized something wasn't right about the Bren Ten they'd found by Peter's body. Why would he have left the gun there? He might as well have painted a target on his back with a big red arrow pointing to it.

He said, "We'll wait for your lawyer, then, Mr. Hart."

CHAPTER 47

Maestro, Virginia
Tuesday morning

It had to be fate, Griffin thought, when he saw one of Maestro's half-dozen taxis pull in front of the hospital doors as he limped out on his cane. An elderly man helped a woman out of the back, then leaned in to give the driver some cash.

The driver eyed Griffin. "You look kinda pasty, son. You sure you're not going the wrong way? Out instead of in?"

"I'm definitely out," Griffin said, and climbed carefully into the backseat. He hoped the aspirin Dr. Chesney had finally given him would kick in soon. He laid the cane over his legs. He gave the driver Salazar's address on Golden Meadow Terrace.

They pulled up to Salazar's house ten minutes later to join four other cars overflowing the driveway. "Fancy address," the driver said. "What's going on?"

"Don't know yet," Griffin said.

"Hey, that's the sheriff's Range Rover. I sure hope he wasn't the one who dragged you out of the hospital."

"Nah, this is all my idea."

Dix walked out onto the porch and watched the taxi slowly pull away, the driver leaning his head out the window to see all he could. Griffin was limping only slightly, not putting all that much weight on the cane.

Dix said, "Saw you coming. You're not looking bad."

"Nope. I'm good to go."

Dix said. "I told Anna you'd wake up and come here, fire steaming out of your ears, ready to crawl up our butts for leaving you."

Now, there was a visual. Griffin grinned at him. "Have you got the cuffs on Salazar?"

"Well, not yet. Come on in, you'll see for yourself. Can you make these three steps?"

When he finally negotiated the three steep steps, he had to stop a moment, knowing Dix was looking at him and wondering if he should say anything or keep quiet. Dix kept quiet.

Griffin stepped into the hallway of Rafael Salazar's house for the first time since Saturday, when he'd come to see a bunch of women cleaning up from the party Friday night. Only three days ago.

"Come in here, Griffin," Dix said.

Griffin made his way into the large living room and stopped dead in his tracks.

The room was trashed. Sofas, chairs, and coffee tables were ripped apart and hurled by angry hands to the floor, paintings ripped from the walls and slashed with a sharp knife. Devastation and destruction. Griffin said, "Don't tell me your guys did this?"

Dix gave him a ghost of a smile. "Nah. You should see his music room, all those beautiful antique guitars, the Steinway, all the music and books, smashed, ripped up."

"Where's Salazar?"

"No sign of him."

Griffin hadn't once thought Salazar wouldn't be here. "He ran?"

"It's difficult to tell, since his bedroom is as trashed as the rest of the house. His closet, too. Even the suitcases were torn open."

Ruth and Anna walked into the room. Ruth said, "Hi, Griffin. Can't say I'm surprised to see you. You got any ideas what the people who did this were looking for?"

Anna was speaking to two of Dix's deputies behind her. She turned to him and couldn't help the big smile from blooming. He looked to be fine, maybe a little stiff, maybe in a little pain, but she knew he'd manage. "His car's still in the garage, tires and spare slashed, seats ripped open, and glove box yanked out."

Griffin looked at each of them. "What do you guys think?"

Anna said, "I called Mrs. Carlene, Salazar's secretary. She told me he's late for a class and his cell phone isn't working. I'm thinking it's a falling-out of thieves, and whoever did this believed Salazar was holding back something, so they took him and went to work to find whatever it was he wouldn't hand over."

Dix said, "Maybe some of Salazar's clients, some gang members, turned on him for some reason? Or is there a partner we don't know about who thought Salazar was double-crossing him?" He dashed his fingers through his hair, making it stand on end. "He could be anywhere by now."

Anna said, "Or maybe he's dead."

Dix picked up the twisted remnants of a flute. "We'll know soon enough. I gotta say, I didn't expect this when we drove up."

"I expected Salazar to meet us at the front door, smoking one of those nasty cigarillos of his, all supercilious ennui, and wave us in," Anna said.

Griffin turned to her as she was speaking, but she was staring down at her scuffed boots, the same ones he'd seen her wearing last night when she'd applied pressure to his leg while he'd tried not to groan. He said, "Suppose it wasn't a coincidence Salazar disappeared the same night we were attacked, Anna? It was a spectacular distraction. Made it easy for him."

"If that's so," Ruth said, "everything we're seeing

here could be a ruse, too, to cover his flight. He didn't give us the chance to serve him, or to question him."

Anna was shaking her head. "I saw his music room, the destruction of his beautiful guitars. He wouldn't do that. No, someone else did this."

Dix said, "Either way, Salazar is finished here. I doubt even his adoring students are going to clean this up for him."

Griffin said, "Has anyone spoken to Dr. Hayman?"

Dix said, "After we searched I phoned him, asked him if he'd seen his brother. He said he hadn't and that he was worried, since they were to have had coffee together this morning, and demanded to know what was going on. I told him only that his brother wasn't here and his house was trashed. He was understandably very upset, but he said he couldn't imagine who would do this. I told him we would find his brother and left it at that." Dix paused a moment, then added, "I'm as sure as I can be that he knows nothing about any of this or his twin's criminal activities."

Griffin was shaking his head. "Two brothers, admittedly not raised together, but how could one not know what the other is?"

CHAPTER
48

The Hoover Building
Washington, D.C.
Late Tuesday morning

Savich made it back from the Harts' to the Hoover
Building in forty minutes. Traffic hadn't slowed yet,
though snow started to fall like a thin white veil as he
drove. The forecasters had threatened more in a couple of hours, and he was glad to beat the worst of it.
Ollie met him when he stepped into the CAU.

"Did you question Mr. Sleeson?"

Ollie nodded. "A retired gent with a beard down to
his navel, really pissed, since he'd reported his precious
SUV stolen on Sunday evening and hadn't heard a word
until I called him.

"Unfortunately, he wasn't any help, didn't see who took it, didn't hear a thing. You should know Delsey's hopping mad, says she's being kept prisoner in your house and it's not fair. She'd have come with me to Maryland to talk with Mr. Sleeson if I'd let her. But not to worry. Coop had her under control when I left. Oh, yes, she tried to call her brother to complain, but couldn't reach him. She might call you, but I think Coop will talk her out of it, get her going with his jokes."

"Thanks, Ollie. What else we got?"

"Melissa Ivy has arrived. She's in the interview room with Mr. Maitland."

"Good. I'm glad he was available. If he asks, tell him I'm in my office. I've got something important to take care of."

Savich went into his office and studied MAX's screen. He smiled and called Dix.

Dix answered on the third ring.

"Noble here."

"Dix, Savich. I think we're in business. Here's what MAX found. There's a thousand-acre parcel of hilly, undeveloped, essentially worthless land outside of Maestro. It was sold by a Mr. Weaver last summer for more than it was worth to a land trust. Not unusual so far, but MAX found the trust had no other domestic holdings, and was owned by an SFB Industries, which appears to be a front company owned by yet another corporation, American Colonial Trust, incorporated in the Cayman Islands. Things get murky here, but MAX found a welter of front companies owned by AZT. One of them is yet another finance company that's under investigation for ties to the Lozano crime family, Salazar's family."

Savich could practically see Dix's manic grin. "Bingo, Savich. If it was Weaver's, I know the parcel and so do you. There's a limestone cave on it. Remember Winkel's Cave and our hairy adventures?"

Not pleasant memories, Savich thought. "Winkel's Cave—there's both a front and a back entrance on Lone Tree Hill. And the cave's big, certainly big enough to house drugs and gang members."

Dix said, "We knew they had to go somewhere, but this is the perfect hideout. There's nothing out that way, only an unused road in ruins and rough terrain. This is it, Savich, this has got to be it. I want you to buy MAX a beer."

Savich paused. "You guys be careful, Dix. These MS-13 gang members, they're dangerous."

"I know," Dix said. "Yes, I know. We will."

Savich was about to leave his office when Judy Garland sang out "Somewhere over the Rainbow." He looked down at caller ID. Bo Horsley. He didn't have time, he didn't—no choice. He said, "Hi, Bo. You calling to tell me more about the *Jewel of the Lion* exhibit?"

"The exhibit says it all without me heaping on praise. I wanted to tell you I've got you and Sherlock a lovely town house in Chelsea to stay in while you're here. Friends of mine are heading for Paris for a couple of weeks—why not Tahiti, I wanted to ask them, since it's

February, but hey, their choice. You guys can come, right?"

Savich said, "We haven't had a chance to talk about it yet. We're still trying to dig our way out of this mess down here—you said we were up to our necks in alligators, and you're right, that's the perfect way to put it."

"Well, let me add another draw. Not only am I trying to get my nephew Nicholas Drummond here—you remember, he's the youngest muckety-muck at Scotland Yard? One of his colleagues, Detective Inspector Elaine York, is here in New York as the minder for the Crown Jewels, especially the Koh-i-Noor, since it's the centerpiece of the entire exhibit. She's one smart cookie, fun, and I think you'll really like her. Best of all, she's a vegetarian, Savich, a kindred spirit. Anyhow—"

Savich looked up to see Mr. Maitland waving at him. He said quickly, "All good inducements, Bo, and thanks for setting up a house for us. I'll get back to you, okay?"

"You got it, boyo. Good hunting."

Savich left his office and walked toward the interview room where Peter and Stony had sat at the table with him only two days before. Mr. Maitland met him outside the door. "She's a beautiful girl," he said first thing, "with a story to tell. Hope you get the truth out of her, Savich. You know her better than I do."

Savich nodded, walked into the interview room, and closed the door behind him. Lucy Carlyle stood back against the wall, watching over her.

Mr. Maitland was right, Savich thought. Melissa Ivy indeed looked beautiful this morning, the deadening shock in her eyes from a few hours before a thing of the past. Her face was no longer pale, her eyes no longer vague, and her long blond hair was glossy, falling sleek and wavy around her face. She wore eye shadow, a lovely shade of pale green that matched her sweater.

"Ms. Ivy," he said, nodded to Lucy, and sat down.

"Agent Savich."

"I see you're feeling better today. Glad you could come in so quickly after you called this morning. Director Maitland tells me you're certain now you saw someone at Peter Biaggini's apartment last night, though you told us then you hadn't seen anyone. Tell me why this is."

She sat forward, clasping her hands in front of her. Even her manicure was fresh, her nails a soft pink. "I'm sorry, but last night, after I found Peter and then you came, I couldn't think. All I could see was Peter and how horrible his head looked and so much blood everywhere. My mind wasn't working."

That was the unvarnished truth. "I understand you remember someone now. Before you tell me, Ms. Ivy, I have some questions for you myself. Had you ever seen the gun that killed Peter before, the one on the floor? Had Peter, Stony, anyone, had it in their apartment, or mentioned a gun like that in your presence?"

She shook her head, sending her hair swaying beside her face. "No, none of them had a gun. All they liked to talk about was computers, or economics or banking, computer games, sometimes, but never about guns."

"Did any of the three mention a camera at the Hart residence, a surveillance system, recordings of any kind?"

"The Harts have that? You mean they watch you with hidden cameras?" At his nod, she said, "That's creepy. I visited there a few times." And he could see her thinking, wondering if she'd ever done anything she shouldn't have while at the Hart house. "I don't think any of them knew, maybe even Stony. At least he never mentioned it."

"Now tell me what you remember at Peter's apartment last night."

He watched her swallow once, clasp her hands in front of her on the table. "When I arrived at Peter's apartment building, I automatically went over to get Peter's mail. He always forgot, and so he gave me a key and asked me to open his box and bring me his mail whenever I was over. I was standing by the row of mailboxes, sorting through some mail, when I heard someone coming down the stairs. I turned my head and saw this person all bundled up, out of breath from running down the stairs, I remember thinking, and then he walked out the front door. He didn't look at me, maybe he didn't even see me, he was in too much of a hurry. I watched him stop right outside the glass doors, like he was pulling himself together, and then he walked away. I lost sight of him. I didn't think anything about it at the time, and I forgot him until I was in bed last night."

"Can you describe him?" Savich said.

"He was wearing a long coat that was too large for him, I think. It was dark, maybe dark brown. I'm sorry, but I didn't really pay attention."

"Was he tall? Short?"

Melissa gave Savich a helpless look and shook her head.

"Did you recognize him?"

"No, sir."

Savich pulled a photo of Wakefield Hart out of his pocket. "Was this the man?"

"No, sir, that's Mr. Hart. Mr. Maitland already showed me his picture, and I told him it couldn't have been Mr. Hart. I've met him several times. I would have said hello to him. Mr. Maitland showed me a whole series of photos, but I didn't recognize any of the men on them, except for Mr. Hart and Mr. Biaggini."

So Mr. Maitland had shown her photos of all the principals. Savich sat back, watched her a moment. He rose. "Excuse me, Ms. Ivy." He motioned for Lucy to follow him outside.

"Tell me what you think, Lucy."

"She's drop-dead gorgeous, she's fluent and reasonable, and I don't know if I believe a word she said. If she'd seen this man in the coat, wouldn't she have told you that last night? Could shock have really made her not remember? It's a pretty big deal, Dillon, seeing this man. On the other hand, why should she lie? This is about her boyfriend's killer. Wouldn't she want him caught?"

"Good question."

Bob Dylan's whiny nasal voice sang "Like a Rolling Stone" from Savich's cell. Savich excused himself. "Sherlock, what's up? Did you dig up some bloody clothes?"

"Nope, Dillon. The only thing we found was a

skeleton of a dead parrot wrapped in blankets. Tom picked up a trace of blood with Luminol inside the washer under the back of the lid, but not enough to identify whose blood it is. It's not looking good in the yard. Three techs are in the woods, looking around. Seems to me if someone dug in the woods, it'd be pretty obvious. Oh, and Wakefield Hart's lawyer is here, accusing us of harassing a grieving family. He had them bring the girls down, and they're sobbing in their mother's arms, all huddled in the living room to show us what cruel jerks we are."

"I don't suppose Tom found any video disks from the webcams in the living room?"

"Not yet, but we found another camera, well hidden in the study."

Savich didn't hold out much hope. "Once the techs clear the woods, cut Tom and the forensic team loose. I need you back here to speak to Melissa Ivy. She's saying now she remembers seeing a man running down the stairs before she went up to Peter's apartment."

"How could she have forgotten that fine tidbit, even as upset as she was? I'll be there as soon as I can, Dillon."

CHAPTER
49

Savich walked back into the interview room to see Melissa Ivy staring down at her clasped hands, no expression on her beautiful face. She looked up at him, gave him a tentative smile.

He said, "This is Mr. Griggs. I'd like you to work with him to give me a picture of the man you saw."

She blinked long lashes and looked distressed. "But, Agent Savich, I only saw the man for a moment, really, and not all that clearly, and I—"

"You said you saw him long enough to be certain it wasn't Wakefield Hart. Please try for us. Mr. Griggs is good at this. Jesse, this is Ms. Ivy. I'll come back when you're done."

Savich left Jesse Griggs, their best sketch artist, alone

with Melissa, and stepped out of the interview room. Lucy, Dane, and Ollie were clustered together, all talking nonstop. He raised his hand. "Someone please call me when Jesse is finished with his sketch, all right? Excuse me a moment."

He walked into his office, closed the door, sat down, and tried to clear his brain. Since they'd been called to the Lincoln Memorial, they'd spent their time reacting, first to Tommy's murder, then to Stony's suicide, and finally to Peter's murder. They'd been pulled one way, then another; it was time to stop playing catch-up, time to focus in. He went back to the beginning, to Saturday morning, with the call from Ben Raven, let each scene unfold slowly in his mind. He didn't analyze them, only let them flow over him to get impressions, to let his gut ring in.

It all had to be of a piece, had to be. One overriding motive that had resulted in both Tommy's and Peter's murders. But what? The gun in Peter's apartment pointed a neon arrow right to Wakefield Hart. But any of the boys could have taken that gun from the Harts' attic. It might already have been in Peter's apartment last night, though he doubted that. The murderer had come to kill, not talk. And now Melissa Ivy was saying the man she'd seen in Peter's apartment lobby wasn't Mr. Hart?

Stop. Back up. The one thing Savich was sure of was that Tommy's murderer was a man. A woman could have shoved Tommy Cronin out of a two-story window, perhaps, a fall that had broken so many of his bones, but he couldn't imagine a woman hauling him to the Lincoln Memorial, stripping him naked, and displaying him at Lincoln's feet. That took a good deal of strength. Two people, then? He shook his head at the utter debasement of the act.

He pictured each of the men he'd met in the past three days, not all that many, really, and had one of them been Tommy's killer? Or was he still off the mark, despite all the evidence against Hart? It could have been an acquaintance, a student at Magdalene who hated Palmer Cronin enough, perhaps on his own father's or mother's behalf, to strike out in rage at his grandson. He saw Palmer Cronin's aged grieving face, then August Biaggini's face when his son had treated him with such contempt on Sunday afternoon, and finally, Wakefield Hart's face, set and angry, ready to do battle for his son that same afternoon.

He let his mind return to the victims, picture them in death. Tommy Cronin's dead, bone-white face, Stony's peaceful face, then, finally, Peter Biaggini's, covered in blood.

Savich saw Stony's face clearly in his mind, saw the bewilderment, the horror when they'd accused him of uploading Tommy's photo. No, Stony hadn't done that, but he knew who had, and it had shaken his world. A user of people wouldn't have cared so much. Was he the innocent victim in all this?

His thoughts drifted and time passed until he realized he was circling back on himself, torturing and distorting his own thoughts to make them fit the facts.

He still had too few of them, and he would have to find more.

His cell played Bob Dylan again.

"Dillon? Delsey here."

He went immediately on alert.

"No, no, everything's okay here. Remember my pilot, Agent Davis Sullivan, who flew me in from Maestro? He's here, and I'd like to go to the Bonhomie Club with him tonight."

"Maybe that wouldn't be too smart, Delsey."

"Maybe Davis and I could come to the CAU and talk about this with you?"

Savich smiled into the phone. "Tell you what, invite Davis over for dinner tonight. Tell him I've got an idea I want to talk over with him."

He punched off, leaving Delsey midsentence trying to wrangle more out of him. His phone buzzed a message. From Bo Horsley. *Heard about kid's murder. Call me when it's finished.*

Jesse stuck his head in. "All done, Savich. Wait till you see the sketch."

CHAPTER
50

Maestro, Virginia
Tuesday morning

Thank heaven Rob and Rafe were in school, Ruth
thought, as a dozen DEA agents in Kevlar vests piled
into her house with her husband, Anna, and Griffin to
talk strategy. There were eight men and four women
among them, all talking, all pumped, downing cups of
coffee at a manic clip from two huge urns and lacing up
their hiking boots. Their MP-5 assault rifles were a
daunting sight piled by the front wall, black satchels next
to them holding additional magazines. She looked over
at the piles of headlamps and flashlights everyone would
need.

They were going to war. In a cave. She felt a spurt of

fear for Dix, quashed it fast. If anyone could handle himself, it was her husband. She looked over at him, speaking to Mac Brannon, who was in charge of the operation. Anna had told her that her boss, Mr. Brannon, was a hardnose, but not unfair, and thankfully he didn't seem to be a do-it-my-way-or-else type thus far, but who knew? He was creeping up on fifty, tall and fit, with a salt-and-pepper crew cut and a rock-solid stubborn jaw. He seemed absolutely in control.

Griffin was speaking in a low voice to Anna, who looked very unlike the waitress at Maurie's Diner this morning. Her long hair was braided in a single tail, wound around a couple of times and fastened at the base of her neck. She was wearing black, like her fellow agents. She looked honed to the bone and tough, a major league butt-kicker among a herd of butt-kickers in Ruth's living room. Griffin looked relaxed enough, Ruth could see, and showed no signs of being in pain since he'd taken some aspirin a short time before. She knew Anna didn't want him to go, but she was smart enough to keep her mouth shut now that she'd figured out he'd be in on the op if he had to crawl, which he wouldn't have to do, thankfully. He looked as pumped as all the other agents, and ready, despite the cane. If Mac Brannon also eyed that cane askance, he didn't say anything.

"People, listen up."

Everyone quieted, turned again to Mac Brannon.

"If our intelligence is right, today we're going to hit

the biggest drug distribution operations in Virginia. And we're going to take a bite out of MS-13. I've discussed strategy with Dix and Ruth, who know the cave well. We've also got three spelunkers with us—raise your hands, guys—thank you. So if you get into trouble, ask them for help.

"We're fortunate that Ruth and Dix have been through both entrances of Winkel's Cave, front and back. We'll be splitting up, and when both teams are in position, we'll go in together. They'll have no way out.

"Anna, you're Team One leader. Claus will be your guide inside the cave. Ruth expects the front entrance to be barred, probably chained. Claus will be bringing a hydraulic rescue tool he borrowed from the fire department along to cut through any locks or chains you might find. If you can't get through, you'll still have the exit covered for us, but this is unlikely, since the gang would want both exits available to them.

"I'll be Team Two leader. Dix and Ruth will fill us in on what to expect when we reach the rear entrance of the cave. We don't know how many gang members will be inside, don't know if Salazar will be there. Remember, they attacked Griffin and Anna with automatic weapons last night, and grenades. You will be fighting in an alien environment, one that will require discipline and concentration. I want no casualties, so keep focused. Let's suit up and get it done."

Three minutes later they were climbing into the SUVs assigned to them and heading out onto the road.

CHAPTER 51

The Hoover Building
Tuesday noon

Jesse Griggs handed Savich the sketch he'd made of the man Melissa saw in Peter Biaggini's apartment lobby.

Savich looked at the sketch, then at Melissa Ivy. She met his eyes, her eyes as blue and limpid as a paradise lagoon. He said, "You're sure this is the man, Ms. Ivy?"

"It's close. But I told you, I barely saw him, so—" She shrugged.

"He looks," Jesse said slowly, "a lot like the news anchor on the CBS six o'clock news."

Savich's expression didn't change. Jesse was right. He felt a spurt of anger, then calmed. What game was she playing with them?

He leaned over the table, his hands flat, and said not six inches from her face, "You realize, Ms. Ivy, that if you're lying about any of this and keep it up, you will go to prison for obstruction of justice? By the time you get out of jail, you'll be too old for TV. You understand me?"

Melissa pressed herself against the back of her chair, to get as far away from him as she could. She looked terrified.

Good. She couldn't play them well if she was terrified. "I'm waiting, Ms. Ivy," Savich said. "Your choice."

She rose straight up in her chair. "All right! But I didn't lie. I came here to help you. I didn't realize I was describing Scott Pelley's face on TV. I watch the news show every night, and I got confused. I told you, I didn't see the man well. I'm not lying about seeing him, though, swear it." She lowered her face in her hands and burst into tears.

Savich straightened, nodded to Lucy. She sat beside Melissa, lightly rubbed her fingers over her arm. "Come on, Melissa. You'll make your eyes all puffy and your mascara will smear. Who knows what kind of photos or footage you'll be in today, and you won't look very good. That wouldn't do, now, would it? Come on, now, get yourself together, and trust me on this: telling the truth is the only way to go or you'll spend tonight in jail."

Slowly, Melissa Ivy raised her face to Savich, looking, he thought, like she was ready to enter the Miss America pageant. Her mascara was perfect, and her unshed tears sparkled like diamonds. She looked gorgeous. She leaned toward him, clasping her hands tightly in front of her. "I didn't make it up, Agent Savich. I did see someone. But I did make up some of the sketch, I guess."

"Why?"

He saw her thinking madly, her brain squirreling around, and wondered if she would treat him to another fiction. Finally, she raised her chin and looked him square in the eyes. "I didn't get all made up like this for you, Agent Savich. I thought since I'm a witness I might be interviewed by the press. I loved Tommy and Peter, and I've lost both of them. Their funerals are tomorrow. I thought there might be a chance for me to, you know, get some coverage in the news, get myself known at some of the news stations as a promising young student."

She was fast, he'd give her that, and not a bad actress.

"That's very resilient of you, Ms. Ivy, especially considering neither Tommy nor Peter is around now to tide you over with money until you graduate. I imagine you'll be down to hocking the earrings Tommy gave you for Christmas soon, won't you?"

She stared at him, pinned, biting her bottom lip. He saw her lipstick there was gone, not that it mattered.

"You should be glad you didn't do a good job with faking that sketch. If you had told the media you'd helped us with a sketch of the murderer, you might have risked your own life. This way, you've just wasted only a bit of our time."

He watched the myriad emotions chase across her face. Primarily, he saw, she was appalled she'd gotten herself in this fix. He watched her and waited.

She looked everywhere but at him. Finally, she lowered her face and whispered, "You're right, Agent Savich, it's not a secret I don't have any money. I'm doing what I'm good at, trying to keep going somehow. And I'm afraid."

"Is there a reason you haven't told us, Ms. Ivy? Something you know?"

"No, nothing like that. But everyone I know is dying, and no one knows why."

He said, "You have a right to be scared, Melissa, but not to be stupid. Instead of trying to scam us, you can help us."

"How?"

"I'm going to search Peter's apartment today, and I'd like your help in searching yours."

CHAPTER
52

Winkel's Cave, front entrance
Team One

Claus parked the lead SUV on the shoulder of Wolf Trap
Road, which ran north and south about a hundred yards
west of Winkel's Cave. They had driven in slowly, all
eyes alert for any movement, but no one was surprised
they didn't see anyone, not out here in the sticks three
miles out of Maestro. There had been a couple of der-
elict houses spaced far apart, visible through the falling
snow, but no sign of life.

The second SUV pulled up behind them, and everyone climbed out. They circled Claus, huddled together,
their breaths mingling white puffs in the still air. They

knew the light, lazy flakes wouldn't last long. They were in for another heavy snow in a couple of hours.

Claus pointed. "The entrance to the cave is a hundred yards in through the maple and pine trees. There's a rough path, but there'll be a lot of rocks hidden by the snow, so be careful." He checked to see that everyone's flashlight and headlamp worked. They checked their weapons and the extra magazines in their belts. They were ready. Claus nodded to Anna.

Anna said, "We didn't see any signs of tire tracks coming in, but since it's been snowing for a while now, they could be covered up. Best to assume they will have guards stationed near the front of the cave, even though Dix and Ruth think it's closed down. Surprise is the key, so we'll go in quiet, split up, and come at the cave entrance from opposite sides. If the sheriff is right and it looks abandoned, Claus will cut through the iron gate with his combi-tool and we'll follow him in."

Claus cleared his throat, so nervous and excited he could scarcely get enough spit into his mouth. He cleared his throat again. He'd already told them, but he couldn't help repeating it again. "An explosion was set off in the cave last year—someone trying to cover up a murder—so the passage leading toward the rear entrance was caved in last time I was here. We'll be climbing down before we get to it, and you may start to encounter some sharp debris from the explosion, shards of limestone and dolomite, rocks and dust. It may be slippery from the dust, so follow my lead."

Anna picked it up. "As we've already discussed, some of the gang members have to be using Winkel's Cave as their living quarters, if only to defend their stash at night. We'll hope they cleared the debris away to give them access to more room and another exit." Anna looked at each agent's face, most of whom she knew, some married, some with kids, some drinking buddies or movie buffs, but all were smart, tough people. "We have ten minutes before we head into the cave." She looked at her watch. "Let's move out."

She nodded to Claus, and he stepped down into a snow-filled ditch, holding the heavy cutting tool in both arms, and walked toward the thick woods. The agents filed in behind him. Anna stayed with Griffin at the back of the line, since with the leg wound the going would be slow. She knew he was grateful Brannon hadn't decided to leave him behind.

They made their way quietly through the thick pine and maple trees, as silent as the falling snow dusting them and the trees around them in white. The morning was pure, that was the word that came to Griffin, and there was no wind. It was, he thought, like walking through a winter postcard—well, walking a bit on the slow side, and there might be people shooting at them soon.

A twig snapped beneath Anna's hiking boot. She froze. He whispered, "It's okay, only a field mouse could hear that." Griffin knew he was holding Anna back, Anna the team leader, stuck staying back with him.

"Wipe the frown off your face. You're doing great," she whispered, her breath cold on his cheek. "Don't worry, Captain America. We're going to make it to the cave on time. I'm thinking they'll come running into our arms."

"Right into your Kevlar? Got it on tight?"

"Sure, and you?"

"I'm good to go. I figure since we didn't bite the big one last night when they blew up our cars, we're sprinkled with magic dust. It only looks like snow."

She couldn't help saying it. "I want you to promise me you won't hot-dog. I'm the team leader here, all right?"

He gave her a blazing smile.

Claus raised his hand, and everyone stopped. He pointed across a small clearing.

About twenty yards in front of them was Winkel's Cave. It was set into a hillside, surrounded by weeds and undergrowth, and offered a tall, narrow opening covered with an iron-barred gate. A large sign was nailed next to the opening: NO TRESPASSING. It looked deserted, no footprints in the snow, nothing. They listened, heard more nothing.

Anna went to stand by Claus, and pointed at each of them in turn, assigning them to either side of the cave entrance. She and Claus walked slowly to the barred gate along the side of the hill, the agents covering them. They would be blind for a moment if there was anyone inside the cave watching them from the darkness. She turned on her flashlight and peered through the bars. There was no one there. It was time. She whispered, "Claus, get the gate opened." She stepped back.

The hydraulic cutter snapped the thick chain holding the gate, and it clunked to the ground, hitting a pile of rocks. It sounded like a cannon shot in the silence.

Anna checked to see everyone had turned on his headlamp. She met each agent's eyes, nodded. She looked at her watch, raised her hand. "Let's go. Talk in whispers, and only if you need to," and motioned to Claus to lead them in.

Anna held up her hand again when they were all inside. There was no sound except their quiet breathing. The ceiling was high enough so they could walk upright, even Rodney Bengal, who was six foot four. They went around a corner, walked down a couple of steps, avoiding scattered rocks. Claus stopped, and everyone closed in behind him. The darkness was absolute beyond their headlamps. And quiet, Griffin thought. It was the quiet inside the cave that surprised him the most. He clearly heard Anna's breathing.

Around them was an incredible sweep of spectacular draperies, towering stalagmites. Claus whispered, "Don't touch them, they're fragile, and loud if they fall." He realized then that if any shooting started, there'd be destruction all around them. "Stay close."

As they moved down a twisty passage with a low ceiling, Claus whispered, "We're going to have to bend down ahead for maybe ten feet or so, then the ceiling will rise up again. It's narrow there, too, but don't worry, it'll soon widen out."

The cave walls closed in, and soon most of them were bent double. Griffin gritted his teeth and bent. To his surprise, his leg didn't have much to say.

Claus said, "We're going to have to crawl here, but it's not a long passage, no more than twenty feet."

He could do twenty feet, not a problem, Griffin thought, and crawled.

Claus stopped, and everyone stilled. "This is the passage that caved in last year," he whispered. "You see the debris along the sides? It was completely blocked, but they've cleared it. We'll get through now."

Anna said quietly, "Wait up. I hear something."

CHAPTER
53

Winkel's Cave, rear entrance
Team Two

Dix turned his Range Rover right off onto a single-lane road gouged with deep ruts and piles of rocks and fallen branches. There was no banter among his passengers, no conversation at all. The only sound was the rhythmic click of the windshield wipers brushing away the light snowfall.

They passed a couple of old wooden houses set in hollows of land a good way back from the road, surrounded by trees, snow piled high around them and over the old cars parked in the driveways. The whole valley was pristine white and silent as the snow fell lazily from a gray sky.

Ruth pointed. "That last house belonged to Walt McGuffey. He died last year. His heir showed up, looked at the house, closed it up, and left. It's not far now."

The road dead-ended fifty yards later.

Dix said, "We can't go off-road in the snow. So pile out, people. We got us a ways to walk now."

The snow drifted so deep here it was inside their boots within fifteen steps of the road. Dix paused. "Upslope to your left is Lone Tree Hill. See the single oak tree standing on top of the rise? It's been there since before I had feet on the ground. On the far side of the hill, about a hundred yards away, is where Highway 70 runs. There's a dogleg on a country road exit off the highway there, so you can't see beyond it from the highway. They've got to be parking their vehicles under the trees there when they bring in their supplies, drugs, food, whatever they need, right over Lone Tree Hill.

"Once we climb up over this small rise, you'll see a steep gully at the base of the hill where the cave entrance is. We'll have only scraggly trees and some blackberry bushes for cover, and we'll use them as much as possible. Be aware that if they have lookouts high up on the hill, they could see us at any time. Stay quiet."

Brannon motioned to his agents, and they formed a single line behind Dix.

Dix crawled up to the edge of the rise, waved everyone to stop. He went down on his stomach in the snow, pulled out binoculars, and passed slowly from the top of Lone Tree Hill down into the deep gully in front of them some thirty yards away, then up the other side of the gully where the entrance was, some six feet up a gentle slope, thick with snow-covered scraggly trees and bushes, just as he remembered it. He didn't see a guard, but he did see lines of boot prints in the snow, partially covered with the fresh snowfall but still visible, forming a trail going up Lone Tree Hill and disappearing over it, and coming back down the hill and across the gully to the cave entrance. Foot traffic, recent and heavy. Were they moving drugs out, or were they out of tuna fish? He scooted back to where the agents were squatted on their haunches, bunched together.

He said, "The entrance is about six feet up the hill-side. The boot tracks lead right up to it. They've covered the entrance with tree branches, so they have a limited view out. We'll split up and come at the entrance from both sides of the gully."

Ruth said, "Dix and I will go in first, because it gets hairy real fast inside the cave. Remember, push hard to the right, because you'll be on a ledge with a nearly sheer wall of rock below you about two feet to your left. I've told you about this already, but let me emphasize again, this entrance is dangerous. When you go into the cave, hug the wall on the right. If we take gunfire, hit the ground and stay away from the ledge on your left."

Mac Brannon looked around. "If I had to pick the perfect hidey-hole, this'd be it. Easy to access from the highway and not more than an hour and a half from Washington." He grinned like a bandit.

While the agents crawled down the side of the bowl, fanning out, Dix whispered to Brannon, "You need to stay back, and trust that Ruth and I will take care of things." Dix knew to his boot heels there would be at least one guard, probably right inside.

The agents came in from the sides, silent figures clothed in black, now dusted with white. There was no movement they could see, no voices they could hear. There was no sign of anyone.

Dix stood on one side of the entrance, Ruth on the other, his MP-5 in his hand. He smiled at her, then lifted the branches out of the way.

CHAPTER
54

Winkel's Cave
Team One

Anna and her team held perfectly still in the winding passage and listened. It was a ghostly sound that echoed to them from the distance off the cave walls, an alien and frightening sound to some of them as it fell and rose and wailed in the silent air. To Anna, it sounded familiar and beautiful, and she knew immediately what it was.

"Bingo," she whispered.

It was the distorted sound of a guitar being tuned. Soon they were listening to a classical guitar being played with incredible technique, the notes frenetic but perfectly controlled. Anna recognized it as "Rumores de la Caleta," one of Salazar's signature pieces.

She turned off her headlamp and tunneled the flash-light between her palms so only a narrow beam of light aimed at her feet to show her where she was stepping, and made her way to the front of the line. She motioned for everyone to cut their lights and keep back. She walked forward ten steps through inky blackness, turned a sharp corner, and nearly walked into a huge stalagmite shaped like an eight-foot spear. She realized she'd seen it because it was illuminated from behind by an artificial soft gray light. So they'd brought in a generator, or batteries. There was light ahead. She switched off her flash-light, went back, and beckoned for the team to follow her. They slipped to their knees, flattened, and looked down a path that curved sharply to their right.

She motioned for them to stay still while she shimmied on her elbows to get a closer look. It was the huge vaultlike limestone chamber Ruth had told them about, illuminated by electric lanterns that threw distorted shadows on the walls. Its ceiling soared upward, with groups of stalactites fashioned in incredible shapes hanging down like chandeliers. But many of the limestone formations within reach had been wantonly torn apart and hurled carelessly across the chamber, and now lay in scattered chunks across the cave floor.

Anna started when she saw a low limestone arch that covered an indented niche in the far wall of the cavern, stacked floor to ceiling with what had to be kilo bricks of cocaine. She'd made her share of drug busts and she'd seen bricks of pure cocaine before, straight from Mexico or Colombia, cocaine that hadn't yet been cut by local dealers. But she'd never seen so much of it in one place, except in a picture. It had to be worth millions of dollars.

On the opposite wall were stacks of bagged marijuana in even larger plastic bags, and a jumbled pile of weapons, from AK-47s to .38 Specials. Next to the guns were stacks of canned goods and dozens of bags of tortilla chips, cookies, a store's worth of junk food. She saw a half-dozen coolers, portable heaters, Coleman stoves, and two Porta Potties. All the comforts of home.

She smelled chicken noodle soup cooking over one of the Coleman stoves. There were air mattresses and blankets stacked against a wall and strewn about on the floor.

She saw Salazar, sitting in a director's chair, his head bent low as his long fingers moved over the guitar strings. He was dressed in jeans and a thick crew sweater, boots on his feet, looking quite comfortable. She realized he was playing softly, but the incredible acoustics in the cave amplified the music, exploded it outward. His music would cover the sounds of their movement.

On either side of Salazar sat three collapsible tables, and there were men sitting at two of them, playing cards. Two of the men were eating the chicken soup she'd smelled. She counted ten of them, plus Salazar. They all looked rather bored. Only a few of them appeared to be listening to the music Salazar was playing. She supposed they'd had to live with it since he'd moved in. During the previous night?

Bored or not, they looked like hard-asses, and they each had a SIG556 SWAT semiautomatic rifle close by, with a thirty-round magazine, reliable as sunrise and meant to kill hard.

She looked down at her watch. Brannon and his crew should be ready at the back entrance.

Anna whispered to all of them, "Ease up and take a good look. Locate all ten of the gang members. Look for available cover. Then we'll hold here until Brannon's team sets up a cross-fire."

CHAPTER
55

Winkel's Cave
Team Two

There was a yell from inside the cave, and it gave Dix time to flatten against the hill, then automatic rifle fire spewed bullets out of the rear entrance. One rifle, one guard. Dix waited until he finished off his magazine, stepped forward, and fired into the cave.

They heard a scream that echoed back to them and faded as the man fell over the edge and crashed down on the rocks and the river below.

There was silence again. Dix said over his shoulder, "They had to have heard that, so they might come at us. Remember, press against the right-hand wall. Let's get this done."

CHAPTER
56

Winkel's Cave
Team One

Anna's team heard the burst of automatic fire coming from the rear of the cave. She hadn't realized they were so close.

"Go!"

They fanned out through the front opening of the big chamber, went down on their stomachs, and took cover.

Anna yelled out, "Federal agents! Drop your weapons or we will shoot!"

Some of the gang had already grabbed their weapons, realized they were cornered, and froze for an instant in shock and surprise before one of the men yelled, "Take them out!"

Salazar simply sank down to the floor when the gang opened fire, his guitar cradled against his chest, and crawled behind a big slab of limestone. *Good,* Anna thought. She didn't want that beautiful guitar to get destroyed. All of her agents opened fire at once, and she saw one gang member who was shooting wildly toward them was hit, three bullets to his chest. Griffin had come up behind her, and when he fired his MP-5, another man went down to his knees and fell onto his face.

They saw Dix and his crew run in through the back entrance of the chamber, firing steadily, saw another gang member's forehead bloom in red. The men scrambled behind tables, behind the Porta Potties, but they were flanked and found no cover.

The noise was deafening.

It was over in under two minutes. Ten gang members lay on the cave floor, dead or wounded. One DEA agent had a shard of flying limestone embedded in his arm.

The agents held their fire and looked around the vast chamber, making sure all ten men were accounted for. The silence was broken only by moans and curses. It had been a bloodbath.

"Don't shoot me!" They all heard Salazar's voice, saw him rise slowly from behind the slab of limestone, cradling his guitar against his chest. "Don't shoot me!" he shouted again. "I am Professor Salazar, and I have been their prisoner, do you hear me? They came and took me, trussed me up and blindfolded me and brought me to this place. You have saved me from these men." He spared a glance at the dead and moaning men scattered all around him. He looked scared out of his mind, his face dead white except for a splatter of blood from one of the gang members near him. "Please. I will tell you everything I know."

There was a sudden yell. "Die, then, you lying pig!" A gang member lying on his side six feet from Salazar pointed a .38 and shot him. The bullet exploded through Salazar's guitar and punched into his chest. Dix was closest and fired twice. The man grabbed his neck, his blood fountaining out between his fingers before he slumped down, his head falling against his weapon.

Salazar lay moaning on his back, blood covering his chest, his guitar in shards next to him on the ground, the strings loose and broken, the beautiful wood scattered like pieces of shrapnel.

Brannon shouted, "Dave, see to Salazar. Okay, guys, careful now. Disarm and cuff the wounded."

There was no victory cheer, no high fives, only heavy breathing, relief on every face as the agents went from man to man to find any still alive.

Griffin examined each man's face. The man he and Delsey had seen running down the alley the other night wasn't among them.

CHAPTER
57

DEA agent Dave Parmenter, also a paramedic, went to his knees beside Salazar. "It's bad. We need an ambulance, Dix, right away." As he spoke, Dave was already pressing his hands with all his strength against Salazar's chest.

Griffin said, "We should call in a helicopter." He started hobbling as fast as he could back toward the passage, but a DEA agent raced past him to the cave entrance and a cell connection.

Some of the agents got the two wounded gang members ready to walk or be carried to the front of the cave; another covered the dead with blankets.

Salazar still lay on his back, unconscious now, and next to him was a broken stalagmite streaked with blood.

It was Dix who carried Salazar out on his back. They

were all standing outside the front cave entrance, Salazar still on Dix's back, when the helicopter blades whumped in overhead and the pilot brought it down in a narrow clearing, with feet to spare between the blades and the pine tree branches. Two medics jumped out of the helicopter, eased Salazar onto a collapsible gurney, and slid him in. "We can fit the other two wounded," the pilot called to them, and the men were loaded in. Dave climbed in with them, and the helicopter lifted off.

"Got to admire that pilot," Mac Brannon said, watching the helicopter blades whip so close to the tree branches that snow went flying.

The snow had stopped falling for the moment, and the sun glistened off the white hills, making the world look perfect again.

Dix straightened and twisted his back around, trying to loosen up. "I'd rather not do that again," he said. "I hope Salazar makes it. I'd hate for my back to have suffered for nothing."

CHAPTER
58

Henderson County Hospital

"I hate this place," Griffin said, staring around the emergency room, the walls painted what was supposed to be psychologically soothing pale green but looked more like week-old artichokes to him. Only he and Anna had come to the hospital; all the other DEA agents had stayed at Winkel's Cave, doing an inventory of all the drugs and overseeing their removal. His last view of them was high fives and huge smiles. As for Anna, she couldn't stop smiling, either, a huge blazing smile. "An op that went perfectly," she said for the third time, rubbing her hands together. "Can you believe it, Griffin? It went perfectly!" She was manic, adrenaline still pumping a wild cocktail in her blood. "I'm guessing at least five hundred kilos of cocaine. It's the biggest bust I've been in on. I wonder how long they've been delivering drugs at Winkel's Cave?" On and on she went, questions pouring out of her mouth. She was right, it was an amazing operation. And all the agents had survived, plus they'd closed down a big distribution center and wiped out the MS-13 gang activity in the area. At least for a while.

Anna pulled off her black wool cap and grinned up at him. "Did I tell you you're amazing, Griffin? You made it through the cave, even that one gnarly section. Let's find Dr. Chesney so she can look at your leg. You've got to get it strong again; otherwise, you'll never be able to hold my weight." Whatever that meant.

He lightly laid his fingers over her mouth to shut her up. He could feel her manic smile beneath his fingers. She said through his fingers, "I'm going to check on the status of the wounded gang members."

She was back in two minutes. "One gang member is on his way to surgery, two gunshot wounds, leg and belly. Will he tell us anything? Doubtful, since gang honor demands they keep quiet. We'll see."

"What about the other one?"

She shook her head.

Griffin watched her pace back and forth in front of him, unable to keep still. Griffin sat there smiling up at her while he rubbed his throbbing leg. She leaned down and kissed him, then she was off when she saw Mac Brannon walk into the ER with Dix and Ruth. He watched her talk, gesticulating with her hands. It had felt odd not to be in charge of an operation, but he couldn't complain. Everything had gone according to plan. It was a miracle. He wondered what Anna would say when she came crashing down from the ceiling.

He thought about a cup of hot black coffee. He thought about how he hated hospitals, even when they were warm and comforting. And his leg started aching like a rotted tooth, but he could stand that. He had no intention of letting Dr. Chesney poke around anymore.

Anna and her boss were still in animated conversation. He didn't know where Dix and Ruth had gone to. He made the trek to the cafeteria, bought himself a cup of coffee, and listened to techs, doctors, nurses, cafeteria personnel, and a score of visitors talk about the huge drug bust in Winkel's Cave. He sat down and stretched out his leg and began to lightly rub it. He wondered idly if Salazar would survive surgery. At least he'd been alive when they'd wheeled him in.

He leaned his head back and closed his eyes. Here he'd been driving across the country, enjoying seeing relatives and friends, excited about his new assignment with Savich in Washington.

Three days ago it had all changed. You never knew what life would dish up, like a gorgeous DEA agent named Anna who'd shot an alligator when she was nine. He called Savich to fill him in on what happened.

Anna joined him, and they went to the surgical waiting room on the third floor. They sat together, not speaking now, because Anna's adrenaline levels were crashing, neither of them knowing if Salazar would live or die. Mac Brannon was sitting across from them, his cell phone attached to his ear.

Salazar had been in surgery for two hours. An OR nurse came out periodically to give them updates. Salazar was holding his own; he might make it. *Then again, he might not* were the unspoken words.

Griffin looked up to see Dr. Chesney staring at him, as grim-looking as his mother when he'd pissed her off by leaving no gas in her car. He'd hoped Dr. Chesney was home making snow angels in her front yard, but no, there she was, looking at him from the waiting room doorway, her toe tapping. He gave it up and smiled at her. What followed was five minutes of questioning in an empty patient room, Anna standing beside him. He'd asked her to leave, but that hadn't worked. Dr. Chesney said, "Okay, let me see the leg. Drop your pants, Agent Hammersmith."

Anna, curse her, was grinning as he pulled his pants down and sat himself again on the side of the bed. "Nice boxers," she said. "I've always preferred commando, but black's good, too."

Dr. Chesney gently lifted the bandage from his wound, but it still hurt. "You're lucky," she said after poking around. "The stitches have held, despite all the grief you put them and yourself through. Take some more aspirin when you need it. Like right now."

Anna brought him a cup of cold water from the fountain, and Dr. Chesney stood over him until he swallowed the aspirin.

She lightly touched her palm to his cheek. "No fever.

Good. Take care of yourself, Agent Hammersmith," and she walked briskly out. Not a moment later a code red came over the loudspeaker.

"It's time for another update," Griffin said, and limped to the nurses' station, Anna behind him. Imagine a world-famous classical guitarist, a professor at Stanislaus, and, to top it off, a big-time drug dealer. He wondered how long it would take the media to flood Maestro, Virginia. They met the OR nurse in the hall. "He's out of surgery, but his prognosis is uncertain. He's still unconscious, so there's no reason for you to remain. The surgeon told me to tell all your agents to go out and prevent snow accidents. As for you, Agent Hammersmith, he said you were luckier than you deserved, that if you'd ruined Dr. Chesney's excellent work by crawling around in Winkel's Cave, she'd stake you in the snow and leave you."

There was another code red over the loudspeaker, and Griffin thought, *Oh, no, not Salazar.*

CHAPTER
59

Savich parked his Porsche a half-block down from Peter
Biaggini's apartment building on Willard Avenue, and
they walked through the softly falling snow to its pristine lobby. They used the stairs and followed the long
hallway to the last door on their left to find Mr. August
Biaggini looking at the yellow FBI crime scene tape
crisscrossing the open doorway. He stood unmoving,
staring in, as if uncertain what to do.

Sherlock lightly laid her hand on his arm. When he
turned, his face was curiously blank. She said, "Sir, I'm
Agent Sherlock and this is Agent Savich. Let me say we
are very sorry for the loss of your son."

"Yes, I remember you. They won't let me in. My wife is asking for Peter's blue suit to bury him in, but they won't let me in."

The beautiful lilting voice they'd heard two days before was flat, as if he were moving and speaking simply out of habit, with no emotion at all.

Savich said, "I'll speak to the forensic team leader. Wait here a moment with Agent Sherlock."

Savich ducked under the tape and met Jennifer Whipple in the large entryway. "Hey, Dillon, I called in about the father waiting outside. I mean, I can't let him in, now, can I? He could contaminate the scene—"

"It's okay, Jennifer. I'll stick with him. He wants one of Peter's suits for his son to be buried in."

"I know." She swallowed, her eyes darting toward a tech who was dusting for fingerprints in the large living room. "Okay, we're done in the bedroom."

Savich went back to the hall, where Sherlock and Mr. Biaggini were speaking quietly; rather, Sherlock was speaking and Mr. Biaggini was standing with her, unresponsive, his eyes unfocused.

"Sir, if you would come with me."

"Do you know who did this to my son, Agent Savich?"

"We will know soon, sir," Savich said.

Savich wasn't about to take Mr. Biaggini to the bedroom, since the floor was covered with dried blood, the walls and furniture splattered with it. He met Sherlock's eyes.

She said, "Sir, why don't you describe the suit you want and I'll fetch it for you."

Mr. Biaggini knew, Savich thought; he knew why Sherlock didn't want him going into the bedroom where Peter had died, but he said nothing. He described the clothes his wife had requested, his voice a whisper.

He remained with Savich in the beautiful entryway with the gorgeous wooden floors. "I haven't been here that often. I forgot how much light comes in. I think Peter liked that."

"Yes, even with the snow it's full of light," Savich said. "Did you furnish it for him?"

"My wife did. She's a fine decorator. Can you help us be sure to have Peter's body as soon as possible?"

"I'll check with the ME myself, and I'll call you."

"Director Mueller called me personally as well, after Peter's body was found. It was such a . . . shock. I mean, Tommy, Stony, and now Peter. All of our boys. They knew each other nearly all their lives, and now all of them are dead. What happened, Agent Savich? Why did this happen to my son?"

The man who looked so much like Savich's father stood looking back at him, his deadening pain sitting on his shoulders like a black cloak.

Savich said again, "We'll know very soon, sir, I promise you."

Mr. Biaggini nodded, and Savich showed him into the living room.

A tech was sitting at Peter's computer, set on a desk near the wide windows. He looked up toward Savich, and frowned when he saw Mr. Biaggini. "It's all right," Savich said. "What have you got?"

"Agent Savich, it looks like we've got encrypted files here. I doubt we'll be able to get into them."

Mr. Biaggini's cell phone rang, and he turned to answer, his voice lowered to a whisper. He pocketed his phone after a brief conversation and turned back to Savich, his face again expressionless. "My wife is asking for me. She is in bed—our physician prescribed sedatives. I must go, there is so much to be done, and my wife shouldn't be alone—" His voice stopped midsentence, and then, "We have to prepare for two funerals tomorrow. And when will Peter's funeral be? It's enough to take your soul, if there even is such a thing. It was only two days ago that I was with my son in your interview room with you at the Hoover Building. I never saw him again after that day." He took a deep breath. "I know you did not think highly of my son, Agent Savich. He was not pleasant." He paused, as if searching for words. His voice strengthened. "I told his mother as little as I could about it. She was so proud of him, though he let her know he held her in contempt.

"I don't think his sisters care all that much that their brother is dead. They're shocked, of course, but I wonder if they loved him. He had contempt for them, too, you see, believed himself above them, and he showed it."

Sherlock walked into the living room, a Barneys plastic garment bag over her arm.

Mr. Biaggini gave her a ghastly smile. "Thank you for his clothes, Agent Sherlock." He looked from one to the other of them. "Peter was an amazing child. We loved him so, and gave him too much, I guess, most anything he wanted, even though money was tight then." He shrugged. "It doesn't matter now. He was my son and he was my heart and I would do anything for him, make everything right for him when he made a mistake. I am partially to blame he didn't learn from his mistakes; I mean, there were never consequences for him. He became more supercilious, more arrogant. I remember I cried on his sixteenth birthday because I realized he didn't love his mother, he didn't love me or his sisters. What he seemed to love was power, over his friends, over all of us."

"Sir, did Peter say anything unusual to you or to your wife, express anything but sadness when Tommy was killed?"

Mr. Biaggini stared off into the living room, toward the large windows at the falling snow veiling the world. "Of course, we don't—didn't—see Peter every day. I thought, though, that he seemed sad about Tommy when we spoke to you at the Hoover Building."

"Do you know why Melissa left Tommy and started up with Peter?"

Mr. Biaggini sighed, stared down at the beautiful light-wood floor. "From what I knew about her, I imagine it had to do with money."

"You gave him a regular allowance, did you not?"

"Yes."

"Was it a large allowance?"

"Not really. I paid for his apartment, all his utilities. He had all the money he needed to entertain girlfriends.

"I should go now, to be with my wife. Please find out

who killed my son." He nodded to them and looked lost for a moment before he focused on the doorway, his son's burial suit draped over his arm.

When he was gone, Jennifer Whipple walked into the living room as Savich was examining the encrypted files on Peter's computer. "I didn't want to say anything with Mr. Biaggini here, but we found a whole lot of cash in a manila envelope in a flour canister in the kitchen. Fresh one-hundred-dollar bills. About twenty thousand dollars, I'd say."

But no disks.

CHAPTER
60

Henderson County Hospital
Tuesday afternoon

The code red wasn't for Salazar.

Twenty minutes later, they saw him being wheeled into the recovery room through the closed glass door of the surgery hallway. He was on a ventilator, with doctors, nurses, and technicians on all sides, and more lines running into and out of him than seemed possible. A bag of blood under pressure was dripping into a line in his neck, and the large white bandage around his chest was stained pink. He looked bad, Griffin thought, and he was unconscious.

One of the doctors stopped to speak to them. "Come back in three or four hours, Agents. If he survives, he should be more responsive then." It was odd, Griffin thought, but he looked both pissed and relieved.

Griffin leaned against the pale green wall of the waiting room. "If and when he wakes up, he's going to tell us how innocent he is, and we know that's not the case. And when we coach other gang members, they won't talk, either; the gang has too much of a hold on them, inside and outside of prison."

Anna said, "Even though Salazar was their cover, arranged to buy the land around Winkel's Cave for them, one of them didn't hesitate to kill him when he said he would talk to us if we didn't shoot him."

Griffin said, "Worse mistake he could have made. Everything was unraveling, but they followed orders. I have no doubt they only pretended to take him prisoner after they trashed his house, hid him in the cave until they could be sure to get him safely away. But he broke the code they live by—if you become a threat to the higher-ups, if you talk, you die."

"Let's get some coffee," Anna said. When they reached the elevators, one of the doors opened and Anna nearly swallowed her tongue. There stood Dr. Elliot Hayman, director of Stanislaus. She hadn't even thought to call him to tell him about his brother. His face was tight with panic, but when he saw her, contempt bloomed. "Ah, Ms. Castle. I don't suppose that is your real name, though, is it? You're a federal agent?"

"Anna is my real first name, and yes, I'm a DEA agent."

Dr. Hayman's face was white with anger, and when

he spoke, his voice shook. "I know that my brother was shot. I won't ask why you couldn't be bothered to call me, his brother, to tell me, but now would you explain how could this happen? Who shot him? Is he alive?"

Griffin said, "He is out of surgery and is in the recovery room, Dr. Hayman, but his condition is very serious. He's still unconscious. He was shot in the chest by one of the men he was involved with."

Contempt rivaled disbelief. "No thanks to any of you, I found out my brother was shot. Agent Brannon confirmed it when he saw me in the lobby. He said my brother was shot in a nearby cave. Convenient to say he was not shot by one of your agents, isn't it?"

Anna said, "It's the truth, sir. There are many witnesses."

"And you, Agent—"

"Parrish, Agent Anna Parrish."

"Are you proud to see my brother shot? Proud that you betrayed his trust and betrayed me and Stanislaus?"

"I was doing my job, sir. It was you who invited him here to Stanislaus."

"Yes, that's right, but what has that to do with drugs? Rafael plays the classical guitar, for heaven's sake. He doesn't peddle drugs on street corners." Both Anna and Griffin saw the lie in his eyes, the pain and grief of betrayal confirmed.

Griffin said, "You suspected he was involved with drugs, though, didn't you, Dr. Hayman? And you knew, of course, he spent many summers in El Salvador with the Lozano family."

"I have no intention of answering your ridiculous questions, Agent Hammersmith. Why should I?"

Griffin knew he had to push harder to see the truth. "Because you are also a member of the Lozano family. It is a short step to you from your brother, to you from the family business in El Salvador—drugs, extortion, prostitution, guns—and now to the Lozano organization expanding to the United States. The reality is that your brother came to Stanislaus to a position that would put him above suspicion. He arranged to purchase the land around Winkel's Cave and coordinated the distribution of cocaine, marijuana, and guns with a violent gang with ties to El Salvador called MS-13. Perhaps you've heard of this gang?"

They both saw the horror on his face, heard it in his voice. "Mara Salvatrucha." He raised blind eyes to their faces. "My brother was working with those animals? This is a fabrication. Why are you blackening my brother's name, my mother's name?"

If Anna hadn't been certain Dr. Hayman was not involved in any of this, she was certain now. But he'd guessed what his mother's family was involved in and hated it; his disgust was honest and gut-felt. But how could a man accept that his twin brother was one of the monsters? She said, "Professor Salazar was with them in the cave, sir. We believe he had them trash his house so he could claim they had abducted him. When he offered to confess it all to us, one of the gang members shot him."

Dr. Hayman looked pale, the confident, self-assured

academic gone as well as his rage, leaving him looking pinched and confused. "I know nothing of this, nothing."

He began pacing, still in his lovely gray cashmere winter coat. He looked like someone had punched him in the face. "So they've managed to ruin me at last, ruin me utterly, my brother and Maria Rosa, who took him away to Spain with her when we were children and left me here with my drunken criminal of a father. She wanted to save herself from being beaten to death. She did not care that she was leaving me in his care, damn her to hell.

"Of course, she couldn't leave me out of it. There were hints, I'm not stupid, but I chose to ignore them, as I did not tell her my father never struck me as he had her, that indeed, he was proud of me.

"Yes, I chose to think we were all civilized. When Maria Rosa mentioned Rafael would very much like to come to Stanislaus as a visiting professor for a year, I did not suspect there was anything more to it, none of this drug business, surely not those violent gangs from El Salvador." He paused, stared blindly at nothing in particular, and said more to himself than to them, "Of course I cannot keep my directorship at Stanislaus; I will not even be able to teach anywhere. The government will hound me, try to implicate me in all this, even though I am innocent." He focused on Anna now. "You know I am innocent, don't you?"

"I imagine you are." Anna also wanted to say, *But you knew, you had to know he was here for another purpose, you had to,* but she only stood quietly, watching him. It was out of her hands now.

"Ah, but what kind of man am I, worrying about myself while Rafael may be dying? I must call Maria Rosa in Spain and tell her what has happened. She will blame me, of course. It is like her. Will she admit to me what she has done? Will she admit she told Rafael to get himself kidnapped to cause confusion and distraction until she could rescue him? She never tells me anything, so why should she begin now?"

He walked back to the elevator, not looking back.

CHAPTER
61

Ward Place, N.W.
Washington, D.C.
Tuesday afternoon

The falling snow helped mask the lousy upkeep at
Melissa Ivy's redbrick apartment building. They walked
past the triple row of black mailboxes up to the third
floor and down the battered wooden hallway to apartment 3B.

Melissa opened the door immediately, since Savich
had called her ten minutes before.

She'd changed since the morning into more comfortable clothes, her midriff and navel not on display, perhaps
in deference to Peter's death. Instead, she was decked
out in loose dark blue sweats, her pink UGGs back on

her small feet, her hair in a single thick braid that fell over her shoulder.

"I've already looked for videos that aren't mine, but I haven't found any."

Savich smiled at her. "Tell you what, Agent Sherlock will look around while we talk, how's that?" He didn't wait for an answer, simply nodded to Sherlock and walked to the sofa.

He heard Sherlock moving around in the kitchen. If there were any videos or compact disks Peter had secreted away here in Melissa's apartment, Sherlock would find them.

"Tell me, Ms. Ivy, did you notice if Tommy and Peter had any more money than usual lately?"

She blinked her marvelously thick darkened lashes at him. "More money?"

"Yeah, more cash. On display, for you to see."

She pursed her pink lips. "Well, Tommy took me to buy my Christmas present and said I could have whatever I wanted, that I didn't even have to look at prices. Of course, that was a crazy thing to say at Tiffany, so I looked for something I thought he could afford, and asked for these earrings. He did pay cash, I remember, because I saw him pull the bills out of his wallet, all hundreds. I asked him if he was trying to impress me with that stash, but he only smiled and told me I was beautiful and I deserved it. You mean like that?"

Savich nodded. "That's exactly what I mean. When was this?"

"A week before Christmas. I remember because Tiffany was really crowded. It was so fun, actually buying something expensive in there with all the rich people."

She sounded like an orphan, and he wondered if she wasn't laying it on a bit thick. Probably.

"Did Tommy usually have lots of cash with him?"

"No, that's the first time I ever saw so much. He usually paid with a credit card, but after that we went to a couple of really expensive restaurants, and he paid cash there, too. Why, Agent Savich?"

He only smiled and asked her, "Then why did you leave him, Melissa, for Peter? Sounds like Tommy treated you well, gave you an expensive Christmas present, bought you whatever you wanted." He pointed to the pearl earrings in her perfect ears. "I'd say he was head over heels in love with you."

She searched his face, as if suspecting him of sarcasm, and seeing none, she shrugged. "His grandparents hated me. His Aunt Marian hated me, too. His sisters, though, thought I was beautiful and wanted me to do their makeup. Tommy told me not to worry about it, said we didn't need his family, but I knew he did, and that I'd never fit in with them. Then Peter was there and he wanted me, too, and his parents were really nice to me."

He heard Sherlock move into Melissa's bedroom.

"What about Peter? Did he have a lot of cash?"

"Peter always seemed to, even before we went together. He paid for nearly everything in cash. I asked him once if he wasn't afraid of being mugged and having all that money stolen. He laughed, said cash was better than having The Man know everything he paid for, whatever that meant."

He looked toward the pile of compact disks next to her stereo. "All music?"

"Yes. When you said you wanted to look for a video, I looked through them all first. I listened to the ones I wasn't sure about. They're all music, I'm positive."

He and Sherlock left Melissa's apartment an hour later with nothing to show for the effort.

Then Sherlock mentioned the SUV Delsey had seen in their neighborhood, and Savich remembered. "I've asked Davis Sullivan over tonight for spaghetti. After dinner we've got work to do."

"I'll make you a deal," she said. "You make the spaghetti sauce, and I'll let Sean help me make an apple pie. What have you got in mind for our after-dinner work?"

He grinned at her as he gunned the Porsche's engine. Ah, sweet music to his ears. "We're gonna rock 'n' roll."

CHAPTER
62

Georgetown, Washington, D.C.
Tuesday evening

Savich let out a contented sigh when he was finally seated at the dinner table with Sherlock, Delsey, and Agent Davis Sullivan, Delsey's pilot from Maestro and her date for tonight.

He said, "Davis, I hear you're not new to the Bonhomie Club. You visited with Quinlan and Sally?"

"Yep, heard our boy play. He makes that sax wail."

"Who's playing tonight?"

"Ariel," Davis said as he spooned some of Savich's meatballs and sauce over his spaghetti. "I could sit for hours and listen to her play. Talk about floating you in the clouds; she mellows you out better than any recreational drug back in college, not that I ever tried any, naturally, or inhaled."

Delsey said, "I thought you liked Vincent and Big Escape, people with nose rings and tattoos."

He patted her hand. "I love it all, even that retro stuff you like to blast. Sherlock, the spaghetti and meatballs sure smell good. Thank you."

"Nope, not me. Savich is the spaghetti impresario in this household."

Davis grinned at Savich. "If the sauce and meatballs taste as good as they smell, Savich, you've got to give me your recipe. Here, Delsey, load up." He passed her the meatballs and sauce and spooned Parmesan on top of his spaghetti. "I haven't heard you play yet, Savich. Quinlan told me you sing country and western and play the guitar? And you write a lot of your own stuff?"

"He sure does," Sherlock said as she forked up a bite of spinach salad. "We promise we'll invite you next time he plays."

Delsey took a bite of her spaghetti, closed her eyes, and murmured, "I'm having a spiritual moment here. Dillon, this is seriously excellent."

Davis said, "That's it, then, I gotta have the recipe, keep the cute girl here in my corner."

The garlic toast was passed around, room made on everyone's plate for a bite or two of spinach salad, the Chianti poured. Sherlock felt herself begin to relax. She hadn't realized how tense she was. She took a deep breath, felt her shoulders ease. She watched Delsey and Davis argue and laugh, and they sounded pretty relaxed, too. Relaxed and relieved.

Davis raised his wineglass. "Here's to the incredible drug bust in Maestro today. And no agents were seriously wounded."

After everyone drank, Delsey said, "I'm still amazed it was really Professor Salazar. I don't understand it. He's a world-famous classical guitarist; he's feted everywhere he goes. And he's a drug lord? I still can't get my brain around it. The gods blessed him with everything."

Savich said, "I've learned that for some people family trumps everything. He's a Lozano, don't forget, weaned on the Lozano family business by his mother."

Delsey said, "I'm going to punch Griffin out the next time I see him. I can't believe he was crawling through that cave hours after he was shot in his leg. I was letting him have it when Anna grabbed the phone away and said the wound wasn't bad at all, and not to feel sorry for him." She grinned over her forkful of spaghetti. "Then they both laughed."

One minute Delsey was chewing on the incredible garlic toast, and the next she was standing over the DEA agent dead in her bathtub, then hurled into the stark terror when the gang member was straddling her, holding the knife to her throat in her bed at the B&B. She'd be dead if not for Griffin. She hadn't fallen apart, she'd controlled her fear, she'd handled things, she'd been ready to fight back, and now it was over.

She was alive, Griffin was alive, Anna was alive. She didn't have to fight her fear anymore. She trembled suddenly, felt the shakes start deep in her belly, as cold as the snow falling steadily outside the dining room windows. She hated the thin-as-paper voice that came out of her mouth. "It's all my fault; if I hadn't drunk like an idiot Friday night, then—"

"Then what?" Sherlock said. "The DEA agent's body wouldn't have been in your bathtub?"

"Well, that's true, but if I hadn't gone home early from that dreadful party, I wouldn't have seen a body and I—you—all of us would never have been involved."

Davis chewed a meatball and swallowed. He leaned into her until she looked at him. "Hang it up, Delsey. None of it is your fault. You're blaming yourself for going home to your own place?"

He eyed her, saw that everything he had said was like *blah, blah, blah* in her ears. He put his arm around her and gave her a good shake. "Look at me."

She looked.

"Your brother made it through this, and so did you. They broke up a huge drug-smuggling operation today, seized millions of dollars' worth of drugs and weapons destined to be sold to kids on the streets. They captured or put an end to the people responsible. That's as good as it gets for us. You helped with that. You should be proud of your brother, and of yourself."

So stark, yet it worked. Delsey managed to nod and felt the ice in her belly begin to melt.

"That's better. Now eat some more of Savich's incredible spaghetti. The meatballs, Savich, they're better than my mom's, I swear."

Delsey opted for a green bean on her plate and held it in front of her, frowning.

Sherlock said, "Go ahead, Delsey, you can eat the green bean and think at the same time."

She picked at a piece of garlic toast instead, the green bean still staked to her fork, her spaghetti untouched. "Sherlock, I'm so sorry about last night. I mean, I put Sean in danger, and you guys—"

Sherlock rolled her eyes. "Sean is all right. He decided the evil Incan mathematician, Professor Pahuac, had tried to break in after all. That's a character from one of his video games, and since Sean is very good at clubbing the professor with a canoe paddle, Sean said he'd go outside and stomp him. I told him Pahuac had probably already hightailed it back to his evil cave in Machu Picchu."

A bit of laughter, a good thing. Davis put a fork of twirled spaghetti to Delsey's mouth, and she opened up and in it went. She chewed, thoughtful.

She said, "Since the gang is all broken up in Maestro, maybe Davis and I can go to the Bonhomie Club after all; it might be good."

Savich said, "Someone has come after you twice now, followed you out here from Maestro. You saw that stolen SUV pass by right outside here this morning."

"You mean you don't think it's over, even with Salazar shot?"

"I don't know, Delsey, but I've dealt with gangs like

MS-13 before. What they do can seem chaotic and disorganized, or it can look that way because they follow their own rules, not ours.

"You were never a threat to them except as a witness linking two of them to Agent Racker's death, and through him to Salazar and the whole operation. They made some big mistakes that night, and in a gang like MS-13, if you make a mistake that threatens the group, you fix it, eliminate the witnesses that made you a weak link in the chain, or the gang will cut you out themselves. Someone in the gang may still be under orders to kill you, or die himself. If that's true, we have to stop them."

"How are we going to do that?" Delsey asked. "What are you planning, Dillon?"

"Right now, Delsey, let's not worry about that. Let's all enjoy this good dinner and Davis's lame jokes. Sherlock made an apple pie for dessert."

Davis's eyes glittered even though he tried to hide it, at least from Delsey, but Sherlock recognized that look. Sullivan and Dillon had indeed been planning something, but she and Delsey would have to wait to hear what Dillon had in mind. Dillon appeared to be enjoying his dinner. No meatballs for him, of course, and not all that much spaghetti, either. He was saving room for the apple pie.

CHAPTER
63

The Bonhomie Club
Washington, D.C.
Tuesday night

Marvin the Bouncer listened to Ariel's flute float out over him soft and sad into the snowy night as he stood in the open doorway of the Bonhomie Club, his arms crossed over his chest. He was wearing only jeans, a denim shirt, and a vest, a man impervious to the cold. He wanted the patrons to know that even though he was from Savannah, he was no stinking wuss. Truth was, it was cold and getting colder, under thirty degrees now for sure, and snow was coming down steadily, white and thick as his granny's lace curtains, in the lights around him. They always had lots of lights around the Bonhomie

Club entrance, but outside their circle, it looked black as pitch, except for an occasional halo of light from the two streetlamps that still worked. The other streetlights were out again, smashed by some pork-brained kids. The neighborhood was supposed to be gentrifying, and Ms. Lilly had told him everything was right on schedule with Washington's hundred-year plan.

He turned a hairy eyeball toward Sherlock—who'd told him to call her Delsey tonight—and Agent Sullivan, who was supposed to be her date. They'd gotten out of Sullivan's truck, seemingly alone, and were trying to walk normally, tough because they probably had their SIGs pressed against their legs. Savich had told him about some Latino gang trying to kill this woman Delsey, but he still couldn't believe any yahoos would try to kill her here of all places, or would the idiots not realize the FBI was expecting them? If those tattooed morons couldn't figure out there'd be half a dozen FBI agents hiding around the club, they deserved all the pain that was coming to them.

Savich was in charge, so Marvin wasn't worried. And because he wasn't worried, he hadn't told Ms. Lilly what was going on. Savich had agreed that wouldn't be a good idea. She was hunkered down in her office playing poker with some hotshot ragweeds from Pittsburgh, and very probably winning big.

He met Sherlock's eyes, gave her a slight nod. He had his Dirty Harry big-ass .44 Magnum in his pocket, ready for action. He saw Agent Davis Sullivan turn slightly, speak to Sherlock.

Davis said low, "We're giving them all the chances they could want. I'm thinking the gang has been called off or written Delsey off as too much trouble. I also think Delsey's going to belt all of us for not letting her come out tonight and play."

Sherlock said, "She's got Sean to play with, well, along with Lucy Carlyle and his grandmother. It could still happen, Davis. Stay alert."

It helped, Davis thought, that it was cold and snowing, so Sherlock was all bundled up. Even though she didn't look a thing like Delsey, what with that hood pulled over her head, no one could tell if she was Delsey or Godzilla.

"Delsey kept saying she's the Trouble Magnet, so if we wanted trouble, she should be with us." He gave his head a shake and said, as if the words were being pulled out of his throat with pliers, "The girl's kinda cute, though."

"That's what she said about you, Davis, or something close to that."

Davis called out, "Hey, Marvin, is that Ariel playing?"

Agent Dane Carver shouted from behind them, off to their left, "Under the black Toyota!" Both Sherlock and Davis dove to the ground and rolled, pointed their guns toward a row of parked cars on the street, Marvin right beside them, trying to pull Sherlock under him with one big hand and aim his gun in the other. Even though Marvin was a civilian, it didn't occur to her to tell him to get away, not Marvin. There was a single shot, then a long burst of gunfire from all of them, and a yell. There was silence for a bare second before Savich called out, "You shot him, Dane. Sherlock, you and Davis okay? Marvin?"

"Yeah," she said. "Regular snow angels. Marvin? He's a lovely, very big snow angel. Hey, Marvin, get off me, I can't breathe."

There were two more shots from the night, unexpected, and then Coop shouted, "Another one down, over here." They waited, then searched the street. There was no one else.

Savich looked down at the two tattooed young men in turn, both painfully young, both moaning and clutching their wounds. One of them was close to the sketch of the man Griffin and Delsey saw in the alley in Maestro, the same man who'd tried to use the extension ladder to break into his house last night, if he had to guess.

Savich prayed they'd survive and one of them would talk. He heard sirens approaching as he leaned down and searched one of the young men's pockets. No wallet, no ID, nothing, and so he couldn't believe it when his fingers closed over a cell phone. He pulled out a small flashlight and looked at it, Sherlock, Davis, and Marvin leaning over his shoulder. It was a throwaway, but it was a start.

Marvin was pumped. He slipped his gun back into his pocket and announced, "That all happened in a drunk second, didn't it? It's really fine to see these morons whupped right outside my club. Stupid is as stupid does, right, Sherlock? Sorry I nearly squashed you."

She grinned up at him. "Hey, thanks for protect-ing me."

Marvin patted her cheek and walked back into the club to deal with all the excited voices he heard coming from inside. He closed the door behind him. He was bombarded with questions, but simply raised his hands and said, calm as a judge, "It's all over, folks. The FBI are outside, and they've asked everybody to stay inside here for a minute. Everyone can have a beer on the house while we're waiting."

There was a cheer, and he quickly nodded to Ariel. She looked a bit on the pale side, true, but she was game, he thought, proud of the tiny Croatian woman who hardly spoke a word of English but played like an angel. She put her flute to her mouth, and her achingly beauti-ful melody was instant balm. The buzz still circling the room quieted, and the patrons slowly returned to their seats and their free beers—not the imported beer, though, the cheap beer on tap. Ms. Lilly's people knew her well enough for that. They didn't want to get punched in the nose.

Sherlock heard Ariel begin her flute solo again outside the club. As usual, Marvin impressed her. He was ready for anything they could dish up. Sherlock wondered where Ms. Lilly was. Surely she'd heard the gunfire. "Uh-oh," she said. "Speak of the devil, here comes Ms. Lilly."

"A force of nature, that woman," Davis said as they watched the owner of the Bonhomie Club come steam-ing out, a man's coat pulled over her white satin dress and her five-inch stiletto heels, her magnificent bosom leading the way. She wasn't happy.

She threw back her head and yelled over the sirens, "Dillon! Where are you, boy? You brain-dead or something, bringing trouble here, to *my club*? And now our local law enforcement is going to come here and try to roust me? Thank you so much! Come over here, I'm gonna kick your fine butt!"

Sherlock heard Dillon laugh, then shout, "I'll be there in a second, Ms. Lilly; we got us two perps here who wanted to hurt Sherlock. We got it taken care of. Everything's over. We had agents all over the place, and nothing happened inside."

"I'm going to thump Marvin's head, not telling me what was going to happen."

"I'm surprised it did happen, actually," Savich called back. "We'll have these bozos out of here in a minute." He looked back at her again.

Of course there were always worries, but why say that to Ms. Lilly, particularly after half a dozen cop cars arrived and there were endless explanations and reassurances that the FBI had things under control. Savich assigned an agent to each wounded man and watched the EMTs load them into the ambulances with the cops looking on. He turned to see Sherlock touching his coat sleeve. "What was on that phone you found in the kid's pocket?"

"A phone number. The area code includes Maestro. Let me calm Ms. Lilly while you check this out. Then we'll call Ruth."

He wondered how he was going to soothe Ms. Lilly's feathers, and not just figuratively, he noticed, since she was wearing two peacock feathers stuck in her big chignon, her signature 'do. She stood waiting for him.

Savich didn't have a chance to call Ruth. His cell sang out Billy Ocean's "When the Going Gets Tough." It was Melissa Ivy. He smiled at Ms. Lilly. "My sincere apologies, Ms. Lilly. I've got to take this call, but to make it up to you, I'll play one night for free."

She tapped a stiletto heel in the snow. "Only one night? What do you think I am, pretty boy? As easy as those baby bangers you took down here?"

"All right, two nights for free."

She smiled at him and patted his cheek, pulled the coat around her, and tottered back through the snow and into the club, headed back to her game of Texas Hold 'Em with people who should know better than to sit across a table from her with money.

"Savich here, Ms. Ivy. What's happening?"

"Agent Savich, I was listening on my computer to one of my music CDs I like that Peter had put together for me just a few days ago—you know, to help me feel better. I normally play it on my CD player, but this time I played it on my computer, and I noticed the last file on it was a video of some kind. When I played it, I saw it was Mr. Hart in his study, talking on the phone. I think it's the video from that surveillance disk you were looking for."

He would have rubbed his hands together after hearing that, but his cell rang again, almost immediately. It was Dane Carver calling from the emergency room at Washington Memorial. The Latino Dane had shot in the shoulder who'd been lying with his eyes closed, moaning on a gurney in an ER cubicle, had suddenly reared up, grabbed a scalpel from a tray near his gurney, and sliced his own throat before Dane could even register what he'd done. "My fault, Savich, my fault. It happened too fast—and the blood, I didn't realize how much blood there was in a single human body, and it fountained out all over everything, including me."

"Tie the other one down, Dane."

"Already done. Ollie will keep on him, you can count on that, and if anyone can get him to talk, it's Ollie."

Savich said, "Ollie's good, but you're better, Dane. Go get yourself cleaned up and deal with this, all right? You get anything out of him, you got a week's vacation in the Virgin Islands."

Savich heard an attempt at a laugh. Good, maybe the thought of sun and sand with his wife, Nick, would get Dane focused again.

CHAPTER
64

It was close to midnight when Savich and Sherlock drove to Melissa Ivy's apartment through the steady veil of snow. There was only the occasional car on the road, so it took only eleven minutes. They'd both been tired from the adrenaline rush from the Bonhomie Club, but no longer. It was Sherlock who knocked on Melissa's door.

The door whipped open, and Melissa's face was manic with excitement. She was wearing cat pajamas and big fuzzy slippers, and she was waving a disk at them. "I found it! I found it!"

In a moment, she'd slipped the disk into her computer and they were looking at her computer screen, waiting for it to boot. As she worked the mouse to click the commands, she said, "I usually listen to music on my iPod, but this time I was on my computer doing a class assignment and I loaded in this disk that Peter had burned for me to listen to his favorite music. That's when I noticed there's an extra file on the disk that doesn't play on my CD player, a video file. Take a look."

And there it was, a video file from the surveillance system at the Harts' house.

They watched Wakefield Hart seated at his desk in his study on his cell phone. Both his voice and the picture were sharp and clear. "Yes, Raj."

Raj? It became clear soon enough that Raj had come from a board meeting at an investment firm—Bowerman and Hayes—and he was telling Wakefield how they were putting together a buyout offer for Lancer Inc., a large supplier of transponders to the military with a forty percent premium over the market value of the stock. The buyout would be announced publicly in two weeks. Hart ended the conversation assuring Raj he would get his usual share of the after-tax profits.

They watched Hart punch off his cell, slip it in his pants pocket, and leave his study, smiling and humming.

"What does it mean?" Melissa said. "I know it has to be illegal, but what does it mean?"

"It means," Sherlock said, "that Mr. Wakefield Hart was profiting from insider trading, and his insider at Bowerman and Hayes was this Raj." At Melissa's blank look, she added, "When one company buys out another publicly traded company, they need to make it attractive enough to all the company's shareholders, and so they offer a higher price per share in the marketplace, to make enough of them happy. I'm sure we'll find trading logs at Mr. Hart's broker showing he bought up a whole lot of shares on Lancer Inc. before the buyout was announced. He probably made millions off this one trade. It sounds like he and this Raj have pulled this off before."

Savich said, "It also means with trading logs, phone records, and especially this video, that Mr. Wakefield Hart would be prosecuted by the Justice Department and spend the next twenty years of his life in prison. I'm betting he was willing to do just about anything to avoid that."

Savich's cell belted out "Wild Thing."

"Savich here."

"Agent Hiller here, Savich. Sorry to call you this late, but I thought you'd want to know we've got a screaming match going on at the Hart house."

"We'll be there as soon as we can. Are the daughters there?"

"No, they left earlier with a woman, Mrs. Hart's sister, I believe. There's only Mr. and Mrs. Hart in there, flailing at each other."

CHAPTER
65

Hart home
Tunney Wells, Virginia

They met Agent Hiller by a huge oak tree in the front yard of the Hart home, snow falling lazily around them. "They've quieted a bit, but she was screaming at him that he killed his own son, yelled some nasty names, and slammed out of the living room. She went back in a minute ago."

Savich nodded. "Thanks. Keep an eye on things out here, all right? If there's any trouble, call in backup and come in after us."

Savich pressed on the doorbell.

There was no "Who's there?"—only Hart, heaving and red-faced, jerking open the door and staring at them. "What the hell are you doing here? It's one o'clock in the frigging morning!"

"We want you to tell us about Raj, Mr. Hart," Sherlock said pleasantly, and she stepped forward. He took a step back into the large entry hall automatically, his face for an instant confused, then frozen with shock.

"That's right, Mr. Hart," Savich said, stepping forward and sending him pedaling back. He held up the disk. "We saw this video of you speaking on your cell to your buddy Raj about the Bowerman and Hayes buyout of Lancer Inc. Turns out Peter left a copy with his girlfriend, Melissa Ivy."

Hart was shaking his head now. "I don't know what you're talking about. I want both of you to leave." But he didn't move, as if he couldn't, only stood there, his hands fisted at his sides, struggling with the panic showing on his face.

"Peter must have told you he wasn't going to let you kill him like you did Tommy, didn't he? Told you he'd secreted the disk someplace safe? Didn't you believe him?"

Mrs. Hart stood in the doorway to the living room. Even from this distance her eyes looked glassy from drugs. She must have taken more when she'd stomped out of the living room a little while before. She crossed her arms over her chest and smirked. "Insider trading? White-collar crime is your specialty, isn't it, Wake? But murder? What's on the disk that's so damning you had to murder Tommy? What, he was blackmailing you?"

"Shut up, Carolyn, shut up! You don't know what

you're talking about. I didn't murder Tommy, I didn't murder anyone. I don't know anything about that damned disk, I don't—" Fear bloomed wild in his eyes. Savich grabbed Hart's arm to keep him from bolting. "Let's all go into the living room, Mr. Hart. You can tell us all about it."

Carolyn Hart yelled at her husband, "It's over, you bastard!"

"I agree, Mrs. Hart," Sherlock said, and took her arm and led her into the glass-walled living room, with Mrs. Hart craning her head about to look at her husband. It was silent in the room except for Mrs. Hart's heavy breathing and the crackling of a fire that burned brightly in the fireplace.

Sherlock released Mrs. Hart's arm. "So you have information your husband killed Tommy Cronin? You know Tommy was blackmailing him because he and Peter had that video on the disk?"

She stared at Sherlock. "I heard him screaming one night that Stony had fixed the damned surveillance system, and he was banging his fists against the wall in his study he was so furious. I asked him why that was a problem, but he wouldn't tell me. Then he ran into the control room behind and tore out the system, tore it out with his bare hands, and he never stopped cursing. He frightened the girls."

Savich said, "You had no idea, did you, Mr. Hart? Stony liked to fix things, decided to fix the surveillance system and didn't tell anyone. Maybe he thought it was funny to spy on his family with his friends when they were bored. I'd have to say he was surprised when he saw his father committing a major felony. Tommy, Peter, Stony, all of them must have been having a fine time until they saw you on this video.

"They all knew banking and finance, knew exactly what you'd done. Stony probably made Tommy and Peter swear they'd never say anything, but Peter was Peter, wasn't he, Mr. Hart? A greedy manipulator. I don't doubt it was Tommy who called you, demanding money. Peter would have put him up to it."

"This is all nonsense, all of it."

"Shut up, Wake! That is exactly what happened, isn't it?" She looked like she would have run at him, but Sherlock again held her in place.

Savich continued, "Tommy was flush with cash in December, as was Peter. They got that cash from you, after Tommy sent you a copy of the disk. I'll bet he promised he'd give you the original and you'd never hear from him again.

"But Peter wouldn't let this gold mine go, and you did hear from Tommy again, so you met him at your office on M Street, which just so happens to be on the third floor of the Hampton Building, and you threw him out your window."

Hart listened, saying nothing, fists at his sides, shaking his head back and forth.

"Quite an idea to leave his body at the Lincoln Memorial, to send us off in the wrong direction, at least for a while. But you overthought what you did next. You thought you understood your son Stony's anonymizer software, you thought no one on earth could ever trace anything sent using it, but the thing is, Mr. Hart, you didn't understand as well as your son did, and we traced the photo you uploaded of Tommy Cronin's body back to Stony's computer.

"And that brought Tommy Cronin's murder right back to you."

Carolyn Hart was panting now, nearly hysterical with rage. "Even I didn't think you uploaded that horrible picture from Stony's computer yourself! Stony wasn't even involved. Stony knew you'd done it, knew you'd killed his friend, and he couldn't bear it and he killed himself!"

Hart kept himself in tight control. "Shut up, Carolyn. You have no idea what you're talking about. They have no proof of anything at all."

Savich shook his head at him. "No proof, Mr. Hart? We found a lot of cash in Peter's apartment. Your cash, Mr. Hart, because he didn't withdraw it from his own bank account. He didn't have that kind of money. Neither did Tommy. But you made a large withdrawal from your brokerage account in early December, deposited it in your bank account. Then you made three large cash withdrawals, two in December, and one yesterday, Monday. What happened, Mr. Hart? Peter called you, didn't he? He told you he had copies of the disk, too. Knowing Peter, he would have tried to persuade you it wouldn't do to try to kill him, as you killed Tommy, that he had copies hidden away."

Hart walked to the middle of his modern living room

surrounded by falling snow and pulled out his speaker's voice, smooth and deep. "I want you out of my house. I'm going to call my lawyer."

"Feel free," Sherlock said. "But before he arrives, you might as well know our lab will be looking for trace evidence in all of your cars. If you used any of them to haul Tommy's body to the Lincoln Memorial, they'll find it. We're going to track your whereabouts, and Tommy's, on Friday night, and we'll be searching your office and the concrete sidewalk under your office windows. A human body that falls onto concrete from that height leaves traces. Your phone records, and Tommy's and Peter's—there will be calls you have no good explanation for. You cannot hope to get away with killing them, Mr. Hart."

"But I didn't kill Peter, I tell you. I didn't kill that little bastard!"

Sherlock said, "Then why, Mr. Hart, was your gun lying beside Peter's body?"

"I told you, it's been missing for years, anyone—"

"Did you panic, Mr. Hart, run before you could get yourself together to search Peter's apartment?"

"My wife and I were here last night together! And Friday night as well. Ask her!"

Hart looked at his wife, standing beside Sherlock, looking vague and stupid to him from all her drugs. She was his only chance, and he knew it.

Mrs. Hart said slowly and precisely, "He could easily have slipped out Friday night; last night as well. We have separate bedrooms, you see." She looked at him appraisingly, as if they both knew something Savich didn't, as if challenging Hart to say what he would.

Savich saw Hart's face go slack, saw defeat in his eyes.

"Of course, Mr. Hart," Savich said, "it could be you are telling the truth about Peter. Melissa Ivy saw someone leaving Peter's apartment building, not well, but well enough to think it wasn't you she saw, but someone shorter.

"So let me paint another scenario. Since Mrs. Hart can't vouch for your being home that night, you can't vouch for her. It could have been Mrs. Hart who drove to Peter's apartment last night, Mrs. Hart Peter let in, not realizing she knew and guessed enough to blame him for Stony's death, for Tommy's death, too. Peter would have pleaded for his life when he saw the gun, told Mrs. Hart everything about the video, about Tommy's blackmailing you, that it was you who had killed Tommy. But she knew Peter well enough to know he'd put Tommy up to it, that he would never have done such a thing by himself.

"That's when she realized if she shot Peter, you would be blamed for it, that all the evidence would point to you, particularly if she left your gun next to Peter's body. All she had to do was to vouch for your being with her that night, as any good wife would. All she had to do was wait, knowing the FBI would find a copy of the video, and that we would arrest you, not her, Mr. Hart."

Another long look passed between husband and wife. Carolyn Hart said to him, her voice low and despairing, "Our son, our precious Stony, he did nothing wrong.

And now we have only our two daughters. Would you leave them out in the world without a parent? Do the right thing finally for one time in your miserable life."

Hart looked at her again, then said very quietly, "I did kill Tommy and Peter. I killed both of them."

THEY WEREN'T HOME UNTIL DAWN. Sherlock lay on her back in the dull gray light, exhausted and sad. Had Wakefield Hart really killed Peter, and dropped his own gun there beside Peter's body? And did it even matter, since Hart was willing to swear to it now? At least the two Hart daughters would have a parent to raise and nurture them. And there was closure.

CHAPTER
66

Maestro, Virginia
Wednesday morning

Gabrielle DuBois was packing. They could see her suit-case open, impossible to hide it even with her standing in the doorway, blocking them.

She eyed the three of them, then said, her accent thick, "What is it you are doing here? What do you want?"

Griffin said, "You seem to be in a big hurry, Ms. DuBois. Where are you going?"

"Not that it is any of your business, but I am going home." She shrugged, and crossed her arms over her chest, not moving. She wore loose black sweats and thick white socks on her feet. Her hair was in a ponytail, and she was wearing bright red lipstick. "I do not approve of Stanislaus any longer. I had such high hopes, but I was deceived. Look at what has happened here in your countryside—a cave filled with cocaine, a murder, Professor Salazar shot. Even you, Agent Hammersmith, shot in the leg. Thank you, no, I will return to France, to civilization. I am afraid to remain here."

"That's not very nice of you to say," Griffin said. "What about Professor Salazar? He's hurt very badly. Doesn't he need you? I thought you were in love with him and he with you. Why aren't you at his bedside at the hospital?"

There was no explosion of French expletives, only a lovely Gallic shrug. "I was deceived by Professor Salazar as well. He toyed with my affections. He prefers your sister, I think. It seems he is nothing more than a common criminal, in any case. I no longer care what happens to him."

"Interesting that you are the only student with urgent plans to leave the country, don't you think?" Griffin asked. He stepped forward, but she didn't oblige him and back up. Instead, she leaned into him. "I do not invite you into my apartment."

Anna pulled her creds out of her pocket. "We haven't actually met properly, Gabrielle. As you can see, my real name is Agent Anna Parrish, DEA, and I've been working undercover here at Stanislaus. And your own name is not Gabrielle DuBois, but Claudine Renard."

Griffin was pleased to see Gabrielle flinch and her face go pale, but she recovered quickly, even managed a sneer. "I do not know this Renard person."

Griffin said, "Sure you do, Gabrielle—excuse me, it's Claudine—isn't it? Claudine Renard, longtime student of Madame Maria Rosa Salazar of Madrid? That will make it impossible for you to leave the country, since you entered illegally under an assumed identity." Anna simply shoved her back and moved in, Griffin behind her. He shut the door.

Gabrielle stumbled, managed to right herself. She shot Anna a venomous look. "All right, so you have forced your way in, and you are the law. They are rude and pushy everywhere. But I am not impressed, Anna. I don't care who you are. I want you to get out."

Griffin said, "I'm afraid that's no longer up to you, Ms. Renard. A gang member we've identified as a José Ramirez was shot last night at the Bonhomie Club in Washington, D.C., while lying in wait for my sister, Delsey. I have his picture on my cell phone. He is the same man Delsey and I saw running away after the attack on her at the B&B here in Maestro. Unfortunately for you, he was carrying a disposable cell with your number on it. Careless of him not to toss it, but he was like that, wasn't he? I guess he didn't think it would be necessary. He was one of the men who called you for instructions from Delsey's apartment, too, wasn't he?"

"Vous est dingue! Vous avez perdu la raison! C'est completement fou!" She waved her hand in his face. "This is lunacy, it is madness, do you hear me?"

Anna pulled a sheaf of pictures from her jacket pocket. "I appreciate your fluent French and your dramatic gestures, Claudine, but they won't fly now. Take a look at these." Anna handed her the pictures. "Once we knew who to ask about, we sent a photo of you to the Spanish police, asked them if they could identify you, match your photo with anyone in their files of the Lozano and Salazar family contacts. There you are at a recital at about age eighteen, I'd say, standing next to Maria Rosa Salazar, accompanying you on the piano. You seem quite happy. She taught you voice, and no doubt brought you into the Lozano family business. Odd you never mentioned her. Did you even study with Professor Salazar here at Stanislaus at all, or spend all your time on the drug business?"

Gabrielle looked wildly toward her luggage.

Anna said, "Forget the gun you have tucked inside that luggage, Claudine. You're not getting anywhere near it. Now, you were at Salazar's party last Friday night. It was you, wasn't it, who ordered two of your thugs to take Agent Racker out of there and find out what he knew?"

Gabrielle kicked out fast and hard against Griffin's wounded leg. She made a mad dive for her luggage as he went down. Anna grabbed her ponytail and jerked her back against her. She held her Glock against her temple. "After you're tried and sentenced here in Virginia, Claudine, I doubt you'll ever get to see France again at all."

Griffin stood slowly, his leg thrumming like a metal

drum. He looked down at his cane, in two jagged pieces on the floor. "Now, Agent Parrish, don't you think you're being overly harsh? Maybe Ms. Renard can cut a deal with the Justice Department, tell them all about the Lozano family and about Maria Rosa."

CHAPTER
67

Savich home
Georgetown, Washington, D.C.
Two days later, Friday evening

Anna accepted a slice of pizza from Griffin and bit in.
There were half a dozen pizza boxes scattered on every
available surface in the Savich living room for the dozen
people—DEA, FBI, and the sheriff of Maestro—and
most of them Griffin hadn't even known a week before
and now they were his friends.

Sherlock patted her mouth with a napkin and sat back
in her chair. "Let me ask you, Agent Brannon, who gets
the credit here, the DEA or the FBI?"

Mac Brannon looked from Anna to Griffin, took a

swig of beer, and grinned. "I guess with what's probably going to happen between these two"—he nodded toward Griffin and Anna—"we'll have to consider it a joint success." He raised his beer bottle and toasted Savich. "Now that I think of it, though, Savich here did some of the prep work, but the DEA did all the heavy lifting. I don't remember any FBI dweebs, or you, Sheriff Noble, out there hauling away the guns and drugs."

"We dweebs are glad we could help you get there, Mac," Savich said, and picked up another slice of his vegetarian delight.

Dix said, "I hate even smelling that stuff. Believe me, I was glad to leave it to you." He turned to Anna. "I'm going to miss you pouring me coffee every morning at Maurie's Diner."

Anna patted his arm. "I'm going to miss you, too, Sheriff, and Maurie, of course. He was a great boss. I was afraid he was going to cry when he found out who I really was and that I was leaving, but I distracted him by telling him to give my best to his beloved mama. Dix, you've got a lot of great folk in Maestro. Please tell everyone I enjoyed spending time with them."

Sherlock slipped a sleepy Astro a bit of sausage from one of the pizzas. "I'm glad Salazar made it. Maybe between him and Gabrielle—Claudine Renard, I mean—you can get enough information together on Maria Rosa to make the Spanish police happy."

"She buried their identities as deep as she could, but not deep enough," Anna said. "I feel sorry for

Dr. Hayman, though. He's already resigned from Stanislaus."

Delsey said, "I, on the other hand, can't wait to get back to Maestro and Stanislaus. What, you thought I wouldn't want to go back there to school, Griffin? Of course I do. I want to finish my degree. The only thing I can't see doing is going back to live in my apartment next to Henry. Ruth is going to help me find a nice, safe apartment close to campus."

Anna sat back in her chair and announced, "Sorry, Delsey, no more school for me. Nope, it's time for a vacation. I was undercover for a long time, and wait-ressin' is hard work. I've got to admit, though, that all the tips from Maurie's really supplemented my income. Mr. Brannon said I've earned a long break."

Griffin was thinking how sexy her voice sounded laced with her syrupy slow Southern drawl when Savich said to him, "And you're officially off duty, Griffin, until your leg heals. Are you planning a vacation, too?"

Griffin nodded. "Actually, Ms. Parrish and I have decided to take our vacation together. Rome, the Colosseum, playing Christians and lions, and all that. It will be out of season, maybe a bit on the chilly side, but there shouldn't be any fighting with hordes of other tourists at the gelato stand."

Anna looked at his impossibly beautiful face, with his nose just a little bit off kilter. "I'll just have to figure out if he's going to be a gimpy Christian or a gimpy lion."

Or maybe, she thought, as everyone laughed, she

could take him to Maui instead. She could only imagine how good he'd look in swim trunks and lots of sunscreen she would apply herself. She gave a little shudder and turned down the last slice of pizza, thinking of her little polka-dot bikini.

CHAPTER
68

Georgetown, Washington, D.C.
One week later

Savich slipped his cell phone back into his pocket and watched Sherlock toss a piece of popcorn in a high arc to their manic dog, Astro. Astro took a flying leap off the living room carpet, caught the popcorn two feet in the air, dropped back down, chewed for a millisecond, and raced back to Sherlock, barking for more. It was a game that had no end until the popcorn was gone and they'd proved to him that it was gone, usually by letting him carry the empty bowl around in his teeth.

Savich picked up *The Washington Post*, pointed to a photo of the Koh-i-Noor diamond in its setting in the

Queen Mother's crown. "You and I haven't had a chance to talk about the *Jewel of the Lion* exhibit at the Met next week. I spoke with Bo Horsley, you remember, my dad's old partner?"

"Oh, yes. Did he congratulate you on saving the world?"

"I spoke to him before there was any saving, but he did email me with a 'well done' this morning. I think I told you he's heading up the private security for the *Jewel of the Lion* exhibit at the Met. Not only has he got us a town house in Chelsea, he wants us to go to the opening gala as his guests, eyeball the Crown Jewels and the Koh-i-Noor diamond, and rub elbows with the rich and famous. He's trying to talk his nephew, Nicholas Drummond—Bo called him the youngest muckety-muck at Scotland Yard—to come over. His added inducement was Detective Inspector Elaine York, a colleague of his nephew's who's the official 'minder' for the exhibit. He really likes her. Also, she's a vegetarian."

Sherlock rolled her eyes. "He have any more perks to offer?"

Savich grinned at her. "That's about it. He did add in his email that Nicholas is not only a detective chief inspector with Scotland Yard, he's also a computer expert, probably better than me. He says it's about time we met. Maybe we could duke it out. I could hear him laughing with that shot."

Sherlock said, "Wait a minute. We've got Nicholas Drummond, a Brit who's with Scotland Yard, and yet his uncle is American FBI. How does that work?"

"Bo told me Drummond's mother, Bo's sister, is American, starred in a TV sitcom here in the late seventies, early eighties. She met his father, a Brit, in L.A., they married, Nicholas was born here, and then they went back to England, where they stayed. Drummond's grandfather is a viscount. An English peer—isn't that a kick?"

"I wonder if Drummond's as cute as you are."

"No," Savich said. "No way."

Sherlock grinned up at him. She nodded to the open copy of *The Washington Post.* "I wouldn't mind seeing the Crown Jewels, and the idea of having our own house—sure, let's go. Take MAX. I want to see if he recognizes this Nicholas Drummond as a kindred spirit or kicks his royal butt to the curb."

Keep reading for an excerpt from
the next FBI thriller by Catherine Coulter

POWER PLAY

Now available from Jove Books

Buckner Park
Chevy Chase, Maryland
Middle of March
Saturday, late afternoon

She always ran at sunset. She rarely ran all-out, rather she maintained a smooth, steady pace because this was her thinking time. Thankfully, it wasn't freezing cold on this early evening. The two-lane trail wound in and out of oak and maple trees, the terrain not too extreme. She loved how the light played through the still-naked tree branches, and how quiet it was with so few other people out in the park this time of day. Quite different from running along the Embankment in London—a challenge, since there were always people to watch out for. Here or in London, it was still her precious thinking time. Diplomatic protocols with endless snafus, relations with Her Majesty's government, and now too often about people who wanted to blow up their neighbors, or London, still fighting out thousands of years of hatreds seemingly bred into their bones. Sometimes there were victories, but few they were, and far between. She was good at her job, but there was always something to work through, something to make her brain ache. But not today. Today she was trying to figure out what suddenly happened in her life that had brought her here. As she ran, a constant prayer looped through her brain that she'd left the danger back in England.

Her breathing was even, her muscles warm, and she relaxed into the repetitive movement. She focused on the quiet, even heard a blue jay, the sounds of small animals moving about in the underbrush near her, the slap of her running shoes on the trail, smooth and steady.

After another quarter mile, the trail turned back toward Nickerson Road, with its two lanes and light traffic. She ran parallel to it for a hundred yards or so. George's face flashed in her mind. He was eating spaghetti, of all things, and smiling at something she'd said, and she felt the familiar punch of grief, raw and deep.

And that was the question she always came back to. What had she done that would make someone want her to pay with her life? With George's life? No matter how she turned it over in her mind, she simply couldn't think of anyone who possibly hated her that much.

She heard a car approaching on Nickerson Road. In

that stark moment she heard the engine revving, the car accelerating toward her. She twisted to look, stumbling on a clump of rocks at the edge of the trail and falling sideways, flailing her arms to keep her balance, but still she fell hard. The car was close now, nearly on her, and it was coming fast. She didn't think, simply rolled into the bushes near several trees. She smelled the exhaust, felt the heat of that beast as it flew past her.

She heard the car brake hard, pictured the driver turning around to come after her again. She jumped to her feet and ran into the woods off the trail, the only sound in her ears the frantic beat of her heart. She plastered herself against the back of an oak tree and waited.

Ready to find
your next great read?

Let us help.

Visit prh.com/nextread